PREY

Emergence

T. Purcell Dodge

PREY: Emergence

Copyright © 2019 by T. Purcell Dodge

All rights reserved. No part of this book may be reproduced or transmitted in any form or by any means without written permission of the author.

Cover Design: **Kent Holloway**

This book is a work of fiction. Names, characters, places, and incidents are products of the author's imagination or were used fictitiously. Any resemblance to actual persons, living or dead, business establishments, events, or locales is entirely coincidental. The opinions therein are not the opinions of the writer, nor are they suggestions for action.

Paperback ISBN 978-1-7331421-0-6

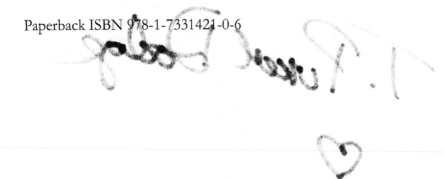

For my Momma
Who fiercely insisted I follow my dreams
Even when they terrified her.

For my Da
Who happily acted out characters
And inspired me to create.

For my Person,
Who has been my constant since I was seventeen.
She is as delightfully exquisite as any muse.

For my boys,
Who gave me purpose
When everything seemed darkest.

Acknowledgments

Thank you for taking a chance on my book. This story has been a labor of love and I can't wait for you to join the complex and beautiful world that is the Proactive Resources for Evidentiary Yields family. I truly hope that the PREY series continues for a long time. You taking a chance on this story, means the world to me. Please continue to give me your support. In return, I promise to continue giving you the characters that I love. Reviews help me know if I'm doing something right, or not. If you have a moment to write a review for me, I'd very much appreciate it.

Stay in touch with me.

Find me on Facebook at "T. Purcell Dodge". Follow me on Instagram at t.purcelldodge. Post pictures with #PreyForUs so I can see you reading my book. Reach me via email at trish.dodge.87@gmail.com, I'd love to hear from you.

This story is an amalgamation of many years of toil, heartbreak, soul-searching, and my hope for the world. I hope showing people from all different walks of life learning to complement each other in order to achieve something spectacular can impact the world positively. Reach out in friendship to someone today. Smile at a stranger. Listen to a different point-of-view. You don't have to agree with someone to respect their choices. Love with your whole heart, no matter who, or what, it is you love.

I want to thank my Da, who has always been my soundboard, my champion, and one of my greatest fans. This story would never have been created without him.

My Momma, (whose steadfast, unconditional, love and support have changed my life in so many ways) has been the heart of this project.

Without her pushing me to keep trying, this work would never have survived my self-doubt.

My dear friend, Stephanie Cornish, who created art for this story. The hours I spent with you while you created inspiration for me, are some of my favorite memories attached to this story.

Kent Holloway who created the stunning cover for a first-time independent author, thank you for all your help and advice.

Rebekah Snygg-Carrasco, you will always be my first muse and my person, without you, creativity is lacking. You are my go-to for help with characterization and plot. I love you.

Matt Dodge, you helped me find my soul again. There are no words to describe my love for you. I know what love is, because of you.

Chapter 1

Shadows danced in the flickering light of the lone street lamp on the curve of a path through Central Park's trees. A young woman slowed from her jog, glancing at her watch, she pulled her earbuds from her ears with one hand. Her blonde ponytail bounced as she hopped up and down on the balls of her feet to stretch her calf muscles.

The trees painted the pavement with stationary black lines. A shadow moved behind her, casting its shade beside her as she walked slowly, staring down at her hands, trying to untangle the cord of her earbuds with a quiet curse. She stopped walking directly under the lamp as she managed to finally get the cord untangled. The shadow stopped when she did, the darkness pooling at her feet went unnoticed as she placed her earbuds back into her ears.

She looked up at the light as it flickered with pink flushed cheeks and sweat shimmering on her forehead. "Stupid piece of crap," she grumbled as she walked slowly from the safety of the ring of light on the pavement. The shadow followed through the light, but she was too busy picking a song on her iPod to notice the danger. She selected a song and shoved the music player into her armband, her head already bobbing to the music.

She entered a darkened section of path and the shadow lunged forward, moving rapidly toward her, like a shark to blood. The glint of a blade caught the shreds of light from the moon as the man brought it around the woman from behind at throat level. He almost got the blade to her flesh before she grabbed his wrist with her right hand and elbowed him hard in the solar plexus with her left. As the air whooshed from his lungs, the woman stepped back, under his arm, twisting his wrist as she moved until she was behind her attacker. She realized she had miscalculated her maneuver when his arm wouldn't continue past his torso.

She cocked her head and peeked over her attacker's shoulder. Her blue eyes fell on the shaft of the knife sticking out of his gut only a moment before the man moaned and fell to the ground at her feet.

"Oops," she grimaced and moved to render first aid as her coworkers suddenly appeared from the surrounding trees.

Chapter 2

"Give it to me straight, guys, how much trouble are we really in?" A woman with deep auburn hair, pale green eyes, and a cute button nose was sitting at a high-tech computer station with three separate monitors.

Her question was aimed at her comrades, who were sparring on a mat in front of her. One looked like he could have stepped from a samurai movie if he hadn't been wearing Adidas shorts and a sweatband. His distinctly Japanese features were complemented by his neatly fashioned top knot, which may have looked hipster on anyone else. The smooth skin of his bare chest glistened with sweat as his wiry physique allowed him to spin a kick at his opponent's face.

The much taller, lanky, black man with kind milk-chocolate eyes stepped away from his friend's foot with a laugh, "What's with you and straight things, Mere-bear?"

The redhead shrugged, "I like to know what I'm up against, no matter how hard." She grinned at him and winked.

"I don't know, Mere," the handsome Asian man responded, ignoring the inuendoes his friends were making. "It's not like she had much choice in the moment. The only thing that could have been better is if she'd twisted to the front instead." He glanced at the woman and continued, "But that probably would have broken his arm. Either way, he's getting hurt."

"Do you think Whit expects us to be psychic now?" Mere asked, inspecting her nails and biting her bottom lip in thought.

"She really should have gone to the front," the black man responded as he tried to grab his sparring partner, "that would have taken her away from the blade."

"It's a matter of preference, EmEm!" The Asian man stood up from his crouch with a faintly angry expression, "She had control of the weapon, that's all that matters."

"We can debate grappling all day long, Will, it doesn't change the fact that a man was stabbed who didn't have to be," EmEm also stood up and shrugged his shoulders.

"A serial rapist was injured," Mere corrected with a scowl, "forgive me if I don't shed any tears."

"Injured with his own knife," Will added, shaking his head, "and if you report to Whit that she should have made a different decision, I'll fight you one hundred percent."

The black man shrugged his shoulders again, "Whitlock hasn't asked my opinion on the matter, and I won't give it unless asked." His chocolate eyes narrowed as he looked at Will, "But I won't lie either."

Mere sighed heavily when both men squared up again on the mat, as though they'd settle the argument there, "Boys. Let's focus on the task at hand," she motioned to the Mobile Command Unit behind her. It looked like a famous band's tour bus, a huge black vehicle with black tinted windows, "How do we eavesdrop without getting caught?"

Will grinned, "Why do you think we moved the mat so close to the office window?" He lunged forward and soon the men were a flurry of strikes and kicks.

"OOPS?!" A booming male voice rattled the office window enough that Will and EmEm stopped sparring, mid-strike, and turned to stare at it, trying to discern what was happening behind the tinted glass and blinds of the back room.

Inside the office, a woman with bright red curly hair and luminous green eyes was slouched back in one of the two chairs for clients, she was staring at her boss, who towered in front of her, with her head slightly cocked to the side as though with boredom.

PREY

The muscular black man ran his hand through his short-cropped gray hair with a frustrated sigh and continued in an even tone, "You have got to be more careful. We are NOT in the practice of injuring the suspect!"

The redhead shrugged and put her feet up in the second chair, "In my defense, I just ASSISTED him in stabbing himself. He brought the knife and intended to use it on me. I can hardly be held responsible for misjudging the length of his arm, Whit." She watched him walk around his desk, "I doubt his victims would mind the outcome much." She arched an eyebrow, "Besides, he's gonna live. It's the best of both worlds," she grinned.

James Whitlock sighed heavily and sat behind his desk, rubbing his eyes with one hand as though willing away a migraine. "Is this all the evidence?" He motioned to the small box on his desk and finally looked at her with tired onyx eyes.

She nodded, "EmEm and Tessa got enough footage to put this guy away for good. Will was available for DNA testing, but since we turned the suspect right over to the police, we figured they might want to do at least part of their job for themselves."

A polite knock on the door was followed by the door opening. An apparently world-weary man in a wrinkled suit and dark trench coat stepped into the room, nodding his thanks to Will who had led him to the office.

The Asian man craned his neck to see into the room before the door was shut in his face.

"Speak of the devils," the woman smiled and stood up, "is that all for me, Whit?"

"No, you stay right there," Whitlock stood from his desk and reached his hand out to the newcomer, "you must be Detective Finnegan."

The detective nodded and shook Whit's hand before motioning to himself as he sat in the chair recently vacated by the redhead, "What gave me away?" he laughed.

The woman stepped around her boss' desk to lean against the wall by the window behind him. "The roguish devil-may-care smile, matched with the agency assigned badge, gun, and wrinkles," she answered in a bored tone as she peeked out of the blinds, the light shone on her pale face highlighting the dusting of freckles across the bridge of her nose.

Finnegan shrugged his acceptance of her statement, staring at her momentarily before turning his attention back to Whitlock, "Do you have our casefile for us?"

Whit handed the other man the small box from his desk, "Right to business, I can appreciate that. Here is the video and audio from last night as well as all the clothes our agent was wearing."

"So, tell me truthfully," Finnegan took the box and held it up as though judging the weight of its contents, "is that how your company usually operates?" He shoved the box into the pocket of his trench coat, "When your organization was suggested by his subordinate, the Commissioner was under the impression that the suspect would be turned over unharmed." He looked back and forth from the imposing man to the woman, he felt bold with a desk separating them from him. "He's facing a shit-storm if the press ever catches on that we hired you to apprehend a suspect, let alone that he was stabbed by the company we paid to capture him. This is New York City. The NYPD isn't in the habit of asking for help from anyone."

Whitlock's fists came down like sledgehammers on his desk as he leaned forward menacingly and growled, "It is not our usual practice." Shoulder muscles bulged beneath a perfectly pressed dress shirt, "However, it should go without saying that my agent had to protect herself any way she could. That man was the one with the weapon, my agent was unarmed."

The woman smirked at the detective when he looked to her quickly, feeling threatened. She winked.

"Nevertheless," the larger man continued as he stood upright again and smoothed the shirt over his core with both hands, bringing Finnegan's attention back to him. "I can understand your Commissioner's discomfort. I am aware that he only accepted our services because of a recommendation by Officer Gwen Grayson and we do not want to sully her reputation, so when we send him our sizeable bill, we will deduct five percent."

Finnegan nodded quickly, "Sounds fair to me, I'll let him know. Is your agent's information in this box?" He tapped his pocket, "We'll have to know where to send the subpoena."

"That's not how this works-" the woman started, but Whitlock held up his hand, silencing her.

"We were hired to catch a serial rapist who brutalized women in your jurisdiction," Whitlock's voice held no niceties. "Our only goal is to assist you with the evidence required to capture that man." He appraised the detective carefully, his hand stroking the perfectly maintained beard on his chin. "You have video-graphic evidence of the same MO, you have his DNA, and you have the seven other cases to tie him to using these pieces of evidence." Dark eyes glared into pale blue ones, "My agent is off limits to you. As far as I'm concerned, she doesn't inhabit the same plane of existence as you, and you certainly will not be subpoenaing her." Whitlock made fists so tight that his knuckles popped before releasing that tension and merely standing with his hands at his sides, "Especially since your need to do so, would merely be due to your lack of police work on the cases aforementioned." A small tug at the corner of his mouth was almost a smile, "If your Commissioner wishes for our transaction to remain anonymous, he will comply with the contract he signed."

Finnegan's eyes were wide, his Adam's apple bounced as he swallowed hard. He stood up and opened his mouth to speak but was cut off.

"Gage will show you out," Whitlock motioned to the door and turned his back on both the occupants in his office, opening the blinds to his window.

The redhead pushed off the wall with a bored expression marring her features as she motioned for the detective to exit the room before her.

"What did he call you?" Finnegan asked when he found his voice as she followed him from the room.

"Gage," she responded as she closed the door behind her, "as in baggage without the bag," she motioned to herself with a grin, "I'm a whole lot of mess."

"Why did you rate being in the room during our business?" Finnegan tried to seem like he was merely curious, but there was a tone to his voice that made Gage bristle.

"Because I was the agent who helped the animal you were ineffectively pursuing stab himself in the gut," she responded pertly, leading him through the large vehicle, past several monitors and assorted expensive equipment.

"You?" Finnegan was noticeably surprised, "That girl was blonde."

Gage snorted, "You're right. She was. She also doesn't exist." She opened the door into the warehouse where Will, EmEm, and Mere were standing, obviously still trying to eavesdrop.

"You have red hair," Finnegan said slowly as he followed her down the stairs.

"I t'ought you'd prefer red hair and freckles," she responded with an Irish accent, smiling shyly, and fluttering her lashes at him. It was then that he realized her freckles were too uniform. "You strappin' Irishman."

The laughter from her friends made Finnegan feel like an idiot.

"There's something wrong with you people," the detective stated as his gaze swept the group. "Do any of you function normally?"

"Define normal," Gage responded, smiling at the friends she considered family, "if being victimized and relying on incompetent jackasses like you to solve the crime, is normal, then count us out." She motioned to the open garage door.

"I am not incompetent!" Finnegan sputtered angrily.

"Tell that to your boss," Gage responded. When the detective seemed like he was about to continue the argument she cut him off, "No, really, go tell that to your boss. Our business is concluded, you're now trespassing."

Finnegan stood frozen for a moment in shock, then shook his head as though waking himself up, before he turned to walk out the door. He called, "Watch your six, kids," over his shoulder, "if you burn your friends like this, I can't imagine how pissed your enemies get."

"It's cool," Gage called after his retreating form, "they stab themselves eventually."

Finnegan left the garage to the sound of laughter.

"Now," Gage turned to her compatriots, "who wants to get their drink on?"

Three hands shot into the air.

"Sorry to put a hold on the celebration," Whitlock appeared in the doorway of the RV, "but there's still a matter of business to handle."

Gage sighed and turned to face her boss, she took in his appearance for the first time all day; noting that his sleeves were neatly rolled up to his elbows and the buttons at his throat were open, giving him the appearance of a hard-working businessman. The tattoos on his forearms and his carefully sculpted beard, shot through with grey, gave him the rougher edge she'd grown used to seeing daily, "What's that, Papa Bear?"

"The matter of where we go from here," Whitlock responded, ignoring the nickname.

"I vote home," Mere stated, "we haven't been home in months. We need to get back and maintain our contacts if we want to ensure they're useful, should we ever need them."

"Not to mention Will really needs to get laid," Gage quipped.

Will blushed and EmEm laughed, punching his friend's shoulder good-naturedly.

"I guess it would be nice to settle and regroup," Whitlock nodded, "we need to contact the Aussies for Mere's rifle anyway. That's always easier at home."

"Not to mention, my garage needs tending," Gage added, "you're only my part-time job. Don't forget that."

"And the street races are next week," Mere piped up, "if I miss another race, I doubt they'd let me back into their good graces."

"That's true," Will spoke up finally, "if we want to maintain all our contacts in the underground race scene, going home now is imperative."

"Not to mention our media contacts, right Little Brother," EmEm nudged Will's shoulder and winked at Mere who was grinning.

Will sighed, "Okay, yes, I would love to see my girlfriend in person after four months on the road with you animals." He met Whitlock's gaze, motioning to Gage, EmEm, and Mere, "Do you see what I have to put up with?"

Whitlock actually smiled, making him look far less haggard, "I know what you put up with because I see everything. I also know that you usually have just as much to do with the shenanigans." He clapped his hands once and nodded, "It's settled then, we'll head home to Miami in the morning."

Cheers erupted but were cut off when Whitlock continued, "Gage, make contact with the Aussies as soon as you can. We still need that rifle. Let's try to run down some leads on that West Virginia shooting case, on the off chance we decide to go there next."

Gage saluted, "As long as you recognize that my time will be spent predominantly in the garage, and living the delightful lifestyle afforded someone with my status."

Whitlock rolled his eyes, "Yes Gage, I recognize that you'll be at clubs, illegal street races, and parties. Just don't forget you're supposed to be making contacts we can use later."

Gage smiled brightly before singing, "I got friends in low places…"

"Will," Whitlock cut off the woman's song, "check in with Lina and verify that the media has been quiet, please. We don't need this incident up here to be attached to us. Make sure Gwen is clear as well. I don't want her to have any blow-back from helping us out."

Will nodded, "Absolutely."

"Check in with Lina," EmEm snorted, "don't forget to ask Lina after you two *reconnect* is what he really means."

The laughter was immediate and even Whitlock smiled in agreement before turning to Mere, "You just concentrate on racing. If we get you to the standards of Lorenzo Gambino than you can start making real contacts for us."

"She's already good enough," Gage cut in, "it's the having to up and leave so often that's hurting her credibility."

Mere smiled her thanks.

"Finally," Whitlock continued, "there's the issue of those ruined cars we received as an incentive from the latest victim's family here. I think we should just sell them for scrap, not worry about fixing them."

Gage put her hands on her hips, her jade eyes flashing, "You promised me that Gran Torino. You can NOT back out now! I already ordered the parts it needs."

Whitlock chuckled, "Fine, we'll transport the Torino to your shop but the other two we're selling as is for the cash. Agreed?"

Gage shrugged, "I don't care as long as I get my Torino."

"Good." Whitlock turned to go back into the RV, "Enjoy your night, we'll leave in the morning."

The four friends cheered but their merriment was immediately cut short when Whitlock turned around and said, "Oh, I almost forgot, we'll be vetting a new member when we get home."

"Awwww," Mere groaned, "you KNOW that never ends well."

"It's rare that we find someone with the skill set we need who can get along with us," Will added.

"Not to mention I thought we were doing well with the team we have," EmEm nodded his agreement with Will and Mere.

"Well it's a good thing it isn't up to you, isn't it?" Whitlock's tone was almost gleeful.

"Dick," Gage muttered under her breath as Whitlock disappeared into the RV.

"I heard that!" His voice came back muffled.

"You were supposed to!" She shouted back at him before laughing and turning to her friends, "Quick, let's go find a bar before Tessa gets back and stares at us all disapprovingly."

"All in favor?" Will called out, grabbing his shirt and jacket from off the chair by the computer station Mere had vacated.

"AYE!" They all yelled and ran from the building laughing.

Chapter 3

The smell of gasoline and oil permeated the small garage. A young girl with sand-colored curly pigtails leaned over a car's engine with a rag in hand, her tiptoes barely brushed the stool she was using to reach under the hood.

"Okay, that's where the oil goes," she pointed, "that's where the washer fluid goes, and that's the battery," she smiled proudly up at the man who was standing beside her.

"Very good," he nodded with a smile, "but what about the tip-over?"

The little girl's pigtails quivered as she shook her head in confusion, her jade eyes questioning, "You never told me about a tip-over before!"

The man kicked the stool out from under her and laughed when she squealed. He caught her in the air and spun her around until she was laughing breathlessly, "It's the tip-over!" He shook her gently, "The tip-over got you!"

"Daddy, stop!" She squealed amid giggles.

Then everything was dark. She was alone in the middle of a room and all she could hear was the opening and closing of doors from far away.

Blood was seeping toward her from all sides slowly.

"Hello?" The little girl's voice was so tiny and scared as it bounced off the walls, echoing back upon itself over and over again.

Dark green eyes fluttered open. Gage stretched her arms above her head and yawned.

"Dreaming those sweet dreams, you love so much?"

The feminine voice came from the hallway, so Gage chose to ignore it as her eyes closed once more and rolled onto her stomach, cuddling against her pillow.

"I thought you were rebuilding that Gran Torino this morning."

The voice was getting louder, which slightly annoyed her, "I already did it," she mumbled into her pillow. "Couldn't sleep so I started early. I went to bed at six am, so go away, it's still sleepy time."

"Now that you're back in town for a bit, word on the street is Lorenzo Gambino is going to come to ask the infamous Gage to help him with a project."

Gage opened one eye and stared at the girl standing in her doorway.

"It's true." The young redhead held up her hands in mock submission, "I swear."

"Are you aware of just how much I hate you right now?" Gage groaned.

"Well, it's about seven in the morning, so yes, I have a pretty good idea." The redhead laughed lightly and turned on her heel, "But I made pancakes, so I'm hoping to win back some bonus points."

"With chocolate chips?" Gage asked hopefully as she pushed herself up from her bed and stepped to the floor with booted feet.

"Yes, extra chocolate chips," the voice sing-songed back as Gage pulled off her shirt and threw it behind her onto the floor, "now change out of your yesterday clothes into your today clothes and get your cute ass out here!"

"You know Tessa, you probably should stop acting like my MOM," Gage called as she kicked off her boots and pulled the belt off her jeans, "since you're like seven years younger than me."

"But I'm so much more mature than you are, Kitten."

Gage slipped out of her jeans and tossed them on her bed with a shrug, muttering, "I guess that's probably true." The smell of pancakes made her stomach growl, so instead of pulling on clean jeans, she strode down the hall in her bra and panties, "Where's the food?" She stepped into the kitchen, nodded her head at the people sitting around the table and grabbed one of the pancakes from off the plate at the center of the table.

Her young friend stood in the center of the kitchen with wide blue eyes, "You are such a freak," she sighed, shaking her head.

Gage shrugged, "What?" She looked down at herself as she rolled the pancake up and took a bite, "It's just like a bikini."

"Yeah," a young man, who was painfully nondescript, grinned from his place at the table. His dark hair was slicked back from his pale face.

Mere rolled her eyes from next to him, "Look, Derek, everyone knows about you, you don't have to pretend seeing a girl in her bra is exciting."

"I'm NOT gay, Meredith!"

Gage snickered as she took another bite of her rolled up pancake.

Mere motioned to her friend, "It's very obvious that any straight man, hanging around us for extended periods of time, would have long ago tried to tap that."

Gage looked down at herself then looked back up, "It's true," she said with her mouth full of half-eaten pancake as she winked at Mere, "I'm freaking hot."

Mere laughed at her friend before turning to Derek, "The only logical explanation is that you're hot for EmEm." She held up her hands as though surrendering, "No judgment, we've all had love affairs with our roommates, there's no reason to be embarrassed."

Derek's face was crimson and he sputtered, trying to figure out a good retort. EmEm drank his glass of milk with an amused expression on his face.

Gage snorted at the spectacle.

"Get out of here, before you cause problems," Tessa laughed and swatted at her half-naked friend with a dish towel.

"Fine." Gage said with her mouth full of another bite of pancake. "Whatever," she strode out of the kitchen and back down the hall to her room, where she shut the door and finished her pancake before going into her small bathroom for a shower.

"WHERE THE FUCK IS MY MONEY?"

Gage stepped from the shower, toweled off and quickly started getting dressed, ignoring the fact that her jeans stuck to her still wet skin. She cinched her belt and pulled on a tank top before towel drying her hair as quickly as she could and moving from the bathroom toward the angry voices.

"Look, I don't know what you're going on about, but you can just wait downstairs in the garage, where someone would be happy to help you," Tessa's voice was small but firm.

"I WANT MY FUCKING MONEY BACK!"

Gage stepped into the kitchen to find Tessa and a man arguing. "I'm sorry Eduardo, do you have some sort of malfunction I should know about?" She asked with her jade eyes narrowed in anger, "Because coming to my home to whine like a bitch is not what I like from my customers." She moved until she was between Tessa and the shouting man.

"I won't be your customer anymore," Eduardo Espinoza snapped, "my brother's engine gave out."

Gage arched an eyebrow, "Your brother's sex life has nothing to do with me."

"Very funny, Bitch," Eduardo spat, "his engine blew up. The engine YOU put in his car."

Gage crossed her arms over her chest, "And you want to blame me because your brother ruined a perfectly tuned car? How does that work?"

"I want my money back," he stepped toward her menacingly.

She tried not to let her amusement show on her face as she held one hand up at his chest level, "Look, if you can prove the car's problem was my fault, I'll be happy to refund your money." Gage cocked her head slightly, "But we both know your brother is a moron who can't drive, so it was most likely driver error."

"You dare disrespect my family?"

"Oh, I dare," she nodded, "and I don't know who you think you are, but this is my home. The garage is downstairs, if you had a problem you should have called for an appointment like everyone else." She cracked her neck, "If you EVER try to threaten me again, by word or actions, I will end you." She glared at him then with an overly sweet tone she asked, "Okay?"

He smiled meanly, "What is it a little girl like you could possibly do to me?"

Gage returned the smile with an innocent one of her own, staring down at him in amusement because he was several inches shorter than her, "Why don't you come at me sometime and see, Sugar."

"It seems to me, the lady would like you to leave," a deep male voice Gage didn't recognize interrupted the discussion.

"Gambino," Eduardo turned to face a man who was leaning against the counter beside Tessa, "no one asked for your input."

"How is it possible I didn't see you there?" Gage's eyes were wide when she realized Lorenzo Gambino must have been there the entire time standing right behind her.

"You were otherwise occupied," the muscular Italian man smiled, his arms crossed across his chest, "it's okay, I'll forgive you."

Gage arched an eyebrow then turned her gaze back to the disgruntled customer, "I'm through with you now, please leave, or you'll be escorted from the residence."

Espinoza let out an angry huff, "This isn't over."

"Actually, it is," she responded, "take your shit to a new garage. I don't want you near my shop again. You have a problem with that? Sue me." She didn't wait for him to respond, instead, she turned her attention to Tessa, "Where'd Meredith and the others go?"

"We needed milk," Tessa answered.

"So they went…" Gage trailed off, her head cocked to the side.

"To the gun range, of course," Tessa sighed and picked up her purse, "you two are going to be the death of me."

Gage grinned, "But you're so young. You can't die before us, that's why we brought you here."

Tessa rolled her eyes, "I'm going to the grocers, you play nice."

"Yes Mummy," Gage stuck her tongue out at her friend. When she turned back to the door, Eduardo Espinoza was gone, "Oh good, he CAN take a hint."

"Which is shocking," Lorenzo stated, still not moving from the counter, "since he's really not that bright."

Gage laughed as Tessa left and closed the door behind her. "So, to what do I owe this honor, Mr. Gambino?"

"I'm looking for Gauge," Gambino straightened and stood in front of her, offering his hand to shake, "and you can call me Enzo."

Gage smirked and shook it once before crossing her arms over her chest, "So, tell me, why do you need to speak to Gauge?"

"I may have a job for him," Enzo put one hand in his jeans pocket, "do you know where I can find him?"

Gage laughed lightly and looked him up and down, taking in the expensive leather jacket and designer jeans hugging his muscular physique, "What makes you think Gauge cares about your job?"

"You know my name," Enzo smiled as he changed the subject, returning the hooded gaze with one of his own, "don't you think I should know who you are?"

Jade eyes surveyed his cocky grin, "You know who I am, at least, you've heard of me. You've just lost some key facts."

"I think I'd remember something so beautiful."

Gage laughed lightly, her hands dropping to her hips, "Well, Mr. Gambino-"

"Enzo," he interrupted.

"Enzo," she amended with a sly smile, "Gauge, is not a man. Gage is me." She held out her hand to him to shake his hand again, "It's a common misconception."

"Well," he took her hand and held it longer than was polite, "I guess I'm just an idiot then."

"No," Gage pulled her hand back and shoved it in her pocket, "just a typical man, assuming only someone with a dick can be good with cars." She shrugged, "It actually tends to work to my advantage."

Enzo stared at her with wide eyes for a moment.

"What?" She asked with an arched eyebrow.

"You're just not what I expected," he answered.

"I get that a lot."

Chapter 4

"So," Tessa walked into the kitchen with two brown paper bags in her arms, "what did Mr. Gambino have to say once he found out the brilliant Gage is a chick?"

"Enzo's cool," Gage said with her eyes still closed. She was lounging in a bikini on one of the poolside chairs on the patio.

"Oooo," Tessa set the bags down and came out through the open slider, "ENZO, is it?"

Gage opened one eye and looked up at Tessa, "You're in my sun."

Tessa moved to her right until her shadow no longer fell across Gage's face, "You gonna tell me?"

"He still offered me the job," Gage answered as she closed her eye again, "so he must not think the whole me not having a dick thing is that big of a deal."

Tessa laughed and shook her head, "What's the job?"

"He has a classic Mustang he wants to be rebuilt internally. He also asked about some airbrush work on the hood, if you're up to it. He wants a badass phoenix."

"He can't have this done in his own garage?" Tessa's voice was disbelieving.

Gage opened her eyes and sat up, "He said it takes more finesse than he has," she smirked, "and he's so muscular, it must be true," she sighed appreciatively.

"You're hopeless," Tessa sighed and walked back inside, putting away the groceries, "completely hopeless."

"Where's Mere when I need her?" Gage responded as she stood and walked into the room, "My appreciation of the three-legged species is lost on you."

"Damn straight," Tessa laughed, "I don't understand how you two are so crude."

"Comes with the territory," Gage shrugged and pulled a box of cookies from the paper bag.

"What's this?" Tessa asked, shocked, "You're helping me put away groceries?"

Gage arched an eyebrow, ripped off the top of the box, and pulled out a cookie, munching on it with an innocent smile.

"I should have known," Tessa rolled her eyes and finished putting away the groceries, "you are such a dork."

Gage shrugged, "There's a race tonight, wanna go? It's the first time the whole team will be together and home for a race in almost two years."

"I have school tomorrow," the redhead put a hand on her hip and cocked her head to the side with attitude, "some of us are trying to better ourselves."

Gage swallowed her cookie and grinned, "And some of us are already perfect," she curtsied and walked back out onto the patio, "you should blow off school for once. Come party. It'll be good for you."

"No," Tessa sighed, "it would involve drinking and dangerous behavior."

Gage turned to stare at her friend, "Are you sure you're nineteen? Because you act like you're forty."

The redhead rolled her eyes and left the kitchen. As she walked down the hallway she called, "Are you going to work at all today? Or just eat your cookies and get fat?"

Gage looked down at her flat stomach and pinched at it, making a face, "I'm NOT getting fat!" When her friend didn't respond Gage put her box of cookies down and called worriedly, "You don't REALLY think I'm getting fat do you?"

Tessa's laughter echoed down the hallway.

PREY

~*~*~*~*~

"Why are you doing sit-ups while eating cookies?"

Gage continued to do her sit-ups between bites, "Because Tessa said I'm getting fat, so I've decided to burn off the sugar WHILE eating it." She smiled at Mere who was leaning against the wall with an amused expression on her face.

"I heard Gambino came by," Mere changed the subject, "was that before or after Espinosa came demanding his refund?"

Gage sighed heavily and stood up, her sweatpants riding low on her hips, showing the elastic of her yellow bikini, "I actually think it was during. He was here when Espinosa went ape-shit," Gage smiled dreamily, "he even tried to defend my honor."

Mere laughed, "You have honor?"

"No, that's why he tried," Gage responded with a chuckle of her own.

"So, what's the job that Gambino can't do in his own people's garage?"

"Well," Gage put the box of cookies on the counter and strolled toward the door, motioning for Mere to follow her, "he claimed that the job he wants done involves more finesse than he's capable of maintaining."

"So," Mere said casually as the two women walked down the stairs, "what's your read on the real reason?"

"What?" Gage looked over her shoulder pretending to be shocked, "You think Enzo is lying?"

"Enzo huh?" Mere arched an eyebrow.

"Yes," Gage sighed, "but word on the street is he's involved with someone," she pouted, "too bad I don't believe in home-wreaking."

Mere shook her head as she followed her friend into the main garage, "Seriously Gage, what's the real reason?"

"I think he doesn't want it connected to him," Gage responded, her tone all business, "I think he's fully capable of doing all the modifications he specified, but he doesn't want this car in plain sight, he wants this done on the down low, which I assured him we can do."

Mere shrugged, "Sure, no big."

Both women stopped walking when they heard growling from two sources. One was a deep gravelly sound the other was higher and throatier.

"I came by with the key and met your welcoming party," Enzo was standing in the far corner of the garage with a ring of keys hanging from one of his fingers. His hands were up in surrender and two dogs stood growling at him. One was a Doberman pinscher; the other was an exact copy of the big dog but at the size of a Chihuahua.

"They don't normally get protective during the day," Gage strolled forward, "were you snooping?"

Enzo sighed, "I may have wandered by a couple of times before coming in," he smiled, "I was trying to gather courage to see you twice in one day." He looked her up and down, taking in her bikini top and tattooed torso, "Butterflies huh?" He smiled again as he referred to the twin tattoos on her stomach by her belly button, "I like that."

Mere laughed, "You like butterflies?"

"Fair enough," Enzo's smile turned sheepish, "I mostly just like the skin."

Gage arched an eyebrow before snapping her fingers. Both dogs immediately ceased growling. "Killer, Tiny, go play," the dogs ran past the women on the command. Moments later the sounds of squeaky toys could be heard.

"Killer, huh?" Enzo rubbed the back of his neck with his free hand, "That's one BIG scary dog you got there."

"Nah," Mere smirked, "the big one's Tiny."

Enzo glanced back and forth between the two women, both of whom shrugged.

"We have ironic senses of humor," Gage explained.

"So, the 'Stang, as we discussed," Enzo tossed Gage the keys.

She caught them with her right hand and held them out to Mere, "Take it around back for me?"

Mere took the keys and nodded her head, walking past Enzo. She looked back at him over her shoulder and turned around so she was walking backward. She mouthed 'oh my God' and nodded her appreciation slowly.

Gage's smile broadened as she tried not to laugh. When Enzo turned to see what was funny, Mere was already out of the garage.

"So, you decided you'll sign the contract?" She asked, turning his attention back to her.

"Yeah," he nodded, "I decided it's the least I can do, after all, the price you quoted me is way too low."

"How do you figure?" She asked as she strode by him to the office, "You already have all the parts, it's just a matter of getting the parts into the car."

"Which will take a while," Enzo answered, "most shops charge by the hour for labor."

"So do we," Gage answered, "we're just quick. We know cars here. They listen to us."

"Cars listen to you?"

Gage turned to look at him, "You know, if you really listen, and I do mean listen hard, you can hear a car practically screaming out to be loved." She smiled a bit as she stared past him at the Gran Torino she'd just rebuilt, "Every car has a soul, as long as you're good to the car, the car will be good to you."

"So, what you're telling me, is you're crazy."

Her gaze went back to him and she laughed, "Sure. Crazy, brilliant, it's all relative."

"Well, I've heard that you're the best-"

"I am," she answered and opened a drawer, pulling out a piece of paper, "if I can just get your signature, you can be on your way."

Enzo took the paper from her hand and took a pen from the cup on her desk before bending over to use the wooden surface to sign it, "You going to the race tonight?"

"Yeah," Gage responded, "Mere, that gorgeous firecracker who took your keys, is in it. She'll be wiping the floor with her competition, pretty soon she'll be racing you," she smiled, "better watch your back."

Enzo straightened, his dark eyes shining with laughter, "Oh I'll do that." He handed the signed piece of paper to her, "I'll see you tonight then."

She nodded, "Your car should be ready Friday unless our artist is available for your hood before then. If she's available, I'll send you mockups and let you choose your design. The timeframe would be based on her availability. Right now, I believe she's unavailable, I'll call you if that changes."

"I look forward to the call," Enzo answered.

"That was a terrible flirt," Gage scolded, "you're better than that."

Enzo sighed, "I know. I'm sorry."

Gage laughed, "Now run along before I sick Killer on you."

Enzo smirked and arched his eyebrow, "All right. I'm going."

Gage waved flirtatiously at him as he strode away.

Chapter 5

"I have absolutely NOTHING to wear!" Gage shouted as she threw the last shirt that was hanging in her closet on her floor. She waded through the piles of clothing to her dresser and began pulling clothes from the drawers.

"What do you mean?" Tessa stared with wide eyes when she came into Gage's doorway, "Holy crap Gage, what the hell are you doing?"

"I don't have anything to wear!" The older woman whined as she looked at the shirt in her hand before throwing it to the ground.

"What are you talking about?" Tessa motioned to the floor, "Look at all that. There has to be something in there you can wear."

"No," Gage shook her head, "I hate it all. Nothing is good enough, we're going shopping."

"I can't," Tessa shook her head, "I have homework."

"Fine," Gage sighed, "I was going to buy you something fancy. But if you won't go then-"

"HONEYS I'M HOME!" A faux Ricky Ricardo voice called as a door slammed.

"MERE!" Gage pushed past her younger friend and rushed down the hall, "Bal Harbour bitches, we're going shopping for hot clothes, my treat!"

"Oooo," Mere clapped her hands, "race clothes?"

"I want to make Enzo drool all over his girlfriend," Gage answered proudly, "and possibly find a suitable booty call."

The two older women laughed as Tessa entered the room and rolled her eyes, "You really are hopeless, Gage."

"Are you coming or not?" Gage turned to the redhead, "Free things are fun, and we can poke fun at the bimbos."

"No, I told you, I can't," Tessa shrugged, "sorry. But you go."

"We will," Gage responded. She opened the door to the stairway leading to the garage and called, "KILLER! Pick out a bag, we're going shopping!" The growling yelp that floated up the stairs made her call, "Stop complaining you punk, just DO it."

"Oooo," Mere grinned brightly, "can we go to Rosario's for a late lunch?"

"Certainly, my dear," Gage glanced over her shoulder and wiggled her hips, "I take care of MY dates."

"Yay for Sugar Mamas," Mere laughed, "and I don't even hafta give you sexual favors."

Gage laughed and shook her head, "To the bedroom!" She called and pointed in front of her as she ran down the hall to her room, "Now I need to find a shopping outfit!"

There was a squeak as a black bag was pushed through the dog door onto the kitchen floor. The bag was followed by the miniature pinscher who stood beside it, waiting.

"Which one did he pick?" Gage called.

"Black Louis Vuitton," Mere called back.

After a few moments, a crash, and a curse, Gage walked back into the room wearing a tight pair of black jeans with an electric blue halter top, "Good boy!" She cooed at the small dog that immediately pulled his lips back in a grimace, "Oh don't give me that face," she scolded, "you know you enjoy scaring the blondes." He barked once and ran in a tight circle around the bag, seeming to almost dance.

"You really should come Tessa," Mere glanced at the youngest woman, "it'll be lots of fun, and on Gage's dime."

"I wish I could-"

"You either come shopping now, or we're kidnapping you tonight," Gage scooped up her dog and placed him in the bag, sliding the straps over her shoulder, "so make your choice."

"I'm not going to either," Tessa answered, "I'll be writing my paper, bring me back something from Rosario's."

Gage arched an eyebrow and looked at Mere who smiled mischievously, "Kidnapping it is," they said at the same time before letting out maniacal laughs and exiting through the patio door, sliding it closed behind them.

Tessa rolled her eyes and sat at the table, opening her laptop and beginning to type.

~*~*~*~*~

"What about this one?" Gage held the miniskirt against her waist, "Does it say 'delicious and available but not a whore'?"

Mere arched an eyebrow, "That says 'I'm cheap, use me.'"

"Hmmm," Gage looked down at it thoughtfully for a moment then sighed, "nah." She hung the garment back on the rack, "I guess that's not what I want to say."

Mere laughed good-naturedly, "You crack me up."

Gage shrugged, readjusting her bag on her shoulder, "Killer is fucking snoring. It's obnoxious."

Mere's laughter resumed, "You're the one that took him out during his normal nap time. There haven't even been any purse-puppies to make fun of today."

Gage sighed, "Which is upsetting, because you know how I love watching the little girls cry."

"True," Mere nodded, "shopping has been a let-down today, it's upsetting."

"All in all, a very unfulfilling day," Gage agreed as she strode around the sale's rack. "Wait, what's this?" She dug into the hangers and held something below Mere's line of vision.

"What is it?" The younger woman craned her neck to see.

"Ai Mami, this is Puuurrfecto!" Gage made it sound like a purr and held up the candy-apple red soft leather tight jacket, "You MUST have it."

Mere's eyes lit up and she held out her arms, "GIMMIE! GIMMIE!" She caught the garment when Gage threw it and had it on and zipped in a matter of moments, "Oh, so soft."

"Yup, that will bring you luck tonight, you are going to have it," she winked at her friend, "I insist."

"Well," Mere stroked the sleeves, hugging herself, "if you insist."

"I do, I do," Gage laughed, "now find me SOMETHING!"

Mere saluted her friend, "On a mission. Roger that," she cocked her head, "or should it be copy that?" She chewed her lower lip thoughtfully.

"I don't care if it's roger or copy," Gage responded, "I need to get LAID, Mere. You GOT me?"

Mere laughed, "Desperate nymphomaniac," she nodded, "roger."

As they began scouring the store once more a group of three bleached blonde girls came strolling in, chattering in the high-pitches that made birds cower.

"Oooo," Gage smiled, "yummy." She nodded her head toward the girls. Each of them had a bag that had a small furry head peeking out. Gage looked down at her own bag, "Oooo Shnookums, there's some puppies here for you to see." Killer opened his eyes, yawned, and blinked up at her.

"Ready?" Mere asked softly.

"SO ready," Gage nodded and walked with her friend arm in arm, "like OH mah GAWD," she shrieked in a token Valley-girl tone, "can you believe what he said to me then?"

"No way," Mere said back in the same type of tone, "not what I THINK you're gonna say."

"I think you think what I thought it would be," Gage answered matter-of-factly.

"So, what you think I thought you'd think it'd be is wrong?" Mere asked as they strolled up to the other girls who were by now staring at them.

"SO wrong," Gage responded. "What I think you think I thought it'd be was not even a little what HE thought I'd think it'd be."

"Oooooh," Mere nodded then smiled brightly at the three girls, "oh mah GAWD! Look at those sweet babies!" She waved her fingers at the Chihuahua and two Pomeranians before handing the price tag from her coat to the sales clerk.

"Just darling," Gage answered as she handed over cash for Mere to pay the clerk for her jacket, "what're their names?"

"Mine's Sugar Baby," the blonde with the Chihuahua answered, her manicured fingernails scratching her dog's ear.

"Snicker-doodle," the second answered as her caramel colored dog began to yip.

"And mine's Dash," the last one said, "named for Kim Kardashian."

"Oh my GAWD KIM!" The three squealed.

"We're like SO excited for her new line, aren't you?"

"Like TOTALLY!" Gage nodded with a fake smile still plastered on her face as Mere handed her back her change. She zipped it into the front of her bag.

"You should like TOTALLY see her puppy," Mere pointed at Gage's bag, "he's like, the most adorable thing EVER."

"But he's totally shy," Gage sighed and pulled her purse off her shoulder, "you hafta get super close and kinda peek in, real quiet."

All three of the blondes nodded with their eyes vacant of any real emotion.

Gage held her purse out slightly and the three girls all leaned in, shushing each other anxiously though none of them spoke. "Ready?" Gage asked in a whisper.

They all nodded.

Gage popped open her purse and Killer sprang from the bag at the three girls, growling and baring his small teeth. All three girls shrieked and jumped back. One fell over a display of shoes, her Pomeranian yipping insanely as it hit the ground. It got free of its bag and bolted for the back of the store.

"YOU'RE FREE DASH!" Gage called, laughing hysterically, "DASH AWAY!"

Mere grabbed Gage's arm and the two of them ran from the store laughing with Killer running behind them barking.

"GOOD BOY!" Gage scooped her dog up and the two women ran down the block before slipping into a different store.

Chapter 6

The smell of burning rubber, exhaust, and gasoline swirled in the air like a cheap hooker's perfume. The crowd got high from the scent that gripped them like a fist and dragged them to the finish line as the end of the first race neared. Mere didn't see who won. She didn't care. She heard the crowd whooping and cheering and the squealing of tires that always brought goose bumps to her flesh. Those tell-tale signs meant the first race was over.

"You know, it doesn't matter how many of these things I go to," EmEm said from the passenger seat, staring out the window, "I'm always surprised by the level of depravity."

Mere laughed, putting her window up as she pulled her car close to the mass that seemed to pulse with excitement. She turned the key, pulling it from the ignition and pocketing it in her new jacket as she climbed from her candy apple red Nissan 370Z. When she closed her door, she couldn't help but smile at how perfectly her jacket matched the car's paint. She pulled a tube of lipstick from her pocket and looked in her side mirror to coat her lips in the exact shade of her car's paint. It was specially made for her, the price was a bit extreme, but as she smacked her lips and took in her appearance, she decided it was definitely worth it. Plus, every race, she'd always worn it, and never lost. Maybe luck wasn't real, but it couldn't hurt to pretend. She pulled her auburn hair back into a high ponytail.

"Of course, by now I should be used to it," EmEm continued as he walked around the front of the car, smiling at her as she straightened. "My witchy woman," he nodded at her, "I don't know how you don't get attacked constantly, looking so fine."

"It's my resting bitch face," Meredith scanned the crowd, searching for anyone she knew. They still had two more races to watch before it was her turn. These beginning races were for the less experienced. She linked arms with EmEm and walked through the crowd, most of the people moved out of her way as she walked. She smirked, knowing it was her reputation making them move, not EmEm's formidable stature.

Mere tried not to sneer as they finally came to the break in the crowd and found three smoking cars huddled together at the finish line. They all had body damage and a number of other problems that she was too bored to name even in her head, "Amateurs," she muttered as she shook her head and rolled her eyes before turning back the way they'd come and heading back toward her car.

"Hey MERE!" A female voice was calling her, "EmEm!"

Mere turned to her right, scanning the faces to find the one who had called her. A pretty Latina woman with long brown sugar hair, who looked completely out of place in the crowd of street race fanatics, was trying to force her way through the crush of bodies. She looked up at Mere and EmEm with pleading brown eyes and motioned to all the bodies.

Mere laughed and called out, "What's shaking Lina?"

A few of the fans in the crowd recognized Mere and moved to let Lina through.

"Not much," Lina responded with a smile of thanks when she finally made it to Mere's side, "I must admit I'm loving the new coat."

"Thank you," Mere grinned and EmEm spun her as though they were waltzing to show off her new clothing, "courtesy of Gage."

"Oooo," Lina nodded, "tres chic." She smiled at her friend, "and those lips, full of fire as always."

"In every way," Mere laughed.

Lina laughed too, "So where is your patroness? Will she be gracing us with her presence?" She smiled mischievously, "And more importantly, will she be allowing Will to shirk his garage duties and come play?"

"Indeed," Mere looked up when the deep guttural rumble of an American made muscle car permeated the sounds of whining engines and squealing tires, "I'm sure that's our fearless leader now in her new toy."

"She really worked a miracle on that old thing, didn't she?" EmEm's awe was apparent in his voice.

"New toy?" Lina turned and caught a glimpse of the newly renovated Gran Torino, "Her and her American muscle," she said sadly, shaking her head.

"We spent two hours today arguing over Imports or American," Mere muttered, "we should start that argument again, now that it will be two to one." She elbowed EmEm in the gut playfully, "God knows this one isn't any help."

"I don't care if a car is imported or American, I just like nice cars," EmEm said defensively, "I don't see how that's a problem."

Lina laughed, "While I do enjoy a good import, I must admit, Gage did wonders on that car. Will told me it was practically a shell."

Mere nodded appreciatively, "I never said she wasn't magic, I just think she should only use her powers for good, to fix imports."

~*~*~*~*~

Gage climbed out of the driver's seat of her favorite new acquisition and closed the door behind her, running her fingers down the hood lovingly. She turned and grinned at the handsome man who climbed out of the passenger seat, "She drives like a dream Will."

"I know," he laughed, his brown eyes sparkling, "and she would have been just as good if you'd waited and let me help."

Gage shrugged with an innocent smile, "My bad? I got excited once the paint was done."

Will shook his head as he opened the back-passenger door and looked down at the occupant who sat pouting, "You might as well come out and enjoy yourself. No one will take you home till you at least pretend to have a good time, Kid."

Tessa glared up at him and climbed out of the car, slamming the door and turning her glare to Gage when the older woman arched an eyebrow in the redhead's direction.

"You should have just come of your own volition," Gage shrugged, "it's your fault you didn't get to prettify."

Tessa rolled her eyes and crossed her arms over her baggy T-shirt.

Gage straightened her knee-length skirt that had a slit all the way up dangerously high on her right thigh and grinned when she saw Mere and Lina, "CHICAS!" She threw her arms out as though wanting to hug them and kissed at the air the way the Valley Girls did, "MUAH! MUAH!"

"Hola!" Lina called back to the older woman, waving and blowing several kisses at the newly arrived trio.

Mere laughed and rolled her eyes, "We already got our Valley Fix today, Gage."

Will grinned at the sight of Lina and walked around the Torino, "Hey Babe." He put an arm around her waist and kissed her temple lightly, "We kidnapped the kid outta bed," he pulled her against his side and whispered, "she's pissed."

"Aww," Lina laughed lightly and looked at Tessa's somber expression, the girl was in sweatpants and an oversized T-shirt, her hair pulled up in a messy bun. "I suppose if I'd been kidnapped, I'd be pissed off too." The Latina pulled her car remote from the pocket of her jeans, "I have some spare outfits and makeup in my car if you're interested," she let the remote dangle from her index finger and held it out in an offer to the younger girl. "Leftover freebies from my photoshoot yesterday, I was going to bring them over to the flat anyway."

Tessa looked at Gage who was staring at her expectantly and sighed, "I don't suppose you'd let me take your car home would you."

Gage, Mere, EmEm, and Will all looked at Lina.

Lina shrugged her shoulders, the remote still hanging from her finger, "I'm not going to come chasing after you like a banshee if you take my car for a small joyride and just happen to end up back at home, if that's what you mean."

"I will," Gage held up her hand, "and I'll just make Will pick you up and carry you right back, so you might as well just stay and have a good time."

Lina arched an eyebrow at Gage before glancing at Will, "I think I missed the memo about you being the personal servant to other women."

"She paid me fifty bucks," he shrugged and bumped fists with EmEm, "perfect for date night."

Lina shook her head, but her lips were twisted into a small smile.

Mere laughed at Tessa's forlorn face, "You hafta cheer me on anyway," her words were punctuated with the squealing of tires. "There's only one more race before I go."

"I have a paper I should be writing," Tessa complained.

"Bull shit," Gage rolled her eyes, "that paper is not due for two weeks. You're just being annoying and whiny. You need to chill out and be a kid," she pushed Tessa toward Lina, "go make some bad decisions."

Tessa frowned and said, "I guess I'll go *prettify*," as she took Lina's keys. "Where is it?"

Lina nodded her head over her shoulder, "Directly behind us. You won't be able to miss it. It sticks out like a sore thumb, just like me!"

Tessa nodded and headed in that direction.

Will laughed, "A sore thumb huh?"

"That's how I feel every time I come to one of these things," Lina leaned more of her weight against him.

"I've never wished to be a kid sucking his thumb before," he grinned down at her, "but I'm reevaluating my wish strategy."

Lina rolled her eyes at him but chuckled, "Mi Amor, extremely original."

He shrugged and tickled her side with the hand he had resting on her hip, "I can't help it, you're irresistible."

Gage and Mere exchanged looks and made faces, EmEm pretended to vomit.

"Get a room," Gage sighed and turned back to her car, opening the back driver-side door and allowing Tiny and Killer to leap down.

"Don't hate," Lina laughed at Gage as her body jerked away from Will's fingers when they pressed into her ticklish side. "I suppose you can't help loving to cuddle with me. I'm just so darn cute and all."

"This is all the darn cute I need," Gage rubbed Tiny's head and grinned.

Will laughed, "You're MUCH cuter than the mutt, Babe."

"I would hope you would think that I'm more attractive than a dog," Lina responded, "if you didn't, I might be a tiny bit offended."

Tiny looked up with pricked ears and gave a growling yowl-like sound before leaning against Gage's leg.

"Ha," Gage scratched his ear, "you should know by now not to use his name in a sentence when you're around lover boy."

Mere nodded, "He'll get his ass bitten again."

Gage and Mere looked at each other with a smirk, "Actually do it," they said together while EmEm laughed and motioned from the dog to Will, as though he was an air-traffic-controller.

"No!" Lina yelped, "That's horrible."

Will glared at each of his friends in turn, "That's right, my lady likes my ass unbitten."

Gage rolled her eyes, "It's not OUR fault Tiny has taken a dislike to you. Everything was fine until you laid claim to Lina."

"Probably it's because you took away his favorite cuddle mate," Mere added.

"She does spend a lot less time at the flat now that you two live together," EmEm said matter-of-factly.

Lina pushed her dark side-swept bangs from her eyes, "I still love Tiny," she spoke as she crouched and stared at the dog leaning against Gage's leg. "Are you going to pout or come see me?"

The dog grumbled a bit but stepped forward until he was within arm's reach and cocked his head to the side.

Gage laughed and shook her head, "You better go get to the start line Mere, I hear the screaming of hoochies."

Mere nodded, "I'm on it."

"Good luck!" Lina called before turning her stare back to the dog. "Come on now," she cocked her own head to the side, mirroring him, "you're not really mad at me, are you?"

"She doesn't NEED the luck!" Gage yelled after her friend.

"'CAUSE I GOT THE SKILL!" Mere shouted with a little dance.

"Pink slip it!" EmEm called before turning back to watch Will's plight unfold.

Tiny seemed to sigh and glared up at Will who held up his hands in surrender, "Hey man, I'll share her if it means you won't bite me."

Lina smiled, "Come on, you know you're still my main boy."

"Hey," Will frowned when EmEm punched his shoulder in glee, "I said I'd SHARE."

Gage laughed and picked up Killer, "But Tiny is so much cuter."

"Relax," Lina laughed as she turned her head slightly to speak to Will over her shoulder, "I still love you, too. Tiny was just my first cuddle buddy." She pouted at the dog, "You really aren't going to love on me?"

The dog stepped forward and kissed her face once before resting his chin on her shoulder and glaring up at Will.

"Now see," Lina laughed and rubbed his ears fondly, "I still love you."

"He's looking at me like he wants to eat me," Will said quietly, staring down at the monstrous dog.

Gage laughed, "That's 'cause he does," she said pertly, "I'm going to find a good spot to watch Mere whip ass and take names. She promised to try to get me a muscle car." She held her hand out to EmEm, "Coming darling?"

He moved closer to her so she could link her elbow with his, "Absolutely, let's go."

"You wouldn't hurt Will and make me sad, would you?" Lina said sweetly as she pushed the dog back and cupped his face, rubbing her nose to his.

Tiny let out a huff of air that sounded surprisingly like a sigh before licking her face once more and chasing after Gage.

"You know that dog is going to kill me in my sleep, right?" Will asked as Lina stood up.

Lina laughed and looked at her boyfriend, "I guess it's a good thing you sleep with me, so I can protect you. Don't worry, I'll take your mind off the fear," she winked at him and smiled brightly.

"Mmm," Will placed his warm hands on her hips and pulled her to him, kissing her deeply before pulling back slightly and saying, "promises, promises."

Lina laughed lightly and tapped his chest with her fingers, "You know I keep my promises. Let's go find Gage and cheer for Mere."

Will nodded with a grin of his own before letting his arm once more encircle her waist and ushering her through the crowd. His grin swiftly left his face however when both dogs came trotting over.

"I guess Gage thought they should hang with us," Lina laughed at her boyfriend's face.

~*~*~*~*~

Gage and EmEm caught up with Mere just in time to see the younger woman's exasperated sigh.

Gage said, "What's wrong chick-e-dee?" at the same time EmEm said, "Who needs their ass kicked?"

"I got pushed back into a different race," Mere said with a broad grin.

"That's AWESOME!" Gage returned the grin as EmEm swept Mere into a huge hug, "It was the jacket wasn't it."

Mere looked down at the leather when she was placed back on her feet and shrugged, "Probably," she laughed.

Gage shook her head and opened her mouth to assure her friend that it was the driver, not the attire, when all the color drained from her face and she took a step back from her friends, "Oh my God," she whispered.

Mere laughed and scolded, "We're not being Valley Girls anymore," the teasing smirk disappeared when she glanced at her friend's face, "What's wrong? You look like you've seen a ghost."

EmEm scanned the crowd in confusion.

Gage licked her lips slightly, "I think I'm going to be sick," she practically whimpered.

Mere's green eyes surveyed the crowd, trying to find the source of her friend's discomfort, "Why? What's wrong?"

"Is that Alejandro Sanchez?" Gage asked under her breath, "What is he doing here?"

"Ale-who? I don't know who that is," Mere stared at her friend with concern before glancing at EmEm who matched her confusion, "Should I know who that is?"

EmEm shrugged and shook his head.

"No." Gage turned from the crowd, "I need to go. Now. I need to leave right now."

"Okay," Mere took her friend's arm, "I'll go with you. Let's go."

"Don't be stupid," Gage pulled her arm from her friend's grasp gently, "you still have to race. I'll be okay, you stay here."

"You sure?" Mere studied her friend's face. The tension in the blonde's body was unnerving. Gage seemed afraid, a fact that scared the younger woman, "Because I can withdraw from the race. My cred won't suffer."

"Are you nuts?" Gage scoffed, "You just got moved up a bracket. You're racing."

"I can go with her," EmEm said to Mere, "no problem." He turned his gaze to Gage, "Just tell us what the hell is going on."

"EmEm, there's a hot Hispanic guy in a button-down shirt at your six O'clock," Gage's jade eyes darted around, "stall him."

EmEm looked at her in confusion for a second, but her tone held no room for discussion, so he sighed and turned around. He physically ran into the man his friend had described as Gage took off at a run in the opposite direction.

"WAIT!" Mere chased after her, "Gage! Damn it! What's going on?"

Gage whirled to face her friend and caught her by the shoulders when she almost ran into her, "Just do me a favor okay?"

"What?"

"That hot guy is about to come up to you and ask about me. Tell him nothing. In fact, try to find out what he knows, but don't believe a word he says to you. I'll explain everything later, I swear." With that said she turned and literally ran to her Torino, climbing in and driving away.

Mere turned back toward the races and jumped when a Hispanic man who was standing directly behind her smiled and held out his hand to her, "Hi there, my name is Alex Santiago, what's yours?"

Mere took his hand for less than a second before pulling hers back and crossing her arms across her chest, "My name's Meredith," she responded, studying his face as she tried to figure out why he scared Gage. She saw EmEm behind him shrugging his shoulders in confusion, she shook her head at her friend. EmEm opened the wallet in his hand, looking through its contents.

"Nice to meet you, Meredith," his smile was charming and his warm milk chocolate gaze was soothing, "do you know Bridget Grayson?"

"Yes." Mere responded hesitantly, "Do you?" She paused a moment, "Well obviously you do, I meant HOW do you know Gage?"

"Gage?" Alex arched an eyebrow, "Is that what she goes by now?"

Mere cursed angrily at herself mentally but kept a forced smile on her face, "I meant Bridget. How do you know Bridget?"

"She was the love of my life," he responded softly, "until she left me for no reason. I've been looking for her for a long time."

Mere stared at him in shock.

"I can tell she's never told you about me," he sounded almost hurt.

"I'm sorry, I just-" Mere sputtered, "I mean- I didn't-"

"It's okay," he smiled at her discomfort, "do you know where I can find her?"

"No." Mere stated quickly. "Well, yes, I do, but I'm not going to tell a stranger where to find my best friend."

He held up his hands as though surrendering, "Easy. Take it easy. I would never ask you to compromise your friend." He dropped his hands to his side, "I just want to see her again."

"Why are you here?" Mere changed the subject.

"I came to Miami to find Bridget," Alex answered. "I came from Texas, where she and I were together for five years."

"Wow," Mere was shocked again, "five years?"

"She really never told you about me?" that hurt tone had returned.

EmEm beckoned her with the wallet before pointing at the race finishing.

"Look, I have to go race now." Mere shoved her hands in her pockets, "If you want, you can give me your number. I'll make sure Bridget gets it, then she can call you if she wants to see you."

"Fair enough," he smiled again and pulled out a metal business card tin, he removed a card and scribbled two phone numbers on it before handing it to her, "good luck on the race."

"I'll make sure she gets this," Mere held up the card before shoving it in her pocket and pushing past him to get through the crowd to her car. "Lucy," she murmured under her breath, "you got some 'splaining to do."

Chapter 7

Mere burst through the door into the flat and looked around. "Gage?" She listened for an answer. When she didn't get one, she spoke louder, "GAGE! WHERE ARE YOU?"

"My room," a small muffled voice responded after a moment of silence.

Mere stormed down the hallway and into Gage's room practically shouting, "What the HELL was *that* all abou…" she trailed off when she realized the room was empty. Her eyes scanned the small room, taking in the piles of discarded clothing and the furniture which was in disarray. "Um, where?"

A small sigh came from somewhere in the room.

"Gage?" Mere turned to look behind her and found the room to be completely empty, "Where the hell are you?"

The door to the closet creaked slightly and Mere could see the toe of Gage's purple sock against the grain of the wood.

"Are you *hiding* in the closet?" Mere asked in disbelief as she moved toward the door.

"Not hiding," Gage said softly, peeking up at her friend when the younger woman came into the doorway, "just sitting is all."

"On the floor," Mere stated, staring down at her friend's huddled form, "in the closet. You're one of the most claustrophobic people I've ever met."

Gage shrugged and pulled her knees to her chest, wrapping her arms around her knees, "So maybe hiding." She rested her chin on her knees, "But only a little, the door was open."

"Hiding in the closet," Mere said again in disbelief.

"Yes, smart one," Gage rolled her eyes, "in the closet."

"Get out of the closet," Mere stepped back, "this instant!"

"You want me to come out of the closet?" Gage snickered to herself.

"Stop being a smart ass and get out of the God damned closet!"

Gage sighed unhappily, "But I like the closet. It's warm, and just the right amount of dark, and-"

"OUT!"

"Why?"

Mere was trying to keep the panic gripping her throat from making her voice squeak, "Why are you afraid?"

"I just like the closet," Gage responded, "I'm not afraid."

"I have NEVER seen you act the way you did at the race," Mere answered.

"Shit!" Gage scrambled to her feet and stepped into the room, "Did you win?"

"Of course I fucking won," Mere scoffed, "now explain. You promised you'd explain!"

Gage wiped her hands on her shirt and looked around her, "Didn't you drive EmEm to the race? Where is he? Did you leave Tiny and Killer there?"

"Yes, I did." Mere stated, "EmEm is a big boy, he can take care of himself. Lina and Will can take care of the dogs, you need to talk to me. Now. Stop changing the subject."

Gage swallowed and looked at her friend, "Did you talk to him?"

"Who?" Mere asked.

"Alex."

"Yes," Mere pulled the business card with his numbers from her pocket, "he gave me this. Said you were the love of his life back in Texas."

Gage made a face and took the card, looking down at it, "Did he say why he was in Miami?"

"Said he was looking for you," Mere responded, "that you left for no reason, and he's been searching for you ever since."

Gage snorted, crumpled the card in her fist and threw it at her vanity. The small ball of paper bounced off one of the canvas blocks perched in wait for a wig, "Yeah, I'm sure he was real broken up about me leaving."

Mere didn't respond, she merely stared at her friend expectantly.

Gage looked up and sighed, "Look, Alex was a chapter in my life I'm not proud of. I was very young. I made stupid decisions. People got hurt. I left because it wasn't healthy."

"Wow, that's awesome," Mere grumbled, "you managed to tell me absolutely nothing about the situation while pretending you're disclosing some great secret. EmEm stole his wallet. Alex didn't have anything interesting in it, except his ID and cash. We've got his address too, if you need it."

Gage nodded, "Thanks for the info." She met Mere's expectant gaze, "At the moment, that's all I'm prepared to disclose. I'll tell you all about it someday, but right now I'm tired."

Mere sighed, "I hate you."

Gage nodded, "I know. But it's okay, 'cause I love you."

Mere shook her head and turned on her heel, "I won a Camaro and I don't want it. I was gonna give it to you, but if you're gonna be a bitch…" she trailed off as she walked out of the room.

Gage smiled, "What color?"

"Orange."

"I love you Mere-bear," Gage said as she closed the door quietly.

"Love you too," Mere sighed and shook her head.

~*~*~*~

"She's not coming back," Tessa sighed as she scratched Tiny's ears, "*is* she?"

Tiny whined low in his throat and looked over at the small redhead who was sitting on a curb with a dejected look on her face.

"I didn't think so."

Killer ran across the parking lot, his small legs a blur. He leaped up into Tessa's lap and yapped at her, snapping his teeth.

"What's that?" Tessa asked, "You'd like me to strangle your mommy?" She smiled at the small dog, "Absolutely, I can do that."

Killer cocked his head to the side, staring up at her.

"That's not what you asked?" Tessa asked with a chuckle, "Are you sure? I'd really like to do that for you."

Killer cocked his head to the other side.

"What were you trying to-" she was cut off by the sound of three people frantically whistling.

Killer barked and began to run in circles on Tessa's lap.

"There you are!" Lina cried as she came out of a crowd of stragglers, "TESSA!" She stopped walking, surprised, "What are you still doing here?"

Tessa frowned at the woman, "Well, apparently Gage ran off before the race, and Mere stopped long enough to collect her winnings and zipped off after her."

Will came to a stop behind Lina, "Mere gave me the keys to her new Camaro," he held them up. "You can drive it home, instead of making me drop off EmEm and go to the garage before walking home."

"This way Lina and Will can just drop me and go home," EmEm added before leaning toward her and whispering loudly, "they can shack up quicker."

Tessa nodded and stood up slowly, brushing herself off, ignoring EmEm's off-hand comment, and grumbling, "I'm not going to speak to them for at least eight days."

Lina smiled, "I'm sure there's an explanation sweetie, no need to get too upset. After all, everything turned out okay."

Tessa sighed and took the keys from Will, "Where's it parked?"

Will motioned over his shoulder with his thumb, "Over by the Happy Meal Billboard. You gonna be okay, Kiddo? Want me to drive you home?"

"I can drive," Tessa responded before slapping her thigh for the dogs to follow her, "you guys go home."

Will chewed his lip thoughtfully for a moment watching the girl move through the crowd with the two dogs trailing behind her.

"She's fine," Lina bumped her shoulder against his, "stop worrying, you're not her big brother."

"We might as well be her big brothers," EmEm interrupted, "this whole situation is weird as hell."

"I just don't know why Gage would have left Tessie here," Will wrapped his arm around Lina's shoulders, "she pretends to be irresponsible, but she loves that kid. We all do."

"I'm sure there's an explanation," Lina said again, "everything's fine. You can figure it out tomorrow when you go in to work." She smiled up at him, "Now are you coming home with me? Or what?"

Will grinned down at her, "Mmm, with an offer like that, how could I refuse?"

"Hey! Take me home first!" EmEm covered his eyes with his hand, "I don't want to see your lovey crap."

Chapter 8

Gage lay in her bed, staring at the ceiling. She was still fully clothed in her tight skirt and fancy top. Her fuzzy purple socks were pulled up to mid-calf and her heeled knee-high boots lay forgotten in a heap on the floor. She heard a car door slam outside and sat up, "Shit! Tessa!" She heard clawed feet running up the stairs from the garage and shortly after, Killer hurled himself onto her bed.

Gage hugged the small dog and looked into his face, "Is she very angry?"

A door down the hall slammed making Gage jump slightly.

"Yup," Gage sighed and scratched Killer's ear, "she's angry."

Killer licked Gage's face and hopped down from the bed. He left the room slowly, no doubt going to report to Tiny that their mistress was okay.

"Love you puppy," Gage called quietly after his retreating form.

The sound of music came from Tessa's room and Gage sighed, "She's not gonna talk to me for like eight days."

~*~*~*~*~

Mere stepped from the shower and wrapped a towel around her body. She heard music coming from Tessa's room and shook her head, "That girl is going to give us the silent treatment," she said to her reflection in the steamy mirror. She wrapped a second towel around her hair and piled it on top of her head. She swiped her hand across the mirror to rid it of moisture and inspected her perfect skin in her reflection.

She looked down when her phone beeped. She picked it up and looked at it before rolling her eyes, "So not interested Derek," she muttered as she placed the phone back on the counter. She pulled the towel from her hair and dropped it on the floor before combing through her tresses with her fingers. She began the long process of rubbing leave-in conditioner into her hair. She listened carefully to the noises of the house while she worked. Tessa's music got louder, and no sound at all came from Gage's room.

Mere chewed her bottom lip in thought and opened the bathroom door when she'd finished with her hair. She peeked down the hallway and saw that Gage's door was slightly open. She crept silently down the hallway, wincing each time her bare feet touched the cold wood floor. When she reached the doorway, Mere used her pointer finger to push open the door a little more and peeked into the dark room.

The bed sheets were rumpled, "Damn it," Mere muttered, "where the hell is she?" She arched an eyebrow when she saw the clothes Gage had been wearing in a heap on the floor, "Is she naked?"

Mere turned and hurried back to the bathroom to grab her phone before going into her room and closing her door. She started texting before the door was even closed.

~*~*~*~*~

"Hey, Babe?" Will called from the kitchen, "You want this leftover Chinese?"

Lina laughed from where she was laying on her bed, "Go ahead, help yourself."

Will strode back into the bedroom, one hand holding the carton of Chinese food and the other scratching lazily at his bare chest, "You sure you don't want some?" He asked as he lay down on the bed beside her and pulled a noodle from the carton with chopsticks.

"I'm fine, thanks," Lina smiled at her boyfriend before turning her attention back to the computer in her lap. "I just want to finish this paragraph, then we can sleep."

"Who the hell wants to sleep?" Will asked with a crooked smile and a wink.

Lina rolled her eyes, "You're insatiable."

"Yup," Will nodded and slurped a noodle, "I missed you."

They both looked at the bedside table when a phone buzzed.

"That yours or mine?" Will asked.

"Both actually," Lina reached over and grabbed the phones with one hand. She dropped both phones between them on the bed and went back to typing.

Will picked up his phone and flipped it open, "Mere says Gage is missing and possibly naked."

Lina arched an eyebrow and glanced at him, "Crazy say what?"

"She wants to know if Gage called us," Will answered as he typed his answer into his phone, "maybe I should run over there to make sure everything's okay."

Lina nodded, "Do you want to do that?"

"No," Will practically pouted as he typed more, "I'm going to tell her to check the pool."

He lay back against his pillow and waited until his phone beeped again. He flipped it open, "Crisis averted."

"She was in the pool?" Lina asked.

"Yup."

"Naked?"

Will sat up excitedly, "You offering?"

She laughed and went back to typing, "I still can't believe you have a flip phone."

He shrugged, "It serves all my needs. I can make phone calls or text. I don't need anything else. Plus, it's lasted me five years already, how often do you have to replace yours?" He looked at her expectantly as he continued eating his noodles.

Lina arched an eyebrow at him, her fingers still typing away, "Often, but you've never been curious about all the apps out there? Or wanted to take amazing pictures?"

Will made a face and finished chewing before answering, "I actually enjoy the people I surround myself with, I don't need brain-numbing games or apps to waste my time. Plus, I don't have to take pictures, the best photojournalist I know lives with me."

"Awww," Lina looked back at her computer screen, "flattery will get you everywhere."

"Everywhere?" Will perked up with a little smirk.

Lina saved her document and closed her computer, "Yes, everywhere," she said huskily and put her computer on the side table.

Will looked from his food, to his girlfriend, and tossed the container over his shoulder onto the floor.

Lina laughed, but scoffed, "You're cleaning that up!"

He crawled on top of her and growled, "I'll do it tomorrow."

Chapter 9

Gage swam laps until she couldn't anymore. When her shoulders burned and her legs were numb, she floated on her back in the center of the pool, staring up into the black as pitch sky.

"So, you gonna talk to me or keep being a punk ass?"

Gage dropped below the surface momentarily in shock before popping back to the surface, "Holy SHIT Meredith."

"I've been here for the last twenty-seven-hundred laps," Mere answered from her seat on one of the lounge chairs. "It's not my fault you're insane and too pig-headed to notice anything but causing yourself physical pain."

Gage stuck her tongue out quickly before she swam slowly to the stairs, "For the record, my ass is not punkish and I am not causing myself physical pain."

"You just swam laps for at least an hour straight without stopping," Mere responded, "if you aren't in pain, you're high."

"I'm not high," Gage muttered.

"Then you're in pain," Mere snapped, "how about telling me what's got you so spun?"

"I don't want to talk about it."

"That doesn't mean you shouldn't," Mere responded, "maybe this insomnia is brought on by your stubbornness."

"Don't be silly," Gage muttered as she stood at the bottom of the stairs for a moment, "You know I don't sleep."

"You don't really think I'm silly," Mere stated matter-of-factly, "you're afraid I'm right."

"Not really," Gage climbed into the warm night air, "I just needed to relieve some aggression."

"Remember the part about the swimming for over an hour?" Mere scoffed, "That's not simple aggression."

Gage shrugged as she grabbed her towel and wrapped it around herself, "Felt like aggression," she responded as she lay on her lounge chair.

Mere sighed heavily before saying, "Promise me that you'll catch some rest."

"I promise," Gage responded, "go back inside. I swear we'll talk about this soon. I just have to get my head around it first."

Mere sighed as she stood, "Fine. Don't go back in the pool. I don't want you to drown."

"Yes, Mami."

Chapter 10

Tired eyes with barely visible hunter green irises stared into a cracked mirror. The pupils were dilated and blood red veins masking their whites. Bridget's sweat-damp hair curled at her chin in a layered cut that once was cute but now looked dirty, limp, and lifeless.

She blinked slowly, that action alone took more energy than she felt she could muster. Her hands were shaking involuntarily. Her chest felt like it was caving in with each slow pump of her heavy heart. She knew what she had to do, but it was taking all she had to stand, let alone walk away. Her stomach churned again, but she had nothing in it to spew forth into the stained toilet that beckoned from beside her.

She could hear someone in the next room. A chair scraped across the floor. Bridget swallowed hard, blinked again, and turned to the door. She pushed against the piece of wood with shaking hands and stepped into the next room.

"I'm leaving." Bridget was angry that her voice sounded so small. So pathetic. Instead of firm, like she knew it should be.

"What the fuck do you MEAN you're leaving?" His fury ripped from his throat with the force of hornets buzzing in the air around her.

"I can't do this anymore," she whimpered, preparing for the sting.

"Do what?" He didn't move from his seat by the circle table.

"It isn't healthy," she swallowed again and shoved her shaking hands in her jeans' pockets, "he's going to kill me."

"Now you're being melodramatic."

Realization dawned on her and Bridget's heart dropped into her shoes, "You called him."

"He has a right to know you're tripping."

Bridget shook her head, tears welling in her eyes, "You've killed me." She turned from the man she'd considered her friend and found her nightmare, clad in khaki pants and a baseball T-shirt, standing in the doorway.

"Hey, babe." Alex smiled at her in that disturbingly charming way he had about him. "Where are you going?"

"Please," Bridget whispered, "please just let me go. I can't do this anymore. I just want to go."

Alex's smile deepened to a toothy grin as he cupped the nape of her neck with his left hand and pulled her face to his, "You're not going anywhere, babe." His right hand stabbed a blade into her torso, beside her belly button and twisted as he growled, "If I can't have you, no one can."

The scream caught in her throat as the white-hot pain tore through her deadened senses.

"God DAMN it, Gage, wake the FUCK up!" Will shook his friend roughly, contemplating slapping her.

Gage jerked awake so hard that she fell from the lounge chair onto the concrete poolside.

"Are you okay?" Will reached for her but she flinched away from him, averting her eyes and bringing her hands up to shield herself. "Hey," his tone became far gentler, "it's okay," he held his hand toward her as though calming a wild animal, "you're okay. It's just me. I'm not going to hurt you."

Gage swallowed hard and wiped at her face, "I know Will. I know you wouldn't hurt me." She cleared her throat and sat up, "Sorry. Bad dream."

"I'd say that's the understatement of the God damned century," Will responded with some of his normal bite.

Gage smiled slightly, "What are you doing up here? I thought you were banned from the house for drinking all the whiskey, or something stupid."

Will glowered at her, "Well I *was* in the garage when I heard you screaming like someone was fucking slaughtering you. So I came to help." He motioned with his head to the large wrench that was on the ground beside her.

"Aw," Gage smiled sadly, "you were gonna protect me? That's cute."

"Shuddup," Will grumbled.

"Go on back to work," she stood up, "I'll be down in a few minutes."

"Maybe you should take the day, Boss."

She shook her head and started to walk toward the back door, "I'm fine."

Will grabbed his wrench and stood, turning to go back down the stairs on the side of the flat.

"Oh, Will?" Gage turned back to her friend.

"Yeah?" Will glanced at her.

"You're not getting paid overtime for groping me in my bikini."

"Yeah," Will shook his head and rolled his eyes, "you're welcome, Boss."

When he disappeared down the stairs Gage whispered, "Thank you."

~*~*~*~*~

"Gage is losing it," Will stated as he closed the door when he got home that night.

Lina laughed lightly, "Babe, a person can't lose something they never had."

Will walked into the kitchen and stared at his girlfriend with scared dark eyes, "I mean it," he said softly.

Lina stood from her chair and moved to him with concern. She placed her cool hands on his cheeks as though checking for fever, "What happened?" she asked quietly.

"When I got to work this morning, she was screaming bloody murder upstairs." He shook his head when she smirked, "No. I mean, literally, like she was getting murdered. She was in pain. Screaming."

"Was she okay?" Lina asked, her eyes widening with concern, "Did she-"

"She was dreaming, Lina," He interrupted her. "She was dreaming and screaming like she was dying."

"It was just a nightmare then."

"When I woke her up, she was terrified. She was shaking and cringed away from me."

Lina arched an eyebrow.

"She was AFRAID of me," Will insisted.

"What are you trying to say?" Lina asked gently.

"I've only known one other person who dreamt like that," Will responded, "my Dad used to have nightmares that left him screaming in a cold sweat," he was staring at the floor intently, "I don't think it was a nightmare. It was a memory."

Chapter 11

The soft sounds of Cello music wafted through the flat.

Gage stood in front of her full-length mirror, staring at her reflection. Her black jeans effectively covered her legs and her black leather boots gave her an extra few inches of height without being too noticeable. Her black tank top was untucked and hanging loosely. She lifted its edge and stared intently at the twin butterflies that were tattooed beside her belly button. Her fingers traced the ridge of flesh that the ink disguised.

She took a deep breath and released it slowly as she tucked the shirt into her jeans. She attached her holster to her belt in the small of her back and pulled her SIG Saur from her vanity's drawer. She checked the weapon and placed it into the holster before pulling on her leather jacket and zipping it up, masking the weapon. She cracked her neck and braided her hair quickly.

When she was done, she coated her lips with Chapstick and shoved the stick in her pocket. She applied some makeup to her eyes then stared at her reflection again. She'd made her eyes look almond. Purposely giving herself an almost Asian appearance. She grabbed her sunglasses and put them on the top of her head before leaving her bedroom.

She strode away from the sounds of her friends in the other rooms and silently left the flat. She entered the garage and whistled shrilly as she grabbed the keys to her pickup from the wall. Killer and Tiny came to her side instantly, knowing what was happening. Gage smiled at Killer, "You're still too small baby," she said softly, "you guard the home front." When the dog whimpered, she bent down and scratched his ears. "Go on." He let out an angry puff of air and ran back the way he'd come.

"Let's go Tiny," Gage motioned to the brown 1951 Ford F1, "we've got business to handle. Time to turn off the emotions."

Tiny growled slightly and tilted his head.

"Don't give me any of that," she scolded him. "I'm fine." She opened the driver's door and he leaped into the cab, moving into the passenger seat where he sat erect. She climbed into the driver's seat and closed the door. "I'm fine," she said again as she stared at herself in the rearview mirror.

Gage tossed her sunglasses into the glove box, before pulling a green shoulder-length wig out, and settling it on her head. She twisted it while she studied herself in a small mirror on the dash until she was satisfied that it was on properly. She glanced to the passenger seat where Tiny was staring at her.

"How's it look?" She asked.

Tiny cocked his head and let out a small whimper.

"That bad huh?" She snickered. "Good thing it's just for some Aussies then," she scratched Tiny's ear, "shall we go?"

Tiny barked once and turned his gaze to the windshield expectantly.

Gage turned the key in the ignition and couldn't help but smile when the engine roared to life with a guttural grumble, "You know, you're the only truck I'll ever love," she cooed and stroked the dashboard of the classic truck. "My beautiful lady," she kissed the steering wheel before putting the truck in drive and hitting the gas.

~*~*~*~

Mere walked sleepily to the kitchen in her sports bra and shorts. She yawned and rubbed her eyes, blinking several times to clear her vision as she made her way to the fridge.

She could hear Cello music and decided to blame that for the ungodly hour that she was awake. "Tessa, you're so lucky I completely forgot you at a race that you didn't even want to go to," she muttered as she pulled the milk from the fridge and took a few swallows straight from the carton before calling loudly, "otherwise you'd be in so much trouble right now!" She placed the nearly empty carton back in the fridge and scratched the back of her neck as she surveyed the room. "This place is a wreck," she decided. She walked toward the cereal boxes on the kitchen table. There were three different boxes on their sides, spilling their contents across the table.

Mere wrinkled her nose at the state of it. As she walked by, she knocked over the only upright box. She smirked as she heard the Froot Loops rain onto the floor.

"Gage!" Mere shouted, not caring that it was 5:30 in the morning. When she received no reply, she arched an eyebrow. "Ooooooooh Gaaaaaaaaaage!?!" The Cello music stopped abruptly. "I didn't call you Tessa." Mere responded to the sudden lack of music, "Go about your business ignoring me." The cello music began again.

"Princess?" Mere knocked on Gage's bedroom door lightly, "Wakey, wakey, eggs and bakey my sweet." She knocked slightly louder, "Gage?" Mere tried the doorknob and found the door to be locked. "What the hell?" She muttered to herself before shouting, "Gage this door has never been locked as long as I have known you. Open it this instant!"

There was no reply. Mere continued to pound on the door for several minutes until the Cello music stopped. Tessa stomped angrily from her room, cello in hand, and handed Mere her bow. The petite redhead then stood on tiptoe and ran her fingers along the top of the door frame. She located a small metal push key and handed it to Mere. Then the redhead snatched her bow back, slammed her door behind her, and once more began to play.

Mere blinked once, looked down at the small metal key in her palm, and then looked back at Tessa's door. "THANK YOU!" She used the key to pop the lock on Gage's door and opened it. A quick scan found the room to be completely empty. "I swear to GOD if she's dead in the pool, I'll fucking KILL her!" Mere ran down the hall and onto the pool deck.

The pool was a mirror of the beginning of dawn. All of the chairs were empty. "I hate her," Mere said matter-of-factly, "yup. Just hate her." She nodded to herself before walking to her room all the time muttering to herself.

~*~*~*~*~

"What's making you spit the dummy?" A tall man with dark hair and a bushy beard lounged on a crate inside an abandoned warehouse. "She'll be apples, Mate." He tipped his black cowboy hat so it covered his eyes, "No need to be this way over a seppo."

"This isn't just about a bloody seppo," a second man paced anxiously and ran a hand through his lighter brown shoulder-length hair. He glanced at the second man, "IS it."

The darker man shrugged and adjusted his cowboy hat, "Dunno Mak. Seems like you just wanna have a naughty. Don't let bizzo mix with stickin' your donger where it don't belong."

Mak stopped walking and glared at the other man, "I never knew you was such a knocker, Buck."

Buck smirked, "No worries."

"You just lair it up, Bastard." Mak resumed pacing.

Buck laughed and stood up when he heard the door slide open to the left.

"You know," Gage walked into the warehouse as if she owned it, "I never have ANY idea what the hell you two are talkin' about." Her green hair shone in the morning light.

"G'day sheila," Buck grinned, "I reckon that's bonzer. Just havin' a blue."

Gage stopped walking and stared at him. She blinked once and said, "How does one *have* a color?" She shook her head in exasperation, "Never mind." She glanced at Mak while saying, "Don't call me Sheila."

Mak stared at her with a kind of concern in his eyes. She wasn't her normal blasé self. Her banter didn't have the same bite. She seemed tired. Her eyes didn't shine with humor like they normally did, they were dull, almost pain-filled.

"Stop staring at me," she said after a moment, "you're making me nervous."

"Perving," Buck laughed as he lay back down on the crate.

"We ever going to meet the real you?" Mak asked, motioning to her get-up.

"Probably not," she responded pertly.

"Does anyone know the real you?" Buck asked cheekily.

"Probably not," she responded again impatiently, "can we handle business now please?"

"Where's the bitzer?" Buck asked.

Gage sighed and whistled the opening tune from *The Good, the Bad, and the Ugly* shrilly. Tiny trotted into the warehouse opposite where Gage had entered, he sat down, erect, roughly ten feet away.

"Bailing us up?" Mak asked.

Gage stared at him blankly, "Huh?"

Buck stood from where he'd been lounging and walked to Tiny. The dog continued to stare straight ahead at his mistress, with his ears perked in her direction.

"I'm a little pressed for time fellas, can we please just get this over with?" Gage turned from them and walked toward the crate that Buck had just vacated, "I assume this is what I'm here for?"

Mak stared at her back in shock, at a loss for words momentarily, "Uh, yeah." He looked at Buck in confusion, "Yes. Everything's there, just as you requested."

"Six boxes of ammo?" She asked.

"Eight," Mak corrected.

"On account of you being such a good customer," Buck laughed. He was crouched by Tiny, reaching his hand toward the dog. When the hand was within inches, the dog bared his teeth and growled low, so Buck would move his hand back and Tiny would return to serenely sitting. Buck continued to tease the dog, making him bare his teeth, then return to normal, then bare his teeth.

"All the specifications as we discussed?" Gage asked as she picked up the rifle with an impressive scope and held it to her shoulder.

"For you?" Mak asked.

"Not to big note Mak here, but he found the fair dinkum. I'd have got bog standard, this one's exy," Buck finished, still teasing Tiny and laughing at his sport.

Gage stared at Mak and blinked a few times, "All I understood in that entire statement was your name."

"This model is expensive with the modifications and all the specifications," Mak said with a grin.

"I have the cash, obviously," Gage stated as she lifted the rifle again and scanned the shadows with the weapon's scope.

"You even know how to shoot that properly?" Buck teased her.

"I'm a terrible shooter," Gage answered.

"Pig's arse!" Mak exclaimed, "I've seen you hit bullseye after bullseye, fifteen meters out, with a handgun from the quick draw."

"You misunderstand me," she chuckled, "I'm an excellent shot, I'm a terrible shooter. I have awful habits and I never decided to break those habits because I got too damn good despite them."

"Like what?" Buck looked up from teasing Tiny, curious.

"I only shoot with one eye, for starters," Gage closed her left eye and looked from one man to the other, the rifle pointed at the ground, "I can't even leave my left eye open or I'll miss."

Both men laughed at the face she made so she decided maybe she could push her luck a bit.

"Has anyone else on the East Coast been looking for anything similar?" She brought the rifle back up, her right eye to the scope, "Particularly the whole hard to trace part?" She caught sight of a wisp of shadow that made her jump, lower the weapon, and advert her gaze momentarily, her heart racing.

"Maybe," Mak responded, trying to ignore her discomfort, "we're not in the bizzo of dobbing customers in."

Gage replaced the rifle into the hard case that was in the crate before she looked him in the eye and said slowly, "Okay." She unzipped her jacket and pulled out a thick envelope, holding it out to him, "I'll take the rifle. I'll call if I need anything else since you're not looking to be more helpful."

"Are you okay?" Mak asked, not reaching for the envelope.

"What?" Gage backtracked slightly, "Huh? Why? I'm fine."

Buck stood from his crouched position, "He's right. You're acting like you've got kangaroos loose in the top paddock."

"How long have you worked with us?" Mak asked.

Gage glanced from Buck to Mak and stated, "I don't know, two years?"

"In those THREE years," Mak corrected her, "you have never once turned your back to us, or lost your train of thought, or made a mistake, or showed up late."

You DID order eight boxes," Buck added, "not six."

Gage nodded slowly, "Okay, how long have we been friends?" Mak opened his mouth but she cut him off, "The answer is we're NOT friends. We're business associates. So, either you fine boys take my money, and I take this lovely piece of sexy death," she closed the case and fastened the latches. "Or I take my money elsewhere."

"Are those the only choices?" Buck asked.

"Sadly, yes," Gage nodded, "unless you're willing to enter into a deeper relationship."

Mak perked up instantly and Buck laughed, walking to them exclaiming, "Now he's gonna crack a fat."

Mak blushed and sputtered, "That's not-"

"I don't know what the hell that means, so don't get your panties in a twist," Gage interrupted.

Buck snorted and Mak cleared his throat and said, "What did you have in mind?"

"We've worked together enough that you know I'm not looking to screw you-"

"That stands out like a dog's balls," Buck elbowed Mak, "makes this one cranky."

Gage rolled her eyes, "Discretion is important to me too," she continued, "I'd pay top dollar for the occasional ear to the ground."

The Australians stared at her blankly.

"You give me information," she said slowly, "I give you money, but I don't tell anyone."

"I could give you the drum, but you'd have to hit the turps with us," Buck stated.

"No idea what you're saying," Gage stated.

"Come on! Let's get rotten!" Buck exclaimed, throwing his hands up and dancing a little.

Gage blinked and looked from Buck to Mak who made the motion of drinking with a handsome grin.

"I only go drinking with my friends," Gage responded once she understood the suggestion, "but if you find out who has been looking for an untraceable .338 Lapua Magnum with similar specifications as mine, let me know." She picked up the rifle case, "That information checks out, and the first round is on me, and my girls."

"You know," Mak stated, ignoring Buck smacking his arm excitedly at the mention of 'girls', "we could try to be mates."

Gage laughed a genuine laugh, "Fine. You wanna be friends?" She turned to Mak and put a fist on her hip, "You need a haircut, you look like a girl."

Buck laughed and Mak made a face.

Gage turned on Buck, "YOU need a shave, bushman. I mean come on, some nice stubble might work okay, but the all-out scraggly critter that's crawled onto your face and died is just *not* attractive at all."

Buck stopped laughing, "Holy Dooley. She can't be our cobber. She called me a bushie."

Mak glanced at the other Australian and shrugged, then turned back to Gage, "So if we do that, you'll be our mate?"

Gage arched an eyebrow, "You don't want to be friends with me boys, it never ends well."

Buck smirked, "Spiffy, he just wants to root."

Mak punched his partner's arm hard enough to make Buck yelp and turn away.

Gage blinked a few times then said, "I don't have any idea what that is, but I'm thinking it's naughty." She smirked at Mak, "I'm flattered, but I don't like girls."

Buck snorted and walked over, he took the rifle case from Gage and headed out of the warehouse the same way she'd come in, Tiny finally stood from his spot and trotted after the man.

Mak sighed, "I can assure you I'm no sheila."

Gage held up the envelope again and waved it in front of him, "You want the money, hunny?"

He stared at her for a moment until she shuffled uncomfortably under his scrutiny then he smiled a half smile and took the envelope. "It's all here, right?"

"If it isn't, you know how to contact me," she responded.

Buck walked back into the warehouse with Tiny behind him, watching him, "All loaded up."

"Fantastic." Gage whistled and Tiny turned around and left the warehouse. "Later boys." She waggled her fingers in a flirtatious wave as she left.

"Not to skite," Buck said, "but she clearly sees my donger as an icy pole."

Mak looked at him sideways before locking him into a headlock and punching him.

Chapter 12

By the time Gage had arrived back at the flat, Mere had assembled the entire PREY crew, minus Whitlock, around the kitchen table.

"What the hell is this?" Gage closed the sliding door and faced her friends, "An intervention?"

"Where were you?" Mere's tone was accusatory.

Gage cocked her head, her body stiffening with anger, "I was doing my job, Meredith." She set the rifle case on the table, "Or did you forget that I was tasked with acquiring your rifle?"

Mere's face clouded with confusion momentarily, but then she said, "You've been acting weird. Don't pretend you haven't."

"So, your way of saying you're concerned is to gang up on me?" Gage snapped.

"We're not ganging up on you," Will said quietly, "we're here because we're worried about you."

"Plus, we all have to go to the office today to vet that new guy anyway," EmEm added half-heartedly.

"I'm just here for the food," Tessa sipped her hot tea and avoided everyone's surprised gaze.

"She's still mad at us," Mere said matter-of-factly with a dismissive wave of her hand.

"The fact of the matter is we just want you to know that you can tell us anything," Will interjected, "we're here for you, you're our fearless leader, and we love you."

EmEm nodded his agreement, "Plus you're the glue, if you fall apart, we all do."

"No pressure, huh?" Gage pulled her wig off and headed to the hallway, "You guys are way off base, I'm fine. I'll meet you at the office."

When she made it to her room, she closed the door behind her and breathed a huge sigh of relief. She appreciated her friends' concern, but she wasn't ready to divulge the gritty details of her past. Especially considering most of them held extremely strong beliefs which wouldn't allow much compassion.

Gage tossed her wig onto her bed and walked to her vanity. She sat in front of the mirror and stared at her reflection, wondering if there would ever be a good time to explain herself.

A knock on her door made her jump. She played it off and called, "What is it?"

"Do you want a ride? We're due in fifteen minutes," EmEm's voice was soft like he was trying to purposely be nonconfrontational.

"I'm good." Gage responded as she started to wipe her makeup off, "I'll meet you there."

"All right," he clearly wanted to say more, but he didn't. He stood there for an extra minute before walking away.

Gage finished wiping her face clean and began reapplying with a different technique to contour her face and make her eyes pop. Then she put in blue contact lenses and pulled on a white blond wig that fell down past her shoulders. She situated the fake hair over her own until she was satisfied with the fit and look, then she stood up and changed her leather jacket for her denim one. She checked her reflection in the mirror and changed her mind. She kicked off her boots, removed her holstered handgun, and stepped out of her pants, leaving them in a heap on the floor, she changed into a short pleated khaki skirt. She stepped into a pair of high heels and inspected her image again. She smiled at herself and nodded her approval before tucking her firearm back into the small of her back, clipping the holster to her waistband.

She grabbed her keys out of the pocket of her discarded leather jacket and walked back out into the main area. Everyone was gone and the rifle case was also missing. Gage grabbed an apple from off the counter and walked down the stairs into the garage. She took a bite as she walked to the front door and flipped the "open" sign to "closed for grub".

When she exited the building and turned to lock the door, she could sense someone watching her. It immediately made her prickle and whirl to search her surroundings for the offender. She didn't find anyone on the street and didn't see any occupied cars, but the feeling continued to grow in her gut, so she quickly locked up and hurried to her blacked out Suburban parked in the alley beside her shop. Once she was safely inside with the doors locked, she looked around again. She saw a red pickup truck pull out of a spot on the street and drive slowly by her shop. She couldn't see the driver, but she couldn't help but feel like whoever it was, was the source of her discomfort.

She waited for the strange truck to disappear, then started the engine of the Suburban. She really wanted to follow the pickup to see who the driver was working for, but she had to go to the office or Whitlock would get involved in her current personal situation. She didn't think any of her friends would go to him for insight on her, which was lucky since he could answer any questions they might have. She didn't want to give him any reasons to intervene.

She made the quick drive to the office in silence, deep in thought. When she pulled up to the gate and typed in her passcode, she was actually surprised she'd made it unscathed, she couldn't even remember what route she'd taken. It was a good thing she drove to the office so much that it had apparently become second nature.

She drove down into the parking garage and ignored the shadows produced as the sunlight was gradually choked out into the flickering lights of the underground concrete box.

Gage pulled into her designated spot and hopped out of the vehicle. She locked the doors with her remote and strode into the elevator that was only ten feet away. She hit the button for the fifth floor and rode in silence to her destination.

The elevator stopped in the lobby and a man in his early to mid-twenties stepped in, he was wearing 511 tactical khaki pants and a polo shirt. His blond hair was cut short in a crew cut and he was clearly used to commanding attention with his presence.

He glanced at her with clear blue eyes before pressing the already illuminated five and standing with his back to the wall, right beside her.

She met his gaze when he glanced her way but now stared straight ahead in awkward silence as the elevator climbed slowly.

"Do you work on the fifth floor?" He broke the uncomfortable silence with a soft Southern accent.

"Yup," she responded curtly, her toe-tapping anxiously.

He looked her up and down with his peripheral vision as if she couldn't notice, "Isn't the only business on that level Proactive Resources for Evidentiary Yields."

"Yup," she responded pertly, making a popping sound on the p.

"Oh," he said awkwardly. He rocked on his feet as though trying to figure out what to say next when the elevator jerked to a stop and the doors opened.

Gage strode from the elevator, straight behind the front desk, and sat in Tessa's chair, waiting to greet the man she'd ridden up with in the elevator.

When he walked slowly from the elevator, she gave him a gracious smile and cooed in a pronounced Southern drawl, "Howdy, you must be Jerimiah Edward Braxton the third," she stood from the chair and held out her hand to him.

"My friends call me Brick," he said slowly and shook her hand.

"Since we're not friends, I'll call you Biscuit," she responded with a smirk. "Right this way Biscuit, I'll introduce you around."

"Please don't call me that," he said as he followed her.

"I can call you JEB instead," she called over her shoulder, "initials are fun."

"No, don't do that."

She led him into a large gymnasium where Will and EmEm were unrolling mats to lead training later in the day.

"This is our main training space, where we practice beating the shit out of each other," she waved her hand to show the size of the space. "If you'll direct your attention to two of our founding members," she smiled at her friends. "This is EmEm, he's Asian, so clearly he's our crazy awesome martial artist, Brainiac, tech-savvy genius." She motioned to EmEm, "This is William, resident thug master, he knows all the gangs in the area, is an impressive dancer and shoots handguns sideways."

"Eminem?" Brick asked.

"He's neither a rapper nor a milk chocolate candy," Gage responded before holding up her hand as though to block her lips and whispering loudly, "however I do have it on good authority that he melts in the mouth faster than the hand."

She kept walking with Brick following her, looking more and more confused, "Hi fellas, I'm Brick," he said, holding out his hand.

"No time for niceties, Biscuit," she grabbed his hand and started to drag him from the room, "oh shit, I think I mixed them up a bit," she paused momentarily and cocked her head to the side.

"Their names, or their specialties?"

"Yes," she smiled and walked from the room leaving EmEm and Will laughing.

Brick followed her into the kitchen area where Tessa was making coffees.

"This is Tessa, give her your coffee order, she'll make it for you while we're touring," Gage smiled at the redhead and winked.

"Uh, just black coffee please," he sputtered as he chased after Gage, who was already on to the next space.

"You'll need these," Gage handed him safety earmuffs and clear eye protection, she'd already put in foam earplugs and had on designer sunglasses.

He put on the glasses and hurriedly put on the ear protection as she was opening the door to the range where Mere was loading two different handguns.

"This is Hot Pants," Gage shouted as Mere began shooting, "she's our resident bitch gun expert who likes to drive fast. She prefers that over the handguns though," she pointed to the rifle she'd procured from the Aussies which was perched on a shooting block beside Mere.

He reached out to touch the rifle and Mere smacked his hand with one of her now empty handguns.

"Careful Biscuit, she'll chew you up and spit you out," Gage laughed.

Mere snapped her teeth at Brick and smirked when he arched an eyebrow.

"Continuing on," Gage left the range through the second door and walked down a hall, she pulled out her earplugs and pushed her sunglasses up on her head. "This is the technology Mecca," she strode into a room completely covered in monitor stations with several computers. "We can search any server we have access to from all over the world in this room."

Lina looked up from her monitor and smiled, "Good morning."

"This is our press correspondent, and resident Will charmer," Gage motioned to Lina, "She likes justice, the truth, and all things normal reporters hate nowadays."

Gage breezed past Lina and out the door, back into the hallway. She entered a room with a large table and padded chairs and plopped into one of the chairs before motioning across the table to another chair.

"Tell me about yourself, Biscuit."

He sat down and stared at her for a moment before saying, "I was a corpsman, I served five combat tours attached to a Marine Corps unit in the Middle East, and now that I'm out, I'm looking for something to keep me busy. I'm good with firearms, love saving lives, and don't like criminals."

Gage nodded, her hands folded in front of her on the desk, "Interesting. How old are you and are you currently in a relationship?"

Brick faltered, "I'm not sure how that's pertinent to this interview."

"It's pertinent because we have several attractive people all working together in extremely close quarters, sexual tension is commonplace and we need to know if you're going to fit in okay."

"I can hold my own in any situation," he responded with a smirk, "plus, I'm old enough to consent."

She arched an eyebrow and nodded, "Interesting choice of words." She smiled and leaned forward, fully aware that the tank top she was wearing gave him a good view of her cleavage, "Your prowess will undoubtedly be tested."

"Can't wait," he responded cheekily.

Tessa came into the room and gave Brick his black coffee, "Whitlock is ready for you now."

Gage hopped up and headed out of the meeting room, "Excellent, thank you, Tessa."

Brick took a sip of his coffee and put it down on the table before following Gage.

"What?" Gage motioned to the cup when she reached the door, "Not good enough for you?"

Brick went back and picked up the cup, "It's actually quite good, but I figured it was rude to carry a cup around."

"But less rude to leave it and expect someone else to clean up after you?" Gage asked. "Interesting," she said before he could respond and left the room.

Brick sighed and followed her, carrying his cup.

Tessa couldn't help but snicker as he left the room.

Gage came to a stop outside Whitlock's office and knocked lightly on the door, when Whitlock responded, she swung the door open and motioned for Brick to enter.

When Brick walked into the room, she slammed the door behind him and walked back down the hallway, laughing.

EmEm and Will looked up when Gage entered the room.

"How completely mixed up is that poor boy going to be?" Will asked, his dark eyes twinkling with laughter.

"I mean, is it our fault if he's clearly a racist, chauvinistic, horn-ball who doesn't pay attention to details?" Gage asked with a neutral accent and a grin.

"You're awful," EmEm laughed, "he didn't seem so bad."

"He accepted that you shoot guns sideways without a second thought," Will pointed out.

"I mean, I do." EmEm responded, "I don't know what the hell to do with those things."

"Ah, scary death machines," Gage whined in a high-pitched voice, "stop it, get it away from me! The thought of such violence makes me chafe."

Will laughed when EmEm threw a towel at Gage's head. She ducked under it and did a little spin before popping back up and strutting to the side of the room.

"It really wouldn't hurt to have a medic on the team," Will said.

"Oh, don't call a Corpsman a medic," Gage said in a growling tone, "terrible insult, Sir. Not acceptable!"

"We can't all be Army brats," EmEm laughed, "We don't know the difference."

Gage threw a plastic practice knife at EmEm and it caught him in the chest, "Marine brat! How dare you! Semper Fi!"

EmEm glared at her before reaching down and picking the knife up from the floor, "Again, don't know the difference."

She kicked off her high heels, put up her fists, and bounced on the balls of her feet, "Should I learn you the difference, son?"

"Anytime!" He answered and threw the knife at her.

She deflected the weapon with her palm as she twisted away from it, "Be careful what you wish for, Grasshopper," she smiled as she again assumed a fighting stance.

"GAGE!" Whitlock's booming voice echoed in the gymnasium.

Gage smiled sheepishly and turned to face her boss, "Yes, dear?"

"Why must you torture every prospective hire I find?"

She shrugged, "I'm just drawing out his inappropriate characteristics," she responded. "No offense," she winked at Brick, who was standing beside Whitlock.

"How is that not offensive?" Brick muttered.

"Who are you to decide about inappropriate characteristics?" Whitlock questioned, clearly unamused.

"Hey Biscuit," Gage responded, "can you name one of the female's in this building?"

"You mean besides you and 'Hot Pants'?" He asked, "Tessa."

"Ah yes," Gage nodded, "Tessa. Whom you gave an order, the moment you met her."

"You told me-" Brick started but Whitlock held up a hand to silence him.

"Luckily, it doesn't matter how much you screw with this young man's head," Whitlock interjected, "I have the final say on his employ, not you."

Gage shrugged, "I mean if you want to meet your white boy quota, I feel like you could at least choose someone who doesn't stick out like a sore thumb."

"He does kind of scream military or cop," Will said, motioning to Brick.

"I have other clothes," Brick responded.

"And you chose those for a job interview?" Gage arched an eyebrow, "Interesting."

Mere walked into the room behind Whitlock and Brick, "Are we hiring the square?"

"Seriously?" Brick asked, "What the hell is wrong with you people?"

"We're a very close-knit group of people," EmEm answered, "we each have a niche in this family, xenophobia is common in such an environment."

Gage sighed heavily, "No, no, no!" She glared at her friend good-naturedly, "EmEm, you're a thug remember?"

"Oh, right," EmEm cleared his throat and made his voice deeper, "you ain't one of us, Cracker."

"Much better," Gage nodded.

Whitlock actually cracked a smile before he once more assumed a stone-face, "Brick, as far as I'm concerned, your resume speaks for itself. You're welcome to join our team if you so choose." He shook the young man's hand, "Take a few days to decide if you can put up with these brigands and give me a call to discuss your pay."

Brick nodded, "I don't really need any time to decide."

"Please," Whitlock held up his hand, "really evaluate your situation, this job isn't one to take lightly. There's an inherent risk, as well as an inability to have a stable home life, what with the constant moving. I know you're used to that, coming from your prior service, but please take at least a day. Not to mention, you'll have to rely on these people to have your back."

Brick shrugged, "Okay."

"I'll walk you out," Will said and motioned to the door closest to the front desk.

"Give him the man to man!" Mere shouted.

Will shook his head with a grin as he followed Brick out the door.

Once they were gone, Whitlock stared at Gage for a moment before pointing at her hair, "Platinum huh?"

She curtsied.

"I've called in a favor to Gerard," Whitlock continued, "you're in the next fight circuit if you're up to it. I have a lead to follow."

Gage bowed low, "At your service my liege," she said dramatically before straightening and asking, "when is it? If you don't mind me asking."

"Tomorrow night." Whitlock responded, "Can you be ready by then?"

"I'm always ready to kick some ass," she responded, "which fighter am I this time?"

Whitlock laughed and turned to leave.

"That's not at all disconcerting," Gage said to EmEm, who shrugged.

Chapter 13

"Sweet T?" Gage asked incredulously as she stared at the robe Whitlock brought her.

"I thought you could connect with your Southern roots," Whitlock gave her an uncharacteristic grin, "all the fighters are using fight names."

"Yeah, FIGHT names Whit!" Gage shook the robe at him, "You do something mean! Like Berserker or Mauler, shit, at this rate, Bunny would have been scarier, at least then I'd have sharp pointy teeth. What can Sweet T do to you? Diabetic coma? Cavities?"

"I thought you enjoyed irony," Whitlock was far more amused than Gage liked.

Gage stared at him for a moment longer before saying, "You better make sure they play *Another One Bites the Dust* before each of my fights." She turned to the mirror and stared at her reflection before grabbing a washable hair dye from her dresser and heading to her bathroom.

"It'll be done," Whit promised, "I'll see you in an hour, outside. We'll ride together."

"Yeah, yeah," she grumbled as she slammed her bathroom door shut.

~*~*~*~

"SWEET T TAKES DOWN ANOTHER OPPONENT! THIS GIRL IS ON FIRE TONIGHT!"

Gage bounced on the balls of her feet and cracked her neck as the other woman's manager and the referee dragged her unconscious body from the makeshift caged ring. The only thing she hated about these underground fights was that most of the fighters weren't actually trained fighters, they were brawlers.

Even though they were talented in their own right, you couldn't place a peewee football player on a field with a professional player and expect results. Gage had been training in several forms of martial arts since she could walk. She was especially fond of Brazilian Jujitsu.

She was already four fights in and hadn't broken a sweat yet.

"NEXT TO THE RING, SPITFIRE!"

Gage listened as some Irish jig music started to play and a brawny redhead started marching toward the ring with her fists in the air. The crowd liked her, they pumped their fists and shouted as she passed.

The energy was palpable. Gage watched her opponent carefully as she climbed onto the platform and entered the cage. Spitfire was easily six feet tall and had at least sixty pounds on her. Size didn't concern Gage. She'd taken down much larger opponents before.

She started bouncing again as *Another One Bites the Dust* began to play. She closed her eyes and nodded in time with the music. When the bit of song ended, she opened her eyes and zeroed in on her opponent. When the starting whistle sounded, she flew at Spitfire.

The redhead was surprised and flung a wild haymaker at Gage's head. Instead of simply dodging, Gage stepped to the side and grabbed the other woman's hastily thrown punch. Gage twisted and brought her leg up, hooking across her opponent's body and using momentum and body weight to bring them both to the ground. When they fell together, Gage was twisted around Spitfire and had the woman in a painful armbar within seconds of hitting the mat. Spitfire struggled and tried to punch with her free hand, but the blows lacked the strength necessary to force Gage to release.

Gage slowly lifted her hips, forcing Spitfire's elbow the wrong way. Finally, the redhead tapped on Gage's leg.

"WINNER! BY SUBMISSION: SWEET T! THE SOUTH IS RISING AGAIN!"

Gage rolled her eyes as she rolled back away from Spitfire. This announcer clearly thought highly of his witty banter, it annoyed her.

She glanced at the crowd and wasn't disappointed, they were all on their feet, cheering her. She stood up and bowed to them. They ate it up with glee.

She caught sight of Mak and Buck in the crowd and did a double take. The Australians were at the bar, each nursing a full mug of beer. They didn't really seem to be interested in the fight, which made her wonder why they were here. Though, it did make sense for them to be doing business in the illegal underground fighting circuit. She couldn't help but smile when she realized Mak had cut his hair to chin length and Buck's beard was well maintained.

Gage's eyes scanned the crowd for Whitlock and found him in a far corner, speaking to a small man in an expensive suit. Her boss didn't seem very happy, she cocked her head and tried to read their lips, but then *Another One Bites the Dust* began to play and she had to bring her attention back to the ring.

~*~*~*~*~

"I'm telling you, I swear that's our seppo," Buck smacked Mak's chest with the back of his hand.

"I don't think so," Mak shook his head, staring intently at the woman with brown-sugar colored hair, a purple sports bra, and black shorts. A tattoo of butterflies on her stomach, by her navel, made him cringe slightly, "I don't see her being the butterfly type."

"It still cracks me up that you're so freaked out by tiny bugs," Buck elbowed Mak. "I think you're just scared to know she could whip your ass," he laughed as Sweet T took down another opponent, this time with a savage kick to the head that dropped the other fighter like a sack of potatoes.

Mak shrugged, "I reckon it could be her, it's not like we know what she really looks like." At that moment, she met his gaze and his pulse raced, "Yup, that's definitely her. Do you think that's how she really looks?"

"Who knows?" Buck grinned, "That girl's a chameleon."

"We have money on her right?" Mak asked, his eyes still locked with Gage, who winked at him before breaking eye contact and playing up the crowd.

"Course we do," Buck scoffed, "Sweet T? Seriously? How could we resist a name like that? We're Australian gunrunners, how often do we run across a similar irony?"

Mak smiled and said, "Good," before draining the remainder of his beer and starting to push his way through the crowd to get a better view.

~*~*~*~

Gage finished her Jameson with a gulp and sighed in happiness as the smooth whiskey burned its way down her throat. She pushed her empty glass across the bar, winking her thanks at the bartender before cracking her neck and tucking her chin against her chest, closing her eyes to drown out the noise of the crowd. She felt the Australians approaching more than she heard them.

"Not to be a sticky-beak, but why'd you never tell us you're an ass-kicker?" Buck draped an arm across her shoulders in an act of familiarity that made her tense slightly.

She smirked, ducked under his arm, grabbed his wrist and twisted his arm up behind his back. He yelped in surprise making her laugh out loud before letting him go and patting his shoulder, "It was need to know." She grinned at him, "You didn't need to know."

Mak looked her up and down from behind with an appreciative smile, "So is this your real look?"

Gage shrugged and looked down at her sky-high heels, mini skirt, and a tank top, as she turned to face him, "More or less."

"More less, right?" Mak shook his head, "I don't see you as a Southern Belle."

"Joke's on you!" Gage exclaimed, "Texas, born and bred."

"You're saying you're a cowgirl?" Buck was still rubbing his elbow but his dark eyes were amused.

Gage arched an eyebrow at him, "I can ride anything with legs, but you probably shouldn't make sexual innuendos to your partner's infatuation." She winked at Mak, "Nice hair-cut, but you still need a few more inches gone to be taken seriously, Darlin'."

Mak blushed and ran his fingers through his longish hair, "Why do you think you're my infatuation? Maybe I'm just curious by nature."

Gage let her face fall, "Oh, I was hoping you wanted to find somewhere to relieve some tension together, but since you don't, I guess I'll just go back to pummeling bitches."

Buck laughed when she flounced past the stunned Mak like a debutant on the way to her ball.

She was chuckling to herself when her path was suddenly blocked by Whitlock's perfectly tailored suit jacket. She stopped short before she ran into him, "What's up, Papa Bear? Get done what you needed?"

"Unfortunately, this lead was a dud," Whitlock grumbled, "at least you seem to be enjoying yourself."

Gage shrugged, "I don't mind relieving some aggression and making some money."

"Well wrap it up so we can make our exit," Whitlock seemed distracted.

"What's up?" Gage asked.

Whitlock looked down at her, "I saw an old friend, he may have information I need to check on, then we'll leave this place in the rearview."

Gage laughed good-naturedly, "I love it when you use car metaphors, but they're usually for Mere's benefit. What's got you so topsy-turvy?"

Whitlock shook his head and said brusquely, "Don't worry about me, just figure out how to get yourself out before the second round without losing respect." He pushed past her and made his way through the crowd.

She watched him leave with her head cocked, trying to figure out his weird behavior, when she felt a cold chill run down her spine. Her gaze swept the crowd of people, looking for the source of the twist in her gut that was steadily tightening. She couldn't shake that feeling that someone was watching her. It shouldn't surprise her that she was being watched, she was the focal point of tonight's show, but something felt different now. An overwhelming taste of salt flooded her senses. It only intensified when she licked her lips and swallowed hard against the swirling in her guts.

"You look like you're gonna liquid laugh," Mak's deep voice was behind her.

She was surprised by the swell of comfort that warmed her from his proximity. She took a step back so that her body brushed his arm, "Just stand here a minute," she said quietly. She hoped it sounded like a request, not an order, so as an after-thought she added, "Please."

He gently rested his hand high on her hip, letting his arm wrap around her comfortably, as if they were lovers, "Whatever you need," he responded.

The heat from his gentle embrace made her chest ache. She was about to shake him off when she recognized Alex in the crowd and her whole body bristled.

His arm tightened around her and his blue eyes searched the crowd, looking for the threat she'd obviously spotted, "What is it?"

A group of three scantily clad women came over, all excitedly chatting and trying to shake Gage's hand. She smiled distractedly and tried to respond to their questions, but her gaze was steadily on Alex as he made his way through the crowd with four or five peons in tow.

"Who is he?" Mak asked quietly when he realized who she was watching. He quickly assessed the well-dressed businessman and the men clearly guarding him. He could tell they were armed and noted three of the five guards likely had prior military experience from the way they carried themselves.

She shivered when his breath tickled her ear, "No one important," she responded.

"Do you know of anywhere in the area to get our drink on?" One of the girls, a brunette, asked with a bubbly voice, "I mean, I know you're Southern, but do you know the area at all?"

Gage recognized that the question was directed at her, so she smiled tightly and said with a pronounced southern drawl, "I love Craze, it ain't far from here. Great music and even better liquor."

"Awesome!" The blonde grinned broadly, "Are you going there after the fight?"

"Probably not," Gage said distractedly, "I gotta go home to a cold bath."

"Is this your boyfriend?" The redhead of the trio cooed, "Is he going to put you in your bath, or can he come clubbing with us?"

"No wonder you learned how to fight," the brunette added, her dark lecherous gaze raked over Mak's body. Gage felt a twinge of something resembling jealousy chill her spine, but she couldn't draw her gaze from Alex as he shook hands with several men by the cage.

"I bet you have to beat women off him all the time," the blonde chimed in, biting her lip flirtatiously at the Australian.

"Sheilas, I'm not a piece of meat," he answered pertly, though he was clearly enjoying the attention, "and I'm sure not going anywhere without this sweetie, here."

Gage felt a small smile tug at her lips despite herself when she heard her fight name. His play on words was strangely pleasing to her, even though she couldn't concentrate with the way his hand made heat spread through her belly. Her hand gripped his against her hip without her mind telling it to, something in that contact helped ground her even though her heart was racing in her chest.

"Oh my God, that accent!" The brunette squealed, "Say something else!"

Gage had been listening distractedly, but she was physically trying to force her gaze to stop following Alex. Her grip tightened because she knew eventually, he'd notice her staring at him, he'd look at her, he'd recognize her. Her hair was longer than he'd remember, and a darker color, but she wasn't wearing make-up. Her dark contact lenses might give him pause for a moment, but if he really looked, he'd know it was her. He was walking through the crowd around the cage, one more turn and he'd be staring right at her.

She finally peeled her gaze away and met the eyes of the brunette practically drooling on Mak. The girl had her hands on his free arm, feeling his muscles or some foolishness. "Honey, there's no call for you to be fawning all over a clearly taken man," she packed on the southern accent, wrapping her arm around his waist in a show of possession. "You ought to be ashamed of yourselves," she shook her head, forcing her face to darken with jealousy, "can't you tell this man's in love?"

Mak looked down at her with a small smirk being the only indication of the surprise he felt.

"Give me some sugar, Sugar," she cooed at him, tilting her face up. When he arched an eyebrow in confusion, she grinned at him and stood up on her tiptoes to meet his lips with her own in a small peck. She pulled back slightly, surprised by the electricity she'd felt with that small act.

He must have felt it too, because he smiled at her surprise, then immediately pulled her tight against him and kissed her deeply with a passion that actually took her breath away and made her question why she'd never given him a chance before. His arms banded around her like warm steel, making her feel trapped and protected simultaneously.

"Ummm, okay?" One of the girls said before the three of them moved away awkwardly.

Gage continued the kiss even after they'd gone, and Mak wasn't going to stop until she did. When her arms circled his neck, she felt the tension release in her gut. Her guard was dropping as she let herself melt into his arms, her back to the cage. For a brief moment, she completely forgot everything but the spicy taste of his lips on hers and the way his arms felt around her.

"Finally!" Buck's voice broke the spell and Gage pulled back from Mak's grip with flushed cheeks, short of breath.

She looked from Mak to Buck with wide eyes, her cheeks red, before gasping breathlessly, "I have to go." She pushed through the crowd to the exit.

"I hate you," Mak grumbled.

"You been chasin' that spunk for goin' on three years," Buck said in exasperation. "What the bloody hell happened? You have bad breath?"

Mak scowled and knocked Buck's hat down over the dark-haired Australian's eyes, "You spooked her."

"She ain't a brumby," Buck scoffed, pushing his hat back up, "How'd I make her bailout?"

"Make up for it," Mak responded, "go spill a drink on that bloke." Mak nodded his head toward Alex as Gage tried to avoid the man on her way to the exit, which was just past him.

"I don't like wasting grog," Buck whined. Mak glared at him and Buck held up a hand, "Alright, alright. Relax."

Mak watched as Buck stumbled up to Alex's group, pretending to be drunk. The guards around the Hispanic man stepped into Buck's way, and the Australian started making a scene before lunging through the crowd and falling to the ground, his drink flying all over Alex's expensive suit.

While everyone in the vicinity was scrambling to help Alex, Gage slipped past and out the exit. She turned and met Mak's gaze momentarily with a small smile before she disappeared.

Chapter 14

Mere heard the garage door open from in her room. She rolled over in bed and glanced at the clock, which read three AM, before snuggling back into her blankets. Tiny was dreaming at the foot of her bed, his paws jerked and little whimpers escaped his throat. Mere rubbed his back with her foot through the blanket and he calmed down with a groan.

"Silly puppy," she murmured sleepily as she closed her eyes.

When she opened her eyes again, the clock read noon. She yawned and glanced at the foot of her bed, but Tiny was gone.

The flat was unusually quiet, which made Mere assume Gage was still asleep. The redhead got dressed and walked down the hall to the kitchen. Nothing had been moved since she went to bed the night before. Mere walked back down the hall to Gage's room and pushed the slightly open door in to see that Gage's bed was perfectly made. The sounds of machinery in the garage made Mere turn around and head back to the kitchen. She slipped on her shop shoes when she stepped onto the landing and walked down the stairs to the garage, finding Gage's booted feet sticking out from under Enzo's Mustang.

"How did it go?" Mere called, kicking Gage's boot.

Gage rolled the creeper out from under the car, her hair in a messy top knot, "I kicked major ass," she said with a grin, her white teeth shining from her grease-stained face.

"Did you sleep at all?" Mere folded her arms across her chest.

"I'm sure I've dozed for five minutes here and there," Gage responded as she started to scoot back under the vehicle.

"You need to sleep," Mere exclaimed, hooking Gage's foot with her own, "what's going on with you?"

"Chill Ma," Gage held up her hands in front of her as though surrendering, "I was just too hopped up on adrenaline after the fights. I figured I should get some work done on Enzo's 'Stang so we can be in his good graces."

Mere studied Gage for a moment, then her face broke into a smile, "Who did you make out with?"

Gage laughed, "You wouldn't believe me if I told you."

"You're all glowy," Mere laughed too.

Gage rolled her eyes, "I am not glowing. It was just nice."

Mere nodded, "Totally glowing, you enjoyed it a little more than you'll admit."

"Oh, I'll admit I liked it a hell of a lot." Gage grinned, "If we hadn't been interrupted, I probably would have let him have me right there in front of everyone."

"When do I meet him?" Mere asked seriously.

"Never," Gage responded, "I don't even really know his real name."

"Oh my God!" Mere exclaimed, "You slut!"

Gage shrugged and scooted back under the car.

Mere's phone buzzed at the same moment that a loud ping came from under the car followed by a curse from Gage.

Mere laughed at Gage as the woman scooted back out again, she held up her phone and said, "Whitlock is calling us in for a job."

"So much for a damn vacation," Gage grumbled and climbed up off the floor, wiping her hands on a rag.

"Can I catch a ride with you?" Mere asked.

"Yup," Gage threw her rag onto the cart by the car. She turned and yelled, "Yo, Will! You coming with, or driving separate?"

"Coming!" Will's voice came from the parts closet.

"Is Lina coming too?" Gage called, "Or is she going to hide in there like she wasn't just letting you give her a tune-up?"

Lina appeared, her usually tanned cheeks a stunning shade of crimson, "How did you know I was here?"

Gage laughed, "No one, but you, would wear high heels in my shop," she pointed at Lina's feet, "those make a distinct sound, Chica. Even when I'm under a car."

Will appeared behind Lina, "Leave her alone Gage, we were just talking."

Mere snorted, "She talks super close to your neck Will, unless you started sweating red lipstick."

Will slapped his hand to his neck, "You guys are assholes."

"You're the one shacking up on company time." Gage smirked, "Your boss must be too lenient."

Will rolled his eyes and lifted his hand so Lina could help get her lipstick off him, "Let's all ride together, so you can continue to bust my balls."

"Lina didn't already tend to those?" Gage asked.

Lina's face burned so red she looked like a tomato, "Oh my God, Gage, how can you be so lewd?"

"It's a gift," Gage shrugged before turning on her heel, pointing to the door, and shouting, "to the Batmobile!" As she led the group to her Suburban.

~*~*~*~*~

Whitlock looked up from his spot at the head of the conference table as Gage, Mere, Will, and Lina entered the room. He couldn't help but sigh heavily at the sight of Gage's grease streaked face, "You couldn't clean up before you came?"

"Your message said emergency," Gage shrugged, "so I came right away." She glanced at the woman sitting near Whitlock, "Please excuse the unfortunate excretions of my career choice."

The woman nodded hurriedly and looked down at the table as the foursome found seats. EmEm, Tessa, and Brick were already seated.

Gage winked at Brick who shook his head with a small smile.

"This is Elizabeth Beverly," Whitlock began as he stood to draw everyone's attention, "she's the headmistress of St. Peter's Catholic Girls School in North Carolina."

The woman looked up and nodded her head slightly to confirm the information.

"Not to be rude," Mere interjected, "but I thought we were staying home for a while."

"If this wasn't an emergency, we wouldn't be discussing the case," Whitlock responded gruffly.

"I came here because I was told you were the best," Elizabeth stated, her wire-rim glasses quivering from the tip of her nose.

"We are," Gage affirmed, "but we still haven't heard why this particular case is more of an emergency than all our others."

"My girls are being taken and murdered!" Elizabeth cried out.

"Come again?" Will asked, looking from the distraught woman to Whitlock.

"Three students from St. Peter's have been abducted over the last two months," Whitlock put a reassuring hand on Elizabeth's shoulder. "Two of these girls have been located."

Elizabeth sniffled and dabbed at her eyes with her handkerchief.

"Located how?" EmEm asked quietly.

"Lauren Kuretti's body was dumped in a nearby park," Whitlock responded, "evidence suggests she was sexually assaulted multiple times and beaten to death."

Elizabeth let out a soft sob.

"Megan Durant was found wandering down a street, bloodied and drugged. She remembers being attacked from behind by a man, but can't remember anything else." Whitlock attached photographs of the girls to the whiteboard behind him. "Stacy Anderson was the last to be taken and she's still missing. We're hopeful that she is still alive."

"If she is, she's being tortured," Gage stated, her tone carefully neutral.

"Which is why this case is an emergency," Whitlock answered forcefully, "it would appear that local law enforcement isn't getting anywhere in the case."

"What information do we have on the staff?" Gage asked, "Is there anyone with a taste for girls?"

Elizabeth scoffed, "You think because we're Catholic, we employ pedophiles?"

"If I was being an ass about Catholicism, shouldn't I ask about missing boys?" Gage asked.

"I thought you said this team was professional!" Elizabeth leapt to her feet, her shaking hand pointing at Gage.

"I'm asking about the staff, because abductions with such a severe commonality as these, usually happen for a reason. The only common factor is the school, right?" Gage looked at Whitlock, who nodded, "So who at your school is taking these girls?" Jade eyes bore into Elizabeth's face, "Or who at your school knows why they're being taken?"

"We were having a staff meeting when Lauren was taken," Elizabeth snapped, "all the male teachers were present."

"Were all the female teachers there too?" Mere asked.

"Megan said she was attacked by a man," Elizabeth responded haughtily.

"Who was missing from the meeting?" EmEm asked.

"Susan Brannigan was sick that day," Elizabeth retorted, "and Lucinda Montez had to leave early for a personal emergency. But both of them have been with me for five years, they're excellent educators and good people."

Gage leaned back in her chair, staring at the small woman for a moment before asking, "Has Susan or Lucinda recently found love?"

"What does that have to do with anything?" Elizabeth was exasperated.

"Miss Beverly, I assure you, there is a method to their madness," Whitlock interjected and motioned to her chair, "please just do your best to answer their questions."

"I'm sorry I'm so emotional," Elizabeth sat down, "I love these children like they were my own." She dabbed at her eyes again, "You're just asking hurtful questions."

"Why are they hurtful?" Will asked.

"Because if the attacker is her employee, she'd have missed something," Gage answered for Elizabeth, who looked down at her hands. Gage leaned forward and caught the older woman's gaze, "We are not suggesting that you are at fault." Her voice was calm and surprisingly kind, "The only people responsible for these atrocities are the people committing them." Her voice took on an edge as she continued, "But you need to give us as much information as you can so we can set the proper trap."

Elizabeth nodded.

"We aren't suggesting you're at fault at all," Will reiterated, "but when the only common factor is the school, it leads us to believe that there is some inside involvement. Are there any subdivisions in the area?"

"Or new students?" Tessa added.

"No, our campus is pretty secluded. There's nothing for at least five miles." Elizabeth answered, "And our only new student was at the beginning of the year, several months ago. She's doing quite well, very social."

"What's her name?" Lina asked, looking up from her notebook where she'd been scratching out notes.

"Caroline Graves," Elizabeth answered, "her mother is a charming woman, very polite, and impeccably educated."

"Have you ever met her father?" EmEm asked.

"I don't believe that I have, now that you mention it," Elizabeth's brow was furrowed.

"These girls who were taken, were they the quiet conservative type, or more 'Hit Me Baby One More Time'?" Gage asked as she leaned back in her chair again, arms folded across her chest.

"Excuse me?" Elizabeth was clearly not impressed with Gage's apparent apathy.

"Did they fit in and follow the rules, or did they rebel?" Brick cut in for the first time.

"Are you suggesting their clothing choices may have led to this?" Elizabeth's voice was rising in pitch.

Mere actually laughed at that and stood up, showing her short shorts and mid-drift baring shirt. "We're the last to suggest clothing choices demand punishment," she stated as she sat back down, "it's important information for us to know while looking through possible suspects."

"It's also important for me to know if I decide to be the next victim," Gage stated, still surveying the older woman carefully.

"Do you really think you could pass for a high schooler?" Elizabeth scoffed, "You're a grown woman."

Gage actually smiled, "You'd be surprised what I'm capable of, and thank you for confirming that these girls were a bit adventurous in the clothing department. Did they have anything else in common?"

Elizabeth fumed quietly for a moment, but she did seem to be thinking.

"Any common friends? Any common hangouts? Favorite classes?" Whitlock asked, "We need to know where these girls may have crossed paths with their attacker."

"Or attackers," Mere stated.

"The police are looking for a man. Why are you so certain that there were two people involved?" Elizabeth's tension was in her voice.

"Why are you so certain there weren't?" EmEm asked, "You seem offended at the mention that there could be more than one perpetrator."

"Because there is no indication there was more than one attacker," Elizabeth cried.

"Our job is to prepare for any outcome," Will stated, "that includes outcomes which seem extreme."

"In actuality, it's not uncommon for there to be two people involved in kidnappings," Tessa's soft voice broke the tension. She'd been staring at the table, listening to the entire exchange, "You never answered if Susan or Lucinda has recently found love." Her bright blue eyes stared at Elizabeth thoughtfully, "So which one has?"

Elizabeth stared back at the young woman with sad eyes, "Susan has been seeing someone, but she won't tell me who," she said finally. "She seems very happy, but she's been out sick a lot over the last few weeks." She looked over at Whitlock, "As for the other questions, I don't know of any other commonalities. These girls were all friends though, they were very involved in the community, and they were full of life," Elizabeth wiped at her eyes again.

"Who else was in their friend group?" Tessa asked.

"And who wanted to be?" Gage added.

"I don't think my girls have ever been exclusionary," Elizabeth answered.

"So, you don't remember how high school works," Gage nodded and stood up, "got it." She glanced at Whitlock, "I've heard all I need to, get me the clothes," she glanced at Lina, "you and EmEm start looking into the names mentioned for me?"

Lina and EmEm touched fists.

"I imagine we can come up with our plan of attack after the Head Mistress is gone," Gage stared at Elizabeth, "do not mention this to anyone." Her voice was forceful, "The only way we can be effective is if no one knows what we're doing."

Elizabeth's eyes were wide as she nodded.

"Whitlock, how about you take Miss-Two-First-Names into your office to discuss fees and necessities, so the rest of us can actually plan this out," Gage opened the door and held it with a fake smile plastered to her face.

Whitlock sighed and motioned for Elizabeth to exit, "Miss Beverly, let's leave them to it."

The woman stood, her offense clearly written on her face, "I don't know how I can trust these people to handle this situation if they're not even mature enough to handle an interview."

Gage's smile turned icy, "If there's a chance to find Stacy alive, we're probably her only hope." Her voice held no real emotion, "Plus there's the possibility that there's a monster on your campus kidnapping girls and essentially raping them to death." She cocked her head, "I'd be more concerned about that, than the maturity of the only people willing to help." She glared at Whitlock as he ushered the speechless woman out of the room.

Gage slammed the door behind them and flopped back into her seat unceremoniously, "Who's in?"

Brick stared at her, "Do you ever NOT say what you think?"

"That sounds exhausting," Gage answered.

"I think we just became best friends," he stated with a grin.

"Um, slow your roll, Tex, that position is already taken," Mere piped up.

"I really don't want to leave, we just got home," Will sighed, "but I guess I'll be back up."

"I can go," Brick interjected.

"We still don't know you," EmEm said, "I don't know if I'm ready to rely on you to watch Gage's back."

Brick shrugged, "The only way I can prove myself, is if you give me a chance to do it."

"That's true," Gage responded. "EmEm, Lina, and Tessa will find everything they can, they'll give us a starting point. I'll go into the school. Mere and Biscuit can be in the follow car." She glanced at Will, "You stay here and make sweet love to Lina," her face broke into a genuine smile.

"I'd be more comfortable watching you," Will answered.

"You'd rather watch me than make sweet love to Lina?" Gage arched an eyebrow.

"That's not- God you're such a bitch," Will sighed.

"I'll be fine." Gage responded, "It'll be good to have medical experience on hand in case we do find Stacy alive." She nodded at Brick, "But you'll have to control yourself around my Catholic School Girl look."

"It won't be easy," Mere said forlornly, "she's sexy in plaid."

Gage grinned and shrugged.

"I think I'll be okay," Brick responded.

"Are you gay?" EmEm asked conversationally.

Brick glanced at the man sitting next to him, "What the fuck, dude?"

EmEm grinned with a shrug, "Just wondering."

"Are you?" Brick asked.

"Sometimes," EmEm replied making everyone in the room, except Brick, laugh.

"Are you sure you're ready to go victim again so soon?" Tessa asked.

Gage chewed her lower lip a second then said, "I don't really have a choice. No one else is qualified."

"Hey!" Mere pouted.

Gage held up a hand to her friend, "The problem here, is someone has to be taken. It's not just beating off an attack or subduing an attacker."

"We could just subdue the attacker then interrogate him," Mere said.

"Then we risk him not talking and Stacy starving or dying of dehydration while we look for her," Brick responded.

"Or, if we're right, and he has a partner, Stacy could die a lot quicker," EmEm added.

"I'll need a tracking device," Gage looked at Tessa. "I'll leave that to you and boy genius," she motioned to EmEm, "preferably something that looks normal, or sewn into my bra or something."

"What if you lose your bra?" Brick asked. He held up his hands in defense when everyone looked at him, "What? I'm just asking. If this guy is sexually assaulting women, wouldn't he undress her first thing?"

"No one will be taking my bra without my permission," Gage responded pointedly, "NO one."

Brick laughed, "I'm not looking for your bra, I'm just stating the obvious. How are you going to protect yourself while you play victim?"

Gage sighed, "Since you're new, and have not seen my impressive work, allow me to explain-"

"She tips on the edge of insanity and hopes we get there before she kills him," Mere interjected.

Gage shrugged and nodded, "Yeah, that's pretty much it."

"I'll rig something up," Tessa said. "I'll make it so you can turn it on when you find Stacy, that way we don't come in too soon."

When Gage and Mere stared at her, Tessa corrected herself, "So Mere and Brick don't come in too soon."

"Are you sure you won't want help?" Will asked, "If there are two suspects, won't you need all the help you can get?"

"Will, why are you trying to leave Lina?" Gage asked. "I think I'll be fine with Biscuit and Mere. Whitlock will be there too."

"I'm sure he'll coordinate with local police also," Tessa added.

Gage made a sound of disgust, "They usually cause more harm than good."

"God love them," Mere added.

"You don't like cops?" Brick asked.

"We like them just fine," Gage answered, "but sometimes the hero complex is too strong to let us do our damn jobs."

"It is rather disturbing seeing you victimized," EmEm supplied.

"Normal people should try to step in to stop violence," Will added.

Gage rolled her eyes, "Tell me more about these fictional 'normal people'. I've always heard stories of their existence."

"The point is, we're on the same side," Will shook his head at her sarcasm, "we've needed the back up before."

"Maybe so," Gage acquiesced, "but your job will be to let me get taken," she said pointedly to Brick, "so don't get all heroic savior until it's needed."

"I'm not a cop," Brick answered, "besides, it might be nice to see you shoved into a trunk."

"He'll fit in just fine," Lina laughed.

Chapter 15

"I love your hair," the voice was startlingly close, making Gage look up from her book.

"Oh, thanks, I braid when I'm bored," she said with a friendly smile as she touched her dark French braid.

"It's so pretty, I wish I could do something like that," the girl had blonde curly hair that was in a wild mane around her tanned face.

"I love your hair," Gage responded shyly, "you remind me of a lion. Fierce and beautiful."

"That is the nicest thing anyone has ever said to me!" The girl sat down across from Gage, "My name's Caroline. I've been meaning to talk to you since I saw you last week. I know it's not easy being the new girl."

"My name's Sammy, and you're definitely not wrong," Gage put her bookmark into her book and set it aside. "Especially with all the crazy press that's been going on," she motioned to the news van in the driveway beside the courtyard. "What is it all about anyway?"

"Don't you own a TV?" Caroline asked.

Gage shrugged, "We don't really have much."

"Oh, damn, you should come to my house after school." Caroline smiled, "My mom doesn't get home until six and she leaves the liquor cabinet unlocked. We can make cocktails and watch reality TV."

"That's so cool," Gage breathed, "you just do whatever you want? What about your dad?"

Caroline shrugged, "He's never home. He pretty much lives in New York City because he has business trips all the time. I'm essentially a product of a single mom."

"Sorry," Gage said quietly and looked down at the table.

"Oh, no worries," Caroline laughed, "I'm used to it. My dad wants me to move to New York with him, but I told him I'm actually starting to like it here." She shrugged, "It'll still be nice to have someone at home with me, that way I don't go missing like my friends."

Gage looked up with questioning eyes, "Should I be worried?"

"Oh shit, that's right. You don't have a TV!" Caroline leaned in as though divulging a secret, "Three girls have gone missing from our school. One is dead, one was found but she still doesn't remember what happened, and the third hasn't even been found yet."

"Oh my God!" Gage gasped, "Do they have any idea who is doing it?"

"The cops are completely stumped!" Caroline whispered, her tan cheeks flushed with excitement.

"Do you have a theory?"

Caroline looked over her shoulder to make sure no one was within listening range, then she leaned in again, "There's a creepy guy with a red van who hangs out by the kitchen entrance. I see him almost every day, staring into my class."

"No way!" Gage gasped, "Have you reported it?"

"I told Miss Brannigan, but she totally blew me off."

"Weird," Gage's brow furrowed, "I wish adults gave a shit about what we have to say."

"Right!?" Caroline nodded as she leaned back. "So, after school today, you want to come to my place?"

"I think my dad has plans today," Gage said apologetically, "but I'll hang out tomorrow if the invite still stands."

"Oh, totes," Caroline grinned as she stood up, "free-standing invite. Just let me know."

"Cool," Gage smiled as she gathered her books and shoved them into her backpack when the end of lunch bell rang. "I guess it's back to the grind," she sighed.

"Don't I know it!" Caroline groaned, "I'm headed to Miss Brannigan's class now. Total bore-fest. If she even bothers to show up."

Gage walked with Caroline to the front door, then excused herself to the bathroom. She checked all the stalls. When she saw they were clear, she said, "Did you catch all that?"

Tessa said Caroline's father is some type of computer mogul. Brick's voice said in her ear. *Her story checks out about him being gone a lot. There's lots of recent flight history and crazy credit card use. He has an alibi for when Lauren was taken but looks like he may have been in town for the other two.*

Gage nodded, even though Brick couldn't see her. "I'm going to check for the red van. It should be there about this time. I don't like that Brannigan discounted it outright."

Do you want us to handle it? You don't want to blow your cover.

"No, I'll do it. I want you guys to be invisible." Gage checked her reflection and put on some lip gloss. "Besides, if it is our guy, I still need him to take me."

Roger that. We're not far if you need the cavalry.

Gage pushed out of the bathroom after the late bell rang and peeked down the hall. It was empty, so she walked quietly down the hall to a side door leading to the courtyard she'd vacated earlier. Once she made it outside, she moved to the large hedge line and stayed in the shadows provided by the greenery.

When she rounded the corner, she saw a dented red minivan with Virginia plates. "Looks like Virginia plates: X-ray, Romeo, Alpha, Tango, Echo, Delta. X-Rated," she said softly. "There's a white male standing outside, mid-thirties with brown hair, average everything. The sliding door is open."

Got it.

Gage moved as close as she dared, staying in the shadows, and tried to see into the darkened windows.

Miss Brannigan came out of the back door, reserved for deliveries and kitchen workers, she looked around hastily to make sure no one was around. She was a thirty-something woman who always wore loose smock-type dresses that had no form to them at all. Her class was by the book and she never had a hair out of place.

Gage watched as the older woman rushed down the steps toward the van, her face a mask of worry and anger.

"What are you doing here?" Brannigan hissed at the man, "Do you want Elizabeth to figure us out?"

He shrugged with a self-assured smile, "I don't really care."

"Are you out of your mind?" Brannigan yelped as the man grabbed her and forcefully threw her into his van. He was in the van after her with the door slammed shut in seconds.

"Holy shit, he just snatched Miss Brannigan!" Gage whispered as she rushed to the van.

She threw open the sliding door and was shocked by the sight inside. Miss Brannigan's feet were straight up in the air, her sensible heels barely hanging on by her toes as the pale buttocks between her legs vigorously thrusted on top of her to a cacophony of moaning and grunting. Her dress was shoved up under her breasts showing a pronounced belly between them when the man hurriedly rolled to the side and yanked on his pants with a yell.

"Oh my God, I'm sorry! I thought you were in trouble!" Gage couldn't help the laugh that caught in her throat as Miss Brannigan's shoe fell off her foot onto her flushed face.

"Samantha!" Miss Brannigan shouted as Gage slammed the door shut again.

"False alarm," Gage snorted quietly, "Miss Brannigan is getting banged out by our mystery man. Also, she's pregnant." The laughter in her ear almost drowned out the teacher's yell.

"Samantha!" Miss Brannigan caught up to Gage as she smoothed her skirt. Her cheeks were burning red, "I'm so sorry. You never should have seen that!"

"Seen what?" Gage asked with a smile, "Your personal life is none of my business. I just thought you may have been in trouble, that's all."

"You're not going to tell anyone?" Miss Brannigan seemed surprised.

"No, why would I? Like I said, it's none of my business."

"You're very kind," the older woman had tears in her eyes, "if Miss Beverly knew I was pregnant out of wedlock, I'm pretty sure she'd fire me."

"Maybe keep those sinful activities off school property," Gage whispered with a smile as they climbed the stairs.

"Absolutely," Miss Brannigan nodded, "you'll understand one day, being pregnant is hard."

Gage laughed as they entered the school, "There is one thing you could do for me."

"What?"

"Write me a hall pass?" Gage smiled innocently.

"I think I can handle that," the teacher laughed.

Chapter 16

Brick looked up from his laptop when Gage came out of the bathroom. "I still can't get over how different you look," he laughed, "I feel like I'm looking through a time-machine at your high school days."

Gage's plaid skirt was rolled up at the waist to make it shorter than regulation. Her knee-high socks were pulled tight around her shapely calves and the small black heels she wore pushed the rules to the limit. Her white button-down shirt was tucked into her skirt with enough overlay to hide the roll making it shorter, and the buttons at her throat were open. Her soft dark curls were in low pigtails at the nape of her neck, drawing attention to her long neck and open shirt. Her makeup seemed understated, but in actuality it made her cheeks look fuller and rosy with freckles across the bridge of her nose. Her eyes were made to look much wider than usual and dark contact lenses made her doe-like expression more impactful. She had false teeth which slipped over her own to make her teeth seem just slightly too big for her.

"Sorry to spoil your day-dream, but my high school days were actually hate-fueled rage-fests of pubescent hormonal drama." She smiled, showing her false teeth, "I was a grungy teenage runaway. That's where I fit into the stereotypes of our work family."

Brick was intrigued, "Interesting, you do this so well, I thought it was second nature."

"It's the plaid," Mere responded from where she was laying on one of the two queen beds in the room, fully clothed, with her eyes shut. "She's just meant to wear plaid."

Brick nodded his agreement, staring at Gage's legs, "It definitely looks good on you, I'll give you that." He glanced up at her amused face and added, "But truth be told, that makeup is too good. You look like a minor. That doesn't do it for me."

"Not even if I turn around, Daddy?" Gage asked with a laugh.

Brick cleared his throat and blushed slightly, "Knock it off."

"Or what?" Gage responded innocently, as she turned around and looked at him with wide eyes over her shoulder, "Will you spank me?"

Brick opened his mouth to respond, but then cleared his throat and looked back at his computer instead, "Miss Brannigan's boyfriend has an alibi for all three kidnappings, so does Miss Brannigan. They're off the suspect list. Her sick days were due to her pregnancy and doctor appointments surrounding that."

Gage sighed heavily, "This is getting boring. What's a girl got to do to get abducted around here?"

"Keep shaking your ass," Brick said without looking at her, "someone will take you."

Mere laughed as she stood up, "I think Lucinda is a valid lead. She hates all things unconventional and sinful." She glanced at Brick and added, "Shake your ass at her a few times, she might snap."

Gage nodded, "Her Chemistry class is the worst. She's so grumpy and rigid. There's no midday van sex for her." She cocked her head thoughtfully, "But she could probably use some."

Brick and Mere both laughed.

"I guess I better get to school," Gage sighed, "I hate this."

"Waiting to get kidnapped must be pretty exhausting," Brick said apologetically.

"No!" Gage responded, "Going to high school! It's damaging my calm! I had my G.E.D. by thirteen, so I wouldn't have to deal with this bullshit." She moved to the door then cursed angrily.

"What? What's wrong?" Mere moved toward her friend.

"I forgot to do my homework," Gage groaned as she stomped out of the motel room. "I'll lean on Lucinda some more. Don't forget I'm going to Caroline's after school today. I'm still curious about her father, something isn't sitting right with me."

Got it. Brick said in her ear, then grinned at her through the front window of the motel room as Gage climbed onto the small white church bus which had just entered the parking lot.

While on the ride to school, Gage decided she should step up her game a notch if she was going to entice Lucinda. She pulled out a non-regulation red lipstick and carefully applied it to her lips. She glanced in the small mirror of her compact and smiled. She closed the lipstick, then pulled out the false bottom on the tube and activated the small electronic device inside before closing the tube back up and slipping it into her backpack's side pocket. When the bus came to a stop at the school, Gage unbuttoned one more button on her shirt, showing the flesh just above her lacy sports bra which effectively hid the ace bandage compressing her breasts.

She strolled down the aisle and winked at the bus driver before making a show of climbing down the stairs. She heard the driver gulp and grinned as she made her way up the front stairs of the large school building. She stopped by Lucinda, who always had morning bus duty, and waved flirtatiously at the driver. He quickly slammed the door shut and drove off with bright red cheeks.

"Get to class immediately, Samantha!" Lucinda snapped.

"Yes Ma'am," Gage sighed forlornly as she strolled into the main hall. Her first class was Mr. Dickinson's History class. "At least there's some man-candy to look at there too," she said dreamily, just loud enough for the older woman to hear.

Gage spent the hour in her class chewing on her lower lip seductively and dropping pens she'd have to pick up. She saw Lucinda's glowering face in the door's window a number of times which made her step up her game by leaning heavily on Mr. Dickinson's desk when asking a question. Even going so far as to lean up against his arm to point to something in her book. His sharp intake of air and refusal to look in her direction made her feel bad for using him this way, but it was necessary to trigger Lucinda.

When the bell rang, she collected her belongings and headed to Mr. Dave's class. He was supposed to be addressed as Mr. Mason per the rules of the school, but his laid-back manner of teaching math made him Gage's favorite at this school. Caroline happened to share this class, so it would be useful in that way also.

When Gage entered the class, Caroline was already seated next to her usual seat. She smiled at the blonde girl as she slid in beside her.

"I love your lipstick!" Caroline said with a broad grin. "I wish I were brave enough to wear that!"

Gage pulled the tube from her backpack as she dropped the bag unceremoniously on the ground, "You're a lioness," she said as she handed it over, "be brave!"

Caroline nodded, "You're right!" She pulled out her compact and quickly applied the lipstick to her lips.

When she tried to hand it back, Gage held up her hand, "You keep it. It looks amazing on you."

Also, keep the bug that's in it. Brick added, ***Nice one.***

"Thank you so much!" Caroline gushed as she checked her reflection in her own compact, "It does look good, doesn't it?"

Gage nodded as the late bell rang and she settled in to watch her math teacher attempt to get high school girls interested in Algebra II. She sat with her knees slightly apart and bedroom eyes staring at her teacher.

He purposely kept his vision away from her direction once he saw what she was doing, but she saw Lucinda's disapproving face momentarily in the door's window of this class too.

"You'd think Ms. Montez would be in her own class, not worrying about ours," Gage whispered to Caroline who giggled and waved at the older woman's scowl.

When the bell rang, Gage collected her things and said, "Are we on for after school today?"

"Oh, sure!" Caroline nodded excitedly, "I'm so happy you can come!"

"Awesome," Gage smiled, "How do I get there?"

"I'll write down my address in Ms. Montez's class," Caroline answered.

"Perfect. If we pass a note in her class, her brain will explode," Gage laughed.

She wasn't wrong.

Caroline passed the folded paper to Gage in plain view of the forty-something archetypal spinster.

"SAMANTHA GRIMES!" The shriek made Gage cringe slightly.

"Yes, Ma'am?" She glanced up at her teacher with a bored expression.

"What did Miss Graves just pass to you?" Lucinda was fuming.

"We suspect it's the stick from up your ass," Gage responded with a sweet smile as the whole class cackled with laughter.

Lucinda's face went crimson and her whole body seemed to shake as she growled, "Excuse me?"

"You're excused," Gage smiled pertly, "are you going somewhere?"

Caroline laughed so hard she almost fell out of her chair.

"You girls think you're above the law!" Lucinda shrieked, "Get to the Head Mistress' office, immediately!"

"Was that just me? Or me and Caroline?" Gage asked, "Who of us is above the law?"

"Miss Grimes, get out of my classroom," the teacher snarled, slamming her hand down.

"Gotcha!" Gage stood up and collected her things, "I'm above the law." She shrugged apologetically at Caroline, "Sorry, it's just me. I'm the only one above the law."

Caroline snorted as she tried to contain her laughter.

"OUT!" Lucinda roared, throwing her notebook in Gage's direction. It fell on the floor and erupted in a flurry of loose papers.

Gage stood still, staring at the papers that floated to the floor, then her gaze went to Lucinda, "Temper much? Jesus."

Lucinda crossed herself and glared at the younger woman, "How dare you take the Lord's name in vain on top of all your other sins today! You must leave this room immediately."

"Pretty sure wrath is one of the seven deadly sins," Gage responded as she strolled past her teacher, to the door. "Which of us is really the sinner here?" She didn't wait for an answer, she called out, "See ya after school, Caroline!" Then she let the door slam behind her as she left the room.

I'm pretty sure that was the most spectacular playing of someone I have ever heard. Brick's voice was highly impressed.

"Yeah, I could kind of tell by all the laughing in my ear," Gage said as she walked down the hallway.

Sorry. He didn't sound apologetic. ***It's safe to say that if Lucinda is the insider, you're on her list.***

"I'm pretty sure she wanted to murder me on the spot," Gage responded, "so I'll walk around tonight and be bait."

Sounds super exciting.

"Story of my life," Gage sighed as she sat down outside Mrs. Beverly's office.

Chapter 17

Gage was walking around in town later that evening before heading to Caroline's house. She came out of the small boutique she'd been wandering in and glanced down the street away from the blue utility van containing her friends.

"The same white sedan has circled this block five times since you went in the store," Brick's voice surprised Gage from behind her as she walked.

"Looking for parking?" Gage asked quietly, barely moving her lips.

Brick glanced at the street which was fairly empty, "Doubtful."

Gage nodded, "Good. Maybe the bait was set properly, go back to the van and watch my ass."

"Your wish is my command," Brick chuckled, "it's a fine ass to watch."

Gage wiggled her hips, continuing to walk down the sidewalk, towards the edge of the small town.

A white sedan pulled across the street and began driving alongside Gage, on the wrong side of the road. She looked over and saw that the driver was a middle-aged man with salt and pepper hair. His smile was charming as he lowered his window, "Are you Samantha?"

She stopped walking and turned to face him, her eyebrow arched, "Who wants to know?"

He laughed and parked, stepping out of the car and holding his hand out in greeting, "Caroline sent me into town to look for you. She said you walk everywhere and she was worried about you making it safely to the house. I'm Gerald Graves, Caroline's father."

"Oh," Gage took his hand and squeezed it flirtatiously in her own. "She didn't tell me her Dad was in town." She smiled and added, "Or so handsome."

Gerald blushed and pulled his hand away, "I've heard all about you though," he chuckled, "would you like a ride to the house? Caroline can't wait to see you."

Gage curtsied, "I'd be much obliged. I'm sure I would have gotten lost along the way."

The man walked around to the passenger's side of his vehicle and opened the door for her.

"Oh my," Gage cooed and bat her eyes at him as she slowly strode around the car, "a true gentleman is so very hard to find these days."

Gerald laughed, "You have a thing for older men, do you?"

"A thing?" She asked huskily, "Sure, I have something for older men. I find experience extremely attractive." She slid into the seat and crossed her legs, pulling her short skirt up her legs slightly as she smiled sweetly up at Gerald. He closed the door and walked back around to the driver's side.

His first action after climbing into his seat and situating himself with his seatbelt on was to reach across her and buckle her seatbelt for her, "Safety first," he said gruffly.

"You smell amazing," she responded breathily as she arched her back slightly then settled into her seat, twirling the hair of her pigtail with a finger.

"Good lord, you really are a little minx, aren't you?"

She shrugged and bit her lower lip before responding, "My parents sent me to an all girls' Catholic school to break my habits."

"Your habits?"

She smiled, "I have a habit of getting what I want. Most adults don't like that."

"Understandable," Gerald chuckled as he began to drive, "please don't teach Caroline that habit."

"She already gets what she wants," Gage responded matter-of-factly. "She wants to stay here. She loves it here. I don't get it. But she's pretty cool. I guess I should congratulate your wife on that though," she looked out her window, using the reflection to watch his jaw clench. "At least that's what Caroline says, that she's basically got a single mom." She looked over at Gerald with wide eyes, "You don't seem so absentee to me."

"I have to make a quick stop," he said tightly as he veered off the main road onto a side street.

"Okay, sure," she answered, watching the van containing Brick and Mere in the side mirror as it turned down a parallel road.

The car sped past several homes in the neighborhood before screeching to a halt in front of a modest house with one light shining from inside. He put her window down slightly then turned off the vehicle, "I'll be right back," he said as he climbed out of his seat. He slammed his door, making her jump slightly. He circled the car and leaned down to her window, "Now, don't you go anywhere, yeah hear?" He smiled down at her, but there was no warmth in his tone or eyes anymore.

"Sure," she smiled then called, "hurry back," at his back as he strode up the walkway to the back of the house.

Well, that was weird. Brick's voice was confused.

"Right?" Gage looked in the side mirror, "There's something real concerning going on here." She stepped out of the vehicle and tried to see into the front window, "Who is he stopping to see?"

I'll go peek in the back. You stay at the car in case he comes back out. Mere will stay in the van to provide your tail if I don't get back in time.

While Brick was talking, Gage walked up to the mailbox to see the address, the name she saw instead gave her pause, "Uh, guys?" She glanced up at the house and said quietly, "This is Ms. Montez's house." She walked back toward the car and pulled out her cell phone, "I think this is a go. Caroline's dad might be working with Montez."

He's her backdoor buddy, Brick's voice was amused.

"Come again?" Gage couldn't hide the disbelief in her voice.

Your boy currently has your teacher face-down on her counter. I guess Miss Brannigan isn't the only teacher getting some sweet love out of wedlock.

Gage made a face, "I definitely didn't see that one coming."

This love isn't so sweet. Brick corrected himself, *I'd more consider it to be hate sex. I'm headed back to the van. This can't last long.*

"Hate sex lasts less time?" Gage asked with a smirk as she leaned over the hood of the car and fiddled with her phone. She glanced up the street and caught the sight of a patrol car pulling over and parking about two blocks up, "What the fuck is local popo doing here?"

Mere's flustered voice broke over the wave. *Whitlock is trying to get them to back down. They're not listening. Miss Beverly told them we suspect Montez so they decided they want to take her in for questioning.*

"If we take them now, we lose the girl," Gage growled.

Apparently, they're under the impression that Montez can be cracked. They're comfortable with the risk of possibly losing their only lead.

"That's nice." Gage sighed, "You have a new job."

Cop Block. What about you? Mere wasn't pleased, *I don't want to leave you without a tail.*

Gage shrugged, "We do what we must. I still have the tracker. I'll pop it when I find Stacy."

If something happens to that tracker, you'll be on your own, Brick growled. *I don't like this at all.*

"If we let those cops ruin this, we could lose Stacy forever." Gage typed onto her phone, spun to face the house when she heard the backdoor slam shut, and muttered, "I like my odds against the perv and the wannabe nun."

"You ready to go?" Gerald's face was visibly flushed even in the low light.

"Sure," Gage smiled, "I was just texting Caroline that we're on our way."

Gerald's face went rigid as he approached her. "You shouldn't have done that," he said coldly as he hit the button on his car remote making the trunk pop open.

Gage backed up until her back hit the car, "Why not?" She squeaked when Gerald grabbed her upper arms roughly.

"You shouldn't have involved my daughter," he growled and pulled her close to him as the van holding her friends drove by to block the patrol vehicle. He dragged her toward the trunk once the van was passed.

"Please, I don't understand, you're hurting me," she whimpered, struggling.

"Get in the trunk," he snapped, "now."

"Please," Gage's fear was real at the thought of being trapped in the tight, enclosed, space. She fed on it and let it fill her eyes, as she mentally prepared herself to allow whatever happened next, to happen. She grabbed his left arm with both of her hands, as though trying to pull his arm away, but in actuality, she was gripping his shirt to prevent her instincts from kicking in. "I'll ride in the back seat," she begged, "I'll lay down, no one will see me. I promise!"

When his fist hit her, she saw stars and stumbled slightly. She hadn't expected the ferocity of the blow, nor did she anticipate him to follow with another punch that connected with her temple and made her lose her balance. She felt him shove her roughly into the trunk, but her head was spinning. The lingering fumes from the exhaust and the heat made her dizzy when he slammed the trunk shut. The panic that gripped her chest as the darkness filled her senses was real. Gage embraced it and let herself kick, claw, and scream. Usually, the fear was an act, but sometimes her situation actually coincided with her true fears, that helped her lose her strength and embrace the inherent weakness which was so attractive to perpetrators.

She felt the car rumble to life and begin to move.

We're still blocking these idiots! Mere's voice sounded like it was in a tin can, far away.

Gage? Where are you? Brick's tone was urgent.

"In the trunk," Gage moaned before allowing herself to succumb to the anxiety attack, which coupled with the blows to the head, managed to rid her lungs of air. Her eyes rolled and she couldn't focus as she slowly lost herself to the darkness.

~*~*~*~

Gage's eyes fluttered open when the vehicle hit a hard bump then vibrated like it was going over a gravel road. She could see through the tail light if she focused, she put all her energy into breathing and looking out into the darkness of the night. She wasn't really sure if she was seeing outside, or just the inside of the light, but it comforted her to think it was the night air, just on the other side of the glass.

The car bumped to a halt and the engine went silent. Gage prepared herself for the impending confrontation. She pushed her hair out of her face and pulled out her earrings, balling her hands into fists with the shiny metal pieces inside one hand.

When the trunk popped open, a blinding light flooded her senses, disorienting her. She felt a fist connect with her chin and forced herself to go limp. Through barely open eyes she saw the light dim as Gerald's head blocked the beam. She felt herself being yanked up roughly and tossed over the man's hard shoulder.

PREY

She opened her eyes, but remained limp, her hands hanging down by his hips as he slammed the trunk shut and carried her toward what looked to be an abandoned mine.

She tried to silently take deep breaths to prepare herself for the trek underground. She realized fairly quickly that there were three separate entrances to the mine. Gerald took her down the tunnel in the middle. She dropped one earring while Gerald was midstride. It landed in the center of the path and glinted in the moonlight. She focused on the sight of that tiny beacon as the darkness closed in.

The light from Gerald's flashlight didn't penetrate the darkness behind him. He walked for a long time, hefting her weight every once and a while to keep her from slipping off his shoulder.

Finally, he stopped and dropped her on the dirt floor of a small cavern so he could light the oil lamp on a small wooden table.

Gage backed into the wall nearest to her, as though the fall had jolted her awake, "What is this? Where am I? What the hell are you doing?"

Gerald sneered at her, "Giving you what you wanted," he responded coldly, "alone time with me."

"Stay away from me, you perv," Gage snapped, pulling her skirt down, "does your DAUGHTER know you're a monster?"

"A monster?" He laughed, "I thought I was a handsome experienced man."

"Not all monsters are ugly," Gage spat out, "though you're certainly losing your appeal." She looked around herself and asked again, "Where am I?"

"Let's just say, no one will hear you scream," he responded with a smug smirk.

"Please," Gage switched her tone to pleading, "No one has to know what's happened so far. If you let me go now, I'll never tell anyone. I swear."

He shook his head, "No, you're too late for that." He stood and began pacing, "All you little harlots keep influencing my Caroline. She would never want to stay here if she didn't have you convincing her."

"You think I have anything to do with Caroline not wanting to live with you in New York?" Gage laughed in disbelief, "Maybe she just knows in her heart that you're a disgusting pedophile."

Gerald flew at her and kicked her side roughly, making the air rush from her lungs.

"Shut up, you little bitch!"

Gage gasped for breath, forcing her gaze to be terrified, "Please. I barely know Caroline. I don't have to be her friend. Hell, I'll leave tomorrow."

Gerald knelt beside her and his hand wrapped around her throat, tightening slowly as she spoke.

"I'll tell her to go with you," she gasped out, "please." A tear ran down her cheek.

Gerald leaned in and licked the tear from her face, then threw her back against the wall before standing up and pacing again.

"You need to go do something about Caroline," Lucinda's voice cut through the stillness as the woman entered the light. "There were deputies in my neighborhood when you took her," she pointed at Gage. "you're lucky they haven't put anything together yet."

"She told Caroline she was with me," Gerald snapped, kicking Gage again.

Gage cried out in pain and curled up into a ball, "Please help me, Ms. Montez," she whimpered, pleading with her teacher.

"There is no helping you, child. You have gone against all of your teachings." She scolded before adding gently, "This is your penance." The older woman turned back to Gerald, "Go smooth things over with Caroline. We can't afford her putting this together. Not with the police so close."

Gerald nodded and motioned to Gage, "What about her?"

"I will handle her until you return," Lucinda stated.

Gage stared at her teacher as Gerald left the cavern with his flashlight in hand.

"Miss Grimes, I wish you could understand where I'm coming from here," Lucinda sighed.

"Please," Gage whimpered, "just let me go. You don't have to do this. You didn't do anything wrong. Please just let me go."

"I'm afraid I can't do that," the teacher sat in the only chair in the space, "I am much more involved than you realize. I'm in too deep now."

Gage shook her head, "Please, you can't believe God would accept this as punishment for flirting."

Lucinda let out a rough laugh, "I'm fairly convinced God would accept any form of penance for your sins child."

"What about *your* sins?" Gage spat, forcing herself into a seated position. "You used your position of authority to help kidnap girls to be raped and tortured."

"No." Lucinda stood up angrily, "I never allowed the sexual indiscretions. That was not in the agreement." She shook her head, "Lauren was a mistake. I have given myself to protect you other girls from that fate."

"How sweet of you," Gage snapped, "you let a monster fuck you so he doesn't rape little girls. You're such a saint."

Lucinda whirled around and slapped Gage's face hard enough to make a red handprint appear, "You have no idea what I've been through. How dare you speak to me like that."

"Seriously?" Gage glared at the older woman, "You helped a madman kidnap your students. You at least stood by while they were assaulted, at most, you participated. But I should feel sorry for you because you've been getting some action on the side?"

Lucinda cried out, "I was a pure woman before this happened. I had to give up that connection to God, to protect you Jezebels."

"You were a virgin?" Gage scoffed. "I should feel sorry for you because you were a forty-year-old virgin who decided to throw her cat at a dangerous man to prevent him from sexually assaulting the girls you helped him kidnap?"

"I was blessed to have met a means to protect the pure girls of St. Peter's, even if there were limits on his choices," Lucinda said quietly, "your type disgusts me."

"The feeling's mutual," Gage snapped back.

"Lucky for me, I don't have to listen to you," Lucinda held up a bottle and poured a liquid onto a scarf.

"What the hell is that?" Gage asked, mild panic settling in her chest.

"Don't be so scared," Lucinda rolled her eyes, "it's simply one of the perks of being the Chemistry teacher," she smiled meanly. "Homemade chloroform. If my measurements are correct, it shouldn't cause any lasting brain damage. I modified my formula after the side-effects Megan suffered."

Gage weighed her options. She could easily overpower the older woman, but she still had no idea where Stacy was, if it was actually chloroform, she could wake up with Stacy and go home. Or, she might never wake up if Lucinda was not a good Chemistry teacher. Gage cursed under her breath as she tried to remember one of Lucinda's lessons.

The teacher stood and walked to Gage's side. Gage crawled back until her back was firmly against the wall, then she sighed and closed her eyes as the cloth covered her mouth and nose. She held her breath and struggled against the woman feebly, grabbing at the cloth with one hand and at her teacher with the other. She made herself go limp and hoped Lucinda would take away the scarf. Unfortunately, the woman tied it firmly around Gage's head.

PREY

Gage's eyes opened slightly as she tried to see where the older woman was in the room, hoping she could pull the scarf down without being noticed. But Lucinda was staring right at her with a sadistic smile marring her face. "That's it," the older woman cooed, "just breathe. It'll all be over soon."

Gage gasped when she couldn't hold her breath anymore, the effects were almost instantaneous, she felt like she was simultaneously flying and falling. Pressure settled in her chest as though a full-grown man was sitting on her. She slid down the wall onto her side, her chest heaving as she tried desperately to catch some air. The more she breathed, the heavier her whole body felt until her eyes rolled and she slipped from consciousness.

Chapter 18

"Give me my people. NOW." Whitlock's aggressive tone was rendered even more effective because it came from his perfectly calm exterior obviously masking the coiled muscles of a former athlete and current warrior.

"Who the hell do you think you are?" The sheriff of the town sat in his cushioned chair. The smug expression on his rotund face was safeguarded by the giant mahogany desk between the two men, "I don't hand criminals over to anyone but the jail."

"What have you charged them with?" Whitlock's tone took on an even more dangerous coldness as he tried to remain calm.

"Right now?" The sheriff snapped, "The paperwork ain't filed yet, but I think obstruction of justice is a good start."

"Obstruction of what justice exactly?" Whitlock asked.

"My men were about to make an arrest when your people stepped in the way," the sheriff growled.

"It's my understanding that your deputies were parked on the side of the road, doing nothing of notice, and my people stopped in front of them to ask for directions." Whitlock's neck was tense as he tried to remain civil. "It isn't prudent to stop behind an officer and approach, so they were only doing what common sense dictated."

"Well, maybe that's how *they* tell it, but it's obviously not what really happened."

"Oh really?" Whitlock asked, clasping his hands in front of him, "So your deputies had their emergency equipment activated indicating they were about to make a high-profile arrest?"

"No." The sheriff stuttered, "They're not required to have their lights on."

"But they obviously had warrants for someone in the neighborhood?" Whitlock asked.

"Warrants aren't necessary if there's probable cause for a felony having occurred," the sheriff answered.

"Did your deputies order my people to get out of the way so they could conduct police business?"

"Yes, and your people said their van didn't work."

"Did you have the van looked at by a mechanic to verify that was a lie?" Whitlock cocked his head. "Because I am fairly certain that the media would love to know that two citizens were unlawfully detained based upon a suspected lie which was never substantiated. Or that they are currently being held without charge and without a lawyer." He continued speaking even though the sheriff had his mouth open and was stuttering. "Furthermore, the public would be quite interested to know that your agency is more concerned with tying up its assets with false arrests of citizens attempting to help a missing victim, rather than attempting to locate said victim. I know I would want to know that the public servants in my area are willing to gamble with the life of an innocent child instead of allowing an outside party to assist in the investigation." Whitlock placed both hands on the sheriff's desk and leaned in, "What would you think of a sheriff who would allow such atrocities to occur under his purview?"

The sheriff's face was crimson, "Are you threatening me?"

"Absolutely not," Whitlock shook his head, his tone even. "I'm simply asking what you think the good people of this municipality would think about such a sheriff. Especially with this being an election year."

The sheriff stared at Whitlock for a moment before picking up his phone and hitting three buttons. He waited a moment then snapped into the phone, "Let 'em go." He listened for a minute then snapped, "Just do as I'm telling you NOW, damnit." He slammed the phone down and glared up at Whitlock, "It turns out, my boys may have been mistaken.

Now, I expect you three to pack up, and get out of my town, before I change my mind."

"That's not going to happen until we find my missing employee," Whitlock's voice rumbled from deep in his chest. "You're welcome to assist, but to be honest, I don't really care if you're involved or not." He turned and strode from the office in time to see Mere and Brick being led down the hallway with handcuffs still on. "Get those handcuffs off my people or I'll have your badge," he snapped.

The deputy escorting the two detainees stared at Whitlock's imposing form for a second with wide eyes before hurriedly scrambling to find his handcuff key.

Whitlock moved to their side like a storm rolling over fields and pulled out a handcuff key from his pocket, "Never mind," he growled, "I'll do it myself." He unlocked the cuffs and tossed them at to the officer who caught them against his stomach. "You'd do well to get the hell away from Sheriff Reed, son," his tone softened some, "I doubt he'll be here much longer."

The deputy nodded and hurried away as Whitlock opened the door to the lobby for Mere and Brick to walk through.

"Well, that's the first time I've ever been arrested," Brick stated as they walked across the parking lot to the van parked outside.

"But not your first time in handcuffs?" Mere asked, her green eyes sparkling with laughter.

"No," Brick acquiesced, "I usually don't mind them so much."

Mere laughed, but then stopped abruptly when she looked at Whitlock's face, "We don't have her signal do we?"

Whitlock opened the back door of the van so Mere and Brick could climb in, he stood in the doorway when they did, "She has completely fallen off our radar."

Her beacon is still intact, it hasn't been damaged, Tessa's voice said from the monitor where she could be seen holding a laptop, *she just hasn't activated it yet.*

Mere glanced at the screen with the younger woman's face, studying the worry twisting Tessa's features, "You can't pick up her earwig's frequency?"

I think it was damaged in the initial attack, EmEm was typing like mad on the computer beside Tessa, *it's been in and out, but all I could catch was a service road for an old mine system east of town. The road services dozens of shafts. I haven't been able to narrow the search. I'm trying to isolate the frequency of her beacon now, even though it isn't activated, I might be able to locate it.*

"Could you hear anything from what you did catch?" Mere asked.

EmEm's face was drawn with worry when he glanced at the camera, *I'm hoping what I heard was part of the act, but she didn't seem very happy.*

She was in a trunk, and now, she's probably in a mine shaft, Tessa snapped. *Our claustrophobic friend is most likely underground right now.*

"Send us the coordinates where you last had her signal," Brick cut in, "we'll head that way and start searching on foot."

Caroline Graves just called 911 and hung up, Tessa stated, *it looks like dispatch called back, and she said it was an accident. They're canceling the call.*

"Maybe Daddy dearest went home," Whitlock stated. He looked at Brick, "You two head to that access road, start looking for any sign of Gage. I'll head to the Graves' residence and see if I can have a chat with Mr. Graves." He cracked his knuckles simply by making fists, then turned and was gone before Brick or Mere could confirm his order.

PREY

"I would NOT want to be Gerald Graves right now," Brick chuckled as he closed the doors of the van and headed to the driver's seat.

Chapter 19

Gage's eyes slowly blinked open, everything was blurry and confusing. Her throat felt like it was full of cotton wrapped in sandpaper. She coughed roughly and licked her lips as she blinked rapidly to try to clear her vision. It was dark. She tried to feel around but quickly realized her hands were bound behind her back. She tested the elasticity of her binds by flexing her wrists and realized it must be some kind of tape.

"Are you awake?"

The voice sounded small and frail.

"Yeah, is that you, Stacy?" Gage felt around as much as she could and realized she was in a cage of some kind. Her whole body ached, but she couldn't stretch out because the cage was small, keeping her in the fetal position.

"She dragged you in here," the voice responded, "are you okay?"

"I'm fine." Gage was touched that this person was so concerned for her well-being, "Are you Stacy?"

"Yes," the voice whimpered, "how long have I been here?"

"Let's get to the more important things," Gage responded in a soothing tone, "are you able to move?"

"I'm in a dog crate," Stacy responded, "all my muscles ache, they never let me out of here."

"Have they hurt you?"

"I'm okay," Stacy's voice was quiet, "are they going to kill me, now that you're here?"

"I'm not going to let that happen," Gage answered, "now that I know where you are, I don't have to play the victim anymore. We're getting the fuck outta here."

"What do you mean play the victim?" Stacy asked.

Even as the girl was asking the question, Gage brought her bound wrists under her butt and slipped her legs through until her hands were in front of her. She bit the tape and ripped it with her teeth, freeing her hands.

"I mean, it's time to get the cavalry," Gage responded and pressed the small button in her bra.

"What cavalry?"

"Where are the bad guys?" Gage asked.

"I think they left for the night," Stacy said quietly, "but I don't know, there's only light when one of them is here. Ms. Montez left after dragging you in, that seems like a long time ago."

"Good," Gage got on her knees and hunched down under the roof of her cage, she felt along the side until she found the front and let out a joyful noise when she realized she wasn't locked in with anything more than the normal mechanisms of the cage. She maneuvered those and pushed the door open before carefully crawling out.

"What was that noise?" Stacy panicked, "Is it them? Are they coming back?"

"It was just me getting out of my cage," Gage responded as she felt along the outside of her cage to find Stacy's, "is this you?"

A hand reached out and touched Gage's fingers, "Please help me," Stacy whispered.

"I've got you," Gage responded and quickly opened the cage, reaching inside to help Stacy crawl out.

The girl cried out in pain as her muscles tried to move but were too cramped and drained from lack of use and dehydration, "It hurts to move." Stacy whimpered in pain, "I don't think I can make it."

Gage dragged the girl out, unceremoniously, "You don't get to stay behind, Buttercup," she stated. "Were you awake when they brought you here?"

"Yes," Stacy yelped.

"Did they make turns," Gage listened carefully, "or just walk straight?"

"Um," Stacy's voice was fading, "I'm not sure."

"Think Stacy. I need you to think hard, or we may get away only to starve to death in an old mine." Gage tried to keep the panic from her voice, but the complete lack of light was making her heart hammer painfully in her chest.

"I don't remember any turns. I think we went straight the whole time."

"Good girl," Gage hefted the girl up by her waist and waited for Stacy's arm to rest on her shoulders, then she started to walk, pretty much dragging the girl who cried out repeatedly. "This isn't going to work," Gage sighed.

"Please don't leave me!" Stacy pleaded.

"That's not an option," Gage responded, "can you stand on your own for a few seconds?"

"I- I don't know, but I'll try," Stacy stammered.

Gage stood the girl up and leaned down to pull Stacy over her shoulders in a fireman's carry. Then she stood up and bore the weight easily, Stacy was skin and bones. "Have they fed you?"

"Every once and awhile," Stacy's voice was cracking, she whimpered, "I'm sorry about the smell."

"Hang in there," Gage ignored the statement, she held one of Stacy's wrists with her hand looped through Stacy's legs so that she could feel around with her free hand. Stacy was crying softly, so Gage added with a gentle voice, "You can't help having normal bodily functions."

Gage's eyes were straining to adjust, but with no light at all, even cat eyes would have struggled to see.

One second she was struggling to see, the next, she could vaguely see a small folding table with an oil lamp and some magazines on it. She quashed the joy she felt at being able to see when she realized there was a faint light source now coming from the tunnel in front of her. She knew if it had been her friends, they would be calling for her, so she quickly went into the opposite tunnel and sat Stacy on the ground. "Stay as quiet as you can," she whispered.

"Don't leave me," Stacy cried quietly.

"I have to go get the light," Gage soothed, "I'll be back, I promise." She touched Stacy's shoulder, "You can do this, Stacy."

~*~*~*~*~

She just activated her beacon! EmEm shouted, making Mere and Brick jump. ***It's a faint signal, but I can tell it's coming from about five hundred yards up the road from you.***

Police haven't located either suspect, Tessa added in the earwigs, ***and Whit hasn't found Gerald yet. Caroline was home alone when he got there.***

"Why'd she call 911?" Brick asked as he and Mere ran back to their van.

She thought someone was breaking in, but it ended up being her dad, Tessa responded. ***She thought he was acting weird, then he disappeared.***

"That was probably him in the car that passed us," Brick said as the van's engine revved and climbed the hill of the road.

Whitlock is on his way to Lucinda's house to check for her, then he will be with you, Tessa responded from the monitor in the back.

You're on top of the frequency now, EmEm interjected.

"On top of it how?" Mere asked, looking around.

I don't know, but your frequency is directly on top of hers, EmEm answered.

"She must be below us," Brick said and pointed into the woods, "there's the car. Let's go."

Mere and Brick put on headlamps and each armed themselves with handguns, once they'd made sure the vehicle was empty.

"Just remember, we'll be underground. Firearms are an absolute last resort," Mere said as she picked up a baseball bat.

"Yeah, you don't have to explain that to me," Brick smiled grimly, "I've seen it."

Mere shrugged and ran to the opening of the tunnel system with her headlamp on.

Brick left his off so that only one light was visible. "There are three tunnels, which do we take?"

I don't know how to help, EmEm's frustration was clear in their earwigs, *the signal is so weak, and those tunnels haven't been mapped in over a century. I'm trying to find the old archives now.*

"It's okay," Brick answered and tapped Mere's shoulder, pointing down the center tunnel, "Gage told us which one."

Mere moved forward and crouched, picking up the earring that had been glinting in the light, "It's her earring. We're going down the center tunnel EmEm. Tell Whit."

Got it, EmEm answered. *Go get our girl before she kills someone.*

"On it," Mere smiled.

Chapter 20

Gage stayed in the shadows as Gerald entered the cavern. He cursed and ran to the cages as soon as his flashlight showed they were vacant.

He whipped the flashlight around the cavern and found Gage cowering against the wall, "Where do you think you're going?" He snapped and strode toward her.

"Oh God, please don't hurt me," Gage cried in terror. Her tone changed to a far harder and more dangerous one as she straightened, she cocked her head, staring at the advancing man in a challenge, "Please, I'm just a little girl."

Gerald slowed and stared at her in confusion.

Gage smirked and cracked her neck, "I almost forgot I don't have to pretend anymore," she stated.

"Pretend what?" Gerald growled.

"Pretend to be your helpless victim," Gage responded and strode forward menacingly, "are you ready to see what it feels like when your victim fights back, you piece of shit?"

Gerald swung his flashlight at her head but she easily ducked beneath the blow and punched his kidney several times when he turned with his swing.

He grunted and moved back as she smiled at him serenely. "Why aren't you hitting me?" She asked in a little girl's voice, "You're a big scary man, right?"

He yelled as he ran at her, she side-stepped and kicked his back as he passed her, making his momentum carry him into the wall. He dropped the flashlight and crumpled to the floor.

"That was really depressing and unsatisfying," Gage sighed as she walked over and picked up the flashlight. She glanced at him and saw some blood on his forehead where he'd hit the rock wall, "Dumb ass."

She turned back to go get Stacy and saw Lucinda standing in the middle of the room with the scarf and an empty bottle.

"Sup, Teach?" Gage asked, gauging her chances to knock the woman out before chemicals were introduced. She noticed the scarf was dripping.

"Who are you?" Lucinda asked with quiet anger making her voice tremble.

"Your worst nightmare," Gage responded.

"Isn't that from Batman?" Lucinda asked, confused.

"Yes, Lucinda, I'm Batman," Gage rolled her eyes with an exasperated sigh, "or maybe I'm an avenging angel, you sick bitch."

"Don't try to justify what you've done to me," Lucinda cried angrily.

"What I'VE done to *you*?" Gage actually laughed at the insanity of the statement. "What exactly have I done to you?"

"You've ruined EVERYTHING!" Lucinda shrieked and ran forward, holding the scarf at face level.

Gage dropped her flashlight, dodged to the side, grabbed the scarf and swung with all her might. Lucinda refused to release her hold on the scarf and was thrown off balance, stumbling back. Gage shrugged at the woman and yanked the scarf, pulling Lucinda forward, into Gage's fist. The older woman crumpled beside Gerald, who was starting to groan.

Gage took Lucinda's scarf, and dropped it on Gerald's face, before grabbing her flashlight and running back to Stacy.

"Stacy? You doing okay, kid?" Her light shone on the fragile girl who was covered in scrapes, bruises, and dirt, among other things.

Stacy nodded with a small smile, "Thank you," she whispered.

"Let's get out of here," Gage grinned, "what do ya say?"

"God, yes," Stacy said and whimpered as Gage helped her stand so she could once more lift the younger girl onto her shoulders in a fireman's carry.

Gage straightened and walked into the cavern, she glanced over and saw Gerald unconscious on the floor, but Lucinda and her scarf were nowhere to be seen. "Fuck," Gage sighed and arced the flashlight to look for the deranged woman. "Keep your eyes open, I don't see Ms. Montez anywhere."

"Oh God," Stacy whimpered.

"Don't worry," Gage responded as she once more wrapped her arm around Stacy's leg and grabbed the girl's wrist so her free hand could hold the flashlight, "we're getting out of here." Her heart leapt into her throat when she saw a light appear around a corner in the tunnel. She stiffened, contemplating if she should drop Stacy, or try to fight while holding the girl. She was still weighing her options when she heard a sound that made her sigh with relief.

"GAGE!" Mere's voice was as relieved as Gage felt.

"What took you assholes so long?" Gage laughed, her dirt-streaked face had splotches of dried blood and scrapes on her cheeks.

"Give her to me," Brick put on his headlamp and moved toward Gage.

"No, I have her, Gerald is unconscious," she motioned to the large man, "you get to drag his ass out." She grinned, "Make sure you hit every rock."

"My pleasure," Brick responded and pulled out zip-tie-handcuffs from his cargo pocket.

"Are you doing okay?" Mere asked quietly.

"Let's just get the hell out of here," Gage responded. Now that she didn't have to focus on the task at hand, the panic was starting to seep back in. The darkness licked the edges of the light, making her heart pound in her chest, "Lucinda was here. Keep your eyes open, there's no telling where the hell she is in this darkness."

"There was only one car outside," Mere said as she led the way, her bat over her shoulder, ready to swing.

"She ran off with her homemade-chloroform-soaked scarf," Gage grunted as she readjusted Stacy's weight.

"Homemade-chloroform?" Brick asked as he dragged Gerald unceremoniously up behind them, "Were you exposed to that?"

"Only most of my time down here," Gage responded, "worry about it after we get the fuck out of here."

"Are you experiencing any shortness of breath, racing heart rate, or nausea?" Brick ignored her request as he pulled Gerald faster to be able to see Gage's face momentarily when she rolled her eyes at him.

"I have a problem with tight spaces," she snapped, "what the hell do you think I'm feeling right now?"

"Fair enough," Brick motioned ahead, "fresh air just ahead."

Gage practically ran the last few steps into the night air. She closed her eyes and breathed a huge sigh of relief. When she opened her eyes, she noticed that there was an ambulance and multiple police cars with their lights activated. The motion from the strobes made her queasy instantly. She stopped walking suddenly, reeled as she got light-headed, and murmured, "Take her."

Brick dropped Gerald and grabbed Stacy as Gage crumpled.

Chapter 21

"I need you to go to the hospital," Brick was looking at his watch while holding the pulse-point in Gage's wrist.

"I'm fine, Biscuit," Gage grumbled, allowing him to fuss over her for a few moments.

"You were exposed to noxious fumes, you could have liver damage," he let go of her wrist, "and your pulse is pretty elevated." He stared at her, "Plus you passed out. I need you to go get checked out."

Gage rolled her eyes and met his gaze stonily, "In your training and experience, is it possible that the cessation of a panic attack, coupled with adrenaline dump and the appearance of strobing visuals, may have had something to do with a temporary loss of consciousness?"

"Why are you such a smart ass? What's so bad about the hospital?" Brick asked, "Erring on the side of caution is never a bad thing."

Gage shrugged, "I live on the wild side. Caution has never really been my thing."

Whitlock strode up with Mere at his side, "Lucinda hasn't been located," he practically growled.

"They're searching the mine with dogs, but there's no sign of her," Mere added.

"There's an officer at her house," Whitlock glanced back at the scene behind him, "but God knows that doesn't mean much."

Gage sat, deep in thought, a scowl marring her face as she tried to connect dots.

"What's wrong?" Brick asked, his head cocked to the side like a questioning puppy as he tried to make sure she wasn't having a medical emergency, "Are you in pain?"

"That's just her face," Mere supplied with a smirk.

Gage playfully narrowed her eyes at her friend before saying, "Lucinda told me there were 'limits' on Gerald's choices of girls to kidnap and brutalize." Her eyes went wide and she jumped up, "Holy shit. Where's the key?"

"We can't get out, we're all blocked in by those cruisers," Brick motioned behind the van to the police cars parked blocking the road.

"Is there someone on Caroline's house?" Gage asked Whitlock.

"She said she was going to go to her friend's house after I left there," he responded. "Why?"

"Tessa, check the bug, is Caroline still at her house?" Gage called into the van.

Yes, the bug's at her house, Tessa responded from the monitor. **There's one deputy assigned there, but I've been calling since you mentioned Gerald's limits and he's not answering his cell phone.**

Gage glanced at Whitlock, the look of realization on his face made her turn and run down the road toward the final police car of the long line of vehicles.

"Gage, what are you going to do?" Mere called after her, "Run there?"

There's no answer at the residence either, Tessa called from the monitor in the van.

"Hey!" Brick shouted as he ran toward the group of deputies standing around, "Move these cars, we need someone to get to Caroline Graves' house, NOW!"

The deputies all glanced at him with annoyed expressions and went back to talking amongst themselves.

"Do you want to catch this bitch or not?" Brick shouted at them.

They ignored him.

They ignored him until they heard the roar of an engine being accelerated harshly and the spray of gravel from rapidly spinning tires coupled with the sound of a police siren as the cruiser at the back of the line suddenly jumped back down the road.

There were several curses and shouts as the crowd of deputies all sprinted to their vehicles and began to pursue the stolen cruiser, which was out of sight before any of them could get to their car.

Brick laughed and headed back to the van, "Did she really just steal a police cruiser?"

Mere shrugged from the driver's seat, "She tactically acquired it. If it's sitting unlocked at a crime scene, I feel like she's really just teaching a valuable lesson. Let's go."

"I'll meet you there," Whitlock called as he moved to his vehicle up by the mouth of the mine.

~*~*~*~*~

Gage looked in her rearview mirror and sighed, "We told you where I was going, you idiots. Where did you go instead?"

The roadway behind her was completely empty. She glanced at the GPS, into which she'd entered Caroline's address before driving away in the cruiser. She was only a minute away.

"Probably should have grabbed a gun," she admonished herself as she turned off the siren and flashing lights. She turned down a driveway that was lined with trees. The wrought iron gate at the end was propped open by large barrel planters with flowers. "Seems kind of pointless," she grumbled as she pulled up to the circle drive by the entrance of the mansion.

She came to a stop behind a darkened police cruiser and didn't see any light or motion from inside it as she slammed the car into park.

She glanced around the car, looking for a weapon, but found none. She pushed the button in the center dash by the floor under the radio, popping the trunk. She quietly turned off the vehicle and shoved the key under the floor mat before moving to the trunk to see if there was anything worthwhile to use for protection. She saw an extra set of handcuffs so she grabbed them and tucked them into her waistband before closing the trunk and running to the front of the house.

The front door was slightly ajar, an unconscious deputy lay in the foyer. His face was ashen, but Gage didn't see any blood or obvious trauma. Lucinda's scarf was on the floor beside him. His sidearm was no longer in his gun belt, making her mentally kick herself again. She leaned over the deputy and pressed the red emergency button on his radio before walking silently into the house, her eyes scanning constantly.

"Please! I don't understand!" Caroline's wails were coming from somewhere up the massive staircase.

Gage looked around but the foyer was just an empty marble room. There was nothing to wield as a weapon. She saw a statue at the bottom of the banister and grabbed it as she mounted the first step, hoping her momentum would be enough to dislodge it. Her shoulder almost dislocated when the statue did not come with her up the first few steps. It was definitely too heavy and also mounted far more effectively than anticipated.

Gage grumbled as she climbed the stairs quietly, with no weapon, listening to Caroline's whimpers.

Lucinda was clearly giving her speech about Jezebels as Gage rounded the corner. Caroline was on the floor, cowering against the wall by a table displaying a massive flower display in an ornate vase. Her frightened eyes darted to Gage making the older woman sigh quietly because Lucinda turned to face the new threat.

"Curse you for actually watching for clues of sneak attack," Gage put her hands up in surrender. "There's no point in continuing this crap, the police are on their way."

"You've ruined EVERYTHING!" Lucinda's hand was shaking, but her finger was on the trigger and the barrel was pointed right at Gage's face.

"I tend to do that," Gage responded before shaking her head, "if I'm gonna die, do you mind if I die more like myself?"

"What does that even mean?" Lucinda's tone was at least an octave too high.

Gage slowly moved her right hand to her mouth keeping her left hand up in surrender. She pulled the false teeth out of her mouth and sighed, running her tongue over her teeth, "That is so much better. You have no idea how annoying those teeth were." She glanced at Lucinda's face, noticing her large teeth and added as she tossed the false teeth onto the floor, "Well, maybe you do."

"You're just evil," Lucinda whispered, "how could you be staring death in the face, and continue to be so vile?"

Gage shrugged, "It's a talent. I a-vase myself."

Lucinda's face screwed up in confusion, "What?"

"A-VASE," it rhymed with amaze, confusing everyone, so Gage nodded her head to the table by Caroline a few times, "I A-VASE myself." She widened her eyes at Caroline who slowly seemed to understand what was going on.

The girl stood up quietly and picked up the massive vase, when Lucinda turned toward the sound of the noise, Caroline swung the vase like a bucket, soaking Lucinda with the water inside as flowers rained down.

Gage sighed and stared up at the ceiling, shaking her head. Lucinda stood sputtering, staring at Caroline, the gun in her right hand momentarily forgotten. It was all the time Gage needed to rush up behind the older woman.

Gage ducked under Lucinda's weapon hand and grabbed the woman's wrist with both hands before standing up as she yanked the arm down. The satisfying crack of bone and shriek of pain from the teacher made Gage smile. The gun slid across the wood floor and bumped to a stop at the wall. Gage moved to once more be behind the wailing woman and handcuffed her hands behind her back, despite the obvious injury.

When she glanced up, Caroline was standing holding the dripping vase, with wide eyes.

"Way to go, Dorothy," Gage grinned, "I was actually telling you to hit her with it."

Caroline dropped the vase and it shattered at her feet, "I- I don't understand."

"You're in shock," Gage said soothingly, "you'll be okay. Everything is okay now. It's over."

Sirens grew in the distance and Gage kicked Lucinda's legs out from under her, making the woman sit down hard. Then she picked up the discarded gun and unloaded it before locking the slide back and sliding the now safe weapon toward the staircase.

Caroline rushed to Gage and wrapped the older woman in an inescapable hug that forced the breath from her lungs.

The deputies started announcing themselves as they rushed in with weapons drawn. Gage slowly managed to get to her knees and held her hands up as best as she could, but Caroline was clinging to her so tightly it was hard to move or breathe.

"Upstairs," Gage managed to choke out and stayed as still as possible with her hands visible as the first few deputies made it up the staircase.

Lucinda was wailing on the floor in a heap, Caroline was hysterically clinging to Gage who was desperately trying to show the deputies she was unarmed.

"Your downed deputy's weapon is right there," Gage motioned with her head to their feet. "She's your wanted subject," she used her head to motion to Lucinda, "she's going to need a hospital to set her arm." She pointed down at Caroline, "This is your latest victim."

One of the deputies holstered his weapon and approached, "I'm handcuffing you for my safety and yours," he stated.

Gage rolled her eyes as she interlaced her fingers behind her head, "Did I take your cruiser?"

He handcuffed her as best he could, trying to untangle Caroline, who continued to cling to her, "No, that was my Sergeant's cruiser."

Gage snorted with laughter, "Oh shit, you better never let him live that down."

The deputy actually smiled, but tried to hide it, "You are being detained at this time."

Gage nodded, "I'm used to handcuffs," she sighed, "though usually they're more appealing, and there's no weeping girls."

The deputy actually laughed at that and peeled a hysterical Caroline off of Gage, directing the girl to a female deputy with a gentle push. The second male deputy upstairs dragged a yowling Lucinda to her feet and walked her down the stairs. The woman was raving incoherently and kicking out at Caroline and the female deputy as they walked down the flight of stairs first.

Gage felt the warm hands of the deputy who had placed her in handcuffs on her upper arms from behind as he helped her stand up. She climbed to her feet then glanced back at him, "Say, Deputy…" she read his nameplate, "White," she smiled at him and leaned back into him slightly, "this is much closer to my usual handcuffed experiences," she winked at him.

Deputy White blushed profusely as he held her arm, helped her down the stairs, and murmured softly in her ear, "I think what you did for these girls is really admirable."

When they got to the first level, she curtsied as best she could, "Just doing my job."

White shook his head as he led her outside by the arm, "There's no way anyone would do what you do just as a job," he motioned to the bruises on her face.

"Maybe I like it rough," she responded absently as she watched an ambulance arrive for Lucinda.

"You strike me as being someone who likes control," he responded, "not being controlled."

She stopped walking making him misstep and face her. She was roughly eye-level with him, staring at him directly she responded good-naturedly, "You're far too observant to be employed by the backwoods douche-canoe for whom you currently work."

He shrugged, "This is a paycheck."

"True that," Gage nodded, "so is what I do. Same thing."

He let out a rough laugh as he led her toward his cruiser, "Not even remotely the same thing."

"Why not?"

"For one, I get to carry a gun and arrest people," he stated.

"Sometimes I get to beat the shit out of people," she countered.

"Fair enough," he acquiesced, "but I don't have to let anyone beat me up to complete my job."

"Maybe the fact that you aren't willing to sacrifice for people is why my company is needed to protect the innocent girls of your jurisdiction," she snapped.

"Oh, I'm plenty willing to sacrifice," he responded, "but I'm not going to be someone's bitch for a job."

Gage stopped walking again, this time with a raging fire in her gut as fury built up inside her like a pressure cooker, "I'm no one's 'bitch'," she growled.

"If you say so," he said smugly, "your face says differently."

"Would you like me to make you *my* bitch," her voice was dangerously cold but her eyes were full of fire.

A small half smirk tugged at his lips, "That's cute little girl, you're handcuffed, and in police custody."

Her face was a stone mask, "That wouldn't even slow me down."

"Gage!" Mere shouted from where she was being detained next to the van. Brick was beside her, also handcuffed and looking extremely annoyed.

Gage didn't look away from Deputy White. She stood rigidly with her hands balled into fists behind her back.

"Gage, please don't kick that kid's ass," Brick called.

"We're in enough trouble as it is," Mere added, "please don't."

Deputy White laughed, "It's cute how your friends think you're so tough."

"I was wrong before," Gage responded coldly.

"Oh, now you realize you can't make me your bitch?" He laughed.

"No, that would be simple," she smiled meanly, "I was wrong before when I said you don't belong here." She cocked her head slightly, "You fit right in, my mistake."

"Is that supposed to hurt my feelings?"

"No, I just make a point to always admit my mistakes," she shrugged, "so am I going in your cruiser, or are you letting me go already?"

Just as he opened the back door of his cruiser, a news van pulled up and a reporter jumped out followed by a cameraman. Whitlock approached them and pointed at Gage, his mouth moving quickly.

The reporter's eyes lit up as she rushed up to Deputy White, "Deputy! Is it true you're arresting the woman responsible for saving the two girls victimized today?"

White's eyes were wide as he stammered, "I'm just following orders."

"Who ordered you to arrest the woman who single-handedly saved Caroline Graves from a mad woman tonight, after finding and rescuing

Stacy Anderson?" The reporter questioned, holding her microphone in the startled Deputy's face. The camera lens bounced from the reporter to the deputy.

"They've also arrested the two people who helped me rescue Stacy," Gage motioned over to where Mere and Brick were standing in handcuffs. "The only crime we've committed is that we were more concerned for a victim than our own well-being," she made tears well in her eyes but she carefully kept her face angled away from the camera, "I don't understand why these deputies are so up in arms just because we did their jobs for them."

"This woman stole a police cruiser from a crime scene in order to drive here-" White interrupted.

"Because they weren't listening to my friend," Gage interjected, motioning to Lucinda with her head, "I was held prisoner by that woman in an abandoned mine! I had reason to believe she was going to attack Caroline, but no one would listen to us."

"How is it that, if she stole this cruiser, she still managed to disarm the suspect and save the victim before any law enforcement professionals arrived on the scene?" The reporter asked.

"Oooo, good question," Gage nodded and looked at White, "I'm curious about that also. Especially since we TOLD you where I was going."

White's face was crimson and he sputtered incoherently.

"Interesting," Gage nodded, "about what I expected."

The reporter smiled at Gage, "I wouldn't worry too much, we'll get to the bottom of this, there's no way any charges will stick."

Gage shrugged and looked at the reporter instead of the camera, her eyes wide and watering, "If I have to go to jail for apprehending two dangerous criminals and saving two innocent girls, then so be it. At least I can rest easy knowing that Stacy and Caroline are safe." She slid into the back seat of the cruiser and sat staring ahead.

Brick and Mere were smiling broadly as their handcuffs were removed and they were told to leave the scene.

"Are we going to the Magistrate or are you planning on illegally detaining this woman?" Whitlock questioned Deputy White, "I'm sure this lovely lady would like to accompany us to whichever destination you choose."

"You're absolutely right," the reporter nodded before turning to Whitlock, "who are you to this woman?"

"I'm essentially her adoptive father," Whitlock responded. Puffing his chest up as he stared into the camera, he continued, "This woman risked her life to save two girls in this community, now she's being punished for taking action while the Sheriff's Office stood by and did nothing of consequence."

"You're going to have to leave," Deputy White motioned to the news van, "this is an active crime scene."

"Answer my question first," Whitlock looked down at the younger man, "are you taking her to the Magistrate or to the Sheriff's Office?"

"My orders are to take her to the office," White responded.

"Son, I hope you realize that you are not protected from the law if you follow unlawful orders," Whitlock said softly.

The deputy swallowed hard and closed the door, locking Gage in, "You're welcome to wait in the lobby until Detective White is done questioning her."

"Questioning her about what, exactly?" Whitlock asked, "How to better do your jobs?"

"You need to leave before you're arrested for trespassing," White answered.

"Since the owner of this residence is currently arrested for molesting young girls, and MY girl just rescued the resident of this home before any of you could be bothered to show up, I'm fairly certain that the other owner of this residence would disagree with you regarding my ability to remain on this premise." Whitlock's tone was even, "Unless you've spoken to Mrs. Graves and she's informed you that I'm not allowed on her property."

White swallowed hard with wide eyes.

"You see, it's hard to lord over someone who actually knows the law," Whitlock's voice was low, but White was painfully aware that the camera was still pointed at them.

"You're welcome to wait in the lobby until my detective is done questioning her," White said again and turned from them to walk around the trunk of his car.

"Let's get to the Sheriff's Office," the reporter said to her cameraman as she ran toward the van, "I want to get a shot of them taking her into the station with those handcuffs on! This is outrageous!"

Whitlock sighed and touched the window, Gage smiled up at him and shrugged but her eyes held more emotion than she would care to admit. "I'll be there when you get out," Whitlock told her. She nodded and leaned her head against the window as Deputy White drove away.

The glass was cold on her forehead which was a welcome distraction from the bubble of anxiety in her gut that still hadn't abated. The constant adrenaline surge was finally starting to calm, making her legs feel like tingling jelly. Gage closed her eyes and focused on her heart rate, she hated being enclosed in small spaces, even spaces which allowed her to see out. She knew she was headed for a tiny interrogation room after she finally got free from the back of the cruiser. The quiet panic, that started roiling in her guts when she first hit the trunk of Gerald's car, was starting to boil over, making her sweat and tremble.

She did her best to keep herself calm, focusing on breathing as the car bumped along the road. She felt nauseated but hoped she wouldn't vomit in the back of the cruiser, though, in her opinion, Deputy White deserved the inconvenience. All the possible outcomes due to her actions raced in time with her pulse. Even as she calmed her heart with her deep breathing, her thoughts raced, at odds with her attempts to remain calm.

When the cruiser finally stopped, she waited until Deputy White tapped on the window before leaning back and opening her eyes so he could open the door without her falling off the seat.

"Have a nice nap?" White asked with a grin.

"Yes, obviously I was sleeping, not trying to calm the violent rage inside," she answered sweetly as she climbed from the cruiser.

"You seem to have experience climbing out of cop cars," White said smugly, "you didn't even need a hand."

Gage ignored his comment and took a deep breath of air, closing her eyes as a breeze hit her face.

"This reporter is still attempting to receive word from Sheriff Reed, or any spokesperson of the Sheriff's Office for that matter, as to why this woman, who should be lauded as a hero, is being held in handcuffs."

Gage opened her eyes and glanced toward the reporter from before until she noticed the camera was directly focused on her, and her mind immediately jumped to who could possibly be seeing the footage. She turned her face from the lens, "Are you going to get me inside or what?" She grumbled at White who grabbed her elbow and led her past the media.

"We have not even been told her name, but you can see the brave face this courageous woman is putting on, even hiding from the camera in an effort to save the Sheriff's Office from controversy. She hasn't even been able to clean herself up after being held captive underground for two days."

Whitlock approached and the camera immediately turned to him when Gage and White entered the Sheriff's Office Building.

"This is the self-proclaimed adoptive father of the woman you just saw being led inside in handcuffs. What can you tell us about this case?"

The reporter's desire for a story was apparent in her demeanor as she shoved her microphone in Whitlock's face.

He stopped walking and stared into the camera, "My daughter has been a student at St. Peter's Catholic school for the last week and a half. She was on her way to visit a friend when she was abducted by Gerald Graves and taken to an undisclosed location. He abused her and only left when his cohort, Lucinda Montez, arrived and drugged her with self-made chloroform."

"How do you know all of this?" The reporter asked with wide eyes.

"When my daughter located Stacy Anderson, alive, she immediately fought for both their lives and managed to make contact with me and two of her friends. Gerald was knocked unconscious, but Lucinda Montez escaped from the scene. I spoke with my daughter there and she told me the story." Whitlock motioned to the building behind the reporter, "My daughter had reason to believe that Caroline Graves was in danger due to something Lucinda Montez said. She, and her friends, tried to tell the deputies at the scene to go check on Caroline, but they were ignored."

"What happened next was a desperate act to save a classmate," the reporter said to the camera, ignoring Whitlock now as she spoke directly to the audience.

Whitlock took that cue to enter the front door of the Sheriff's Office.

"My name is James Whitlock, your Deputy White just brought my daughter in for questioning," he stared at the woman at the front desk. "I'd like to be notified as soon as anything changes please."

The woman nodded with wide eyes, "I'll let you know as soon as I hear anything. Our detective is on his way in now."

Whitlock sighed and rubbed his forehead as though willing away a headache. "You seem like a nice lady," he said as he placed his hands on the desk and leaned in slightly, "my daughter hasn't had any water or food for two days, and she's terribly claustrophobic. Is there any way you could take her some water, maybe crack a window for her?"

"I'll do what I can, Hun, but I can't guarantee anything," she said apologetically, "I'm just the desk clerk."

"Never underestimate your worth," Whitlock smiled charmingly at the woman, making her blush noticeably.

Chapter 22

Gage sat on a hard chair with her forehead resting on the cold metal table in front of her. Her hands were finally free, but she kept them clutching each other in her lap in an effort to ease the shaking that was steadily getting worse. By closing her eyes and focusing her energy on her breathing, she could almost forget that she was in a small box of a room in the basement with only a tiny window up far too high to be of any use. The fact that she was once more underground wasn't lost on her, and her whole body ached from the exertions of the last few days.

She had no idea how long she had been sitting, waiting for the detective, but her stomach was both nauseated and growling with uncomfortable hunger pains. She licked her lips and sighed because she knew she was only making them more chapped with her saliva. They were starting to burn.

The door opened and she looked up with hopeful eyes.

"I'm sorry, Sugar, it's just me," the nice lady from the front desk smiled apologetically, "I wanted to bring you some water," she held up a bottle, "and there wasn't much in the way of food. But I brought you my lunch."

Gage smiled genuinely, "That's very kind of you, will you sit with me for a bit. The company might help me keep my brain off the walls closing in on me."

The woman looked into the hallway then shrugged and stepped into the room, closing the door behind her, "No one labeled you an arrest, so I suppose that would be okay." She sat down in the padded chair across the table and placed the bottle of water in front of Gage before opening her lunch box and pulling out a sandwich.

"This is amazing," Gage picked up the water and drank a small sip, savoring the cool fluid as it soothed her scratchy throat. "I didn't realize how rough I felt until I had to sit still."

"Don't drink too fast," the woman's concern actually made Gage smile.

"What's your name?" Gage took another sip of the water and took the half sandwich that was handed to her.

"So you know who poisoned you with a crappy sandwich?" The woman laughed.

"So I know who to thank, once I get out of here, for being the only spec of humanity I've endured in about a week," Gage responded, taking a bite of her sandwich.

"My name is Mary Beth," she placed a wet washcloth on the table beside Gage's water bottle. "I have a daughter who went to St. Peter's. I can't thank you enough for what you did."

Gage nodded, "Mary Beth, it was my pleasure." She shrugged, "of course, no good deed ever goes unpunished."

Mary Beth nodded, "I hope this will be all over soon, Sugar," she patted Gage's hand reassuringly, "I know your Daddy is real worried about you."

Gage's look of confusion quickly disappeared when the door opened, revealing a man in khaki pants and a polo with a badge hanging on a chain from his neck. "Mary Beth," the surprise in his voice disappeared as quickly as it has appeared, his eyes narrowed slightly as he added, "is there somewhere you should be?"

"Probably," Mary Beth responded as she stood up, "but I was overdue for my lunch break, so I decided to check on this poor girl." She collected her trash and smiled at Gage, "You make sure you come to say goodbye when you leave, Sugar. Your Daddy's waiting for you out by my desk."

PREY

Gage smiled and nodded, "Thank you for the water and the sandwich."

"My pleasure," Mary Beth stopped in front of the Detective, "you going to move so I can get on to where I'm supposed to be?"

He sighed and stepped into the room, "Thank you, Mary Beth."

"Uh huh," she murmured as she walked past him, "you be good to that girl, you hear?"

He closed the door and turned to Gage who was wiping her face with the washcloth Mary Beth had left for her. "I don't think anyone here has actually gotten your real name yet."

"No one has seemed particularly interested in anything I had to say," she responded coolly. "Mary Beth was the first one to even offer me some water. Or human decency of any kind, really."

"I'm very interested in everything you have to say," the man sat in the seat Mary Beth had just vacated.

"First," Gage set down the washcloth and stared at him, "do me a favor. Assume I know all your obnoxious interview and interrogation techniques. Don't waste your breath on building rapport or attempting to trick me. You'll only get cooperation from me, so long as you don't patronize me."

He shrugged, "Fair enough."

"I'm not kidding," she said, still staring at him. "I'm not interested in any of the normal bullshit. I'm tired, sore, pissed off, nauseated, and ready to be far out of this town."

He smiled, "So you think you're leaving then?"

She sighed, "Am I under arrest?"

"Not yet," he answered.

"I'm free to go?" She asked, standing up.

"Not yet," he motioned back to her chair.

"If I'm not under arrest, then you are violating my fourth amendment rights by having me illegally detained and brought here to also be illegally detained." She stood, staring at him, "I'd really like to not have to involve a lawyer with this bullshit, I hate lawyers."

"Well there's something we can agree on," he smiled.

She sighed heavily and sat down, "You can't understand how frustrating this foolishness is to me."

"Tell me about that, has this happened to you a lot before?"

"Are you a cop, or a shrink?" She cocked her head to the side, "Because to be honest I don't trust either of those professions."

"In my experience, people who distrust the police are either on the wrong side of the law or extremely misinformed."

She rolled her eyes, "I've had tons of experience with the police, and very rarely am I left with a good feeling."

"How often had you broken the law?"

Her expression was amused, "I reckon since you don't have my name, you haven't run an accurate criminal history." She smiled, "I actually don't have one. I'm far guiltier of bending laws for a good cause than outright breaking them."

"You took a patrol car," he was surprised by her claim.

"I assume your deputies have body mics?" she asked. When he nodded, she continued, "You'll hear my friend telling your deputies to go to Caroline's house because she was in danger. You'll also hear them laugh and brush off his worry." She shrugged, "My friend was in danger, your deputies weren't going to help her, so I did what I had to in order to save her life from a deranged woman." She stared at him, "Not to mention the cruiser was unlocked and running."

"You just admitted to me that you stole a police cruiser." He was a cat who'd just eaten a canary.

"No sir," she responded coyly, "I just verified that a FOIA (Freedom of Information Act) request will reveal just how inept this department has been in handling this case." She cocked her head to the side, "I wonder how much that reporter outside would love to hear that the Sheriff's Office is railroading the private contractor who apparently single-handedly solved the most illicit case this jurisdiction has ever seen. Not to mention saved two victims and apprehended both suspects all while trying desperately to receive aid from an uncaring Sheriff's Office..." she trailed off and smiled sadly, "It really is quite a shocking story. It's sure to garner national attention."

"Are you threatening me?" His voice was not remotely amused.

She shook her head, "Not at all, just stating facts."

"Let's start over," he sighed, "my name is Detective White. What is your name?"

She stared at him, "Is everyone here named White, or is your son the one who arrested me?"

"Detained you," Detective White corrected.

"If I was merely detained, I would be free to leave," Gage responded scathingly.

"Are you going to tell me your name?" He sighed.

She leaned back in her chair and folded her arms across her chest as she seemed to measure him with her eyes.

"Trying to decide if you could make a break for it?" He stiffened at her gaze.

"No, that's not a difficult task, I could do it if I really wanted to," she continued to stare into his eyes, "I'm trying to measure your mettle to decide if you're just caught up in the bullshit, or if you're part of the damn problem."

"What problem is that?" He asked.

"Illegal seizures, apparent lax procedures, disregard for human life," she stared at him for a moment, "I could go on, but I think you get the point."

He stared back at her, unflinching.

They stared at each other in silence before she finally broke the tension, "I'm desperately hoping your son learned his chauvinistic tendencies from someone else, and that you'll slap the shit out of him when you review his body mic."

The way the Detective's eyes flashed with surprise before once more becoming carefully blank, gave Gage her answer.

"Good." She sighed and leaned forward, resting her hands on the table she continued to stare into the Detective's eyes, "How much of the story do you already know?"

He also leaned forward slightly, "Assume I know nothing."

She smirked, "Like most of the other deputies I've met here, got it."

He sighed slightly, "Are we passed that yet?"

"Passed what?" she asked innocently.

"The snark," he responded, "can we just speak like adults?"

"So, you at least know I'm not a nubile seventeen-year-old high school student," she smiled.

He placed her false teeth on the table, "I'd say you gave up that cover at the Graves' household."

She cringed slightly at the sight of the teeth and rubbed her raw gums with her tongue, "Those were so not ready for long-term use. I've got to work on them some more."

He stared at her, waiting for her to elaborate.

"How are Stacy and Caroline doing?" Gage asked quietly.

"Stacy was severely dehydrated, and a little beat up, but all in all not nearly as bad as was anticipated," he answered. "Caroline is hysterical, and we're having trouble locating her mom, so she's just sitting here crying."

"Jesus, you have her in one of these rooms?" Gage asked, concerned, "Why don't you just throw the poor girl down in the mine with us."

Detective White shrugged, "I don't really have much say over that, but if we find our common ground, I'd be happy to take you to her."

Gage made a face at him, "I thought we agreed there would be no interrogation tricks," she grumbled, "the old 'I gave you something, now you give me something' is so tired."

He shrugged, "If it works, why change it?"

Gage took a drink of her water before explaining her involvement, "Head Mistress Beverly hired my company, PREY, to take on the abduction case because she was afraid of the ineptitude of the Sheriff's Office." She shrugged, "No offense."

He made a face at her before questioning, "PREY? Why have I never heard of that?"

"Proactive Resources for Evidentiary Yields," Gage stated. "A company I helped create to catch the criminals in this country who elude capture, to protect the innocent victims they were maiming and murdering." She sat up straighter, "Generally we catch the bad guys and hand them over to the boys in blue with a pretty bow, like this case."

Detective White pulled out his small notepad and a pen.

"Sometimes it's the police themselves who bring us in, more often it's the victims or their families." Gage took another sip of her water, watching carefully as the Detective wrote something down.

"Why Proactive Resources for Evidentiary Yields?" He asked finally, looking up at her.

"Mostly we just liked the acronym PREY." She smirked, "You know, I pretend to be the noun: prey, to lure out the suspect. Then I switch to the verb: prey and become the predator to prey upon the suspect."

"You often pretend to be a victim?" his tone was unreadable.

"I act as bait, the suspect makes the decision to attack, I don't force anyone into anything."

"How has this not been made into a case for entrapment?" The detective seemed honestly confused, which annoyed her slightly.

"Again," she stated slowly, "I don't force anybody to do anything. I embody the suspect's type of victim, they decide to attack. Not to mention I don't represent any government entity. I'm merely a civilian with special skills."

White snorted slightly at that, "I'll say. You made short work of Gerald and Lucinda. I'll give you that."

"I'll take that," Gage bowed her head slightly at the praise, "now when can we get over this bullshit and let me go home?"

"You still stole a cruiser," he answered.

"I did not steal anything," she responded, "to steal, you have to have the intention to remove something from the owner's possession permanently. I did not go joy riding back home in a cruiser, I used it to convey me to the rescue of your downed man, and an innocent girl."

"You can spin this however you like," he responded, "you still stole the car."

"I returned it in excellent condition, and saved lives," she responded.

"I will talk to the sheriff, but I'm not really sure how this is going to play out," he rubbed his eyes. "I'm pretty sure he'd like to crucify you as a warning to anyone wanting to meddle in police business."

She rolled her eyes before leaning back in her chair again, "Well, you can tell him that there's no way in hell he'd be reelected if he throws the town hero in the clink. The first thing I'll do is give an exposé to that lovely reporter out front, detailing all the time I spent in this town saving those girls and catching the criminals with no help from this inept department. I'm sure she'd love that interview. She'd really love covering my case with the election coming up."

White sighed, "You really know what to say don't you?"

She leaned forward and said quietly, "Between you and me, I'd rather never look into a camera or speak with a reporter. It would be career suicide for me. The only way I can effectively be a victim is if no one knows who the hell I am. If the sheriff throws me a bone on this one, I will have no reason to speak to anyone about this case."

He smiled as he stood up, "I'll present your proposal to Sheriff Reed and let you know what he has to say."

When the door closed behind him, Gage tried to occupy herself with her water bottle, and ignore the fact that the walls really did seem to be closing in on her.

Chapter 23

Whitlock was sitting on the bench across from Mary Beth's desk, his back was straight and his hands were resting on his knees. He stared ahead, listening as doors slammed and raised voices swelled from somewhere within the building.

Mary Beth smiled apologetically at him, "I'm not sure what's going on, but I'm sure it's not about your girl."

He smiled back at her, "I'm just as certain she's at the root of it. She has a way of infuriating people."

Mary Beth looked down at her keyboard and shrugged, "She seemed lovely to me."

Whitlock chuckled and continued to stare at the closed door of the sheriff's personal office which was visible behind the front desk even though a door separated that hallway from the lobby. When it slammed open, Mary Beth jumped, but Whitlock was still as stone, he pulled his cell phone from his pocket and held it on his knee as he waited.

Sheriff Reed stood in the doorway, his chest heaving, making his stomach jiggle. His tan uniform was wrinkled and ill-fitting, drawing even more attention to his crimson sweating face. The vein in his temple was visibly throbbing with what Whitlock could only assume was rage.

"You!" The sheriff pointed a pudgy finger at him, "Get in my office, NOW."

Whitlock stood slowly with a smirk teasing his lips, "Sheriff, have I done something to offend you?"

"In my office," the smaller man snarled before turning to the detective already in his office, "you bring that little bitch in here right now."

"There's no need for that kind of language, Sir." Whitlock admonished as he strode through the door to the hallway in front of the sheriff's office, tucking his phone into his jacket pocket, "We've been nothing but cooperative with you."

"Nothing but cooperative?" The sheriff scoffed, "You people have brought me nothing but problems."

"I think Caroline Graves and Stacy Anderson may have different views on that subject," Whitlock answered smoothly as he stepped into the room.

Gage strode into the room followed by Detective White. She glanced at Whitlock before moving to stand beside him against the wall. Her face was still streaked with dirt and blood, her make-up smudged. Her hair was still in low pigtails, but one was higher than the other and her hair was so frizzy that she looked like she'd stuck her finger in a light socket.

"Apparently, you two believe you can blackmail me into dropping felony charges on this girl, here," the sheriff's hand was shaking as he pointed at Gage.

"It's not really blackmailing," Gage sighed, "more like a mutual understanding."

"You shut your mouth, girl, you've done enough damage," the sheriff snapped.

"Damage, like saving two innocent girls from violent deaths, and single-handedly capturing both suspects," Whitlock responded.

"Yes," the sheriff growled, "coming into my jurisdiction and making my men look like fools."

Gage muttered, "They didn't need help with that part, just everything else."

Whitlock elbowed her and she made a face at him.

The sheriff's vein was throbbing so wildly, Gage stared at it, wondering when it would rupture.

"May I speak, Sir?" Detective White spoke up.

"Sure, why not? Add your two cents in," Sheriff Reed waved his hand dismissively.

"I think the proposition brought to the table is a good one, Sir." White quickly continued when the sheriff's face turned purple, "If this young lady signed a non-disclosure and left the state, there would be no way for the media to truly know what happened here. It doesn't seem like she wants credit for anything."

"Nope," Gage shook her head, "as far as I'm concerned, y'all can say whatever the hell you want. I was just a passerby in this mess. My job relies on a certain amount of anonymity, it's in my best interest to avoid any recognition or cameras."

"Well good," the sheriff was smug, "then that should still apply from the jail with no bond available."

"If I'm sitting in jail, there's no reason for me to be concerned about my job anymore," Gage responded. "Not to mention, I doubt a magistrate would hold me with no bond for this bullshit."

"You don't know how the law works around here," the sheriff's face was starting to return to a normal color as he felt more in control of the situation.

"Are you saying you control the magistrates in your jurisdiction?" Whitlock asked.

"*Of course* I control the magistrates," the sheriff snapped, "I control everything about the law in this county. Nothing happens without my say so. How do you think I've been sheriff so long?"

"Certainly not for the good job you're doing," Gage snapped.

Whitlock sighed and Gage glowered at him again.

"Sir, I really think we should consider this deal," White piped up again, "there's nowhere we can put her where the media won't find her. They'll make her story national news."

"I'll put her under the God damn jail," the sheriff snarled.

"Oh good, now you're threatening to kill me?" Gage's knuckles were white from the pressure of the fists she was making, "You'll find that I'm much harder to kill than I look."

"You're not the first to think so," the sheriff snapped at her.

Gage raised an eyebrow but Whitlock silenced her with a look.

"Sir!" White's surprise was evident in his tone.

"Oh shut up, White," Sheriff Reed snapped and sat down behind his desk, "your two cents weren't worth shit."

Everyone in the room looked at the door when a loud knock interrupted them.

"Excuse me, Wilbur," a beautiful woman in her forties wearing a fashionable dress with black hair in an elegant French twist, entered the room. She looked right past the sheriff, turning in the room to take in its occupants before staring up at Whitlock, "My name is Jennifer Graves, I'm here for an explanation. My daughter Caroline said my husband has been assaulting girls?" Her blue eyes were swimming with tears of confusion.

"Detective White, take Mrs. Graves and explain the situation to her," the sheriff's voice was still tense.

"Is this the girl who saved my Caroline?" Jennifer motioned to Gage who smiled at her.

"Yes," Whitlock responded before anyone else could answer. "This is the woman who saved Stacy Anderson from your husband, then took it upon herself to race across town and save your daughter from her deranged teacher."

"Sorry about your vase," Gage piped up, "but Caroline was really brave. You should be proud of her."

Jennifer breezed through the room and hugged Gage tightly. She was much taller than Gage due to her heels, so the younger woman was awkwardly mashed against the older woman's breasts, "Thank you so much. I don't know what I would do without my Caroline. I'm so grateful." Gage's arms hung at her sides as she was forced to accept the hug. Eventually, the smell of Jennifer's perfume, and the warmth of her embrace, made Gage slowly accept the show of affection. She imagined this is what a mother's hug should feel like. She patted Jennifer's back with one hand awkwardly and looked at Whitlock for help, but he only smiled.

Jennifer pulled back, her perfectly manicured hands lingering on Gage's shoulders, "You must allow us to take you to dinner, Dear." She glanced at Whitlock, "All of you."

Gage smiled sheepishly, "I'm not actually free to go, Mrs. Graves."

"What?" Jennifer whirled to face the sheriff, her blue eyes cold, the tears and confusion forgotten, "Is there a reason the savior of my only child is not free to go, Wilbur?"

The sheriff swallowed, "well, uh-"

"Because I would hate to stop the monthly contributions my family has been making to your election campaign," she snapped, "there doesn't really seem to be any reason I can't take this girl and her friends to dinner." She paused, staring at the portly man with narrowed eyes, "Is there a reason?"

"She has some paperwork to fill out, Jennifer. That's all," the sheriff sputtered, "she'll be free to go in an hour or so."

Gage laughed but stopped when Whitlock glared at her again.

"Is there anything I can bring you, Dear?" Jennifer turned back to Gage.

"I could use a change of clothes," Gage responded, looking down at the rumpled mess of an outfit she still wore, "maybe some makeup. My friends should be outside in the blue van, they can get me something if you can just let them know."

Jennifer shook her head, "Nonsense, Caroline and I will go get you some things and be back in an hour." She glanced back at the sheriff, "One hour."

He nodded at her and looked down at his desk as Jennifer patted Gage's hand and left the room.

"White, draw up a non-disclosure and get their signatures," Wilbur sat down in his chair with a defeated expression. "All four of them," he added as White began to leave the office.

"I'll notify my people to come inside," Whitlock nodded his head courteously as he turned to follow the detective from the room. He motioned for Gage to precede him.

"Good thing you can't be bought, Sheriff Reed. I was worried about your moral compass for a minute there," Gage called sweetly as she left the room.

Whitlock sighed heavily as he followed her and closed the office door behind him. The angry shout of frustration that followed them, even through the thick wood, made him smile slightly before pulling his cell phone out of his pocket again and hitting a button before calling Mere and asking her to meet them in the lobby.

Gage was being hugged by Mary Beth by the vending machines which were just down the hall from her desk when Whitlock stepped into the lobby. He hung up his phone and smiled warmly at the women, "Thank you for all your help, ma'am."

Mary Beth laughed as she pulled back and wiped at her eyes, "Oh hush, my name is Mary Beth, not ma'am!"

Whitlock nodded his acceptance, "Very well. Mary Beth, I appreciate you taking the time to help."

"It was my pleasure," Mary Beth touched Gage's cheek with her cool hand, "this sweet girl deserved it, after everything she'd been through." She pulled Gage into another hug with a weepy laugh, "Don't let them hold you up too much longer, Sugar. Get you something tasty to eat!"

Gage winked at the older woman when she was finally released from the embrace, "I'm thinking steak!"

Mary Beth chuckled, "Good for you, Sugar." She headed back to her desk and called over her shoulder, "Eat some extra for me!"

The door burst open and Mere entered with a beaming grin, "So I'm guessing we have the standard non-disclosure agreement situation?" She passed Mary Beth and moved closer to Gage and Whitlock.

"You got it, Toots," Gage returned the grin, "I love it when a plan comes together."

"Now we're the A-Team?" Brick grumbled, following the redhead.

Gage's mouth teased into a half smile, "This was a rough first case, Biscuit. How'd you like it?"

"I don't like handcuffs," Brick muttered, rubbing his wrists.

Mere pat Brick's shoulder as if he was a puppy, "He did great for his first time. I was impressed."

"Mere loves popping cherries," Gage winked at Brick.

"I usually prefer experience," Mere added, poking Brick in the ribs playfully, "but you were a pleasant surprise."

Brick sighed and shook his head at Whitlock, "Are we going home now?"

Whitlock shook his head, "Once we all sign non-disclosure agreements, we are apparently being treated to a meal."

Brick arched an eyebrow, "So we can't tell anyone what happened here? That's kind of bullshit, don't you think?"

Whitlock stared at the younger man for a moment before stating, "You knew the particulars of this career choice when you applied. If you find that recognition is what you desire, perhaps this isn't a good fit for you."

Gage laughed, "Now that we're starting to like him, you threaten to fire him?"

"Your priorities are all mixed up, Daddio," Mere added to Whitlock, before wrapping her arm around Brick's waist and addressing him, "this job takes some getting used to."

"But there's free food," Gage piped up.

"And you can pretend to be a debonair secret agent to the nubile women," Mere added, letting her arm slip from Brick so she could strut like James Bond and strike a pose.

"Plus, Whitlock recorded the entire incriminating conversation with the sheriff," Gage smiled before glancing at her boss, "didn't you?"

Whitlock cleared his throat, "I may have some audio," he grumbled.

"There are ways around non-disclosures, for those extra obnoxious assholes," Gage winked at Brick.

"Anonymous tip?" Brick's lips slowly twisted into a smile, "I like it."

"Just because we don't want our faces plastered everywhere, doesn't mean we want that criminal reelected," Gage looked up the hallway and saw Detective White motioning to her. She started to walk past Brick and slapped his ass as she did, "We have to have some kind of moral compass."

Brick jumped and sighed, "Obviously."

Mere laughed as she caught up to Gage and wrapped her arm around her friend's waist, walking with her in stride.

"I've learned to just ignore what you can, enjoy what you can, and pick your battles," Whitlock motioned for Brick to follow the women, "it's not worth the headache to try to change them."

Brick actually laughed as he glanced at Whitlock, "That means a lot coming from you."

"How do you mean?" Whitlock asked.

"You strike me as the type who always wants control. Every detail planned meticulously." Brick shrugged, "But then you have a bunch of rowdy kids working for you who thrive on the mess in life."

Whitlock chuckled, "I'm sure we do seem like an odd group from the outside, but each person serves a specific purpose. Hopefully, you'll find that out along the way."

The two men entered a small dank room, which was rather crowded with Detective White, Gage, and Mere already inside it.

"This is my home away from home," Gage addressed them as they entered.

"Looks like fun times," Brick responded, taking a quick look around at the basement interrogation room.

"Quaint," Whitlock added, noting the distinct lack of usable windows. He noticed Gage was rather pale. Her face was drawn.

"Let's get this over with so we can get her outside in the fresh air," Mere spoke, interrupting Whitlock's thoughts.

"Okay, this is a non-disclosure I've drawn up," White placed four sheets of paper on the table, "I can explain the details if you'd like-"

"We all understand how a non-disclosure works," Gage responded hastily, she picked up the papers and handed them to her compatriots, "bonus points, we can also all read. Though I'm sure that is a coveted skill here."

White sighed and waited while they read through the form. He handed Gage a pen when she held her hand out to him.

Gage scribbled her signature and the date at the bottom of the paper then handed the pen to Mere who did the same.

Whitlock signed his form with his expensive fountain pen, produced from the interior jacket pocket of his suit. He held it after he finished and glanced at Brick hesitantly, then put the pen back in his pocket with a tiny sigh of relief when Mere finished with her form and handed the pen to Brick.

"He doesn't share well," Gage said out loud to no one in particular.

Each of the four handed their form to Detective White, who glanced them over and nodded, "Excellent, thank you for your cooperation."

Gage snorted, then cleared her throat, "Do you have a business card or something, in case I get lonely and need to talk."

Detective White rolled his eyes, but produced his card, "You're a peculiar woman. But thank you for your help here."

Gage smiled, curtsied, and purred, "Thank you kindly for the compliment," with a pronounced southern drawl before handing the card to Whitlock who tucked it into his jacket pocket.

"Can we go now?" Mere asked, "If this place is giving ME the heebie-jeebies, I know it's freaking her out." She grabbed Gage's hand and strode from the room quickly.

Whitlock and Brick followed with White bringing up the rear of the group. Once they were back in the lobby, White bid them goodbye and disappeared back into the labyrinth of halls and offices.

"Mary Beth, you glorious lady, I'm out of here!" Gage smiled at the older woman as she and Mere approached the clerk's desk hand in hand.

"Wonderful!" Mary Beth was beaming, "I'm so happy, Sugar. You stay outta trouble now, you hear?"

Mere laughed, "That's impossible. This one doesn't know HOW to stay out of trouble."

The front door opened and Caroline entered the lobby with a shopping bag in her hand, "Sammy!" She dropped the bag and almost knocked Gage over with the force of her hug.

"I'm getting so many hugs today," Gage's tone was neither happy nor angry, but her eyes were pleading for help.

Mere laughed and picked up the bag from the floor, peeking inside before looking at Gage again with a nod of approval.

"I'm so glad you're okay!" Caroline pulled back slightly, but her hands remained on Gage's shoulders, just like her mother had done. "Are you coming back to school? Why are you here? Are they giving you a medal? What happened with my dad?"

"Holy crap, stop!" Gage shook her head, "Too much! Too many questions all at once."

"Sorry," Caroline said sheepishly. "I'm just a little overwhelmed and that translates into constant chatter."

Gage stared at Caroline for a moment before slowly speaking, "I'm here because I had to sign some paperwork. I'm not going back to school because I'm twenty-six, and I don't think they make medals for what I do." She paused, "The situation with your dad is far more complicated than I can explain quickly in the lobby of the Sheriff's Office." She pointed at the bag Mere was holding, "Is that bag for me?"

Caroline's eyes were wide as she comprehended the information she'd just been given, but she nodded.

"Fantastic." Gage pulled back, "Is your mom outside?"

Caroline nodded again.

"You go on out there, I'm going to get cleaned up. Your mom said something about dinner, we can meet you somewhere, just let him know where," she motioned to Whitlock who was chatting with Mary Beth.

Gage motioned to Mere and the two women disappeared into the bathroom as Caroline headed back outside with a shell-shocked expression marring her pretty face.

Gage made a beeline for the sink and started to splash her face with cold water.

Mere closed the door behind her and locked it, she glanced around the small bathroom and realized it must actually serve as a locker room. "Hey Gage?"

Gage looked up, water dripping from her chin.

"There's a shower," Mere pointed with a grin.

Gage's eyes widened and she whirled around to look at the rather sad looking shower. It didn't have a shower curtain but appeared to be functional since water was steadily dripping from the fixture.

"I don't know if I'd trust that," Mere laughed.

Gage shrugged and started to undress, "I'm so disgusting, it would take a lot to dissuade me." She glanced at Mere, "Is there anything I can use as a towel in there?"

Mere smiled, "There are so many treasures in this bag, you'll think Lina did the shopping." She reached in and pulled out an oversized Egyptian cotton towel. "This thing alone had to be a hundred bucks!"

"I'm worth it," Gage laughed, "is there any contact lens stuff in there? I'd hate to waste these colored lenses, they're perfectly good, just really annoying."

Mere hung the soft towel on the hook by the shower and dug back into the bag, "There's a toiletry kit. Lemmie rip into it." She put the bag down and unzipped the small makeup bag, "Bingo!" She pulled out a contact case and some solution. She put the makeup bag back into the shopping bag and unscrewed the contact case and filled it with the solution.

Gage was standing in front of her friend, naked, by the time Mere held out the prepared case. Gage quickly swiped the contacts out of her eyes and into the corresponding sides on the container. "Thank God," she sighed and blinked multiple times as she moved to turn the shower on.

"You're so sexy," Mere laughed, trying to ignore the many scars on her friend's body as she closed the container, and went back to inspect the contents of the bag.

Gage wiggled her butt as she stepped into the shower's stream, "You like it!"

"Speaking of 'things I like'," Mere pulled a green designer dress from the bag, "How did that lady know what size to get you?"

Gage shrugged as she rubbed her face with her hands, "I have no idea, she was in the same room as me for like five minutes. Maybe she's magic."

Mere handed her a small bottle of shampoo from the bag, "Yes, definitely she's magic."

Gage sighed happily and immediately began to scrub herself with the soap. Dirt and blood pooled at her feet the more she scrubbed.

"Also speaking of 'things I like'," Mere pulled Gage's phone out of her back pocket, "you've been very popular, I don't know who's calling you since the name is Dundee, but the ringtone you assigned it is amazing. Brick and I enjoyed dancing to it."

Gage laughed, "I have an amazing sense of humor," she glanced at Mere, "let's leave it at that, shall we?"

Mere shrugged and put the phone back in her pocket. "You're going to look amazing in this stuff," she pulled a sexy pair of strappy high heeled stilettos from the bag. "This woman has impeccable taste."

Gage finished washing the soap out of her hair and turned off the water, "She's a beautiful and stylish woman, she probably just picked things she'd wear." She grabbed her towel and dried off quickly, wrapping the towel around her body.

"Doubtful," Mere held up the dress for Gage's inspection, "this doesn't strike me as 'devoted mom'," the dress was tight, short, and revealing.

Gage smiled, "That looks like so much fun. Too bad I don't have anyone to impress."

"Impress me!" Mere cried and started handing Gage the things she would need to get ready.

~*~*~*~

"What the hell is taking so long?" Brick was leaning against the van, "I'm starving."

Whitlock was standing with his hand in his pocket and a smile on his face, "Give her a break, she's been underground for a few days."

"Yeah, but that lady said she was buying us dinner, it's rude to make her wait," Brick was about to complain further but his mouth dropped open as Gage walked from the building with Mere. The redhead was usually a full head shorter than Gage, but today, she barely made it to the older woman's chest.

"She cleans up nice, doesn't she," Whitlock laughed at the younger man's expression.

Gage and Mere walked right past the reporter and cameraman who were still covering the story. Neither one recognized her in the form-fitting dress and stilettos which helped to completely transform Gage into the sexy woman she was, instead of the nubile teenager she'd been pretending to be. Her hair was blonde again and fell in soft waves around her shoulders.

"Now that I'm feeling much more like myself, where's the meat?" Gage asked. She winked at Brick, "Not that meat, put it away."

"Down boy," Mere added with a giggle.

Brick rolled his eyes, "You look good, but I'm not that impressed," he headed to the front of the van, "can we go eat now?"

"Yes, I'm starving!" Gage linked her arm with Whitlock's, "Meet you there?"

Mere nodded and headed to the passenger seat of the van, "I have a pair of heels in here right? I can't wear flats when she wears heels."

Brick laughed as he started the van.

Chapter 24

Gage sat with her back to the wall of the van's interior. Her legs were stretched out in front of her with her ankles crossed. The monitor systems were all shut down and closed up into the custom designed walls of the van which were like drop-down desks on steroids.

She was focused on her phone, trying to ignore the enclosed space. Brick was in the passenger seat and had his window cracked at her request, but that air barely made it into the rear of the van.

Mere was lying beside Gage, her head in Gage's lap as she slept. Gage was still wearing the dress Jennifer Graves bought her, but the heels were forgotten beside her. Mere's red hair was sprawled across the deep green of Gage's skirt, making her smile and think of Christmas. Gage absently stroked Mere's hair occasionally while the younger woman slept soundlessly.

Dundee: *Pretty sure I saw you on the local news in North Carolina.*

Gage smiled at the text from Mak.

Gage: *I don't know what you mean.*

Dundee: *You weren't dressed up like a school girl, getting arrested? I'm pretty sure I recognized those legs.*

Gage: *Maaaaaybe*

Dundee: *Ha. It's a good look for you.*

Gage: *The plaid? Or the handcuffs?*

Dundee: *I'll let you decided on that one.*

Gage: *Why were you in North Carolina?*

Dundee: *Headed North to see a lead in West Virginia about that weapon you asked about.*

Gage: *Oh really? What's the word?*

Dundee: *I haven't spoken to my lead yet. He wanted to talk in person.*

Gage: *You know just following a lead won't get you drinks with my girls, right?*

Dundee: *How bout just with you, then?*

Gage: *Cute. Let me know when you find out something useful.*

Dundee: *I'm full of useful info. I don't think you should deny yourself a drink.*

Gage actually laughed.

Gage: *You don't need to worry about what I deny myself.*

Dundee: *Fair enough, where should I find you if I have info?*

Gage: *My phone clearly works.*

Dundee: *Reckon I can catch you at Craze?*

Gage: *I'm pretty impressed you remembered that name. It is my watering hole of choice. If I'm in the mood, I usually go there.*

Dundee: *I remember everything from that night.*

It was a simple sentence. Gage was surprised to feel a warmth spread through her tummy and a blush color her cheeks.

Dundee: *See ya soon*

Gage: *K*

She hadn't known how to react. So she distanced herself as best she could from the conversation. It was her usual defense mechanism. A part of her hoped he'd take the hint and back off, but another part hoped he'd accept the challenge of the chase. She wasn't really sure which part she actually wanted to win.

"Who is he?" Mere's voice made Gage jump. "Sorry," Mere laughed, "I just saw you smiling and blushing like the school girl you were pretending to be and I got curious."

"It's nobody," Gage shook her head, "just distracting myself."

"Uh huh," Mere sighed as she stretched across Gage's lap, then sat up, "I can't wait to meet Mr. Distraction."

"Once we get back, I'll have no need to be distracted anymore," Gage put her phone by her shoes.

"Everyone could use a little distraction sometimes," Mere wiggled in a sexual manner.

Gage shook her head, "I'm good. I need to keep my head clear."

"Why's that?" Mere asked.

Gage went still and stared at her friend in the darkness.

"It's just the two of us," Mere continued, "it feels like the perfect time to tell me a story about your ex and why he has you so spun."

Gage sighed, "It's not a big deal. I just don't want to see him."

"You bolted from a race and left Tessa behind." Mere's disbelief annoyed Gage, "I feel like there's more to this than simply not wanting to see someone."

Gage crossed her arms across her chest and snapped, "I can't change your feelings, but they're not my problem."

Even though the dark masked motion, she felt Mere recoil slightly as though she'd been slapped.

"Since you're exhausted and cranky, I'll let that go," Mere's voice was tight, "but you will have to talk to me eventually."

"That's your opinion," Gage responded, closing her eyes.

"I guess you're right," Mere shrugged, "if you want to be a heartless bitch, you could do that instead. I was under the impression we were family."

Gage sighed but kept her eyes closed, "Please, just let it go. I don't want to talk about it."

"Whatever," Mere grumbled then sat for a moment in silence. She was going to make Gage think she was truly angry, and she was hurt, but she decided to change the subject anyway. "What did Caroline have to say when she pulled you to the side after dinner?"

"She blames herself for what her father did," Gage responded.

"That's a pretty harsh notion for a kid," Mere said gently, "what did you tell her?"

"I told her she couldn't control his behavior, nor was she responsible for his depravity. It's easy to blame yourself for things you have no control over, but it's a hell of a lot braver to accept that sometimes people are just fucked up. You can't save everyone. Especially not from themselves."

Mere nodded, "Sounds like good advice."

"It's hard advice to swallow," Gage answered, "I gave her my number in case she needs to talk later."

"That was nice."

Gage shrugged, "Sometimes I think all we do is make more victims, you know? If I can help her move on, that would be something good."

"Everything you do is something good," Mere responded immediately. "How many people do you know who would allow themselves to be taken and beaten in order to save a complete stranger?"

"Oh, I know a few," Gage opened one eye and smiled at Mere.

Mere laughed, "Fair enough. All I mean is that what we do is extraordinary. No one can take that from us."

"I hope you're right," Gage said quietly, closing her eyes again. She couldn't help but wonder who else may have recognized her on the news.

"I'm sensing a need to let loose and have a good time," Mere poked Gage's side.

"What do you mean?" Gage asked.

"I mean we should all go to our place and drink until we're stupid," Mere responded.

"For some of us, that happens much faster than others," Gage smiled as she opened her eyes.

"Some of us are already stupid," Mere shrugged and winked at her friend.

When Gage laughed, Mere continued, "You, me, that dress," she motioned to Gage, "we can have a lot of fun with that dress."

Gage laughed, "Sounds good, Mere-Bear, I could use some stupid in my life."

Chapter 25

Gage walked from the parking lot to the front of the line at Craze. She wore the amazing green dress with a leather jacket over it and even wore the stilettos. She usually erred on the side of more sensible footwear but even she had to admit the shoes made the outfit. Her makeup was carefully contoured to accentuate her cheekbones and draw attention to her eyes. Today her hair was dark and chin length, angled in to complete the look. She approached the bouncer with a broad grin on her face, "Tiny Tim! You lost weight, Baby!"

The hulk of a man smiled in return and rubbed his rotund stomach, "Thanks Gage, I've been on a diet. The Missus is worried about heart attacks."

Gage nodded, "Fair enough, you look great." She motioned to the door, "Are they all in there?"

"Mere is in her dancing shoes," he warned her, looking her up and down appreciatively, "you've got the look for it, but you don't seem to be in the same mood as her."

Gage smirked and shrugged, "I can never keep up with that girl. Is Howie in there too?"

Tim shook his head, "Howie sold the place."

Gage's face fell, "What? Why? I didn't even know he was in the market to sell. What's gonna happen to the place?"

"Supposedly the new owner made an offer Howie couldn't turn down," Tim shrugged and glared down the group of people trying to push past the velvet rope. "He bought it because his girl loves the place or something. Supposedly he's not going to change anything."

"Well that's good I guess," Gage pouted, "I'll miss Howie." She stood on her tiptoes and hugged Tim around the neck quickly, "But so long as you'll still be here."

"You know it Mami, go on in," Tim opened the door for her. When the group in the line started whining, he turned to face them and growled, "Shut up or you'll wait all night." He motioned to Gage, "Perfection goes first, you can wait." He winked at her as she laughed and entered the busy club.

Gage made her way to the booth and table that was always reserved for her friends. It was situated beneath a platform in the center of the dance floor. The platform was where the owner, Howie, had entertained his high rollers. It provided some privacy, but also kept you right in the middle of the action.

The circular booth beneath the platform offered its own bit of privacy without the prestige of the platform. The booth didn't draw as many eyes as the celebrities upstairs.

Gage touched EmEm's shoulder when she approached and he slid into the booth so she could claim the chair he'd just vacated at the end of the table. This was her favorite spot, it offered a view of the front and side exits, as well as the bar.

"Mami!!!!" Mere squealed when she caught sight of Gage, "You're here!" Gage motioned to herself and Mere nodded her appreciation, calling out, "And looking oh so sexy."

Gage smiled in amusement at her drunk friend as she pulled off her leather jacket and draped it on the back of her chair, "Told you I'd be here." She shrugged, "The sexy thing just kind of happens."

"I ordered you a Jameson," Mere shouted over the song, "but I drank it."

EmEm slid a glass of Jameson and coke over to Gage, "I saved you one," he said.

Gage kissed his cheek, "My hero." She sat back, crossed her legs, and watched her surroundings. The crowd, and her friends, were always a source of great amusement to her, especially when alcohol was involved. The normally docile and PDA-shy Will and Lina were making out in the back of the booth, EmEm was dancing in the seat next to her, barely containing his excitement. Mere was drinking anything that was on the table for more than a minute and dancing with anyone who asked her.

Gage recognized Mak at the bar, but all she could see was his back. The brown leather bomber jacket was a giveaway, especially when it was draped on a muscular male back. He'd cut his hair more, but it was still just slightly too long for her taste. He started to turn so she quickly diverted her gaze to her hands on either side of her drink. She picked at the napkin beneath her drink and lost herself to her thoughts for a moment.

The bass of the song was causing vibrations through the whole club which was making Gage's untouched drink seem to dance as she stared at the cocktail napkin she was idly shredding.

She half-heartedly listened to the laughing group of people sitting around her, but her concentration was anywhere but on the frivolity which was supposed to be her focus. She was still uneasy in any space with walls, the fact that the club was packed full of bodies was making her anxious.

The hairs on the back of her neck began to tingle as though she was being watched making her jade gaze sweep the crowded club. When she didn't see any threats, she returned her gaze to the small pile of napkin fluff and tried to ignore the bubbling feeling in her gut. If she didn't look at the tiny space she was inhabiting, maybe she wouldn't feel so claustrophobic.

"GAGE!"

Mere's shout caught Gage off guard and made her flinch before looking up guiltily.

"You seriously haven't heard a word I've said, have you?" Mere chuckled.

Gage shrugged apologetically and turned her attention back to her hands.

"That gorgeous hunk of prize man-meat has been studying you. He looks very interesting," Mere insisted, "all hard and chiseled."

Gage rolled her eyes before looking at her best friend, "If he looks so hard to you, why don't you go chat him up."

Mere looked back at the staring man at the bar, "He clearly likes you," she responded, "his eyes haven't left you since he saw you."

Gage fidgeted, "I know. It gives me the creepy-crawlies."

Mere laughed, "Why would you not jump all over that?"

"Because he doesn't interest me," Gage responded. "He'll come over here all," she switched into a fake Australian accent, "'G'day sheila, you need a nuddy donger'," she switched back to normal speech and resumed playing with her trash, "or some stupid nonsense like that."

"Why's he Australian?" Will asked with an amused chuckle, his arm around Lina's shoulders, "And what the hell is a nuddy donger?"

Gage looked up, startled by her own mistake, "Uh, He's clearly Australian," she motioned to Mak and looked him in the eye, "most brazen crazy men are Australian, I've noticed that."

The table laughed and conversed about the possibilities involving nuddy dongers as Gage purposely moved her body to square up to Mak. She straightened her back and stared into his eyes until he broke eye contact and looked down at his drink.

"Well, Gage is clearly dominant," EmEm smirked, watching the exchange.

"Works every time on dogs," Gage returned smugly before downing her Jameson and Coke and slamming the glass down.

"Need another?" Mere asked.

"Nope, I'm going home now." Gage stood up from her chair, returning it to its rightful position, "I'm bored of this place," she stated as she pulled on her leather jacket and zipped it up.

Mere pouted, "But we didn't even dance or do shots."

"Sorry Mere-Bear, I'm just not in the mood today," Gage turned from the table and started to push her way through the crowded bar.

When Mere turned her gaze back to the bar, a bleached-blonde girl with enormous boobs was standing where the handsome man had been earlier.

Gage focused on the side exit as she made her way through the crush of bodies and flashing neon lights. She smelled sweat and sickeningly sweet mixed drinks. She couldn't help but notice the use of illicit drugs in the edges of the crowd out of the corner of her eye. The faces of ecstasy, with wide dilated eyes and slack expressions, were like a slow-motion movie playing out as the strobe lights kicked on in tune to the throbbing music.

Gage blinked hard to rid herself of that sight and told herself that the hairs on the back of her neck were only twitching because Mak was watching her walk. She knew the high heels probably did wonders for her gait, so she let him stare as she tried to break through the crowd.

The crush of bodies almost seemed to tighten in on her until she felt like she couldn't breathe. It was painfully hot, she tried to unzip her coat, but she barely had the room to lift her hand. The flashing lights started to spin and she felt nauseated as she finally found the door. She slammed her body weight into it, to force it open, and stumbled, coughing, into the cool night air.

The door slammed shut behind her, leaving her in the darkness of the alley to gasp and cough. She closed her eyes and focused on breathing in and out slowly for a few moments as she leaned against the brick wall of the club. She could feel her heart pulsing in her temple so she willed her body to calm down until the throbbing of the bass coming from the building was stronger than her pulse beat.

She took one more deep breath and then opened her eyes.

She hadn't heard him come up in front of her. Hadn't smelled his cologne or recognized the cold smile in the crowd inside. She opened her mouth to scream out as her heart leaped into her throat but Alex wrapped a hand calmly around her slender neck and squeezed. The sound of her scream came out as a squeak and she scratched at his hand feebly with both of hers.

"Now, now, you *just* calmed yourself down," he growled meanly. "Why would you amp yourself right back up?"

She wanted to fight him. She wanted to stab him with the knife clipped to her underwear or break his neck, but the truth remained that for some reason, she was weak as a kitten when he was around. She knew that she could get away. She knew that she could hurt him. She could kill him. Something inside her simply shut down her ability to move, other than to make piteous mewling sounds in her throat, and clutch at his hand.

"Why've you been avoiding me, Bridget?" His tone was almost hurt, but his eyes were as cold as the hand around her neck. "You look real good," he slowly unzipped her jacket with his free hand and leered down at her, making her stomach roil.

She couldn't breathe at all. Her face felt hot as the blood pooled there. Her ears were blocked by the sound of throbbing blood and her own attempts at breathing. Her vision was blurring, her temper flared when she realized hot tears were streaming down her face.

"You knew I'd find you, Babe," he smirked, "it was only a matter of time. You've always been mine. You can't fight that. When I asked around, I was told this is your favorite club. So, I bought it." His free hand stroked her hair, "Then I saw you tonight, in this dress, those heels, like you dressed up just for me." His fingers followed her collarbone and trailed through her cleavage down to the low neckline of her dress.

Her anger smoldered in her gut and she was screaming internally at herself to act. She managed to harden her gaze, her tears forgotten, as her vision started to darken around the edges.

"You going to fight me?" He asked in an amused tone. "You know you can't fight fate."

Her eyes searched wildly for anything she could throw at him as he leaned in, so that to prying eyes they'd look like lovers embracing. She saw past his angled body to a retreating form that she recognized. Her eyes went back to Alex and she kneed him as hard as she could between his open legs.

The air fled his lungs in a whoosh of air that sprayed her face with saliva. His hand loosened on her throat and she managed to push him off her as she ran full tilt down the alley as best she could with the stilettoes on her feet. The less than sensible shoes greatly hampered her speed.

She heard him get up and give chase. She heard herself call out in a strangled squawk she was worried wouldn't carry down the alley, "MAK," and then she was falling face-first with a heavy weight on her back.

Her face smacked into the pavement before she was rolled roughly onto her back and Alex's furious face was all she could see as she felt his fist slam into her solar plexus, making her immediately gasp and cough for breath.

He was sitting on her stomach, keeping her from getting away and also keeping her from catching her breath. He raised his fist again and she closed her eyes, waiting for the pain, her coughs stuck in her throat as she sucked air in quickly.

The pain never came, and then his weight was off of her, followed by some grunting and heavy thuds.

Her eyes flew open when she felt a gentle hand on her face and all the air she'd been holding in rushed out in short gasping breaths.

"Are you all right?" Mak's tone was so much softer and kinder than Alex's had been, it took her brain a moment to catch up.

Gage stared up into his concerned face for a moment as she concentrated on breathing before she realized that Alex was cursing on the ground near her. She scrambled to her feet, allowing the Australian to help her, and then stumbled to the mouth of the alley toward her Gran Torino.

Mak helped her to the car and held his hand out until she gave him her keys. He unlocked the door and motioned for her to climb across the seat to the passenger's side. She did as he bade, staring at the mouth of the alley with fear etched into her face.

Mak slid into the seat of the car and caressed the wheel with his left hand as he used the key to make the metal beast roar to life. He sheepishly smiled a half-smile at Gage as he closed the door and hit the gas, making the car's tires spin.

"Safety first," he stated as he used his left hand to strap on his seatbelt and used his right to steer, leaving the parking lot in a cloud of dust.

Gage didn't know how long they'd been driving, or even where they were. After the first few minutes of driving where the only sound was the engine's grumble, she couldn't help the tears that streamed silently down her cheeks as she stared out the window. She was extremely grateful that Mak was being quiet. It gave her a chance to process what happened. Her throat was on fire and she tasted blood. She was pretty sure she'd bitten her lip when she hit the ground earlier, but she was afraid to look in the mirror. She didn't want to see the pathetic cowering fool she became around Alex.

Her mother had told her when she was very young, that love made you powerless. It was one of the only things Gage could remember about her mother. It had been intended as a sweet comment, at least that's what she'd always thought. Maybe it was still sweet, because of all the things she felt for Alex, love had never really been the classification she believed. Fear made her powerless, but it was fear of herself; of what she'd allowed herself to become in his presence, more than fear of him, that made her devoid of physicality.

"You okay?" Mak finally asked. He'd been watching her out of the corner of his eye for the last twenty minutes while he drove. He hated the swell of masculine aggression that boiled in his belly at the sight of her crying. He wished he'd beaten that asshole more ferociously for the violence he'd witnessed, but at the time, his mind was only on getting Gage out of there.

She swallowed, her face distorting with pain from the motion, and nodded, wiping at her face.

"Are you sure?" He asked gently, "I can take you to the hospital."

She turned and looked at him for the first time since she'd climbed into the car, "I'm fine." She managed to croak out, wincing at each syllable. He did his best not to wince at the sight of her face, her nose was swollen and bloody, bruises were already spreading around her eye and throat.

He reached over and gently touched her throat, he was glad when she didn't shy away from him. "Let's have a Captain Cook," when she arched an eyebrow at him, he added, "that's already bruising," as he put his hand back on the wheel. "We need to get you a warm compress."

She stared at him with a confused look marring her face.

"It works," he responded to her unasked question, "better than ice, so long as the swelling isn't too bad." He pulled into a motel parking lot. "Stay here a minute, I'll see if I can get you a room. If not, you can just bunk with me. Buck's out tonight."

When she balked, he smiled at her, a full and charming grin, "Don't you make assumptions: I'm not that easy. Just because you made me your hero, doesn't mean I'll pash you again," he winked at her, leaving her sputtering and confused.

Chapter 26

"It's really not my fault they didn't have any more rooms," Mak opened the door to his motel room and motioned her to enter, "I'm only here one more night anyway, then Buck and me are moving to a unit."

Gage arched an eyebrow as she entered the room with only one queen sized bed.

"Before you go all sticky beak," Mak continued talking as he followed her into the room, "we're staying in the area for a bit. Plus, I figured it would be nice to have a place to go back to when we're not working."

She sat down at the table, crossed her legs, and watched him walk around the room, picking up clothes and throwing them in a pile on a chair in the corner.

"We don't really go down under much anymore," he continued, "so our land there isn't exactly home. Not to mention it's beyond the black stump, even for Straya," he glanced at Gage, "time to plant some roots somewhere. Might as well be here in the big smoke."

She waited for the break in conversation before she spoke in a raspy tone, "I was actually more curious about you sharing a room with another grown man, and there's only one bed."

"Look at you, immediately going to the bed," Mak winked at her again.

She blushed despite herself and tried to put on a harsh look, but a smile kept trying to force its way out. She knew she looked like an amused child in the midst of a temper tantrum, trying to stay mad despite the laughter inside.

"If you must know," he added, clearly delighted by her reaction, "my brother and I don't ever sleep at the same time. One of us is always up.

But if we were sleeping at the same time for some reason, one of us would use the matilda." He nodded over at the bedroll on the floor, "It feels more like home anyhow."

She couldn't stop the laugh that bubbled up, but she tried, so she ended up snorting, because she thought about the scene in *Crocodile Dundee* where Sue realizes Mick slept on the floor of the expensive hotel, instead of in the luxurious bed.

Mak grinned at her, "What was that?"

She shrugged, but her grin was broad for the first time tonight.

"There's that smile," he said softly.

She bit her bottom lip and turned from him, instead, studying the table's contents, which happened to be maps of West Virginia. She touched one of the marks on one of the pages and immediately noticed it corresponded to the shooting case which Whitlock had been studying for a possible next excursion for PREY.

"Told you I'd look into it," Mak said from beside her, making her jump noticeably. "Shit, I'm sorry," he quickly apologized and stepped back from her, holding his hands out like he was calming a wild horse, "I didn't mean to spook you."

She swallowed and licked her lips looking down at the table, her short hair falling in a curtain around her face. She heard him sit on the bed because the springs of the mattress squealed in protest. Her lips parted as she tried to think of what to say, but no sound passed her lips. She drew in a breath and let it out slowly.

"I know this is none of my business, and I'm out of line for even asking," Mak spoke quietly, "but I've seen you breeze through ten opponents without breaking a sweat. Not to mention some pretty impressive stories from the underground which I can only assume are down-playing actual events."

"Is there a question in there?" Gage asked with a sad smile as she turned her gaze to him.

He ran a hand through his hair, watching her expression carefully, before dropping that hand back down to the space between his knees. "I dunno," he looked at his hands as he absentmindedly fiddled with his fingers, "I reckon the question is, why?"

She was still, staring at him with confused eyes and a calm face. He looked up and met her gaze, adding, "Why did you let that bounce treat you that way?"

She bit the inside of her bottom lip for a moment and averted her eyes, then spoke so softly he had to lean toward her to hear, "You're right. It's not a physical limitation." She shook her head slightly, "He couldn't fight me on my worst day." She swallowed hard and closed her eyes, "It's really hard to explain."

"Give it a go," Mak said softly.

She sighed, "It's complicated. I didn't have a normal childhood. I-" she licked her lips and met his gaze hesitantly, "let's just say that by the time Alex came into my life, I was a broken, lost, girl. He made me feel normal, for the first time in my life. The problem was, he wanted me weak, so I let him convince me I was, because I didn't want to disappoint him. I didn't want to be left all alone again."

Mak swallowed hard, watching the emotions play through Gage's jade gaze. He desperately wanted to hold her in his arms and tell her she'd never be alone again, but even more than that, he wanted her to continue talking.

"For a long time, I let him convince me that he was the best I could do. That his company was worth everything he did because I deserved the pain. Seeing him now, it's like he's the personification of the lowest moment of my life, and for some reason, I'm powerless against him. My brain can't function and I go back to that time of weakness," she held his gaze. "I feel like I can't breathe, I'm trapped, and the whole world is crumbling around me. One look and I'm right back to being that girl who'd just had everyone she ever loved taken from her." She was staring through him now, "It didn't matter that he was an abusive narcissistic sadist, back then all that mattered was he wouldn't leave me. I wouldn't be alone."

She sat in silence for a moment before blinking and looking back at him, "So you're right, it's not physical. It's psychological, and some part of me apparently still believes I deserve it."

He swallowed, staring at her with emotion in his eyes that made her voice catch in her throat. When she looked away from him, he spoke, "It seems to me, that you've got a group of mates now who aren't going anywhere. So maybe you can decide that you're not alone, or weak, anymore."

"I don't know how to fix it," she said quietly, staring at a crack in the wall. "Shit, this is the first time I've actually spoken about this to anyone." She turned her gaze back to him, "How do you do that?"

"What?" He asked, meeting her stare.

"I've just told you more than I've told my best friend," she responded. "I barely know you, but here I am, spilling my guts."

He stood up suddenly, worry in his eyes, "Are you that hurt?"

Gage laughed, "It's an expression, I'm telling you all the things I haven't been able to tell anyone before. Why is that?"

Mak sat back down, making the springs in the mattress squeal again, "Oh," he said sheepishly before smiling at her, "it's Aboriginal magic."

"You used magic on me?" She was amused.

He nodded, "It's an old art, most people don't even know it exists anymore." He leaned in, and whispered like he was divulging a secret, "They call it compassion, sometimes it's called empathy."

Gage snickered and shook her head, "So, you're a master of it, huh? That explains everything."

He nodded, "I'm something of an expert, I studied a long time with the tribe on my family's land in the Never Never." When she just smiled at him, he continued, "Besides, you're not scared of anything that I've seen. Why should you be scared of talking?" He stood up before she could respond, disappeared into the bathroom, and started the shower.

She closed her eyes and took a deep breath, feeling at peace for the first time in a long time.

"I got the shower running for you," Mak's voice broke into her thoughts, "need help undressing?"

She opened her eyes and arched an eyebrow at him.

He shrugged, "I had to try, didn't I?"

She laughed and stood up, "Will you do me a favor?"

"If I can," he responded.

"I have a backpack in the trunk of the Torino, will you get it for me?"

His eyes narrowed, "You want me to get you some clothes to change into," his tone was accusatory, not questioning.

She nodded, "Is that a problem?"

"I like that dress," he responded with a wink, "it's a beaut."

"You can have it," she laughed as she kicked her high heels off, "though I doubt it will fit you," she winked before walking past him into the bathroom. She was struck by how tall he was when she had no shoes on, she barely reached his shoulder, and she wasn't a short woman. She tried to think back, but she was fairly certain this was the first time she'd ever been near him without heels on her feet.

He shook his head slightly when she closed the door. With an amused smile, he headed out the door to get her bag. He found it easily and headed back into the room, glancing around as he did, checking for anything out of the ordinary. More and more he felt like he wanted to be with Gage, but he recognized that might be more complicated than anticipated. He closed and locked the door behind him and headed to the bathroom door.

He knocked, "I have your bag, are you decent?"

He heard her laughter but she didn't answer his question, so he shrugged and opened the door. "I'm happy to be a dag," he put the bag on the floor just inside the door. The steam swirling in the room was cut by the cool air coming from the small window which Gage must have opened before getting into the shower. Her dress, underclothes, and wig were in a heap below the window.

"Good to know you like it hot," Mak said, then added with a teasing tone, "there appears to be some sort of hairy critter on your clothes. Let me know if you need me to kill it," he poked the shower curtain before leaving the room to let her finish her shower.

Gage jumped when the curtain moved but smiled at how nice he was being to her, she wasn't used to accepting help, especially from strangers. Though she had to admit he was more than a stranger, he was at least an acquaintance and maybe even more, if she was honest with herself.

She stood with her face upturned to the hot water, letting it wash over her and clear her mind for the moment. She stood like that for longer than she intended to, but for the first time in a long time, she actually felt secure. She rubbed at her face and arms to get rid of the dirt and blood. "I really gotta stop meeting you like this," she grumbled to the shower, acknowledging that she'd taken more than one such shower this week.

She cut the water off and dried her hair first before toweling off and then wrapping the towel around her body. She quickly French braided her hair and used the thin hair tie which was always on her wrist to tie off the end of the braid. She tucked the end of her braid underneath her hair against her scalp to hide the length.

She toweled off one more time before tossing the towel over the shower bar to dry. She retrieved her bag and dug inside it at the sink. She set a small makeup bag on the sink before pulling out her yoga pants and sports bra. She dropped the bag on the floor and quickly pulled her clothes on, before unzipping her makeup bag and getting to work on her face.

Mak looked up when the bathroom door opened. He was sitting at the little table with his right boot on his left knee, and the map spread in his lap. He looked her up and down, then quickly looked back down to his papers, "I like the look, but if I'm honest, I'm really not a fan of the butterflies."

She looked at her torso in surprise, "Why not? I think it's pretty." She ran her fingers along the twin butterflies which were masking her scar.

"Not my bowl of rice," he responded sheepishly.

"So much so that you don't even want to look at the rest of me, huh?" she asked. Her eyes widened with realization, "Are you afraid of butterflies?"

"I just don't like them," he responded, carefully keeping his gaze on the paper.

She was watching him, "Do I need to put a shirt on?"

"If you're more comfortable as you are, it's fine, I just won't look that way."

She laughed at him until her face was flushed then gasped, "I can't believe you're afraid of a pretty, fluttering insect!"

He glowered at her, making sure to look only at her face, his frustration compounding when he took note that she'd reapplied makeup to mask her face, "They are vile, disgusting, creatures."

"They're pretty," she answered, a smile still twisting her lips.

"They start as caterpillars, right? Ravaging crops, and being general assholes," Mak stated, clearly about to lay out his case. "Then each little asshole creates a cocoon, and proceeds to eat itself until all that remains is a tiny pile of goo." He was passionate about this argument, he put the map on the table and dropped his foot to the floor, leaning forward,

"Then that goo rearranges itself into the shit and corpse eating bastards they come to be."

She was stunned, staring at him.

"That's right, your pretty fluttering insects slurp up flower nectar, sure, but they also like sloshing around in shit, decaying bodies and rotten fruit. Sounds like vile harbingers of death to me."

She was silent, her face frozen in a bemused expression.

"Just don't expect me to love the tattoo," he muttered, trying to save face, he looked down at his map again but wasn't really seeing it.

She considered letting him stew in embarrassment for being afraid of a harmless insect, but instead, she found herself speaking, "Earlier, you said I wasn't scared of anything, but that's ridiculously inaccurate."

He looked up at her, relieved, "How's that?"

"I'm afraid of pretty much everything," she answered, going back into the bathroom and coming out with a tank top on. She tossed her backpack on the floor by Mak's chair. "I'm afraid of enclosed spaces, but I also don't like wide open spaces either. And I only feel safe in a small dark place, but it has to have the door open." She shrugged, "I don't like crowds, but I hate being completely alone. I'm terrified of losing control, but I don't really like being in charge. I constantly worry about being inadequate and losing the people I love due to my own weakness, but I also worry that if I put in too much work, I'll be over prepared and end up letting people get hurt due to my overly exaggerated ego." She stopped talking when she realized that she was babbling and he was staring at her.

"Well that's-" Mak started but was quickly interrupted.

"Weird? Crazy? Completely counter-intuitive?" She supplied, "I know."

"I was going to say interesting," Mak responded, "and a hell of a lot more normal than hating butterflies." He smiled at her and she couldn't help but return it. "On a completely unrelated subject," he paused and cocked his head slightly, "or maybe a completely related subject," he met her eyes, "I find it interesting that you have to make yourself up, every second of the day."

She looked away from him and sat on the bed, suddenly exhausted, "Habit."

"I'd like to meet the real you someday," he watched her, "I think we could get along great."

She smiled sadly and responded, "I wouldn't be so sure," as she lay back against the pillow, "the real me is a mess."

"I don't believe that for a second," he answered and walked into the bathroom. She heard water running for a few moments. He came back with a wet hand towel which he was folding as he walked. "Here," he shook his head when she started to sit up, "just lay back, let me do this for you."

She lay back slowly, eyeing him cautiously.

"Don't give me that look," he admonished as he gently lay the hot compress on her tender throat.

She winced and closed her eyes as the heat began to seep into the ache of her bruise.

"Is it too hot?" He asked softly.

She shook her head slightly but kept her eyes closed.

"Good, let it work, just stay still."

She nodded gently, "Thank you." The sound of her voice was so quiet, he almost didn't hear her.

"Rest now," he said, "you're safe here."

She felt her lips tease into a smile, as she drifted off to sleep, because for once, she actually felt those words were true.

Chapter 27

"It wasn't very polite of you to reject our good customer's offer of friendship, Bridget," Alex's gaze was frigid. "I don't know if I can forgive you for losing that business."

She was huddled in the corner of the room, weak and crying into her knees. Trying to cower beside the filthy mattress on the floor which was the only furniture. Her stringy hair hung in her face when she looked up at him, "He touched me," she whimpered, "I can't do this anymore."

"Can't do what?" His voice was as cold as his eyes, "What you're paid to do? Do I need to find someone else? I can think of ten girls who would love to be my girl. Ten girls who would give anything to be taken care of by such a giving benefactor."

Her eyes were on the floor as she trembled in fear of what was going to come, "I'm so sorry. I just don't want to be touched by anyone," after a split second she added, "but you."

"You love me so much you only want me to touch you?"

She nodded hurriedly, hoping that would save her from his wrath.

"I don't mind sharing you," he stated meanly, "in fact, I prefer to share you. It makes me appreciate all that you're willing to do for me."

Hot tears spilled down her cheeks again and she felt a pit twist in her stomach.

"What do you think about that?" He asked her.

She remained silent with her head bowed in supplication.

"Unless you don't actually care what I want," he crouched in front of her, inches from her, "is that what you're really saying?" He pushed her hair back behind her ear then gripped the nape of her neck roughly, forcing her bloodshot eyes to meet his gaze, "Are you becoming selfish, Bridget?"

She shook her head as best she could, her eyes pleading pitifully, "No, please. I was just startled. I didn't mean to hit him."

"So, you will party with our friend?" He asked.

Her lower lip quivered.

"I'll give you what you need to relax," he added, holding up a loaded syringe, *"I made this myself, just for you. It's a special mix."* He brought it toward her and she averted her eyes because she couldn't move from the grip he had on her, disgusted with the swell of excitement she felt. He laughed meanly, *"You don't want it?"*

"Please," she whimpered, trembling, *"please don't do this. I don't want this anymore. I want to go home."*

"Home?" He laughed harshly again and used his grip on her neck to throw her back against the wall in disgust, *"This is your home, Bridget."* He stood and put the syringe on the cardboard box which served as a bedside table, *"Which foster home do you want to go back to? I'm sure I could arrange to pick up that girl at your last house. You two could trade places. She'll come stay with me, and you can go home,"* he sneered as he stood up. *"How old is she now? Eleven?"*

"No," she whimpered, *"that's not what I meant."*

"Not what you meant?" He asked, *"So you don't want to leave?"*

"No, I'll stay," she whispered, staring at her shaking hands.

"If you want to stay, you have to regain my trust," he responded.

"I'll do whatever it takes," she answered, her tears forgotten. Her emotion was replaced by a dull coldness which spread through her whole body, deadening her senses.

"You have two choices," he answered, *"I can give you this delicious shot I made just for you, and you can give our good customer the best time he's ever had, or I can punish you for your indiscretion."*

She cringed, then looked up at him, *"Punish me. I'm not being your whore anymore."*

He smiled at her meanly, *"Get on the bed."*

She climbed up onto the scratchy sheets of the mattress and lay on her back.

Alex tied her wrists to the top of the bed with fabric which ran beneath the mattress and attached to her ankles at the bottom, then he pulled out his pocket knife and unfolded it. *"I'm going to teach you a lesson. If you scream, you'll be punished longer."* He ran the sharpened blade down her arm, slowly slicing shallow lines into her flesh. She whimpered but made no other sound as she stared up at the peeling paint of the ceiling.

Alex began to slice her skin again, then leaned over her so he could whisper in her ear, "Oh, and when I'm done with your punishment, I'm going to shove that needle into your vein until you're flying high," he pulled back slightly so he could smile at her terrified expression. "Then, I'm going to bring my customer in here and let him do whatever he wants to you."

She struggled against the restraints, but she was so weak, and every time she moved her hand, it pulled on her foot, it was no use. Alex laughed at her attempt and growled, "Because his business means a hell of a lot more to me than some strung out bitch who thinks she's allowed to make decisions."

He brought the knife to her collarbone and when she struggled, the blade bit into her flesh. She screamed and fought her restraints desperately.

Gage sat up with a cry and grabbed her left collarbone, covering the pale scar that twisted along the bone, as bleary jade eyes swept the room in confusion. Mak was already by her side but was hesitant to touch her, especially when she shied away from his presence.

"Whoa! She'll be apples, it's just me, you're safe. It was a dream," he had his hands out toward her, trying to calm her, "you're safe now. There's no one here to hurt you."

She trembled, her breath coming in short puffs as she stared up at him with watery eyes for a moment, before reaching for him like a child for her teddy bear.

He sat down on the edge of the bed, and she threw herself into his arms, holding him tightly with her eyes squeezed shut and her face pressed into his chest.

He pulled her into his lap, shushed her and stroked her hair gently, holding her to his chest and swearing silently to the universe that he'd find the source of her nightmares and kill him, if she'd let him.

When Gage woke up again, she realized she had been sleeping on Mak's chest. She blinked several times to clear her vision and looked up at his handsome face as he slept awkwardly sitting on the bed with his back to the wall and one leg sprawled out on the bed, his other was bent at the knee hanging off the bed.

When she pulled away from him, his arm, which had been wrapped protectively around her, fell to the bed, startling him awake. He jerked into an upright seated position and snatched his Glock 19 from the nightstand beside him. When he realized it was just her moving, he blinked hard a few times and put the handgun back on the bedside table, clearing his throat. "What's wrong?" His voice was raspy with sleep, "You okay?"

She nodded and did her best to ignore the heat in her cheeks, "Sorry about last night, I don't know what that was all about."

He arched an eyebrow at her, "Really? You don't know why you had a nightmare after you were violently attacked in a dark alley?"

She shrugged, "I've been under a lot of stress lately, must have been my imagination kicking in. No need to look at me like that. I'm fine."

"I know about nightmares," Mak said softly, "you don't have to gloss over what you're going through," he swallowed and stared at her intently, "not with me."

"Oh yeah?" She scoffed and tried to ignore the impact his words had on her, "What nightmares do you deal with?"

He shrugged, "I've seen a lot of violence in my life," he cleared his throat, "but generally, my nightmares are about my dad."

Gage almost laughed, but stopped herself, "So we both have daddy issues. A match made in Heaven."

"You have a bad relationship?" Mak asked.

"He chose to go die instead of raising me. Not that he was raising me well," Gage responded humorlessly, "it's a sore spot."

"I'm sorry you lost him," Mak's tone was gentle, "thank you for telling me."

"Such is life," Gage shrugged. She didn't like being vulnerable, so she asked, "What about your dad?"

"What about him?" Mak looked down at his hands, "He's still alive if that's what you mean."

"Why do you have nightmares about him?" Gage asked, honestly curious.

"He was always a rather absent dad," Mak started. "The way he tells it, he was on a drive for two years or so and when he came home, Mum had two babies."

"Are you twins?" Gage asked, shocked.

Mak shrugged, "We don't rightly know. Dad never knew which of us was older but he reckoned we were different ages."

"What does your mother say?" Gage was perplexed.

"Mum hasn't spoken in years," Mak said quietly. "Doctors don't know why, there's no physical reason, she just doesn't speak. Happened right around the same time as Dad coming back, he says it's her guilt, choking her. She told him our names, then just stopped talking."

"Can she write?" Gage was invested in the story now.

Mak shook his head, "She had no reason to be educated. She came from a poor family and was given to my dad at a young age. All she ever wanted, was to be able to read. I tried to teach her, but Dad reckoned it was better she wasn't educated." He hadn't looked up from his hands. When Gage looked closer, she realized they were cross-hatched with thin scars.

"So, you truly have no idea who's older?" She tried to ignore the swell of enraged empathy she felt in her gut at the sight of his scars. "One of you must be someone else's kid if you were different ages, right?" Gage realized what she said and back-pedaled, "I'm not saying anything bad about your mother."

Mak smiled slightly, "Part of me really hopes she fell in love and had a wild fling, it would serve Dad right." He shrugged, "But to be honest, I don't know if he'd recognize the age of a child correctly to save his life."

"You think you're twins?" Gage asked.

Mak cocked his head a bit, "All my memories have Buck in them. I reckon he could be my older brother, but let's be honest, I'm the responsible one."

Gage laughed, "That's true, it would be hard to imagine Buck as your older brother."

Mak nodded, "I doubt we'll ever really know for certain."

"Wait," Gage suddenly realized what his story meant, "you don't know your birthday?"

Mak shook his head, "Never had a reason to, the only one who would have known was Mum, and she couldn't write it or tell us."

"How old are you?" Gage asked.

Mak made a face, "I don't know exactly how old, but we reckon we've got to be around thirty, give or take a couple years."

"You and Buck sat down and figured it out?" Gage's disbelief was apparent.

"Tried to," Mak responded, "people always ask you how old you are, it's pretty hard not knowing. Especially in school, and when we signed on for service."

"Wow, that's crazy," she swallowed, "I'm sorry, that must have been rough. I can't imagine how you can talk so openly about it."

"That's what it's like, being real with someone," he stared at her for a moment before saying quietly, "if you ever feel like trying it more fully, I'll be the first in line."

She paused, shocked, then cleared her throat and grumbled, "Thanks for your help, but I should probably get going. Mere will be worried."

"I responded to her text last night. I told her you were staying with a mate," he said as she stood from the bed and moved to her backpack.

"You did what?" Gage whirled to face him.

"She was messaging a lot. I know you're close, I didn't want you to feel bad when she worried," he responded. "I've seen you put in your code before, sorry if I over-stepped my boundaries."

She stared at him and wondered why she wasn't furious that he had gone through her phone. Or why she felt like she could stay in the small motel room with him all day and be just fine. Or why she had slept the best she had in months awkwardly cradled to his muscular chest.

"Gage?" His eyes were questioning.

"It's fine." She snapped quickly, coming back to reality. "I need to go anyway."

"Or you could stay," he responded with a cheeky smirk, watching her rush around the room, collecting her belongings and shoving them into her backpack, "we can talk some more."

"We've talked plenty," she grabbed her leather jacket and set it on the bed before sitting down on the squeaking mattress to pull on the socks and tennis shoes from her bag.

Mak stood up and stretched in front of her, his shirt riding up slightly when his arms were above his head. The flash of tummy wasn't the chiseled six pack she was used to seeing on the men in her life, but his innate masculinity affected her in ways she hadn't felt in a long time.

She cleared her throat and quickly tied her tennis shoes, trying to ignore him when he pulled his shirt off to replace it with a clean one. His muscular chest and arms were clearly the result of functional exercise, not a life in the gym. She noticed several scars on his torso which drew her gaze, the musculature kept her attention as he bent to grab a shirt from his duffle. When he glanced at her, she felt her cheeks heat up and she quickly pretended she wasn't looking at his physique. She was surprised by her body's response because she was used to lanky playboys who sat at the gym doing sit ups at all hours of the day.

"I don't know why you suddenly pull back whenever you feel like you might actually like me." Mak sighed sadly as he pulled on his shirt, walked back to the table and sat down, oblivious to the blush creeping across her cheeks.

Gage didn't answer as she grabbed her backpack and entered the bathroom to fix her make up. She closed the door loudly behind her.

Mak stared at the door forlornly, wondering if his efforts were for naught. He cracked his neck and remembered how good it felt to hold her. "One of these days I'll break the walls," he muttered, his lips pulling up on one side in a half-smile.

"What was that?" Gage asked as she breezed back into the room.

Mak had looked down when the door opened, "Just talking to myself," he responded.

"Do you make a habit of that?" She smirked.

"Sometimes you have to talk to yourself to find polite conversation."

She rolled her eyes but said nothing. She didn't like the effect he had on her. She couldn't afford to feel comfortable when the danger of her past was so close. She didn't like how he made her open up. She picked up her jacket and put it on then turned to look at him, wondering what she should say.

"One of these days, you're going to be too tired of the façade, and you're gonna wanna be real," he stated it like it was a fact. "When that day comes, just promise me you'll look me up," he looked up at her, his blue eyes were a little sad. "I'll be there for you, no matter where I am."

She sighed and pretty much ignored the statement as she searched the pockets of her jacket. "I must have dropped my phone somewhere. Can you call it for me?"

Mak tried not to let his heart sink at her dismissal and picked up his cellphone from the table in front of him, punching in her number.

"You know my number by heart?" Gage asked him, both amused and oddly touched.

"I don't know about my heart, but yes, I remember your number," he responded.

The loud music of her ringtone filled the room.

Do you come from a land down under?

The song was unmistakable and Gage smiled brightly, "Oh look, here it is," she held up her phone, which had been in her pocket all along. The song continued and she sang along, dancing slightly.

"My ringtone is Men at Work?" Mak was amused, he was trying to feign insult, but even more so he was trying to not sing along.

"Yup," Gage tossed him her phone and he saw that he was listed as Dundee on the screen.

He actually laughed and glanced at her, "Is this meant as an insult?"

She stared at him coyly, carefully masking her emotion, she shrugged slightly.

"Paul Hogan is a national treasure," he stated, "and this is one of my favorite songs. All you're doing is solidifying my affections." He tossed her the phone back and grinned at her, "But by all means, keep fighting your feelings. It's rather amusing for me."

Gage rolled her eyes and slid her phone into her backpack's side pocket as she slung the bag over her shoulder, "What feelings am I fighting?"

"You're clearly trying to distance yourself emotionally by being rather stereotypical," Mak responded, pulling his own backpack onto the table and opening it. "Vegemite?" He pulled a jar from the bag.

Gage burst out laughing, "Are you kidding me? You actually have that in your bag?"

"Well yeah," he looked at the jar then grinned at her, "it's the brekkie of champions and hard to come by over here. So, we pack our own."

"Why doesn't that surprise me?" Gage sighed, "You're ridiculous."

Mak shrugged and pulled some crackers from his bag before leaning back in the chair, "Ridiculously prepared for a bonzer start to my day," he responded with a self-satisfied smile as he began to dip his crackers in the vegemite and eat them. "Obviously this manner of eating it isn't ideal. Some nice toast, a scrape of butter, and then this delicious nutrition right on top is the best way to eat it." He held up the cracker, "But this is much better than a dingo's breakfast."

Gage was bemused, staring at him.

He stared back at her, chewing thoughtfully on his cracker. He swallowed and stood up, "By the way, if you were ever curious about my dancing skills, watch that music video," he motioned in the direction of her phone, "the little bloke in the front taught me everything I know."

She smirked at the thought of Mak dancing in the playfully awkward manner of the music video, but she didn't want him to know that some nights she watched it on repeat, "You can't be serious."

He shrugged, then the operator pumped his long legs and muscular arms as though he was climbing a ladder in place. He stopped after a split moment, but she recognized the dance from the man he'd been referencing in the music video for *Down Under*.

Her hysterical laughter caught her off guard, but the sheer joy she felt couldn't be contained, "You really have no problem making a complete fool of yourself, do you?"

He ate another cracker and packed up the rest of his breakfast so he could return it to his backpack. When he'd finished chewing, he grinned at her and winked. "Made you laugh didn't it?"

She nodded, "I think the only thing that could make it better, is if you were in tactical gear with a rifle."

"Oh, that can be arranged," he smirked, "no worries."

"I have to see that," she answered.

"If you really want to see something," Mak looked over at her with a serious expression, "you should see Buck playing the flute solo, it's a thing of beauty."

"Oh my God, you have to be kidding me," she was envisioning the large bearded man with a flute, and it made her grin broadly.

"Not at all," Mak shook his head, "we did the music video for the talent show with a couple of mates when we were young."

Gage laughed, "I can't believe I never put together that you two are brothers. That show must have been amazing," she shook her head, "come on, I'll take you back to the club to get your car."

He nodded, "My motorbike," he corrected, then added, "hopefully it didn't get towed," as he preceded her from the room.

Gage felt warmth in her stomach at the thought of him riding a motorcycle. He looked good in his jeans and tight leather jacket which was obviously his riding jacket.

"Stop perving," he commented with a wink over his shoulder before playfully dropping his keys on the floor, "oh no! I can't believe that just happened," he bent over in front of her.

She actually blushed, then laughed about blushing.

"Stop looking at my ass," he stated without even looking at her as he stood back up.

"Just go to the car, you dork," she laughed as he sashayed his hips while walking.

Chapter 28

"Did you sleep with the guy at the bar?" Mere didn't even greet Gage when she entered the sliding door by the pool. The redhead stood in the middle of the kitchen with her arms crossed and her head cocked.

"Hello to you, too." Gage made a face, "Yes and no, I guess."

"What does that even mean?" Mere's hands moved to her hips. "I texted you when I got home and you weren't here. I got back, 'I'm staying with a mate'." Mere cocked her head, "A MATE? What the fuck is that, Gage?"

"I assume it's a friend," Gage responded, before clarifying, "the guy at the bar was Mak, one of the Australian gun-runners we use."

"I kind of figured he was one of them when you used the accent to describe him," Mere answered, her tone still rather harsh, "are you sleeping with him? Why wouldn't you just tell me about him?"

"I didn't have sex with him, Meredith," Gage sighed, "I just slept in his bed is all."

"So, he's the one you've been randomly making out with?"

Gage arched an eyebrow, "I'm not running off to make out with him like a love-sick teenager if that's what you're getting at. I kissed him once after my fight to use him as a cover and happened to like it. That's all. I have not kissed him again, nor will I."

"You like him," Mere's tone was accusing, her gaze was hurt.

Gage wasn't sure how to respond, she was getting angry about the aggressive questioning, but also sensed the under-lying hurt feelings in Mere's demeanor. "I don't know how I feel about him," she answered finally. "I think he's hot, and he's an amazing kisser. But he's also an asset to PREY, I wouldn't want to risk that with a fling."

Mere seemed to be wrestling with something internally.

"What?" Gage snapped, then sighed and continued with a friendlier tone, "Sorry. What's up? Spit it out."

"After you left, Alex came by the table," Mere said after a moment.

Gage stiffened and turned to walk to her bedroom.

"Gage wait," Mere followed her. "He said he bought the club because he heard you loved it. He said he was keeping it the same, and he wanted us to know we were welcome to keep using our table, he seemed really sincere. He just wants-"

"That's great," Gage cut her off. When she reached her doorway, she turned to face Mere, "Is there anything else?"

Mere stared at her friend's hurt expression, "I'm just really confused at this point," she responded softly. "I'm supposed to be on edge around this guy, but you won't tell me why, and he seems really nice."

"I guess I thought maybe you'd understand that some subjects are hard to talk about," Gage stated. "I figured you'd have my back without needing explanations."

"That's not fair," Mere frowned.

"You're right," Gage nodded, "it isn't fair."

The two women stood staring at each other for a moment.

"I'm going to take a shower and get to work downstairs, I've wasted enough time lately," Gage took a step back into her room.

Mere cleared her throat and changed the subject, "Will finished up Enzo's car."

"Fantastic," Gage answered, "did Tessa find time for the artwork?"

"She said she could send sketches tonight," Mere answered.

"Will you please call him and let him know? See if he wants the car now or if he would like to wait for Tessa."

Mere nodded, "I'll take care of it."

"Thank you," Gage responded and closed her door. The second the door was closed, she turned and leaned her back on the wood. She let out the gasp of emotion she'd been hiding from the moment Mere had mentioned Alex. Tears welled in her eyes but didn't fall as her hand found her sore throat and she slid down the door until she was sitting on the floor. She wrapped her arms around her legs and let her forehead rest on her knees.

Gage heard Mere say, "You take care of you," softly before the younger woman strode away from the door.

Mere was confused by Gage's stand-offish nature the last few weeks. It was not like her to keep secrets. At least Mere didn't think Gage usually kept secrets, but she was beginning to question everything now.

Mere pulled her phone from her pocket and searched her contacts before making a call.

Hey Mere, Lina's voice was as chipper as always.

"Do a full search on Alex Santiago," Mere said, "EmEm has his ID if you need anything off it. There has to be something we don't know about this guy."

Okay, sure. I'll do it now. Catch you later with what I find out.

"Thanks, Lina, I appreciate you." Mere hung up her phone and headed down the interior stairs to the garage. She went into Gage's office and sat in the leather desk chair for a moment before setting her cell phone on the desk in front of her. She scrolled through her contacts again and selected one as she pulled the file on Enzo's car from the pile on the desk.

Chapter 29

Gage spent her day working in the garage.

It was dark outside when Will stood awkwardly near the trunk of her current project car, trying to decide how to speak to her.

"If you have something to say, just say it," Gage's voice floated from under the hood where she was currently working.

"You've been here for at least ten hours with no rest or food, Boss," he said finally as he strode to her side.

"Astute observation," Gage responded without stopping what she was doing, "you've been working on your detective skills."

Will sighed, "Seriously Gage, what's going on?"

Gage paused for a moment before resuming her work, "I don't know what you mean."

Will stared at her until she glanced up at him. Her eyes were sunken and there was grease all over her face. "You should pack it in for the day, Boss," he said finally.

She arched an eyebrow at him, "I'm sorry, I missed the memo where suddenly you're in charge of the shop hours."

Will blinked his eyes slowly.

"Don't you blink at me," she glared at him, "remember the dynamic we had before, back when you were scared of me? When you reported for work promptly and never spoke?" She turned from him, wiping her hands on a rag, "Let's go back to that."

Will stared at her back, trying not to take her attitude personally. "Oh, you mean back right after my dad died and you brought me into this life to give me meaning?"

Gage stopped walking and sighed, looking at her feet for a moment. She turned back to him and took in his appearance. He looked exhausted, his normally well-kept top knot was loose, pieces of hair framed his face. "Why are you projecting?" She asked, motioning to his appearance, "You're obviously not sleeping. Trouble in paradise?"

Will hadn't moved, "Everything is fine with Lina, but everyone is freaking out about your weird behavior. It takes a toll."

Gage rolled her eyes, "Why is my personal life such an interest, all of the sudden?"

"Since you're displaying disruptive behaviors which endanger you, and you lash out at everyone who loves you," Will responded.

"You'd know something about that," she snapped. She immediately regretted the words, especially when she saw the pain in his eyes.

"You're right," he said when she was silent, "I know what it's like to be drowning in bullshit. I know what it's like to wish everything would just end." He walked toward her slowly, like he was afraid she'd bolt if he came at her too quickly, "I know what it's like to throw yourself into anything so you don't have to think about what's really wrong."

She was breathing hard when he came to a stop in front of her.

"So, what's really wrong?" He asked softly. "You were there for me when I needed someone," he reached out and took the rag from her, "so let me be there for you now. What's going on?"

She stared at him, trying to arrange her thoughts, she wasn't sure what to do. Her hands tightened into fists then unclenched, he'd taken the rag she'd been using to distract herself from fidgeting. A part of her wanted to explain everything, but instead of pouring out her soul, she said, "I don't know why y'all are so convinced something is wrong." She forced a smile, "I like to work. I like to swim. I have bad dreams sometimes." She shrugged, the motion caused the high collar of her shirt to fall slightly, some of the make-up she'd used on her neck had rubbed off on the shirt, revealing her bruise.

She saw his eyes widen and immediately tugged her shirt collar up while turning to walk away.

Will grabbed her arm and pulled her back, he blocked her hand when it came at him to block his view and pulled her shirt back so he could see her throat. "Who did this?"

She shrugged, "I didn't know you liked it rough, Will," she yanked her arm back and fixed her collar again.

"Bridget, your neck is bruised, what the fuck is going on?" His tone was harsh, "Stop playing games and tell me the fucking truth. Now."

Gage licked her lips to give herself a moment to think, then spoke with her voice carefully neutral, "To be honest, it doesn't concern you." She raised her chin slightly and doubled down on her statement, "I don't know why everyone thinks it's cool to butt into my life, but I'm fine. I don't need rescuing. Everything is just fine."

"Bull shit," he snapped, his eyes flashing, "tell me who did that to you."

A small half-smile teased her lips, "A ghost," she responded before turning from him and walking away, "maybe you're right about one thing. I'm done working for the night. See you tomorrow, Will."

Will sighed and shook his head as he watched her leave. After she'd climbed the stairs and entered her flat, he pulled his phone from his pocket and called Mere. "You're right. Something is definitely up."

I'm bringing dinner to your place in twenty. Be there. Mere hung up immediately, leaving him holding his phone awkwardly to his ear as he tried to comprehend Gage's actions.

Chapter 30

"Alex Santiago is a boy scout," Lina stated as she typed on her laptop. She was sitting at the small kitchen table of her apartment, across from Will, and next to Mere.

"He's clean?" Will asked, his hair was still in disarray, wisps tickling his exhausted face.

"Well, yes, squeaky clean," Lina answered, looking up at her boyfriend, "but I also mean, he's a literal boy scout." She turned her laptop around to show a picture of Alex in the midst of building a playground with several children watching. "His Eagle Scout project was to build a playground for orphans." She looked at Mere, "He apparently volunteered with the foster system in Texas for years, as a mentor for the kids." She tapped on her screen and a new picture popped up of Alex with two kids on his lap, "He helped institute a Big Brothers branch in his hometown to help troubled kids." Lina clicked onto another picture of Alex holding a puppy outside an animal shelter, "He is a saver of lost kids and puppies alike." Lina motioned to the screen, "I can't find anything bad. He donates large sums of money to charity every year, including a charity he created, and runs, to help kids in foster care find places they feel like they belong."

"So, he's basically the perfect guy for Gage," Mere stated, "all the projects close to his heart, are her pet-projects."

Lina nodded, "I have truly exhausted all my avenues, all my contacts come back with the same information." She motioned to the laptop, "He seems to be a stand-up guy, with a huge heart."

"Why is she running from him then?" Will asked. "She's freaking out. And someone bruised her throat. I know what I saw."

Mere sat in silence with a furrowed brow.

"What?" Will asked her.

"Last night Gage rushed out of Craze, right?" Mere sat up straighter in her seat, "She was gone all night."

"Alex came by the table with a black eye," Will added then made a face and added, "I wonder where he got that."

"Gage spent the night with the guy from the bar, the Australian," Mere leaned forward, putting her hands on the table, "I would wager a bet that he had something to do with Alex's face."

"You think he hurt Gage?" Lina looked from Mere to Will, "Could anyone do that to her without her letting them?"

"I don't know," Mere shrugged, "he's a big guy."

"She is more than capable of protecting herself," Will responded. "He'd have to surprise her to get hands on her at all, let alone with enough force to bruise her like that."

"I think we should talk to Alex," Lina said slowly.

"I don't know why that feels like a betrayal," Will sighed and put his head on the table.

"If she won't tell us why she's being so weird, we have a duty to figure it out," Mere snapped at him, standing up.

"We won't tell him anything about her," Lina supplied reassuringly, "we'll just try to figure out what's going on. He's clearly the key to everything that's happening."

"This is a terrible idea," Will insisted.

"I don't need your permission," Mere stated as she walked toward the door, "I'm going to text him. He gave me his number last night. We have a right to know what's got Gage so spun."

"Maybe we should go to Whit," Will sat back up, "he knows what she went through in Texas, doesn't he?"

Mere stopped walking and whirled back to face him, "So talking to the puppy-hugging boy scout is a betrayal, but going to our boss, that's cool?"

Will sighed, "Whitlock is family, he's not an outsider."

Mere rolled her eyes, "You battle with your uncertainty-demons, I'll be figuring out what's wrong with our friend." She slammed out the door before anyone could respond.

Will sighed heavily and once more put his head on the table, "Why does life always have to get complicated, just when everything was so good?"

Lina moved to stand behind him and gently pulled him upright in the seat so she could rub his shoulders, "The universe will always throw curveballs, mi amor."

Will groaned and leaned his head back against her middle and looked up at her, "I just want to lay in bed with you for the next few days."

She smiled down at him and kissed his forehead, "First, you need a hot shower. Stinky." She laughed and pulled away from him, heading to the bathroom.

Will smiled and shook his head, before following her.

Chapter 31

The next evening EmEm walked into the gym area of PREY and found Gage pummeling the punching bag so viciously that her knuckles were bleeding.

He approached her slowly, watching as she poured every ounce of power into her onslaught. He knew she was aware that he'd entered the room, but she was completely focused on the flurry of strikes she was inflicting.

He paused and watched as she switched up her attack, adding knees and kicking as she continued to punch the bag.

"Shut up," she snapped breathlessly.

"What?" EmEm looked around in confusion.

"You're about to preach equipment integrity and proper usage," she huffed, never stopping her motions. Sweat soaked her tank top, the bright purple and black bruise on her neck was highly visible in contrast to the pale skin there.

"I mean, maybe NOT ripping up your hands or bleeding all over my equipment would be a good thing," he responded, purposely keeping his eyes on her face.

She stopped punching abruptly, facing him with her hands at her side, blood slowly dripping down her fingers, "You wanna fight."

"What?" He stared at her.

She strode toward him, her face an unreadable mask, "Do. You. Want. To. Fight?"

"No," EmEm took a step back involuntarily.

"Why not?" She snapped, motioning with her hands, "Everyone else wants to fight."

"Maybe you should take a break," EmEm said, his eyes wide and his hands up defensively.

"Why does everyone think I need a break?" she growled.

"You're scaring me, Gage," EmEm said quietly.

"What?" She took a step back, her hands hanging by her sides in defeat.

"You're scaring the shit out of me right now," he responded, "we're all scared. We don't understand what's happening. It scares us."

Gage seemed to suddenly notice the sting from her hands, she looked down at her bloody knuckles, then looked at the punching bag. "I better clean this up," she said finally. Turning from him and walking toward the towels on the far wall.

"I'll get this," EmEm followed her, "why don't you go hit the shower."

Gage glanced over her shoulder at him, "I can clean up after myself."

"You're right," EmEm tentatively reached out and touched her shoulder, "but just because you *can* do something alone, doesn't mean you have to."

Gage sighed, turned, and looked up to meet his gaze, "Thank you. I'm sorry for being so aggressive. I've had a weird few weeks."

"Understatement much?" EmEm smiled and pulled her to his chest in a tight hug.

She tensed initially in the embrace, but relaxed slightly and hugged him back before pushing away and motioning to the punching bag, "Are you sure?"

EmEm nodded, "Go take care of your hands." He motioned to the locker room, "Let me know if you need anything."

She looked down at her hands again and sighed, "Yeah, okay."

Her phone chirped as she was walking and she responded to a text with stiff fingers.

"Everything good?" EmEm asked, watching her walk.

"Yeah, a friend found out information on Whitlock's case," she turned back around and headed to the front of the office, "I'll be back."

EmEm watched her leave, trying to mask the concern on his face.

Gage strode to the front office, carefully closing the heavy door separating the lobby area from the remainder of the building. She listened for the mechanical click and glanced at the keypad, making sure the red light was steady at the top, before she moved into the lobby and sat in Tessa's seat, behind the reception desk. She stared at the elevator with her hands on the desk in front of her.

She wasn't sure how long she sat like that, but her hands were starting to get even stiffer as the blood dried and cracked. She made fists then worked her fingers, watching the flakes of dried blood float through the air.

The elevator doors finally opened and Mak stepped into the lobby. He was holding a thick manila envelope in one hand, and his motorcycle helmet in the other. Her gaze went from her hands to his face, and she immediately regretted it.

"What happened?" His voice was harsh and his blue eyes were a mixture of rage and concern.

She shrugged, "I got mad at the punching bag," she stated as she stood. "You have information for me?"

He stared at her for a moment, gauging her response, before holding out the envelope, "I think I found the gun your shooter used. Buyer information is in here, but there's no guarantee he wasn't just a middleman."

She walked around the desk and grabbed the offering, but he didn't let it go, "What?" she asked in annoyance.

"This is a bad guy," he said quietly, "I don't know if he's the shooter, but regardless, it's a place to start."

She nodded, "Okay."

"It's a dangerous place to start, sheila," he stressed, still not letting go of the information.

Gage pulled it from his grip, "My name's not Sheila," she smiled at him sweetly, "and dangerous is kind of my thing."

"Yeah," he was looking at her neck, "I got that pretty clearly."

She cleared her throat and suddenly felt self-conscious.

"By the by, Buck expects his drink once that checks out," Mak grinned at her.

"What about you?" Gage asked distractedly, "You don't want drinks with my girls?"

"I'd prefer dinner with you," he responded.

She stared at him for a moment, at a loss for words, then stammered, "Like, a date?"

He arched an eyebrow with a small smile, "I don't think that means to me what it means to you, but if you're offering, I wouldn't turn it down."

"Huh?" She cocked her head.

Mak stepped close to her, the smell of his cologne mixed with his masculine stature made warmth spread through her insides, "I wouldn't mind takin' your date, but I reckon I'd like to feed you first. I can get dressed up, you could wear that dress, we could go to a nice dinner like a normal couple."

She cleared her throat and stepped back, not sure what kind of witchcraft he was using that made her want to climb him. "But we're not a couple," she was breathing harder than she'd care to admit, "normal or otherwise."

He shrugged, "It's just dinner. What's the worst that could happen?"

She arched an eyebrow at him, "I'm fairly certain your idea of a nice dinner involves a spit and open fire."

He laughed, "Too right, but I think I could surprise you."

She chewed her bottom lip thoughtfully, "I don't have that dress here."

He shrugged, "So wear something else, I'm not picky." He motioned to her, "Maybe clean those hands, and wash out that dye," he motioned to her dark hair, "I'm fairly certain you're more a blonde bombshell than brunette."

She arched an eyebrow at him, "Actually, I'm a dirty blonde."

He laughed, then grumbled huskily, "I reckon I should have known that."

Gage felt heat on her cheeks, and cleared her throat, "Be back in thirty minutes. You can take me wherever you want."

"Wherever I want?" Mak asked, his meaning clear.

Gage shook her head, "Sorry bud, I'm not easy. You have to woo me."

"Woo you?" Mak asked, "That sounds made up."

Gage smiled, "Dinner."

He nodded, "See you in thirty."

Chapter 32

Mere strode into the expensive restaurant feeling extremely underdressed in her capris leggings and sundress. She scanned the patrons, ignoring the nasty looks she was receiving, until her gaze settled on Alex. He was sitting at a small table, clearly meant for two, sipping a glass of wine as he looked over his menu.

He stood as she approached the table, "Ah, Meredith, welcome. Please, have a seat." He motioned to the chair opposite him so she slid into it, her green gaze carefully watching him.

"I just have a few questions," she said finally.

"I assumed you wouldn't mind eating while we chatted," he smiled warmly, "I haven't eaten all day." He motioned to the bread and cheese platter, "Please, help yourself. It's my treat."

She glanced at the food momentarily before once more locking her eyes on his face, "This is going to sound weird, but what happened between you and Bridget in Texas?"

He seemed genuinely surprised, "I was actually hoping she could answer that question for me." His chocolate colored eyes grew sad, "I was in love with her," he smiled a little, "I think I still am. I've never met a woman like her before." He looked down at his hand which was gripping his knife from his place setting, "She was so beautiful and kind. She helped me with all my various projects and seemed to really enjoy life with me." He shrugged and looked up at Mere, "I was pushing her too hard, I think. She told me she didn't like who she was with me and disappeared." His eyes were hurt, "I thought we were good together, but she assaulted one of our friends before she disappeared. It took me this long to find her. I've been looking since she left."

Mere stayed silent as he spoke, carefully watching him. "So, she just went bonkers and ran away one day?"

"I understand the disbelief," he acknowledged her tone, "it sounds crazy to me now that I'm saying it out loud." He sighed, "But if you know Bridget as well as I think you do, then you know she tends to sabotage her own happiness."

Mere's eyes narrowed slightly, "You think she ran because she fell in love with you."

It wasn't a question so he just shrugged and stared at the redhead.

"What happened to your eye?" Mere could see the bruise, even though someone had clearly tried to cover it with make-up.

"I'm surprised Bridget hasn't told you," he looked down again, carefully placing his knife back where it belonged.

"Told me what?" She asked.

"I ran into her outside the club. I confess, I was pretty excited, and may have gotten too close," he looked up.

"She did that?" Mere asked.

"Oh, no. She was talking to me when a man sucker punched me and dragged her away," Alex took a sip of wine. "She seemed to know him, so I didn't call the police. I assumed it was a jealous lover or something like that."

Mere made a face, "She's not seeing anyone."

"Then who's that?" He motioned to the door.

Mere turned in her seat and saw Gage in a beautiful dress and stilettoes. She was made up just so with her dirty blonde hair in an elegant twist. She smiled brightly at the man from the bar who seemed somewhat uncomfortable in the tie around his neck.

Mere stood up quickly, causing the china on the table to rattle loudly.

"That's the man who hit me," Alex said sadly, "I hope he doesn't use that aggression on her too."

Mere heard what he said, but her gaze met Gage's across the room. Gage's face drained of color when she realized who Mere was with, the pain in her jade gaze was palpable.

The man gently grabbed Gage's elbow and steered her from the restaurant, his blue eyes wild with anger as they bore into Alex.

"He seems to be a very angry man," Alex sighed. "If you have any more questions, you know where to find me. I look forward to seeing you at Craze. Your first drink is always on the house."

Mere didn't respond as she hurried out of the restaurant after her friend.

Gage stormed down the sidewalk with Mak trailing behind her, silently, wondering if he should tell her she wasn't walking toward the truck they'd arrived in.

"Gage!" Mere's voice made Gage stiffen even more. The aggressive tapping of her heels stopped abruptly and Mak almost ran into the back of her. He stepped to the side as she whirled to face the redhead running up to them. She stood perfectly still, her chest heaving with anger, but her eyes awash with pain.

Mere came to a stop a few feet away, unsure how to proceed.

Gage liked how uncomfortable Mere seemed as the younger woman shuffled her feet and waited to be reprimanded, so she continued to merely stare.

"I wasn't here to betray you," Mere said finally, her eyes pleading. She wasn't prepared for the emotion oozing from Gage.

Gage was shaking as she continued to stare, not trusting herself to speak.

"You haven't given me a choice," Mere practically wailed.

Gage's breath caught, but instead of speaking, she merely turned on her heel and began to walk away.

"Gage, wait!" Mere reached out, but Mak put his arm up, blocking her hand.

"Maybe just give her some time," he said quietly.

"Who the fuck do you think you are?" Mere snapped, yanking her hand back.

His blue eyes hardened, "I think I'm her mate. I think maybe you have no idea how much of an asshole you're being right now. So, I also think maybe you should back off and let her process."

"I'm an asshole?" Mere was incredulous, "I'm not the one ignoring my friends, lashing out, and running around with some criminal."

Mak let out a harsh laugh before stating, "Just because she's being an asshole too, doesn't mean you aren't." He cleared his throat, "Look, I'm pretty sure you love her, she's your best mate, yeah?"

Mere nodded.

"So, I'm gonna go out on a limb and say if you actually understood what you've just done, you'd hate yourself." His expression wasn't cold, he was entirely sincere.

Mere studied his face in disbelief, "You know what's going on?" She crossed her arms across her chest, "She told *you* what's going on? She doesn't even know you. You're just some mark who gives her information whenever she snaps her fingers."

"She didn't have to tell me shit," he snapped, "I just pay attention."

Mere stared at him, trying to piece together the real story from the information she'd been given. "Then tell me why I'm an asshole."

A half-smile tugged at his lips, "Nah, sheila. I'm not going to betray her trust." He turned and started to follow after Gage, "I'll leave that up to you."

Mere felt rage boil in her gut, but she wasn't sure if it was from the Australian's words, or if it was because she was terrified they were true. She chased him and grabbed his arm, "How dare you say that to me."

He whirled back and yanked his arm from her grasp, "Why?"

She paused for a minute, confused, "What?"

"Why do you think you can run up and grab hold of me, demanding to know anything?" He asked, "After all, I'm just some criminal."

Mere stared at him.

"Truth is, you're scared I'm right," he answered his own question. "You're scared I'm more of a mate to her right now. You're scared you're losing her." He paused for a second, staring down at her. "Pull your head out of your ass. It's not hard to figure out. If Gage loves you, you must be pretty smart." He turned away from her and started walking again, calling over his shoulder, "Act like it."

"I swear to God, if you hurt her-" she stammered.

Mak whirled and walked back to her, his face like stone, "You mean like you just did?" He yanked at the tie around his neck, loosening the knot, "I know this pure ignorance comes from a good place, so I'm tryin' my best to not hold it against you."

"Meredith? Are you okay?"

Mak's eyes widened, enraged, at the sound of Alex's voice. "I'm only going to say this once," Mak said softly, his eyes carefully looking into Mere's, "distance yourself from that piece of shit." His voice was shaking, "One day, hopefully soon, I'm going to put a bullet between his eyes." The danger in his voice wasn't lost on Mere, "If I had my way, I'd do it right now. But to be honest, I don't want to do anything without Gage's say."

Mere nodded slightly to show him she understood.

"Meredith?" Alex had stopped several feet away.

Mak lifted his gaze, seeming to stare through Alex over Mere's head, "I'll be seeing you real soon," he growled before turning and walking away.

"Well that was unsettling," Alex said as he moved to Mere's side. "Are you okay?"

"I'm fine, thanks," Mere responded, "I'm going home."

"Let me drive you," Alex touched her elbow tentatively, "do you want to call the police? I'll be your witness, that man was being extremely aggressive."

Mere glanced at Alex's concerned face, "I'm fine, thank you. I'll find my own way."

"If you insist," he sighed, "I don't know what that maniac told you, but I hope it doesn't affect our friendship."

Mere forced herself to smile at him, trying to gauge his reactions, "That man won't have any effect on me, whatsoever," she stated finally before heading to the parking lot to get her car.

Alex watched her leave, trying to decide if he should follow her to find Gage's house. She glanced over her shoulder at him, so he waved which she acknowledged with a small smile before once more watching where she was going.

"Got you," Alex said softly before making his way back into the restaurant.

~*~*~*~*~

Mak fumed as he walked, trying to get his anger in check so that he wouldn't go back and break Alex's neck. He realized fairly quickly that he had no idea where he was going, so he paused and looked around to try to guess where Gage may have gone.

His eyes fell on Alex's club, Craze, and a sinking feeling settled in his gut.

He looked for cars and walked briskly across the road to the entrance of the club. There was already a crowded line to get in, but Mak walked right up to the bouncer. "G'day mate," he smiled at the large man, "did Gage come in here? Gorgeous blonde? Frequents this establishment?"

The man stared Mak down for a minute as though trying to gauge his intentions.

"I don't reckon she should be alone," Mak added.

Tim squinted his eyes for an extended period of time, making Mak uncomfortable, before the bouncer finally turned sideways, "She made a beeline for the bar. Watch her back, will you?"

Mak nodded, "Thanks a lot mate," he slapped Tim's shoulder as he went by, "I appreciate this."

The line of people all complained as Mak headed into the club.

"He's Australian," Tim shouted at them as the door closed, "can you compete with that?"

Mak walked through the crowd, making his way to the bar, where Gage was sitting with a half-empty bottle of whiskey in front of her and a shot glass in her hand.

"Hey," Mak announced himself as he approached her.

She tossed back her shot, "Oh hi sexy," she giggled without looking at him as she poured another.

"Jesus, how many of those have you had?" Mak asked, standing beside her, his surprise at her response apparent in his tone.

She downed her shot, shivered, and poured another, "Probably just a few," she giggled into her glass. "Maybe a bunch. A girl's gotta let loose right?"

Mak met the eyes of the bartender who made a concerned face and pointed to the bottle in his hand, showing him that Gage's bottle had been mostly full.

"Maybe slow down a bit huh? Wouldn't want a headache later," he reached for her shot as she brought it to her lips. She dodged him and drank it down.

"So sweet," she cooed, "always worrying about me," she winked at him, "maybe you should take me home."

"I think I will take you home now," he tried to take her glass again.

"Oooo, sexy-time," Gage handed him the glass, but grabbed the bottle and wiggled her hips as she took a swig.

"No," Mak put the glass on the bar, "not exactly what I meant."

Gage smiled at him seductively and said huskily, "You don't want any of this?" Her warm breath on his face smelled of whiskey.

"I'd love to woo you proper," he responded, "but not while you're off your face."

Gage whirled and pressed her back against him, "You don't want me? Not even a little?" She asked as she writhed against him.

Mak grabbed her arms in surprise and made a noise deep in his throat, "Christ, sheila!"

She spun again to face him and stumbled slightly on her feet. His hand cupped her cheek gently to steady her. She stared into his eyes, mesmerized, standing still, "Your eyes remind me of the wide-open Texas sky." Her Southern accent was light, but felt genuine, "They're beautiful."

He smiled, "Back atcha, when you're not wearing contacts."

A small sexy smile graced her face, "How do you know what my real eye color is?"

"Your eyes are green more than any other," he responded, "beautiful, deep green."

She arched an eyebrow and tilted her face up, "You pay that close attention to me?"

He nodded and leaned toward her slightly, she stood on her tip toes as though moving to kiss him, but then she pulled back with a teasing grin and drank from her bottle again.

He made a face as his hand dropped from her cheek and tried to grab the bottle from her, "This isn't you."

She pouted as she blocked his reach, "How do you know what I am?" She held the bottle up teasingly, "I like whiskey."

"You know this isn't smart," he cautioned, "you're in the belly of the beast, and making yourself vulnerable."

She shrugged and took another swig, shivering as the whiskey burned down her throat, "You've been begging me to be vulnerable," she wavered on her feet.

He grabbed her and pulled her to him, "Damn it sheila, put down the bottle."

She melted against him, cuddling into his strong arms, "I'll put down the bottle if you take me home."

"I'll take you home right now," he responded, "let's go."

She glanced up at him with a suspicious expression marring her face, "I don't think you mean what I mean."

"Does it matter?" he was exasperated.

"Yes," she responded, squaring off to face him, "I want to get laid."

He coughed roughly, choking on the air he'd sucked in too fast.

She smirked at him before once more taking a gulp from her bottle, which was dangerously low.

He sighed, "You're going to get alcohol poisoning."

She shrugged and responded, "I've had worse things."

He glanced over her shoulder, saw EmEm across the room and motioned him over.

Mak's gaze went back to Gage as EmEm started to make his way over, a look of confusion on his face.

Gage stared at his face, "You really are a sexy beast."

It wasn't a question, so Mak wasn't sure what to say as he felt his cheeks burn. "I'll take your word for it, sheila."

She sighed, "My name isn't Sheila," as she brought the bottle up again.

Mak grabbed her to him tightly and kissed her passionately before she could get the bottle to her lips.

She tasted like whiskey, but he didn't mind. Her hand holding the bottle slowly dropped to her side. He took the bottle from her, without breaking the kiss. Her arms immediately wrapped around his neck and her now empty hand played with the back of his hair as she fervently kissed him back, pressing against him.

She felt herself melting into him, just like she had at the fight, but just as she felt herself warming and tingling in all the best places, he pulled back from her.

She stumbled, letting out a small gasp of protest, her shocked eyes wide with equal parts surprise and desire.

He steadied her with his warm hand on her hip as he smiled at her. Then he tossed the bottle into the barrel-like trashcan behind the bar.

Her eyes narrowed when she realized he'd played her.

Once the realization had noticeably dawned on her, he winked at her, making her sputter in indignation.

"Gage?" EmEm's tone was surprised as he took in her appearance.

"Right, you're her good mate?" Mak asked. When EmEm didn't respond right away, the Australian continued, "I saw you the other night with her, you work with her don't you?"

"Yes," EmEm responded finally, "sorry, I don't usually see her this way."

Gage was still fuming, her green eyes flashing as she continued to sputter, trying to find the words for her anger.

"Looking normal, drunk out of her mind, or speechless?" Mak asked good-naturedly.

"Um, yes? As in, all of the above?" EmEm asked, still obviously quite confused.

"Right, well, obviously, she's going to need a ride home," Mak stated. When EmEm continued to stand in shock, he continued, "Can I trust you with that, Mate? Or are you rotten too?"

"What?" EmEm glanced from Gage to the taller man, "Oh, no, I'm not drunk. I'll get her home."

"Thanks, mate," Mak shook EmEm's hand firmly.

"Who the hell do you think you are?" Gage snapped finally, her voice an octave too high.

"I'd love to try this again sometime," Mak responded good-naturedly, ignoring her tone, "but I think it'd be best if you went home now."

EmEm put his arm protectively around Gage's waist, "Maybe he's right, you wouldn't be happy if you realized just how drunk you've gotten."

"I know what makes me happy," Gage snapped, trying to pull away from EmEm's grip, but stumbling in the process. "It sure isn't some long-haired, up-tight, douche-bag who's too afraid to get with me."

"Go home," Mak's tone was authoritative, and it made Gage bristle as though she'd been slapped.

"Fine," she stated, grabbing hold of EmEm's arm for balance as she spat out, "fuck you."

Mak sighed, not wanting to admit how much her words stung as she turned on her heel, as best she could, and stumbled away with EmEm supporting her.

The black man looked over his shoulder at Mak with an apologetic shrug before once more focusing on the task at hand.

Mak took a deep breath before turning and walking the other way, back out the front door in time to see EmEm helping Gage into a car. He stood on the sidewalk, watching the car drive away, before disappearing down the alley beside the club. He knew he needed to leave in case he saw Alex again and couldn't control himself anymore.

Chapter 33

Gage's eyes slowly opened one after the other but didn't actually focus on anything. The first thing she noticed was the jackhammer in her skull. The throbbing of her heart in her temples was uncomfortable enough, but then the Sahara Desert in her mouth demanded attention. She rubbed at her eyes with both hands and groaned loudly. She tried to roll over and quickly found out she wasn't in her bed, when she fell off the couch, wrapped in a thin blanket, onto the hardwood floor with a grunt.

"Sorry, Gage. I would have taken you home, but you threatened to cut me if I did," EmEm walked into his living room with a bemused expression on his handsome face.

"You suck," she groaned from the floor.

"There are Tylenol and water on the coffee table," he responded.

"You suck less," she groaned in the same tone as she forced herself into a seated position and drank the whole glass of water.

EmEm handed her a large water bottle as he sat on the couch, "What happened last night?"

Gage swallowed the pills from the table and chased them with huge gulps from the bottle, ignoring EmEm's question.

"Sleeping beauty is finally up, huh?" Derek walked into the room with his keys in his hand.

Gage rolled her eyes and resituated her dress, pulling the blanket off of her, "At least someone here is beautiful."

"Hey," EmEm piped up.

"That's true," Gage cracked her neck, "EmEm is beautiful, you should be used to beauty by now."

Derek shook his head, "What's up with Mere? She's ignoring my calls."

"She's a bitch. Thanks for asking, douche-canoe," Gage climbed to her feet with a groan and cracked her back by twisting quickly. The motion almost threw her off balance because of the hangover, but it was worth it.

Derek rolled his eyes, "Well when you see her, tell her I have tickets to the ballet on Friday."

Gage arched an eyebrow at him, "Dude, why would I tell her that?"

He sighed dramatically, "Damn it, Gage, can't you just do one thing for me?"

"Yes," she nodded, "stop calling Mere. If she was interested in a gay best friend, she'd just adopt EmEm. She's trying to politely let you down easy by ghosting your ass." Gage smiled sweetly, "There, I did something for you."

"Jesus, you're such a fucking bitch," Derek snapped, "I'll be back tomorrow Emmitt, please warn me if your *crew* is here." He said the word with such condescension that EmEm sighed.

Gage knew that she would usually go ballistic, instead, she turned to EmEm and spoke clearly and deliberately, "Do we need to pay you more so you can afford a place with pest control?"

EmEm laughed at Derek's crimson face as his roommate rushed out of the apartment, slamming the door to make his displeasure known.

"Seriously though," Gage squinted her eyes at her friend, "is he two? Or just super flamboyant?"

EmEm shook his head, "He's really not gay."

"Really?" Gage asked, "Because I think that makes his diva nature way worse."

He put his face in his hands, "Jesus, Gage. You're such a bitch."

Gage shrugged and said sweetly, "Well thank you, *Emmitt*, I love to be reminded."

EmEm stood up, shaking his head again, "So you gonna tell me why you got so sauced last night? Or who that dude was at the bar?"

"Nope," Gage looked around for her shoes and found them by the couch.

EmEm sighed quietly.

"Oh, stop it." Gage pointed her shoe at him, "I had some alcohol and made out with a hot dude at a bar, is that really so unlike me?"

EmEm stared at her, "Are you done?"

"No," Gage responded, putting her hands on her hips, each holding one of her stilettos, "I'm sick of all you assholes thinking there's something in my life you need to fix or meddle with, I'm perfectly capable of handling my own problems."

"So, you admit there's a problem, then," EmEm cocked his head.

Gage let out a frustrated sound and snapped, "Leave me alone!"

EmEm held up his hands in defeat, "I'm not prying Gage, I'm here if you need anything, but you do you."

She narrowed her eyes at him.

"Seriously," he continued, "I know you'll come to us when you're ready. I just hope you don't do anything dumb before that time."

She rolled her eyes as she turned away from him, "Joke's on you. I always do dumb things."

"I know," he responded, "maybe this time just let us help before the mess is made."

She paused in her stride to the door, surprised by how much those words stung. She glanced back at him over her shoulder, "Don't worry. I'll clean my own messes from now on."

"That's not what I meant," EmEm sighed at the emotion in her voice.

"It's fine," she snapped as she walked out of the apartment.

"The point is, we all care about you, Gage. Don't shut us out," he called after her.

She slammed the door but heard him say, "Family sticks together," and sighed heavily before walking to the stairs in bare feet with a throbbing headache and smeared makeup.

Chapter 34

Gage climbed the stairs to her flat with her shoes in her hand. She'd put them back on to walk from EmEm's apartment building to her place, but the second her property was in sight, she'd shucked them off again with a sigh.

When she passed the pool, approaching the sliding door into the kitchen, she was surprised to find it slightly open. She debated whether she should just go to PREY to change instead, so she wouldn't have to see Mere. The confrontation that was sure to erupt was already giving her indigestion.

"Gage!" The voice was Tessa's, which was only slightly better.

With another sigh, Gage walked into the kitchen and looked around. Tessa had been baking. It was something the younger woman did when she was anxious. Or wanted something.

"What's with the cookies?" Gage asked, motioning to the kitchen table where the treats were cooling, "And the brownies, and the-" she craned her neck, "I got nothing, what the hell are those things?"

"Mini quiche," Tessa responded with a smile, "I decided to bake today."

Gage stood in the doorway expectantly, her shoes dangling from one hand, dress in disarray, with hair in a twisted mess off to one side of her head. Her make-up was in varies stages of being wiped off.

"Um, you look lovely," Tessa laughed, "what happened to you?"

"I got run over by the whiskey truck," Gage responded gruffly, blinking a few times to try to get her eyes to focus. "So, are you going to tell me what you want? Or do I have to guess?" She licked her lips, "Because I have to warn you, my guesses will suck, I have a headache."

Tessa laughed as if Gage just made the funniest joke, "Why do I have to want something to bake? Can't I just bake?" She held out a plate of chocolate chip cookies to Gage, "Cookie?"

"No thanks," Gage responded, staring at Tessa through narrowed eyes.

"Seriously," Tessa laughed and put the plate down, "I just felt like baking."

Gage made a dismissive noise and moved toward the hallway.

"What are you up to today?" Tessa asked conversationally.

"Going to PREY to work on a lead, then probably logging some hours in the shop," Gage called over her shoulder, "do you have class today?"

"Classes are over for the semester," Tessa responded lightly.

"Oh, shit," Gage turned back to the conversation, "I'm sorry Kid, I completely lost track of time. How did you do?"

Tessa waved her hand, "It's no big deal, I got A's, now I have a break."

"Of course you got A's," Gage smiled genuinely, "I'm proud of you."

Tessa blushed slightly, "Thanks. I appreciate that."

Gage nodded but couldn't help feeling like there was something unsaid in the room. "So, what are you spending your time on now?"

"I've been working on Mr. Gambino's hood," Tessa responded, "it's really coming together, it should be ready tomorrow."

"That's awesome Tess," Gage rubbed at her face with her free hand, "I'm really glad you're making time for your art."

Tessa laughed, "The fact that it makes you money doesn't hurt."

"Well, no, it doesn't hurt." Gage nodded, "but I really just like to see you apply yourself to fun things as much as your schoolwork."

"I know," Tessa trailed off.

"Jesus, Tess, what's going on?" Gage demanded, "If you have something to say, just say it."

Tessa sighed, "I have an opportunity to study abroad," she said slowly. When Gage's face went stony, she quickly added, "it would give me a chance to be on my own, without being all alone. And I could focus on my art and Cello without disrupting you guys. It's a really amazing opportunity. I could finally go to Rome! That's all I've ever wanted."

Gage held up her hand, effectively cutting Tessa off, "Have you thought about what could happen if you're alone in a foreign country?"

The bright happiness left Tessa as if a switch had been thrown, "Yes, Gage. But I'm not exactly a target anymore. Most people don't even know I exist."

"Three years ago, there was a hit on you from one of the most influential families in Columbia," Gage responded. "Now you're suddenly not a target?"

"You said it yourself back then, I was a small fish, they caught my father," tears were in Tessa's eyes, "God knows they made their example out of him. There's no reason to believe I'm still in danger."

"Sometimes I think you forget how the world actually works," Gage's voice was hard, but her eyes were pleading. "You know as well as I do, they didn't only make an example of your father."

"I think my family has paid enough for my father's transgression," Tessa snapped.

Gage sighed, "Yes, I think so too, but that doesn't mean the Escobar family agrees. They had no problem making examples of the rest of your innocent family members."

"Yes, they butchered my mother and sisters," Tessa was openly crying now, "if I had known I would have to live in a prison to stay alive, maybe I would have just let them kill me too."

Gage looked like she'd just been punched in the gut, "I keep you in a prison?" She motioned to the beautiful flat, "I feed you, clothe you, put a roof over your head, and send you to school with cash in your pocket," she cocked her head slightly, "this is a prison?"

"I'm nineteen years old," Tessa responded, "one day you're going to have to let go of the leash."

Gage rolled her eyes, "It's good to know that my efforts are so appreciated. I feel the love." Gage turned and headed down the hallway.

"Please, Gage, just think about it," Tessa called after her.

Gage slammed her bedroom door, making Tessa jump.

Chapter 35

Gage stood in the shower for longer than she normally would. She didn't know if it was because she wanted to wash away the feelings tightening her throat, or if it was because she was hoping Tessa would be gone by the time she was finished.

She stepped onto her bathmat and listened carefully. She heard the road noises from her slightly open window but didn't hear any signs of life from in the flat. She breathed a sigh of relief and quickly dried off.

When she went to her closet to find clothes for the day, she heard doors slamming and sighed heavily. She got dressed in some stretchy black pants and a purple tank top before rubbing some purple wax into her hair. She sat at her vanity and contoured her face to give her a fierce nose and pinched cheeks, then swiped purple eyeshadow on her eyes and completed the look with heavy black eyeliner. She chose some violet contact lenses from her stock and quickly popped them in her eyes. She blinked a few times to situate the lenses, then took in her appearance.

She zipped on a pair of black knee-high combat boots with a chunky heel and tightened the laces. The boots concealed the knives she had hidden against her calves. The whole look was very punk rocker and suited her desire to disappear into a persona. She touched her doorknob hesitantly, listening carefully. She heard both Mere and Tessa's voices arguing.

Gage pursed her lips and thought for a second before turning back into her room and moving to the bathroom. She opened the small window wider and looked out. The roof of the garage jutted out beneath her window. She'd never tried to escape her room this way, but she had considered how to go about it before. She stepped onto the toilet lid and put her left leg out the window, followed by her head and torso, then she pulled her right leg through. Once she was on the roof, she pushed her window closed and walked across the relatively flat roof of her garage to the corner of the building.

The corner of the building had an impressive drain pipe with heavy metal brackets holding it to the brick. She said a quick prayer that it would hold her weight, then shimmied down the drain pipe like a teenage runaway. She only slipped once when her boot missed a bracket. When she was safely on the ground, she went into the garage, grabbed the keys to her Torino and was gone before anyone even realized she was there.

~*~*~*~*~

"Of all the crazy that's she's been spewing, I'm just saying, maybe she's making sense about you going abroad," Mere stated.

"You two are just pissed because one of you would have to actually act like an adult if I'm gone," Tessa snapped.

Mere shrugged, "I mean, that's part of it, don't get me wrong." She took a bite of cookie and said, "But we're also just protective of you. We can't help it really."

Tessa rolled her eyes, "You guys are going to have to let me go eventually, I'm a grown woman."

Mere arched an eyebrow and pointed her cookie at the younger woman, "Yes, you're a grown woman who can bake cookies, paint, and get excellent grades. But can you recognize danger? Or do you rely on us to do that for you?"

"Just because you two keep me under your wings doesn't mean I'm completely useless," Tessa responded.

"You're not useless at all," Mere finished her cookie, "you take care of us and we take care of you." She reached over and selected two peanut butter cookies, "But you've never really had to worry about your safety, we've always handled that for you." She whistled, then continued, "You know that our worries come from a place of love."

Tiny and Killer both burst into the room through the dog door and sat at Mere's feet when she held up the cookies.

"Your love is a little ridiculous," Tessa snapped as Mere fed the dogs each a cookie, then snuck a second one to Tiny while Killer was sniffing for crumbs.

"How do you mean?" Mere's tone was conversational as she tapped her lap and Killer hopped up. The little dog ran in a few tight circles, then lay down.

"I mean, you want me to drink and go to illegal street races instead of doing my homework, but when I suggest an amazing opportunity which will let me be a kid and let loose, you immediately shut it down."

Mere rubbed Killer's ear with one hand and Tiny's ear with the other, "The first allows us to watch over you while you live a little, the second takes you into the mean world alone, to get killed."

"Oh my God!" Tessa practically shrieked, "You two are ridiculous." She threw a bowl into the sink with enough force that it shattered. "Damn it!" She started to pick up the pieces, tears of frustration streaming down her cheeks.

"You can't really blame us for being concerned, can you?" Mere didn't move because she knew Tessa would lash out if she tried to help.

"I get it," Tessa threw the pieces of glass into the trashcan beneath the sink. "my dad fucked up and got a hit put on my whole family. My point is that there's no telling that Escobar even knew I existed. He probably thinks he killed my whole family."

"That's a hell of an assumption to stake your life on," Mere stated slowly.

Tessa whirled to face Mere, "It's my life to stake!"

Mere licked her lips and sat silently for a moment. Tessa stood with her hands on her hips, her face red with anger. Finally, Mere spoke very calmly, "Thank you, Tessa."

"For what?" The younger woman asked in confusion.

"Sometimes I think that because you're so mature, we forget you're a kid," Mere put Killer on the ground. "Thank you, for reminding me that you're still just a teenager," she walked down the hallway to her room with Tiny following her.

Tessa stood in the center of the kitchen, at a loss for words. Killer looked up at her with his head cocked to the side. She glanced at him and grumbled, "Don't you stand there and judge me too. If you want to be judgey, you should just go somewhere else. I don't want to see your face."

Killer made a noise that sounded like a whine mixed with a sigh and left the room through his dog door.

Tessa sighed and shook her head as she went back to finish cleaning up the kitchen.

Chapter 36

Gage didn't look up from the computer screen when the door opened.

"Um, that's an interesting look, even for you," Whitlock stared at her momentarily.

"Do you want the info, or not?" Gage asked bluntly, looking up at her boss.

"Yes, I do. Does it come from a reliable source?"

Gage shrugged, "I got it from our firearm contact, so take it with a grain of salt, but preliminary fact-checking looks pretty promising," she motioned to her screen.

Whitlock rounded the desk to look over her shoulder, "How did he get this?"

Gage shrugged again, "He was motivated."

Whitlock arched an eyebrow at her.

"What?" Gage looked up at him, "I didn't promise him anything but a drink, get your head out of the gutter."

Whitlock chuckled and motioned to the pile of papers in front of her, "May I?"

Gage stood and motioned to her chair, "Have at it, Papa Bear. I'm gonna go find some mischief."

Whitlock shook his head with a bemused smile as he started to look through the papers. There was no picture associated with Mak's suspect, but the description made something in Whitlock tingle with recognition. He heard the door slam as Gage left, but he was more purposefully searching for something familiar in the pile of information.

He looked up to make sure no one was nearby before pulling out his cell phone and calling the same number he tried every month. The mailbox was still full, making him grumble in frustration and shove his phone back into his suit jacket's pocket.

"What are you up to, old friend?" He asked the computer as he looked through the websites Gage had found.

~*~*~*~*~

Gage's phone was singing so often that she finally just turned it off.

"That your boyfriend from last night?" EmEm asked from behind her.

"Not my boyfriend," Gage responded and tossed her phone into her range bag. "Not even my friend," she added as she pulled two handguns from her range bag and loaded them.

"You seemed awful friendly with him," EmEm tried to mask his surprise.

"He's hot," Gage said simply before firing her entire magazine down range into the center of the target.

EmEm shrugged and nodded in understanding before taking her now empty weapon so she could begin firing her second.

"You think I'm hot?"

Mak's voice surprised them both so badly that EmEm pointed his unloaded weapon at the Australian, and Gage's grouping was the worst she'd ever had.

"Whoa, no harm meant," Mak held his hands up in surrender.

"How the hell did you get back here?" Gage snapped, not even looking at him.

"I've been trying to call you all day," Mak responded.

"Yeah, I know. I've been ignoring you all day," she responded curtly, "but that didn't answer my question."

"Well, to be fair, you didn't answer mine either," Mak smiled cheekily.

Gage sighed and looked to the heavens for a split second as she stowed her empty weapon in her bag, "When a girl comes to her place of business for some range therapy, she doesn't like to be interrupted prematurely," she finally glanced up at him. "You already know you're attractive. You don't need me to say it."

"I know that's right," EmEm nodded with a sly smirk of his own as he looked Mak up and down. He didn't even flinch when Gage punched his shoulder, he just handed her the empty weapon he'd been pointing at Mak, sideways.

Mak actually looked surprised at EmEm's flirtation.

"EmEm doesn't have a preference for sexuality," Gage stated conversationally as she stowed the second weapon with the first, "he falls in love with spirits," she glanced at her compatriot, "'spirits' right? Or what's the word you use?"

"I'm drawn to energy, not sexual organs," EmEm responded.

"Yeah," Gage nodded, "he loves people's energy."

EmEm smiled, "Male or female doesn't bother me," he shrugged, "I've loved all sorts of people. If I'm compatible with the energy you put into the world, then I'm all yours."

Mak arched an eyebrow.

"He's a child of the world," Gage stated monotonal, "I wish I could be like him."

Mak smirked at Gage.

"Unfortunately, I just like the 'D' too much to give a shit about energy," she sighed.

EmEm and Mak both laughed.

"But that still doesn't explain how you got into a secured facility undetected," Gage continued.

"I'm not undetected," Mak answered, "I was invited. Your friend is waiting outside so you don't shoot her."

Gage rolled her eyes, and said in an exasperated tone, "That happened ONE time!"

"What?" Mak was actually surprised.

"Every body's a critic," Gage grumbled as she zipped up her bag and slung it over her shoulder. She motioned to the door, which Mak held open for her, much to her chagrin. She rolled her eyes and strode purposefully through the door. She walked right past Mere as she spoke, "Is there a reason you're letting unqualified personnel into our secure office area?"

"Well, when you wouldn't respond to his calls, he started blowing up the main line," Mere responded, pushing off the wall she'd been leaning on. "Since you're avoiding both of us, I figured we could join forces." She followed after Gage, "Especially since you ducked out of the flat like a teenager."

"Didn't want to deal with people," Gage grumbled as she entered the computer lab and put her range bag onto an empty chair.

"Is that why we're awful 'purple people eater' today?" EmEm asked, looking at her ensemble with disdain.

Gage shrugged, "Some people don't mind being eaten."

Mak's ears turned red making EmEm and Mere both snicker as the trio followed Gage through the door into the computer lab.

Whitlock looked up when the door opened and stood when he saw Mak, "Who is this?"

"This is Crocodile Dundee," Gage responded without skipping a beat. She motioned to the papers spread around the desk Whitlock had vacated, "he found that."

Whitlock shook Mak's hand firmly, "It's nice to finally put a face with the name," he said curtly, "though I'm not sure what you're doing here."

Mak nodded, "Fair enough, I'm here because I wanted to be sure Gage wasn't going after that bloke," he motioned to the papers.

Whitlock crossed his arms and stared at the younger man intently, "You know the man?"

"I've worked with him before, in Iraq," Mak responded, "I don't think anyone knows him. But I know he's the real deal. Not someone to be taken lightly."

Whitlock arched an eyebrow, "You fought in Iraq?"

"Among other places," Mak kept Whitlock's gaze. They were the same height, towering over everyone else in the room.

"I wasn't aware you were a soldier," Whitlock's voice was carefully nondescript.

"You didn't get my resume along with all the illegal weapons?" Mak asked.

The room was silent as the two men stared at each other. Whitlock's laugh broke that silence and eased most of the tension. Everyone but Gage joined the laughter.

Gage looked closer at what Whitlock had on his computer screen, "Do *you* know this guy, Whit?"

Whitlock cleared his throat and nodded, "Yes, I do. He was a very close friend for much of my young adult life. We served several tours together both in the Marine Corps and then as civilian contractors."

"Everyone knows you were never young," Mere quipped.

"We were all pretty sure you just appeared one day with a gun in your hand and a scowl on your face," EmEm supplied.

"Don't forget a perfectly pressed suit," Gage said absent-mindedly, still looking over the information.

"If you know this guy, why can't you just call him up?" Mere asked before Whitlock could respond to the ribbing.

Whitlock sighed, "I've tried, he's gotten reclusive in his old age. He no longer responds to his voicemails."

"Reclusive is an understatement. This bloke is bad news," Mak was staring at the back of Gage's head, "he sets traps, has dogs, lives in a sniper nest on top of his compound." He glanced at Whitlock, "You can

NOT just show up on his doorstep and expect a friendly hug hello from your old mate. He takes shots at me every time I go out there."

"You went out there, knowing he'd shoot at you?" Mere asked.

Mak shrugged, "I was motivated."

Whitlock nodded, "Thank you for the heads up, it's appreciated."

"The number I reach him at is in that packet," Mak motioned to the papers again, "if you want to try to call him."

Whitlock perked up, moved past Gage, and sat back down, leafing through the papers until he found one with a number circled. "Perhaps you three could escort our friend here from the building now," he said gruffly.

Gage made a face, "I'm not leaving yet, I want to hear what happens."

Whitlock stared at her.

"What?" She asked, "I'm invested at this point. I want to know if your crazy battle buddy is offing people for sport."

Whitlock continued to stare at her with a deadpan expression.

"Damn it, Whitlock, stop looking at me like that!" She snapped.

"I will inform you if you are needed," Whitlock stated calmly. "Why don't you go pay this man for his intel?"

Gage sighed unhappily.

"What were you promised?" Mere asked Mak conversationally.

"I was going to settle for a proper meal," Mak responded, "but that got interrupted."

Mere looked down guiltily.

Mak sensed her discomfort, so he added, "But Gage promised my brother drinks with her girls, whatever that means."

"I'll call Lina," Mere grinned, "this should be fun."

Gage shook her head, "I'm not going drinking tonight."

"That's fine," Mere responded, "Lina and I will take Mak's brother out, you can go on your date."

Gage looked like she'd sucked on a lemon, "I'm not going anywhere with him."

Mak sighed and put his hand in the pocket of his leather coat.

"Okay," Mere shrugged, "you can just go home and discuss Tessa's traveling abroad."

"What?" EmEm's concern was apparent, "Where's Tessa going?"

"Nowhere," Gage snapped. After a moment, she added, "meet us here in two hours," without even looking at Mak. She walked out of the room and slammed the door behind her.

Mak sighed again, "She's a lot of work." It wasn't a question, it was a statement.

Mere laughed, "That's an understatement."

"Is your brother as sexy as you?" EmEm changed the subject.

"Absolutely not," Mak scoffed.

Mere laughed, "I'll be the judge of that!" She led the group from the computer lab, "Doesn't he have a beard?"

"Beards aren't everything," Mak grumbled as he followed Mere into the front Lobby. Gage was long gone; the lobby was empty.

"Well, I'll assemble the team," EmEm grinned, "this should be an interesting night."

"Are you one of Gage's girls?" Mak asked with a grin as they entered the elevator.

Chapter 37

Exactly two hours later, Gage was sitting at the desk in the lobby filing her nails with a bored expression on her face. Her hair was a straight black wave that flowed over her shoulders. Her face was perfectly contoured and her crimson lips were pursed with concentration as she worked intently. Her eyes were deep brown to complete the look.

Her posture was impeccable as she glanced from her nails to the elevator door when it pinged. Before the doors opened, she looked back down at her nails.

"So now you're doing the Morticia thing?" EmEm asked as he stepped into the lobby. "I mean I love red lips as much as the next person, but that's a whole lot of black, Mami."

Gage shrugged, and held up her hand to inspect her work, "It matched my mood."

"You're wearing leather pants, aren't you," Mere wasn't really asking.

Gage smirked and pushed the chair back so she could cross her booted feet on the desk, revealing her black leather pants.

"It cracks me up that you think those pants are less sexy than a skirt," Mere shook her head.

"I feel badass, not sexy," Gage responded as the elevator opened again.

"Badass IS sexy," Buck's jovial voice boomed as he entered the room. He was the picture of a cowboy with a black cowboy hat perched atop his dark curly hair. His blue jeans were tight in the right places but clearly worn for comfort. His plaid shirt was opened at the throat to show a bit of hair. His broad grin shone from his tan face, nestled in his beard like pearls in a clam.

Mak followed his brother off the elevator with less bravado, but no less charisma.

Buck's dark gaze turned from Gage and immediately settled on Mere. He blatantly checked her out, taking in her tan legs, mini skirt, corset style top, and finally settled on her face, "G'day, sheila," he winked.

Mere laughed, "Wow, you have no shame, do you?"

"Who needs shame?" Buck asked and beckoned her to him.

Mere arched an eyebrow but obliged him and took his offered hand in her own.

Buck twirled Mere then let his arm settle over her shoulders, "You're a beaut. I reckon I'll be drinking with you tonight."

Mere's chuckle was genuine as she wrapped her slender arm around his waist, "Oh, this is going to be fun."

EmEm glanced up at Mak, "You're a damn liar, Boo. Your brother is fine."

Mak shrugged, his blue eyes on Gage, "He has some charms, I guess. If you like midgets."

EmEm laughed as he followed Mere and Buck onto the elevator. "See ya there," he wiggled his fingers and stared at Buck's ass.

They heard Buck good-naturedly ask, "What are you looking at, mate?" as the doors closed.

"Are we going to talk about the fact that you have flowers in your hand?" Gage asked conversationally, her feet still on the desk. "Or the fact that you've cut your hair?"

"It's a peace offering," Mak laid the bouquet of sunflowers on the desk at her feet and ran a hand through his short hair.

"You bought me flowers?" Gage's face was carefully blank.

"If I stole them, would you think it manlier?"

Gage's careful mask cracked when she smiled slightly.

"Yes, I bought you flowers, on the off chance that you might like pretty things," Mak said quickly, encouraged by her smile. He pulled a brown bag out of the pocket of his leather coat, "I also bought you a coupl'a knives, since I know for a fact you like sharp things."

Gage genuinely smiled for a moment, before clearing her throat and standing to conceal the act, "Thanks. You didn't have to do that."

Mak shrugged and handed her the bag, "Well last night didn't really go as expected, so I wanted to make a gesture."

"Oh, you mean how instead of getting laid, you yelled at me to go home like a child?" She asked coolly.

"Look, I don't know what type of blokes you've been familiar with," Mak stated, "but I'm not the type to root a woman off her face."

Gage snorted and shook her head, "You know exactly the type I'm used to, you don't have to be chivalrous to impress me."

"Just because you're used to slags, doesn't mean that's what you should settle for," Mak responded as he pushed the button to call the elevator back. "I'm not going to be anything I'm not," he glanced at her, "maybe try it."

She stared at him a moment, not sure if she should be touched, pissed, or annoyed.

The elevator doors opened and Mak stepped in, "You coming?"

Gage considered letting the doors shut between them, but when she looked into the bag in her hand and saw the knives inside, she couldn't help but grin, so she stepped in too.

"You kind of like me, don't you," Mak said conversationally as he looked up at the numbers as they illuminated.

"Eh," she made a dismissive noise, but she was smiling, and for once, she wasn't thinking about how tiny the elevator felt.

When they got to the lobby of the building, the doors opened and Mak motioned Gage through, "I reckon you were planning on driving yourself, but for once, you're dressed for a ride. I'd love to give you one."

Gage arched an eyebrow at him, "All I wanted last night was a ride, and you sent me home."

Mak laughed, "On my motorbike. If you still want your ride tonight, I'll be happy to oblige."

Gage rolled her eyes, "No chance Dundee, you lost your opportunity."

"I think you'll reevaluate," Mak answered good-naturedly as he led her from the building, "even Mick got the girl in the end."

"How could he not?" Gage asked as she came to a stop by his motorcycle, "He was all that is man: Resourceful, handsome, strong-"

"Australian," Mak cut in with a wink as he handed her a helmet.

Gage shook her head but couldn't help the grin that cracked her face again as she pulled on the helmet. She glanced around, "Did your brother ride over on the back of your bike?"

Mak laughed as he climbed on the bike and looked back at her, "Maybe. Jealous?"

Gage climbed on the back of the bike, putting her feet on the pegs, her knees resting lightly against him.

"You're a pro," Mak called back, "you hold on as tight as you like," he glanced over his shoulder at her, "I could get used to this."

"What?" Gage laughed, "Being in charge?"

"Being between your legs," his eyes were smiling.

She tried to cover the warmth spreading in her guts with an over exaggerated scoff, but when he revved the engine, she leaned into him and wrapped her arms around his waist. She couldn't deny that his muscular back felt nice against her chest. The warmth didn't go away the whole ride.

Buck was dancing with Mere when Mak and Gage entered Craze.

Chapter 38

"Why do we keep coming here?" Mak asked, his jawline tense.

"Because I laugh in the face of danger," Gage muttered, trying to ignore the fact that his reaction made her feel protected.

"Or because you're too chicken to tell your friends you don't want to come here anymore," Mak answered, but his tone wasn't judgmental.

"Right," she nodded, "danger."

Mak shook his head but followed her to the booth where EmEm, Will, and Lina were all laughing.

"What up, bitches," Gage picked up a glass of Jameson from the table and downed it with a shiver.

"Gage!" EmEm grinned, "Welcome!" He glanced at Mak, "And you brought my Boo! I'm so happy you didn't lose him."

Gage glanced at Will and motioned to the dance floor, "I see you've already met Snowy River," she used her thumb to point over her shoulder at Mak, "this here is Crocodile Dundee." She pointed to each of her friends in turn, "That's Lina, Will, and you remember EmEm."

"Who could forget?" Mak asked with a smile, "He's very memorable."

Lina and Will laughed.

"I'm blushing," EmEm stated.

"Gage, maybe you should introduce people with their names, instead of movie nicknames," Lina suggested with a smile.

"Outsiders might think you're racist," Will laughed.

"Oh, I'm a raging racist," Gage stated matter-of-factly, turning slightly so she could see her friends and Mak, "y'all didn't know that?"

Mak purposely glanced at the group of friends in confusion.

"They only stick around 'cause I pay them well," Gage responded to the unasked question. "It makes me seem more," she trailed off, waving her hand as though searching a wheel for the right term, and turned toward EmEm, "what is it?"

"Cultured," EmEm supplied.

"Yeah," Gage nodded, "I got culture, if only in pretense."

Mak had an amused expression on his face.

"Don't laugh," Gage was purposely stoic, "I almost didn't meet you, I thought you were Austrian." She shrugged, "I'm an ignorant asshole, I thought you'd be a giant German brute, obviously, I'm not cool with that. Germans are super scary." She narrowed her eyes, "Then I show up and you're all 'throw anotha shrimp on tha barbie.'" She arched an eyebrow, "It was confusing. I hadn't yet decided on my Australian stereotypes, so I went ahead with our work and just maintained a distance."

"Are you done?" Mak asked.

"Not really," Gage responded pertly, "but if *Crocodile Dundee* taught me anything, it's that you Australians like to be in charge," she motioned to him, "so go on."

"Would you like a drink?" Mak asked.

"Sure," Gage nodded as she sat, "get me a coke, please."

EmEm stood as Gage sat, "I'll help you get a round."

"Not drinking tonight?" Will asked.

"I had enough last night to last me a month," Gage responded, "I thought I'd be good, but to be honest, that shot I just took made me want to puke."

"Mere told us what happened," Lina said softly.

"I don't want to talk about it," Gage muttered.

"I just wanted you to know that it was my idea, and I'm really sorry," Lina continued.

Gage glanced from Lina to Will, "You went along with it, huh?"

"We weren't trying to step on your toes, we're just sailing blind right now. We're worried about you," Will's tone was pleading.

"So instead of just one of my dearest friends making a bad call, it's actually three of the people I trusted most, conspiring against me," Gage stood up, "that's just awesome."

Will slid out of the booth to stand as well, "We aren't conspiring against you. We're just worried about you."

"I'm fine," she said flatly.

"No, you're not." Will responded, "we're not blind. You're freaking out, and none of us understand why."

"Maybe I'm freaking out because I can't handle all of you meddling in my life," she snapped.

"Please," Lina said softly, "just be honest with us."

"Sure, I'll be honest Evangelina," Gage practically growled, "I honestly wish you assholes would mind your own business."

Lina looked down at the table.

Gage glared at Will, "I don't owe you an explanation. Leave me alone."

Will held up his hands in surrender, "Look, just know that we're here when you decide to stop being a bitch, okay?"

Gage nodded, surprised by the tears that momentarily flooded her vision. "I don't need this shit," she said gruffly, "I'm out."

When she turned to leave, Mak was there, "What's wrong?" he asked, his blue eyes staring at her face.

"Nothing," Gage responded, "I don't feel like drinking, I'm out of here."

"You want some company?" Mak asked.

"No. I want everyone to leave me the fuck alone," Gage snapped as she pushed past him, "but no one ever seems to do what I want."

Mak set the drinks he was holding on the table and followed her.

"We messed up," Lina said softly, tears in her eyes when Will sat beside her glumly.

"We didn't have much of a choice," Will sighed.

"Do you still think we should talk to Whit?" She asked.

"No, I guess now we just need to give her the space she wants," Will responded. "Hopefully she'll come to us before whatever is going on blows up in her face."

Lina nodded and took a sip of her drink.

Gage burst into the night air and started walking. It was raining, so there weren't many people outside. She was hyper-aware of her surroundings this time, studying each face near her to evaluate threats as she walked down the sidewalk.

"Gage," Mak called after her as he quickly followed her into the dark, popping the collar on his coat to fend off the rain.

"Go. Away," her tone was vicious.

"Not until I know you're safe," Mak responded cheerfully.

Gage whirled to face him, a few strands of her hair stuck to her cheek from the motion, and her eyes flashed angrily, "I'm not your sweet damsel in distress. You're not the hero of this story. I don't need rescuing."

He stood calmly, "Are you done?"

"No," she snapped, wiping the hair off her cheek roughly, "what the hell is your problem? What part of 'LEAVE ME ALONE' is difficult to understand?"

He nodded, "Fair enough, I'll leave you alone. Once you're somewhere safe."

"You're a real piece of work, you know that?" She shook her head. "What is it about me that makes you think you can interrupt my life? Because I'm this helpless girl you have to rescue?" She pushed his chest with both hands as hard as she could, forcing him to step back, "You tired of being a criminal? You want to feel like a good guy? I'm not a project to make you feel better about yourself."

He stood calmly, listening to everything she said, without speaking. The rain dripped off his eyelashes.

"Answer me," she cried, pushing him again. "What do you want from me? I don't want your help. I don't need rescuing."

"Everyone needs rescuing sometimes," he answered.

"So that IS what you're after," she let out a rough laugh that bordered on hysteria, "you want to save me." She turned from him, splashing in puddles as she strode away, "I'm not going to be saved."

He followed her, giving her space, but continuing to watch over her.

"I know what it feels like to be stalked," she whirled again, facing him.

"I'm not stalking you," he responded simply, "you can say whatever you like to me. Yell at me, hit me, cuss me out," he shrugged, "I'm still gonna make sure you get home okay."

"WHY?" She shouted, frustrated. "Why won't you just give up?"

"I'm motivated," he responded with a little smile.

She shook her head, "You're either an idiot or a masochist, I can't decide which."

He shrugged, trying to mask how much her words were really hurting him, "Come to whatever conclusion you want, just do it somewhere safer than outside this asshole's place."

She stared at him.

"Please," he motioned for her to move on, "if he comes out here, I'm pretty sure I'll kill him."

She shook her head, "I don't need you for that."

"I know," he responded, "you don't need me at all. That's not the point."

"What's the point?" She asked, "I just- I don't understand any of this. I'm throwing rocks at you and you're still standing here, begging for more."

"I don't want to let you down," he responded.

She actually laughed, but it sounded more like sobbing, "Why do you care what I think?"

He took a step closer to her, "Because I've wanted to know you better since I met you," he responded, "because you're beautiful and courageous, and the most capable person I've ever met."

She scoffed and opened her mouth to respond but he interrupted her.

"Shut up." His voice was carefully calm, but that seemed more dangerous than anger somehow. "I let you talk, now it's my turn."

She closed her mouth and stared at him.

"You are the most infuriating person I have ever met, your recklessness drives me crazy," he stepped closer again. "But you're compassionate and good," he let out a breath, staring into her eyes. "I was jaded when you first came into my life," he shrugged, "I'd seen too much bad in the world. Too much death and destruction." His eyes were more emotional than he intended, the rain dripped down his face like tears, "Even through all your bravado and biting humor, you made me realize there was still good in the world. That not everything had to be black and white."

She bowed her head as she listened, feeling guilty for her tirade earlier.

"Hey," he lifted her chin gently to make her meet his gaze, "you're a rare find. You pretend to be this cocky bitch, but you have absolutely no idea how amazing you really are. You already rescued me. I thought it'd be nice to return the favor." He smiled sadly, "I need you to know that you're enough. I know you don't feel like it sometimes, but you are more than I ever dreamed of finding. You're everything I could ever want. I'm not looking for a damsel. I just want a partner."

A tear escaped one of her eyes and trailed down her cheek mingling with the rain, "I'm not worth this effort," she said quietly.

"Yes. You are," he said firmly, wiping her cheeks gently. "I know I'm not a hero. I'm not even one of the good guys," he shrugged, "but something about you makes me want to be better. I'm sorry if that comes across wrong or puts too much pressure on you."

She shook her head and pulled away from his hand, "You're a good man," she responded, "you're probably the best person I've ever met." She met his gaze again, "I don't deserve your affection. I don't want you to be disappointed when you look closer."

He slowly reached up and cupped her cheek with his hand, "There's nothing you could do that would disappoint me."

She closed her eyes and leaned into his hand, "I can't do this," she said softly.

He pulled his hand back, making her feel cold, "I understand. That's okay. I'll be here when you're ready."

"Why does everyone keep saying that," she actually laughed.

"Because there's a lot of people who love you. They just want the chance to help," Mak responded.

"I don't need any help," she answered, some of her fire returning.

"Accepting help doesn't make you weak," Mak said firmly. "Everyone needs help sometimes. There's no shame in it."

Her chin dropped to her chest again, "What if I'm never ready?"

"That's a chance I'm willing to take," he smiled. "You're worth the wait."

She shook her head and said, "You don't know that," as she turned from him and began to walk again.

"Maybe that's the best part," Mak called after her.

She slowed to a stop, her back to him, breathing heavily, face tilted to the sky. The cold rain felt refreshing on her hot face.

"The not knowing," he added.

She wiped her face with her hand and took a deep breath.

"Can I take you home now?" He asked.

She turned back and strode toward him with purpose, her face an unreadable mask.

He stood his ground, not sure if she was about to hit him again.

She threw herself into his arms roughly, wrapping her arms around his neck, and meeting his lips with her hungry mouth.

He immediately wrapped his arms around her waist and pulled her tight against his hard body, the action lifted her feet from the ground as his mouth answered her urgency with his own with no hesitation.

She moaned into his mouth because everything about this embrace felt exactly right.

He leaned into her kiss, letting her feet hit the ground again as one of his hands tangled in her hair even as he held her tightly against him with the other. His hands were insistent, but not forceful. She felt like she was being worshipped, and her whole body was on fire, even though the rain was cold.

She never wanted this to end, his kiss was making her squirm in all the best ways. She wanted him to touch her everywhere, her back was burning where his hand was gently, but firmly, gripping. It was like he was pouring electricity into her and it made all her nerve endings dance. She was lost in him for much longer than she intended to be. This was meant as a consolation prize, as a last kiss goodbye. But now, all she wanted was to stay right where she was, wrapped up in his arms.

Some piece of her came back to the world, from the cloud she was floating on, and she pulled back slightly, trying to catch her breath. When she'd regained some of her composure, she looked up at him and licked her lips. Her voice was a breath when she spoke, "Okay," she took a deep breath and said, "good talk," as she hurried away, leaving him standing confused and breathless in the dark.

Chapter 39

Gage arrived back at her flat and recognized the same red pickup outside on the street. She approached it from behind but realized quickly that it was empty. Her intuition told her not to go inside her shop, so she pulled out her cell phone and scrolled through her contacts. Each name she came to made her grimace. Finally, she decided who to call and hit the send button. He picked up on the second ring.

Donovan.

"Hey Van, it's Gage."

What's wrong?

Gage actually smiled, "Straight to business, I like it. This is gonna sound crazy, but I'm pretty sure there's a guy stalking me."

Call the precinct to report it.

"I know. I would if I was certain, but all I have right now is a gut inclination and the same truck outside my shop several days this week. It's out here again tonight, but empty. I haven't been near the door yet, but something is telling me the guy is in my shop. I don't want to waste police resources if it's nothing."

So, you just want to waste MY time?

"Okay, I guess I'll just go in alone then," Gage responded chipperly.

No. I'll be there in five. I'm around the corner anyway.

"Thanks, Hunny!" Gage cooed.

Shuddup.

Gage leaned on the building across from her shop under the canopy to keep out of the rain. She watched for any sign of life inside. Tessa's car wasn't in its spot, so she knew the girl wasn't home. Shadows kept moving, but Gage couldn't decide if that was because someone was inside, or if it was because she was imagining things. She couldn't hear Tiny or Killer, she wasn't sure if that should make her happy, or scared.

A police cruiser turned onto the street and stopped. Officer Donovan climbed out of the passenger seat and an officer who looked barely old enough to drive hopped out of the driver's seat, put on his hat, and started running toward the shop.

Gage watched with an amused expression on her face as Van called the kid back to him and intensely spoke to him. The kid then moved to the corner of the building, watching the front, as Van walked to Gage.

"Over-zealous much?" Gage laughed, nodding her head in the direction of the other officer.

"Tell me about it," Van grumbled. He'd left his hat in the cruiser. His dark blonde hair was styled in a spiky way that looked both professional, and sexy. He had blue eyes, a chiseled jaw, and the swagger of a confident man. He looked at her strangely, but didn't comment on her appearance, "I can't wait until I'm out of here. I'm so tired of these rookies."

"Where are you going?" Gage asked, "You're pretty much the only cop I actually like."

Van actually smiled, "Aw, shucks, thanks." He shook his head in amusement, "I'm going home to New York. The NYPD just offered me a spot."

"Oooo look at you, Mr. Big Shot!" Gage crooned.

"Yeah, yeah," he shrugged, "I'm excited to finally get back where I belong."

Gage nodded. She pointed to the truck, "This has been outside my shop every day this week. It almost always just happens to leave as I am and is usually occupied by a white male probably in his late twenties."

Van called in the plate and it almost immediately came back as a stolen vehicle. "Well that's interesting," he said, "maybe there's actually something to this feeling of yours."

"Before you go in to clear the building, you should know I have two dogs in there," she said. "I don't know why they're not going crazy right now."

"Do they have a command that will let them know we're friendly?" Van asked.

"How are you at whistling?" She glanced from the building to the handsome cop.

"Mediocre at best," he responded.

"Let me come with you," she stated.

"Not going to happen," he shook his head.

"Van, if you don't want to get mauled, please just let me follow you. I'm not a normal civilian, and probably better trained than that kid," she motioned to his trainee. "If you shoot my dog, I will never forgive you."

"I have no doubt that you'd be an asset, but you're not a cop, so I can't let you help." Van shook his head, "It's just not possible."

"I don't have to go inside," Gage grabbed his arm, "Please, just let me go to the door. If they hear me, they'll leave you alone."

"Why did you call me?" Van asked suddenly.

"What?"

"You never call the police. Last year you beat a guy to a pulp for attacking some stranger, THEN you called. So why are you calling me preemptively?"

Gage shrugged, "You told me, in no uncertain terms, that you'd be very angry with me if I did that again. Now I'm doing the right thing and I'm getting grilled about it?"

Van squinted at her as though trying to read her.

"Seriously!" Gage held her hands up in defense.

"Where are your friends?" Van asked.

"I'm pissed at everyone, so I had no backup," she answered.

Van smirked and shook his head, "You're ridiculous."

Gage curtsied, "Thanks, now can we go see what the hell is going on? I have work to do in my shop."

Van nodded, "You can go to the door, that's it. Understood?"

"Got it," Gage smiled brightly.

Van spoke into his radio as they crossed the street to the front door, then motioned his trainee over.

When they got to the front door, Gage realized the glass had been broken, "Well, I guess I was right."

Van drew his weapon and made three identical announcements identifying himself as the police and ordering whoever was inside to come out.

After the third booming call, they could hear a muffled wailing coming from inside.

"Well that's a new one," Van said and motioned to her with his head, "call the dogs."

Gage whistled the beginning of *The Good, The Bad, and the Ugly* then stood silently for a moment. Killer came running to the door and danced in a circle, barking in excitement.

"You were afraid we'd be mauled by a rat?" Van asked.

Gage made a face at him before calling, "Tiny, you good?"

The deep guttural bark in response made Van arch an eyebrow.

"Now I know why they weren't barking," Gage grinned.

"You want to clue us in?"

"I'm fairly certain you will find your perp in my parts closet in the interior of the shop under the stairwell," she responded.

"How could you possibly know that?" the rookie asked.

"It's the only place in there big enough for the guy I saw in the truck, that has an unlocked door," Gage responded before calling through the door, "Tiny. Stay. You're back up."

The single bark sounded again.

"You're good to go," Gage motioned to the door, "he should stay put."

"Should?" Van asked.

"Please don't shoot my dog," she was looking at the rookie, "he's a good dog, well trained, he will not hurt you if you make sure he knows you're there to help me."

"You stay with me," Van ordered his rookie, "the interior is a wide-open setup, the door she's talking about is on the left, against the wall. Keep your eyes open and your mouth shut."

The rookie nodded hurriedly and tried to pull his flashlight from his gun belt, but it got caught. After a few tense seconds of yanking, he finally managed to get the light out and held it up, his firearm gripped tightly in his other hand as he moved to follow Van into the building.

"The lights are on the wall right when you enter," Gage pointed to the spot from the outside, "then Mighty Mouse can just focus on not shooting you."

Van sighed, "Thanks." He glanced back, "We'll put the lights on, kid, take a breath."

The rookie sucked in a breath and nodded.

"Just remember to breathe," Gage smiled at him, "the adrenaline will try to make you forget. But I'm pretty sure this situation is under control."

The rookie nodded again.

"Here we go," Van opened the door and slipped inside. Gage held the door open for the rookie to follow, then watched through the door as her shop became illuminated and the two officers worked their way through.

She heard Tiny's bark of acknowledgment and the rookie's voice.

Then the muffled wailing she'd heard before became louder as the door into the parts closet was opened.

Moments later Van called out to her, "Come on in."

Gage strode into her shop, picked up Killer, and met the three men by her closet door. The man from the truck was in handcuffs, sitting on the floor, and bleeding from the leg.

"Damn it, my ass hurts, please let me stand," he used the hands which were cuffed behind him to clutch at his butt cheek, which was steadily leaking blood. "That fucking dog attacked me!"

"Yeah, animals tend to defend their territory," Van said in a bored tone as Tiny moved and sat at Gage's feet. The dog was still focusing all his attention on the bleeding man. Gage rubbed his ears one after the other.

"Maybe you shouldn't have broken in," the Rookie added.

"Call rescue," Van ordered.

The rookie started to walk toward the door.

"Where are you going?" Van asked.

"To get my phone."

"If only you had something on you right now that would allow you to let dispatch know we need an ambulance," Van stared at the rookie's radio.

"Oh," the rookie smiled anxiously and started talking on the radio.

"I hate training people," Van grumbled under his breath.

Gage chuckled but was carefully staring at the man on her floor.

"You ever seen this guy before?" Van asked.

"He's the same one I've seen driving the truck," she responded, "but I have no idea who he is, or what he wants."

"I ain't saying shit," the man snapped, spitting in Gage's direction.

Tiny growled deep in his chest and stood.

The handcuffed man immediately began to awkwardly scoot backward while squealing, "You have to protect me! I'm in your custody!"

Van smirked, "Maybe you shouldn't be a dumb ass."

Gage rested her hand on Tiny's head and stared at the man intently.

"Get me out of here, man, I need the hospital," he kicked his foot at Tiny who barked. Once. Eliciting a shriek of terror.

Van laughed, "Man, I'll miss you when I go to New York."

Gage grinned, "Well my cousin is a cop up there, look her up if you need some of the same charm."

"You have a cousin that's a cop?" Van's disbelief made Gage laugh.

"She doesn't approve of all my methods, but she knows I come from a good place," she winked at the officer.

He shook his head with a smile. He noticed flashing lights through the broken glass door and grabbed his suspect by the elbow and helped him stand, "Let's go, chew toy."

"That's fucked up, man," the man said before whimpering with each limping step.

"Look around, make sure nothing is missing," Van called to Gage who nodded.

"What was he up to, handsome boy?" Gage asked Tiny.

The dog looked up at her with his head cocked.

"He didn't do anything but come in, huh?" she smiled.

Tiny made a grunting sound and lay down at Gage's feet.

"You're such a clever boy," Gage cooed. She looked at Killer who was still laying in her arms lazily, "You want to do some work?"

Killer's ears perked up.

"Let's see if that guy left anything in the storeroom," Gage set Killer on the ground. The little dog ran into the abandoned room, sniffing all over.

Gage flipped on the light switch on the outside of the room, "At least he was sitting in the dark, terrified of the monster outside." She glanced at Killer, "I know how that feels."

The small dog glanced up at her, then continued sniffing the room. He kept coming back to the puddles of blood and didn't go anywhere else.

"Nothing weird?" she asked the dog.

Killer yapped, then ran out and lay beside Tiny.

"That dog deserves a steak," Van said as he walked back into the garage.

"He'll get one," Gage responded. "It looks like Tiny got him right when he came in, I don't see anything out of place other than that stuff he probably knocked over running away." She motioned to the floor where several tools were scattered, one of her rolling tool stations was pushed out of its place.

"His name is Victor Hayes," Van said, "there's a warrant out for him for- you want to guess?"

"B&E?" Gage asked.

"Ding ding. You're so clever," he grinned, "thanks for the call. Now I can make my rookie do lots of paperwork."

Gage grinned, "Happy to help."

"You doing okay?" Van was suddenly serious, the concern in his blue eyes gave Gage pause.

"What? Why?" Gage sputtered, "I'm good."

"Don't lie to me," Van made a face, "I'm a cop, everyone lies to me."

"I got some shit going on right now that makes me edgy, and my friends are being dicks," Gage responded, "but I'll be fine."

He nodded, "That I believe." He held out his fist, "I'm a phone call away if you need me."

She bumped his fist with her own, "Let me know what you find out about that guy."

"Will do," Van turned and started walking back toward the front door.

"Hey, Van?" Gage called hesitantly.

"Yo, what's up?" Van turned back.

"Can you do me a favor?" She asked.

"Sure," Van took a couple steps back toward her.

"Can you check if he has any connection to Alejandro Sanchez?"

"Will do," Van answered, "who is that?"

"A guy," Gage responded with a smile.

"You're such a bitch," Van laughed.

"You love me," Gage responded, "I'm adorable."

Van shook his head, "Ridiculous."

"We need to speak to her," the rookie came inside again, rainwater dripping from his hat.

"Kid, where is our arrest?" Van sighed.

"In the ambulance," the rookie answered.

"Did you leave him there alone?"

"I handcuffed him to the bed," the rookie seemed confused.

Van sighed again, heavily, "You're an idiot."

"What?"

Van spoke into his radio and verified that another officer on scene had eyes on the suspect, "Never leave your arrest unattended."

"He's with the EMTs," the rookie said defensively.

"How are you going to feel if he gets free and kills one of them," Van snapped. "You don't leave your arrest." He glared at the younger man, "Understood?"

"I get it," the rookie snapped back, "but I needed to come back in here to make sure you're not letting your friend get away with breaking the law."

Gage arched an eyebrow, "Crazy say what now?"

"Mr. Hayes brought my attention to all the illegal vehicle modifications being done here," the kid's air of superiority made Gage bristle.

"Kelly," Van's tone was both annoyed and cautionary, "do not open a can of worms you cannot close."

"Maybe I need to report that you do favors for pretty girls on duty," Kelly snapped.

"Aw shucks," Gage cooed, with a pronounced Southern drawl, "you think I'm pretty?"

"This is no joking matter," Kelly snapped, "why don't you just explain to me why we should let you go?"

Van opened his mouth, but Gage held up her hand, "It's okay. I'll handle it."

"Handle what?" Kelly snapped.

Tiny sat up, his eyes watching the young cop.

Gage held her hand up to Tiny also, "Stay back Tiny, this kid is too jumpy."

Tiny blinked but continued to stare at the officer, his head tilted.

"May I go into my office?" Gage asked Kelly.

"Don't make any sudden moves," the kid snapped but motioned to the office.

"I'm going to get my keys out of my right front pocket," she said and reached into her pocket with two fingers to retrieve her keys. She walked to her office and unlocked the door, striding in and opening her filing cabinet drawer.

"Hey!" Kelly's hand went to his gun so Van grabbed his arm and held it by the kid's side. "Let me go!"

"I'm your training officer, you idiot. You will NOT draw that weapon," Van snapped.

"Maybe you're just too close to this situation," Kelly struggled.

Gage walked back into the room holding a piece of paper, "Now boys, settle down."

Van pushed Kelly away and glared at him.

"What's that?" Kelly asked, motioning to the paper.

"You are not wrong, some of the modifications my shop does, are illegal for use on the public streets," Gage stated.

"So, you admit it!" Kelly unsnapped his handcuff pouch.

Gage arched an eyebrow, "Down boy, no need for foreplay. The parts themselves are not illegal."

"You still make vehicles illegal to drive on the street."

Gage laughed, "You are all amped up, take a breath." She handed the form to Kelly.

"What the hell is this?" The officer looked at it, then back at Gage.

"That is the form which every one of my customers must sign in order for me to perform any modifications which could be illegal on the road." Gage responded, "If you actually took a second to read it, you would see that it releases my shop from any liability, because it clearly states the vehicles modified are for personal use. They sign a form telling me that vehicle will only be driven on private roads or be shown in car shows."

"You can't honestly believe everyone who signs this actually complies with it," Kelly scoffed.

"That's not my problem," Gage responded, "I have no reason to believe anyone is being deceitful. They sign my form telling me their vehicle will comply with the law because it will never be on the public roadways. Therefore, nothing my shop does is illegal, and you can just strut your pretentious ass out of here." Gage smiled sweetly.

"Maybe next time, ask if this subject has ever been broached before," Van growled.

Kelly folded the form and tucked it into his pocket, "I'll be in touch after I follow up with an attorney."

Gage motioned with both her hands for him to go ahead, "Be my guest."

"Now do as the lady said, and get the fuck out of here," Van snapped, "maybe go keep an eye on your arrest."

Kelly strode out of the garage.

"Jesus, how the hell do you put up with that little shit?" Gage asked.

"I don't," Van grumbled, "I'm sorry about that idiot. I'll be reporting him for his behavior."

Gage smiled, "I appreciate you."

Van nodded, "And I'll let you know about Hayes, as soon as I get our history with him."

"I appreciate you even more," Gage sighed, looking around.

"Do you need any help with the door?" Van asked, "I can come back after my shift to help you board it up."

"That's sweet, but I can handle it," Gage grabbed a broom, "you get your pictures yet?"

"No, but I'll do them, I'm not letting Kelly back in here to fuck shit up," Van pulled out his phone.

"I can get you video from my camera too," she motioned to the camera pointed at the parts closet, "it has night vision."

"That'd be great," Van said as he took pictures of the door. "Do you have Tiny's rabies vaccination paperwork?"

"Yup," Gage walked back into her office and went through her file cabinet. She pulled out a different form and came back into the main garage as Van was walking back from taking his pictures at the closet. "Here's a copy. His vet's number is on there too, along with the information of the school that helped me train him."

"Perfect, thanks," Van smiled. "Good to see you again. Thank you for calling me instead of coming in here and shooting the guy."

"Whaaaaaat," Gage pretended to be offended, "why would I do that? That's just silly."

"Yeah, okay," Van nodded, "whatever you say."

"Who would waste a bullet on that guy?" Gage added with a smirk.

Van laughed as he left the building.

Gage started to sweep up the glass as all the vehicles outside began to move on. "You're getting the biggest steak I can buy tomorrow," she said to Tiny who had moved so that he could see her from where he was laying.

Killer yapped.

"You can have one too," she smiled, "my good boys."

Chapter 40

Mere grabbed her jacket off the booth and waited for the others to collect their things. The evening hadn't been nearly as entertaining as anticipated. The tension hadn't lessened much when Gage left, most of the group just sat, sullenly drinking. Even though the night was ruined, no one wanted to leave until they were sure they wouldn't bump into Gage. The only one who decided to be oblivious to the strain was Buck, who was overtly happy while ensuring that everyone smiled occasionally at his antics.

Buck draped his arm over Mere's shoulders with a broad grin on his face, "You know, you could just come back to my place if you don't want to talk to Gage."

Mere laughed, "As tempting as that offer may be, and as delightful as this night has been," she tweaked his nose playfully, "I think I'd rather have you pining after me."

Buck shrugged good-naturedly, "As you wish, just know, the door's always open."

"To your bed?" Mere laughed again.

Buck looked shocked, "You Americans are weird, you have doors on your beds?"

Mere squinted at him, trying to decide if he was being facetious. She grinned broadly when he winked at her. "You're a mess, Buckley Makenzie," she gave him a small peck on the cheek, "but I actually had quite a bit of fun tonight. You can come dance with me anytime."

Buck bowed low, "An honor which I will happily accept."

Mere shook her head at him but had a small smile still teasing her lips. She turned to head out of the club and noticed Alex walking toward her. She wasn't sure if she should be standoffish, or polite, so she was left standing awkwardly, chewing the inside of her lip.

"Meredith!" Alex's smile was disarmingly charming, "I'm so glad to see you." He waved at her friends, his demeanor warm and inviting, "Thanks for coming everyone. My night is always better when I see you here."

Will stared at the man intently, trying to read him, Lina smiled but cuddled into Will's side.

EmEm acknowledged Alex's statement with a nod of his head.

Buck grinned broadly, "Here's the bounce I've heard so much about."

"I'm actually the owner," Alex said.

"Yes, you are," Buck tipped his hat, "certainly no cobber, that's for sure."

Alex looked confused, "Um, thank you?"

Buck wrapped his arm around Mere's waist and nodded.

"I didn't realize you had a-" Alex began.

"He's just a friend," Mere interrupted. She turned to Buck, "Can you give us a minute?"

Buck shrugged, "You wanna give me the flick for the drongo, I ain't gonna stop ya."

Mere watched Buck move back to stand by EmEm and Lina, but she noticed he was not the same happy-go-lucky man he had been a moment before, he even looked different. She was pretty sure she was now seeing his work persona, the one who went overseas to kill people. Her green gaze turned back to Alex, "How can I help you?"

Alex chuckled, "This is why I like you so much, you're really perceptive."

Mere didn't say anything, she just waited for Alex to continue.

He cleared his throat, "I was hoping you could help me with something."

"I'm not going to help you get to-" Mere started.

"Oh, no, nothing about Bridget," Alex shook his head.

"Okay?" Mere said cautiously.

"There's a benefit tomorrow night, for my charity. It would look pretty bad if I couldn't find someone to go with me to my own party," he smiled sheepishly, "but unfortunately, I don't know many women here who I would actually enjoy talking to for a couple hours. I was hoping maybe you would do me the honor of being my date."

Mere chewed her lip again, thinking.

"Just as friends," Alex said quickly, "I could just really use a friend for moral support as I try to bleed the rich people dry."

Mere arched her eyebrow, "I assume this is a black-tie affair?"

"Yes," Alex nodded, "I know it's short notice, so I'll understand if you say no, but I really hope you'll say yes."

Mere glanced over her shoulder at her friends, Will and Buck were both still on edge, Lina was trying to keep Will calm with her arm around his waist, and EmEm seemed like he was trying to ignore the situation altogether. She turned back to Alex and decided it would be the perfect way to get some more information from him, "Yeah, okay."

"Really?" Alex's face lit up, "That's amazing! Thank you so much, I really appreciate it. Can I send a car to pick you up?"

Mere shook her head, "Just give me the address. I'll meet you there."

Alex smiled broadly, "I'll text you in the morning," he hugged her briefly, "thanks again, you're a life-saver."

Mere smiled slightly and pulled back, "Sure, anything for the kids, right?" She turned from him and grabbed Lina's hand, "Now if you'll excuse us, we're heading out."

Alex motioned to the door, "Absolutely, thanks again for coming. We appreciate your business."

"Gonna give you the chunder from down under," Buck grumbled as he followed the others from the club.

"What are you doing?" Will asked when they made it into the parking lot.

Mere shrugged, "Recon."

"I'm sure Gage will see it that way," EmEm sighed.

"I can't really help how Gage sees our actions at this point," Mere responded. "I need to know what the hell is going on. The only way we're going to know anything, is through Alex, since Gage won't talk to us."

"He's having a lend of you," Buck shook his head, "dirty little root rat."

Mere stared at Buck, "Now I understand what Gage meant, you people make no sense at all."

"Only if you're not the full quid," Buck grumbled.

"I'm not going to be friendly with him," Mere snapped, "but I need information, and he's the only one that will talk to me right now."

"That stands out like a shag on a rock," Buck responded, "you don't think he knows you're desperate?"

"Maybe he does," Mere shrugged, "that's a risk I'll take to help Gage."

"Do you honestly believe that pork pie?" Buck actually laughed in disbelief.

"Um, I have no idea what meat pie has to do with anything in this conversation," Mere said.

Buck sighed, "You're lying to yourself if you think you're doing this for your mate," he shook his head, "you're doing this for your benefit, no one else's." He left her standing in the parking lot as he walked to his motorcycle and pulled on his helmet.

"No one asked you," Mere called after him.

He held up his hands in a why motion before climbing on his bike and starting it up.

Mere turned on her heel as he flew from the parking lot, "Let's go home," she grumbled.

The silence was deafening in the car on the ride back to the flat.

Lina pulled into a spot in front of the garage and stared at the door in confusion, "Um, guys? What happened to the door?"

The others looked and realized the glass door was boarded up with a sign on it.

"What the hell?" Mere climbed out of the car and hurried up the steps to the flat. She knew the others were right behind her. She unlocked and opened the door, but before she could call out, Tessa came down the hallway.

"Everyone's fine," the younger woman said. "Apparently someone broke in downstairs, but Tiny handled it until the cops got here and arrested the guy."

"Who was it?" Will asked.

Tessa shrugged, "Some guy named Hayes? Van wasn't sure of the motive when he called me."

"Donovan called you?" EmEm asked.

"He didn't want Gage here alone or something," Tessa sighed, "he obviously doesn't know her very well. She's in her room and hasn't come out."

"You sure she's in there?" Mere strode down the hallway and knocked on Gage's door.

"What?" Gage called from inside.

"You dead?" Will called from down the hall.

"I live to fight another day," Gage responded, "I'm tired, go away."

Mere heard scratching at the door, so she opened it enough for Tiny to leave the room and go into her room instead.

"Traitor," Gage grumbled as Mere closed the door again.

Mere walked back down to the kitchen, "I'm going tomorrow. I'm sick of all the secrets clouding the air."

EmEm sighed again, "I get that, but shouldn't we let her take the time to figure shit out for herself?"

Mere shook her head, "What if we get a job? How are we supposed to trust each other and work together if we're all on different pages?"

Will stared at Mere, "I don't think this is the next step," he shook his head, "you saw how hurt she was, this is doing exactly the same thing that you saw broke her heart. There's no excuse."

Mere stood still for a moment, when she spoke, her voice was hard, "I'm going to do what I need to, this is the only choice I can make to figure out what's going on."

Tessa looked from one friend to the other, "I have no idea what's happening, but if it will piss Gage off, I vote to do it." When everyone looked at her, surprised, she shrugged and turned to walk back down the hall.

The sound of Tessa's door slamming made Lina jump, "What's wrong with Tessie?"

"She wants to study abroad," Mere grumbled, rubbing her eyes with one hand, nursing a headache, "the conversation obviously didn't go so well."

"We're gonna go," Will said, "let us know if you need help tomorrow."

"I can rig an earwig," EmEm piped up.

"I think I can handle a bunch of rich people," Mere responded.

"It never hurts to have a backup plan," Will cautioned.

"Yeah, thanks, I got it," Mere smiled tightly, "now go away so I can get some beauty sleep." She closed and locked the door behind her friends and waved at them through the glass door before going to her room.

Chapter 41

Gage found herself sitting with Van before his shift had even ended. The sun was just starting to peek above the horizon.

"Victor Hayes is a dear personal friend of Eduardo Espinoza." Van glanced at Gage and noticed she made a face, "I take it you know him?"

Gage nodded, "Yes, he's a punk who was banished from my shop for his behavior not long ago. What was Hayes looking for though?"

Van shrugged, "Your guess is as good as mine. Maybe he was just looking to wreck your shit, or actually hoping to steal some parts, at this point, it doesn't matter. He broke in and damaged property, so we've got plenty to convict him." He held up the DVD Gage had brought with her, "This helps too. I love burying these idiots in evidence."

Gage nodded, "Okay. Thanks, I appreciate you."

She stood from her chair and turned to leave the precinct but Van grabbed her arm gently as he stood, "You want to tell me about Alejandro Sanchez?"

She squinted her eyes at him, "Nope."

"Come on. It's not like you to bring up a specific name unless you know there's something there. Plus, you never wake up this early, unless you never slept," Van stared at her, waiting.

"As I said, I was just curious to know if he had anything to do with Hayes," Gage shrugged, "I'm getting paranoid in my old age, what can I say?" She batted her eyelashes at him, "And I just couldn't sleep knowing I'd get to see you again so soon."

Van shook his head, "If you're in trouble, I hope you know you can come to me."

Gage pat his arm with a smile teasing her lips, "You're a good guy, Van, but I'm just fine."

He looked at her sideways, trying to gauge her honesty.

"Truly," Gage held up her hands in surrender.

"Well, then you should know Alejandro Sanchez goes by Alex Santiago here," Van watched her face carefully. "Sanchez was a major criminal in Texas, as I'm sure you know, but Santiago has no criminal history at all. I was quite interested to see that these two men have exactly the same picture on their driver's licenses."

Gage made a dismissive noise, "He always did love acting innocent," she glanced at Van again, "thanks for the info."

Van nodded, "Is this guy going to be a problem?"

"For you?" Gage asked with a slow smile, "Absolutely not, you're moving to New York City."

Van studied her face, "Be careful, Slugger, I'd miss you if something happened to you."

Gage scoffed, "You won't even be here." She poked his chest playfully with her finger, "You'll be all busy in the big city."

Van shrugged, "Just watch yourself, okay?"

Gage nodded, "I love watching myself. I'm adorable." She struck a pose before walking from the precinct with a smile plastered on her face. When she got to the sidewalk, the smile dropped from her face and she tried to decide where she could go to avoid the most people all day.

Part of her really wanted to call Mak and just spend the day with him, but she didn't pull out her phone. The internal struggle she fought over the subject was almost visible on her face as she climbed in her pick-up truck. She pulled her phone out of her pocket and threw it onto the floorboard in the passenger side of the cab before pulling into traffic and driving nowhere in particular.

~*~*~*~*~

Mere sat in her car, staring up at the mansion whose driveway she was currently occupying. She glanced around, hoping for a sign that no one was home, but she couldn't decide if the residents were inside or not.

With a sigh, she finally exited her vehicle and walked to the front door. She searched her key ring, but then noticed the front door was slightly ajar. She rolled her eyes and pushed the door open, looking around for any sign that something criminal had occurred. All she found was further proof that the occupants of the home had no real regard for how the world works.

Expensive furs littered the floor, a purse which probably cost as much as her rent was strewn on the white rabbit fur couch. A wallet which was barely held closed by the snap lay beside the purse. One of probably twenty credit cards lay carelessly by the phone.

Mere walked past the scene, fighting the urge to take the cash which was undoubtedly in that wallet. It had never been missed when she'd taken it and given it to charity in the past. She crept quietly up the grand staircase to the second floor. She could hear a woman speaking in an unnaturally high pitch down the hallway. She avoided that room and went into the room at the top of the stairs, closing the door behind her quietly.

When no sound of pursuit reached her ears, Mere turned and strode to the closet of the bedroom. She flipped the light switch and a room which was the size of her bedroom was illuminated, revealing hundreds of gowns and expensive pairs of shoes. There was a vanity with a large mirror against the only wall not covered in dresses or shoes. Jewelry was displayed on the wall, surrounding the vanity with no locks or safeguards at all. Mere knew they were real jewels. She grew sick to her stomach at the thought of how much money was blatantly on display. Shaking her head, she moved to a wall of dresses.

Finding a dress which was acceptable for a black-tie gala was actually harder than she anticipated as each time she thought she'd found one, she realized that it was far too low cut, or short enough to leave nothing to the imagination.

Mere hung a royal blue gown with a corset style top and silver embellishments by the mirror, then went back to see if there was anything else she could use.

She'd just pulled a beautiful gold-hued silky slip of a dress when her worst nightmare pushed the door of the closet open.

"Merry? Is that you?" The woman was clearly intoxicated, her once auburn hair was now fried blonde and twisted into a pile on her head.

"Hi Karen," Meredith said with a sigh, "I was hoping not to bother you."

"Oh, Merry! I haven't seen you in so long!" Karen stumbled into the room, her heels not cooperating on the plush carpet.

"I just need to borrow a dress for a thing today, that's okay isn't it?" Mere glanced at the older woman who was standing awkwardly against the doorframe, a champagne glass clutched in her expensively manicured fingers.

"Of course, Honey Bear," Karen smiled, "take whatever you need." She finished her drink and set the glass on the vanity. "There's an amazing black one that would look stunning on you," Karen stumbled to the rack of dresses and started searching them.

"I think I'll just use this one," Mere held up the gold gown. It was simple but had a low back and fitted bodice to accentuate the breasts without being too revealing.

"Oh Merry, show some skin," Karen pulled out a piece of fabric that looked like a bikini with lace over it.

"I'm going to a charity gala for kids," Mere's tone was scathing, "I don't need to 'show some skin'."

Karen sighed and held the dress up to herself, "I just wish you'd even try, hunny. You could do so well for yourself."

"I have done well for myself," Mere stated.

"Are you seeing someone?" Karen's excitement lit up the mask of a face heavy Botox had left her.

"My definition of doing well for myself isn't dependent on a man," Mere snapped.

Karen sighed again, "Oh Merry, I don't know why you get so cross with me. I just want you to be as happy as I am."

Mere stared at the woman before her, the shaking hands and sunken eyes circled with deep bruise-like bags were an indicator. "What pills are you taking now?"

Karen's hand clutched her chest as though the shock of that question pained her, she let the black monstrosity she'd been holding fall to the ground. "I don't know what you're talking about, I'm only taking my prescriptions."

Mere nodded, "Do you take them as prescribed? Or are you self-medicating again?"

"You sound like Richard," Karen waved her hand as though dismissing the notion.

"How is ole Dick?" Mere asked, accepting the answer that had been unspoken.

"Richard is fine," Karen stared at Mere, "he asks about you."

Mere snorted.

"That is extremely unladylike," Karen scolded, "he's your stepfather. You could treat him with some respect."

Mere stared at Karen with a bored expression, "If he actually put a leash on you and took you to rehab like a good husband should, maybe I would."

Karen sputtered, "How dare you!"

"You watched coke disappear up Dad's nose as he shot poison into his veins for years before he finally died, drowning in his own puke." Mere responded, "Now you pop pills and swallow your sorrows with booze, thinking that somehow makes you classier?"

"Watch your mouth, young lady!"

"I'm twenty-three years old," Mere snapped, "not that I'd expect you to realize that since most of your new parts are much younger than me."

Karen adjusted her large breasts and lifted her chin, "It's funny how you can come here and pass your judgments, but you have no interest in refusing Richard's money."

"If Dick wants to try to buy my affections by depositing money in an account for me, that's his business." Mere shrugged, "I never asked him for it, and I don't require it. He can stop any time."

"Well he likes to know he's taking care of us," Karen changed her tone.

"I don't need to be taken care of," Mere responded, "when I did need it, you were off wearing lingerie to entice a rich husband." She looked around, "At least it worked out for you."

Tears welled in Karen's eyes, "I know I wasn't the best mother-"

"You'd have to have been a mother, to be on a scale of awful," Mere cut her off, "I just needed a dress, not a therapy session." She held up the gown as she turned to leave, "Thanks."

"Wait!" Karen chased after her.

"What?" Mere asked and met Karen's gaze, stopping the older woman in her tracks.

"I meant to send you this for your birthday," Karen grabbed a yellow diamond necklace from the wall then selected the matching earrings. "I know it's late, but I want you to have it. It'll look great with the dress."

Mere sighed, took the jewelry, and said, "My birthday is in three months, you didn't miss it."

Karen shrugged, "Well, then it's for last year."

Mere nodded, "Thanks, Karen."

Karen rushed over to the dresses again, "Oh! Wait!"

Mere stared with disdain as Karen pushed the skirts out of the way, "I have to go."

"It'll just take a – GOT THEM!" Karen stood up, a triumphant look splashed on her features as she held up a pair of sparkling gold heels. "These will complete the look, oh Honey Bear, you'll look gorgeous."

Mere forced a smiled, "Thanks, Karen. I appreciate it."

Karen handed Mere the shoes and reached out to brush a wisp of hair from the younger woman's face but Mere quickly recoiled and left, leaving her standing alone in the closet.

Chapter 42

Lina opened the door almost immediately after Mere knocked, she looked flustered and had her purse over her shoulder. Mere could tell she hadn't even heard the knock by the look of shock on her face, "Mere!"

Mere barged in, a messenger bag's strap across her chest, "Sorry to intrude, but I can't get ready at home," she held up the dress and shoes, "help?"

Lina glanced at her watch and made a face, "I'm really supposed to be somewhere."

Mere pouted, "But please? Gage usually helps me with this stuff, I have no idea how to do it alone."

Lina sighed, but smiled, "Okay, go take a shower, I'll cancel my appointment."

"You rock!" Mere dumped her dress and shoes into Lina's arms.

"Whoa, no, take the dress," Lina laughed, "it looks like you crumpled it in a ball, hang it in the room while you shower, it will help it lose the wrinkles."

"See!" Mere took the dress and kissed Lina's cheek, "You save me."

Lina nodded and dropped her purse on the table, "Story of my life," she grumbled as she pulled her phone from her purse, "now go!"

When Mere came out of the shower, she saw that Lina had put a fresh towel on top of the toilet for her. She grabbed the towel and realized it was warm from the dryer. She wrapped herself in it and sighed happily as the remaining tension in her body released. "You're the best person, ever," Mere called.

Lina came in the bathroom, "You owe me fifty bucks. Doctors never let you miss an appointment for free." She smiled at the lump of warm towel which she assumed was Mere, "What kind of lingerie do you have with you?"

Mere peeked out of her towel cocoon, "You had a doctor's appointment? Are you sick?"

"It was just a checkup," Lina shrugged, "but they still charge you to cancel so close."

Mere lifted her bag, set it on the vanity, and opened it, "I'll totally pay you." She pulled out a black strapless bra, "Will this work?"

Lina laughed, "No, black under this kind of dress will stick out like a sore thumb, you need something in your skin tone."

Mere made a face, "Uh, I emptied my bra drawer into this thing," she handed the bag to Lina then resituated her towel and tucked it into itself, creating a wrap dress. "Can you see if anything will work?"

"You better hope something will work," Lina glanced at her friend, "it's not like you can borrow something from me."

"True," Mere sighed, staring at Lina's endowed bosom, "you were far more gifted than I."

Lina laughed again, "I'd trade you the back pain for your killer legs."

Mere shrugged as she investigated her face in the mirror, "The legs are merely from years of ballet."

"Have you ever worn any of these before?" Lina pulled out a jumbled mess of bras and corsets.

"I like the black one," Mere grinned at Lina, "it can have straps or not, that pretty much suits my needs."

Lina rolled her eyes, "Dios mio, I'm taking you bra shopping sometime soon."

Mere made a face, "But they're so expensive," she whined as Lina untangled the mess before her.

"You need proper support," Lina admonished, "you can't wear the same bra every day!"

Mere shrugged again, "I have sports bras too."

Lina shook her head and selected a cream-colored lace bodice with a low back and built-in push-up cups, "This should work."

Mere stared at the fabric like it was a snake, "What the hell is that?"

Lina held it up, "Sexy? Feminine?"

"A straight jacket?" Mere added.

"I'm sorry, do you want to go to this thing, or not?" Lina held out the bodice.

Mere sighed and took it, "You might have to help me with it," she grumbled as she dropped her towel.

"I'll do what I have to," Lina answered as she opened one of the drawers in the vanity and started pulling out beauty supplies.

~*~*~*~

"Babe?" Will called, "Why are you here, I thought you-" he trailed off when Lina came out of the bathroom followed by Mere.

"Wow," Will's eyes were wide.

Mere grinned, "Your lady works magic," she said, motioning to herself. The dress fit her perfectly, showcasing the creamy skin of her back, the yellow diamond of her necklace fell just shy of her cleavage, drawing attention in an understated way. The high slit on her dress allowed glimpses of her shapely legs and the glittering heels on her feet. Her hair fell in soft curls down her shoulders and her makeup was perfectly applied, drawing attention to her sparkling green eyes.

Lina laughed, "You're always gorgeous, Mere, I'm just letting it shine."

"She bippity-boppity-booed the shit outta me," Mere stated proudly, twirling to show Will the full effect.

"Holy crap, Mere," Will wrapped his arm around Lina, "you look beautiful."

"Aw shucks," Mere made an impish face, then looked at her phone, "well, I better get going."

"Do you want me to follow?" Will asked, "I have a tux, I could totally crash it."

Mere rolled her eyes, "I'll be fine. Seriously, stop worrying."

Will sighed, "Well, please let us know when you get home."

"Don't wait up!" Mere widened her eyes as she gathered her stuff, "Thanks again, Lina, you're a lifesaver!"

"Hey, where's my fifty bucks?" Lina called as Mere headed to the door.

"I'll bring it tomorrow!" Mere called and slammed the door.

"I'm never getting my fifty bucks, am I?" Lina asked.

Will laughed, "Maybe in cookies, or a new bag," he hugged her.

When Mere arrived at the address she'd been given, it was already crowded. She pulled up to the valet and smiled at the kid who looked overjoyed to drive her car, "We both know this car is fast," she said quietly, "just don't fuck it up, okay?" She winked at him as she handed him her keys, then headed up the stairs to the mansion which was, unfortunately, not far from where her mother lived.

When she arrived at the front door, a man in a tuxedo greeted her, "Good evening. Invitation?"

"I was invited by Alex Santiago," Mere smiled uneasily, "I don't have a paper invitation."

"Ah, Miss Daley, please, follow me," the man motioned to his comrade who nodded.

Mere licked her perfect red lips and followed after the man who ushered her through the outskirts of the crowd. She grabbed a glass of champagne as she walked by a waiter with a tray of them, she sipped it and made an appreciative face as she followed her escort down a hall away from the crowd.

She glanced over her shoulder in confusion, before looking back to the man, who was stopped by a set of double doors. "Mr. Santiago is waiting for you," the man smiled and opened one of the doors, revealing a library.

Mere stepped into the room and couldn't help the catch of her breath when she took in the room. Floor to ceiling shelves were completely full of books of all kinds, the room smelled like leather and Heaven. She took in a deep breath as she turned, taking in the thousands of books throughout the circular room.

"Impressed?" Alex's voice was jovial as he placed a bookmark in the book in his lap. He was occupying a plush armchair by a roaring fire. He stood, "I am," he motioned to her, "you're gorgeous."

Mere blushed despite herself, "Thank you," she motioned to the books with her glass, "this is amazing."

"I've seen better views," he set his book down and strode to her side with a handsome grin. "At least, now I have," he winked at her and motioned for her to precede him from the room.

"That was cheesy," Mere allowed herself to be ushered from the room, she tried to cover the warmth his praise was giving her by swallowing the rest of her drink.

Alex shrugged and placed a warm hand gently in the small of her back, "I call it as I see it," he seemed sincere, which was confusing Mere.

"I'll have to stay on guard with you," she said casually.

Alex chuckled, "You don't have to guard anything from me, Meredith," he said huskily.

Mere was surprised once more as a blush crept up her neck.

"I wanted to show you this place," he motioned to the books as they left the room.

"Why?" She laughed.

"So you know what I have to offer," he said softly in her ear. His breath made her shiver.

"You have an amazing library to offer?" Mere asked.

"Just one of many perks," he smiled at her, "I had a feeling the books were the way to your heart."

She stared at him, studying his face, "Are you trying to find a way to my heart?"

"I'd be a fool not to try," he responded, his chocolate eyes warm, "you are a stunning woman."

"What about Gage?" Mere asked, carefully gauging his emotional response.

His eyes dropped, "I can't force Bridget to love me." He shrugged, "I know when I'm not wanted. If she's moved on, I guess it's time I do too."

"It took you years searching the globe for her to come to that conclusion?" Mere arched her eyebrow.

"Well, when I came here, I fully intended to find her and win her back," he answered.

"What changed?" Mere's green eyes bore into his.

"I met you," he said quietly and smiled gently.

"I thought this was just a friend helping out a friend," Mere was more breathless than she'd anticipated.

He nodded, "That's exactly what it is," he took her now empty glass from her and replaced it with a fresh one, "but who knows how it could end?"

Mere didn't say anything, but she downed her new drink and placed it on the tray set aside for dirty glasses.

Alex smiled, "There's plenty where that came from," he winked at her again, "want to dance?"

"Um, I don't really do fancy dancing," she said nervously.

Alex laughed, "All you have to do, is follow my lead." He took her hand and led her to the dance floor, "Just relax. Let your body react to mine." He pulled her close and began moving to the music.

She was awkward at first, but she took a breath and inhaled the scent of his cologne; it was intoxicating. The expensive champagne was making her face warm. At least that's what she told herself as she allowed her body to rest against his. She felt like his puppet, but it wasn't an entirely unwelcome feeling. Her body was reacting to his in more ways than just dancing.

They danced for what felt like hours to Mere, they only paused long enough for her to sip more champagne each time the same waiter came by with his tray. All eyes were on them while they danced, making her feel like Cinderella. She was warm and happy while cradled in his capable hands as he spun her around the dance floor.

When his hands began to wander slightly, more than a gentleman's should, she didn't really mind. He was being discreet and it was starting to light a fire deep inside her.

"Mere," he said huskily into her ear as he twirled her to a corner of the room behind one of the huge decorative pillars.

"Yes?" she asked breathlessly.

"You are exquisite, do you know that?"

She tried to laugh but gasped when the bare skin of her back pressed against the cold marble of the pillar, then his heat was pressed against her, and his mouth was on hers. As much as she wanted to deny it, his lips tasted sweet like the champagne, and she was getting intoxicated. The cold behind her and the warmth he provided was making her knees feel like Jell-O. She kissed him back with vigor until they were both breathless.

"I don't suppose we could get out of here," she said roughly when their lips separated.

Alex looked around the room, seeing who had noticed their make-out session, "We could probably slip upstairs," his huskiness made her quiver.

She smiled at him so he started to lead her toward the staircase by the library.

"And finally, thank you so much to our benefactor and host, Mr. Alex Santiago!" The announcement was accompanied by a spotlight on the couple. "Would you come say a few words?" The woman held out the microphone with a broad smile as the crowd clapped.

"Rain check," she whispered into his ear with a smirk.

He sighed heavily but walked through the crowd toward the microphone-bearing woman at the front of the room with a gracious smile.

Mere watched him go, not sure how she should feel, or what she should do.

"You seem pretty friendly with the guy your best friend doesn't like," the voice shocked her back to earth from the cloud where she'd been floating.

Mere whirled to see Van. He was in a tuxedo and his badge was on a wallet hanging from his pocket. His dark blonde hair was styled in the spikey manner he preferred. His blue eyes sparkled and his jaw had a sexy shadow of stubble which he carried well.

"What are you doing here?" she asked, surprised, and a little sheepish to have been caught.

Van motioned to himself, "I'm the sacrificial lamb from the department," he responded.

"I was sorry to hear about your mom," Mere felt herself slowly coming out of the fuzzy stupor she'd been experiencing. Her arms and legs tingled like they were waking from a deep sleep.

"Yeah," Van shrugged, but his blue eyes were emotional, "thanks for the flowers, they looked great at the funeral."

Mere nodded, "What's next for you Officer Donovan?"

"Gage didn't tell you?" Van was visibly surprised, "I thought you guys shared everything."

"So did I," Mere grumbled, "we're not exactly on the best terms right now."

Van made a face, "Interesting."

"So, are you going to tell me?" She asked, exasperated.

"I'm headed home to New York City, I got an offer from the NYPD," he smiled, "which is probably why I got volun-told to come here tonight. I leave next month."

"Congratulations," Mere hugged him, "I'm so happy for you." She pulled back, "We'll miss you here though."

Van nodded, "Well, come visit then," his eyes narrowed, "off the clock, so I don't get indigestion. Watching you guys work freaks me out."

Mere laughed, "Deal."

"Uh oh," Van ducked back slightly behind the pillar.

"What?" Mere looked around.

"Your man just saw me talking to you, he doesn't look very happy," Van responded with a wink. "Think he's jealous?"

Mere rolled her eyes, "Of what?"

"I'm ruggedly handsome and extremely charming," Van pouted. "I'm sure he recognizes that I could steal you away if I wanted."

Mere laughed lightly.

"But he's rich," Van shrugged, "so I'll give him that one." He looked at her, "I'm around if you need help."

"Why would I need help?" Mere asked as she picked up another glass from the waiter as he made his rounds.

"Maybe slow down on those," he arched an eyebrow, "keep your wits about you."

She realized he was right when the sip she took to spite him felt like it went right to her head, making her brain feel like it was made of warm fizz. She looked around and he pointed at the plant beside the pillar. She grinned at him and casually dumped the liquid into the plant.

"I'm pretty sure that's fake, though," Van whispered.

Mere laughed and placed her empty glass onto the dirty-dish tray.

"What's that douche bag doing here?" Van's blue eyes narrowed as he saw Eduardo Espinoza stroll into the room.

"I'm not sure," Mere said when she glanced over and saw who Van was talking about, "he has a lot of money, but he doesn't strike me as the charitable type."

"Jesus, Gage really isn't talking to you, huh?" Van's surprise was written all over his face again.

"What?" Mere's confusion was almost as evident as the momentary pain his words inflicted, "Why?"

"Espinoza's good friend, Hayes, is the one who broke into the shop." Van's expression was hard, "We have no idea why, but I'm pretty sure Hayes only acted on Espinoza's orders."

"Why don't we go ask him," Mere turned to confront the newcomer.

"No," Van grabbed her arm, "let's not make a scene at the froufrou gala."

Mere whirled back to face her friend and pulled her arm from his grasp, "Why don't you ever let me have any fun?"

"Is there a problem here?" Alex's voice was extremely cool. It was a strange change from the warmth he'd exuded before.

"Not at all," Van held up his hands, "I was just keeping your girl from making a fool of herself."

"I'm not his girl," Mere responded and folded her arms across her chest.

Alex glanced from Mere to Van, his face much harder than she remembered, "What do you mean, Officer…"

"Donovan," Van smiled tightly, "Eduardo Espinoza had a friend break into their shop," he motioned to Mere.

"You can prove this?" Alex asked, his chocolate eyes on Mere.

"I can prove that the guy who broke in is an associate of Espinoza, who is too stupid to act alone," Van responded.

"Well, then I don't want him at my party," Alex's gaze turned from Mere to Espinoza and he moved through the crowd like a shark to bleeding prey.

"Uh oh," Van sighed, "looks like he's in alpha-male must-impress-the-girl mode."

Mere glanced at Van in confusion, but her gaze was quickly drawn back across the room when Alex grabbed Espinoza's upper arm and dragged the man back toward the front door.

"Shit," Van and Mere both moved toward the commotion.

"What the hell, man! I was invited!" Espinoza was yelling as he was back-pedaling.

"I don't need any criminals at my benefit," Alex snapped.

"I ain't no criminal, man," Espinoza snapped, nearly falling down the stairs as Alex thrust him outside.

"Tell that to your man, Hayes," Alex growled, his eyes flashing, "you're not welcome here."

Espinoza straightened his jacket, "Forget you man," he turned and walked down the stairs, cursing in Spanish.

Van carefully watched as Alex came back into the room with an apologetic smile.

"I'm so sorry, ladies and gentlemen," Alex held up his hands, "I was informed that man is a criminal, I can't abide a man of poor character in my home." Alex motioned to the orchestra, who started playing again, "Please," Alex motioned back to the dance floor, "enjoy yourselves."

Alex walked back toward Van and Mere, but he was having to weave through the crowd.

Van put his arm around Mere's shoulders, leaned down, and whispered into her ear, "We didn't tell him the name of the burglar."

Mere looked up at Van with searching eyes.

"Maybe we should call it a night," Van's eyes were insistent. "There's more to this guy than we know. I don't trust him. We need to go, now."

Mere realized that she felt unsteady and put her arm around Van's waist. The booze must have gone to her head, but that was confusing because she hadn't had that much to drink. Suddenly the symptoms she was experiencing made her question the content of her drinks.

"Meredith," Alex smiled warmly when he arrived and held out another glass of champagne to her. "Shall we continue our previous conversation? Perhaps, I can give you a tour of my home."

"I'm so sorry," Mere said softly, swallowing, "I should probably go. I think I've had too much to drink."

"There's no need to worry about being tipsy," Alex's smile stayed plastered to his face, but his eyes grew cold when he noticed Van's arm around her. "It's a party, and you don't have to drive home, you can just stay here, with me."

Van tightened his grip on Mere, a quiet challenge that made Alex's smile drop from his face, "I think I'll drive her home."

Mere leaned into Van and spoke to Alex, "Thank you for a lovely evening, Alex. I think it's best if I leave now."

Alex nodded with a charming smile that didn't reach his eyes, "Okay, if that's what you want."

When he moved to kiss her goodbye, Mere turned her face as though she hadn't seen his intention. His lips brushed her cheek, but she was already moving, allowing Van to lead her from the room.

"Great, now I'm a target," Van sighed as he led her away from the crowd.

"You're leaving town," Mere responded sleepily and yawned, "I'm so tired all the sudden."

"Where did you get your drink, Meredith?" Van's tone was suddenly authoritative.

Mere tried to think, but she was all blurry, "Um, the waiter's tray?"

When they made it into the night air, Van spun her to face him. He grabbed her face with both hands to force her to meet his gaze, "Think, Meredith. Did it taste weird?"

Mere shrugged, blinking slowly, "I haven't had expensive champagne in a long time. I wouldn't know if it tasted weird."

"I think I need to take you to the hospital," Van said when she staggered slightly and erupted into giggles. He wrapped his arm around her to keep her from falling.

"No!" Mere shook her head quickly, "I'll be fine. Just take me to your place."

"What?" Van yelped, looking at her like she'd lost her mind, "Why would I do that?"

"You can't take me home! Gage will be so mad," Mere insisted, "and all my friends told me not to come, if they see me like this, I'll never hear the end of it, PLEASE."

Van sighed heavily, "You owe me, Tiny Dancer."

Mere smiled broadly when he used the nickname he'd bestowed on her. She leaned heavily on him as they went down the stairs, "Put it on my tab."

Chapter 43

"Where the hell were you all night?" Will was uncharacteristically upset when Mere strode into the kitchen of her flat, barefoot. She had on a too-big T-shirt over her fancy dress.

"I'm fine. I told you not to wait up," Mere was unamused and disinterested.

"That's it?" Will stared at her, visibly hurt by her blasé reaction.

"Yeah," Mere shrugged, "I told you not to wait up. It's not my fault you apparently camped out at my place waiting for me."

Will nodded, "Just so I'm clear, here, you're combating Gage's weird behavior by mimicking it?"

Mere sighed heavily, "I went to the gala, I danced with Alex, we had fun, I got a little drunk, so I got a ride with a friend."

"Oh my God," Will was looking right through her, "Meredith, did you have relations with Alex?"

Mere laughed, "Have relations? What are you? Sixty?"

"Answer the question," Will glowered.

"No, I didn't, but if I had, it wouldn't be any of your business," Mere responded, "I'm a grown woman. Who I sleep with is my own business."

"Oh, the sweet irony of that statement," Gage's voice made both of them jump as the blonde entered the kitchen from the hallway.

"Morning, Boss," Will said quickly, trying to gauge how much of the conversation she'd overheard.

"I see you're doing the walk of shame," Gage motioned to Mere with her head, "who's the lucky guy?"

"Oh, we're talking now?" Mere asked with more venom than she intended.

Gage blinked and nodded, "Okay, attitude noted." She moved to the fridge and pulled the milk out, pouring herself a glass.

"I just find it so interesting how you've been shacking up with Mak and running around with secrets, but you want to know what's going on in my life," Mere's tone was scathing. She was being fueled by a migraine and bubbling stomach.

"I'm a grown woman, who I sleep with is my own business," Gage responded after downing her milk, "right?" She arched an eyebrow at Mere as she tossed the glass into the sink and put the milk away. "The crazy thing here, is there was a time when you were the only person I wanted to talk to about anything, and now I feel like I'm fighting every time I speak to you."

"Whose fault is that?" Mere asked.

Gage smiled sadly, "Who the fuck knows Meredith?" She started to leave the kitchen but glanced back at Will, "I thought you weren't supposed to be in the flat."

Will shrugged, "I was worried."

"He was just leaving," Mere snapped.

"We're talking about this later," Will said to Mere who sighed and nodded.

"I'll catch you downstairs in a bit," Gage told him, "I know it's Saturday, you don't have to stay if you don't want to, I'm sure I can manage."

Will shrugged, "I don't have plans until later, I'll be here Boss."

Gage nodded, "Thanks."

Will exited the flat via the interior door into the shop. When the door closed the two women stared at each other awkwardly.

Gage cleared her throat and opened her mouth to speak, but then closed it again.

"I hate this," Mere complained, "I miss you."

"I have so much to tell you," Gage rubbed her face with her hands, "I just don't know how."

Mere dropped her shoes on the floor and moved to her friend, she grabbed Gage's hands with her own, "Just open your mouth and talk."

Gage stared at Mere, but then her eyes were drawn to the necklace resting on Mere's T-shirt, "You went and saw Karen, huh?"

Mere nodded, "She's the same mess she's always been. So high, she barely recognized me. It was really hard to see her, but I needed a dress for the stupid gala and it was the only place I knew would have something I could use."

Mere realized what she'd said when Gage's face fell.

"It was just a dance, Gage, well, and a kiss, but it's not like I'm looking to live happily ever after with the guy," Mere said as Gage slowly pulled her hands back.

"You went with Alex," Gage said softly as realization dawned on her. Her jade eyes stared into Mere's lighter ones, "Jesus Mere, please tell me you didn't drink with him."

Mere made a face, "He was very nice and it was a fancy party, of course I had a few drinks."

Gage swallowed hard, looking sick to her stomach, "Did you sleep with him?"

"Why do you care?" Mere asked, "You don't want him, but no one else can have him?"

"That's not-" Gage started.

"I think you just love having him pining after you," Mere accused, "you love the attention."

Gage's eyes widened, "You seriously think I love this?"

"I don't know what to think," Mere snapped, then continued in a softer tone, "I know I like him."

Gage swallowed, the panic gripped in her chest making her words sound strained, "Please, don't."

"Don't what?" Mere asked, "Tell me why you don't want me seeing him."

Gage's hands were shaking and her breathing was in short gasping breaths, "You can't."

"Why can't I?" Mere was practically begging, "Just tell me the truth."

"I can't," Gage whirled and rushed down the hallway toward her room, but Mere gave chase.

"Just talk to me!" Mere grabbed Gage's arm.

Gage stiffened and tried to calm her racing heart, "I have nothing to say."

"You don't care that I went dancing with your ex and made out with him at his expensive party?" Mere asked, trying to catch her friend's gaze.

Gage felt like she was going to vomit.

"GAGE!" Mere's voice made Gage wince noticeably.

"Do what you want," Gage's voice was too high pitched and rushed, "just don't be a complete idiot when you do it."

"What?" Mere finally let go of Gage's arm.

"I don't care what you do," Gage's voice sounded as tight as her chest felt, "just don't be an idiot."

"What is that supposed to mean?" Mere asked.

"Just use your fucking brain Meredith, you're smarter than I am," Gage snapped, "don't be an idiot, like I was."

"To date Alex I'd have to be an idiot?" Mere tried to figure out Gage's reasoning, "Why?"

Gage's bottom lip quivered as she swallowed, "He puts on a good show," she said quietly, "look closer. Don't be blinded by flashy feathers."

"He's a peacock now?" Mere was flustered, "You're not making sense."

Gage shook her head.

"You should be happy," Mere continued, "if he's willing to move on, that means he won't bother you anymore."

A tear streamed down Gage's cheek. She wasn't sure if it was from terror, the pain of betrayal, or sheer frustrated anger.

"I hope you can move on too," Mere said quietly.

Gage shook her head again, refusing to accept the situation.

"Why can't you just be happy for me?" Mere asked.

Gage closed her eyes and couldn't help but remember being an angry teenager, screaming those words at her foster father.

"I'm going to ask him to meet me at Crave, tonight," Mere continued, "you should come. I'd love to sit down with you both in a safe place to discuss all this mess."

Gage opened her eyes and stared at her friend in disbelief.

Mere's eyes were pleading, "Let's figure all this out, and move on."

Gage couldn't help it, she started to laugh. It wasn't a happy laugh, or an amused laugh, it was slightly hysterical.

"Are you on drugs?" Mere spat suddenly, glaring at her friend.

Gage sucked in a breath as though she'd just been punched in the gut, then she turned from Mere and walked away.

Mere grabbed her arm again, but Gage twisted from her friend's grasp this time and slammed her bedroom door shut between them.

Mere heard the click of the lock and sighed, "Van said you've been acting crazy. He said he wouldn't be surprised if you were into something." She was fabricating some of that statement, but she hoped it would goad Gage.

Gage let out an angry yawp and the door shook in its frame from what Mere could only assume was a punch.

"I hope you'll come tonight," Mere called. "If you won't talk to me, at least speak to someone," she turned away and went into the bathroom. "I'd hate to have to plan your funeral because you're too much of a coward to get help," she called, her cold sentiment simultaneously breaking her heart and making her feel vindicated.

Gage sat on her floor with her back to her door, her knees to her chest and her arms wrapped around them. She focused on her breathing, trying to calm her nerves. She heard the shower start, so she stood up and quickly gathered some items into her backpack.

She grabbed her leather coat and strode from her room, not looking at the bathroom as she passed it. She didn't know if her heart was pounding in her chest because of the pain Mere's words had inflicted, or fear for her friend's plight. She remembered how charming Alex could be, she could only hope that Mere was able to see through his façade before it was too late. She wanted to barge into the bathroom and shake Mere. She wanted to scream that Alex was evil. She wanted to explain why, but then all she could hear was Mere's disgust. Her stomach twisted at the thought of admitting she was a recovering addict to her best friend. A friend whose life had been all but destroyed by addiction.

Gage rushed down the stairs into the shop and fed her dogs, "I'll be back later, guys," she gave each dog a pat and stood, "be good boys, okay?"

Both dogs looked up at her with quiet admiration, and doggy sadness as she left.

"I'm not working today," Gage called out as she headed for the door, she was mad that her voice sounded so strained.

"You okay, Boss?" Will came out of the parts closet to see her retreating back.

Gage waved a hand at him dismissively without turning to face him, knowing he would read her emotions and demand an explanation. She pushed through the plywood covered door and beat a hasty retreat.

Tessa came out of the office and glanced to the front door as it closed, "What is she doing?"

"I don't know," Will shrugged, "she left."

PREY

Tessa sighed, "Great, we're finally done with all our custom orders, and she leaves. Who is going to contact all these people?" She waved a stack of papers at him.

Will smiled at her sweetly.

"No, this is not part of my job!" Tessa shook her head.

Will's smile slowly showed his teeth.

"I don't get paid to do clerical work," Tessa insisted.

Will cocked his head slightly and narrowed his eyes playfully at her.

Tessa sighed heavily and turned back to the office, "I hate you all."

"Love you," Will called after her.

"I'm going to tell every single one of them, you'll deliver their car TODAY," Tessa sang happily.

"Don't be evil," Will said with a whine, wrinkling his nose.

Tessa's maniacal laughter was muffled as she slammed the office door.

"So much for a short day," Will sighed and turned back to the shop.

Chapter 44

Brick looked up when Gage entered the locker room. He arched an eyebrow as he buttoned his jeans, "Isn't there a women's locker room?"

"Yes," Gage responded as she walked to the showers and turned one on, kicking off her shoes.

Brick's confusion was purposely apparent. He looked from her to the door and back, "So why are you in here?"

"Because the women's locker room would possibly lead to interacting with bitches," Gage responded dryly and pulled off her shirt and jeans, leaving her in her undergarments. She glanced over her shoulder and saw him staring at her so she turned to face him, her hands on her hips, "What Biscuit?"

He shrugged and pulled on a T-shirt, "Nothing. Just wasn't expecting you to come in and strip."

"What are you doing here anyway?" Gage asked, "We're not working any jobs right now."

"I used the gym," Brick responded, "and I was helping Whitlock out with something."

Gage's eyes narrowed, "He called you in to help him with his case?"

Brick shrugged, "It's not a big deal, he just had a few questions about overseas."

Gage nodded, trying to hide her disappointed expression. The hurt in her eyes was not mirrored in her tone, "Fantastic. I'm glad you're settling into your place," she turned her back on him and pulled off her bra, sticking her hand into the water to check the temperature.

"You take a lot of needless risks, you know that?" Brick asked conversationally.

"Like what?" Gage asked in a similar tone.

"You come in here, strip naked right in front of a man you barely know, and rely on what? Dumb luck? That I'm not some pervert?"

Gage laughed, "I'm not naked, I have on panties."

Brick shook his head and turned his back on her, "Doesn't change the statement."

"You're saying I'm so undeniably sexy that you'll be overcome with desire and attack me?" Gage asked. She glanced back and saw that his back was to her, so she shucked her panties and stepped into the shower.

Brick heard the shower curtain and swallowed, "There are plenty of men who would read this situation differently."

Gage stood beneath the water as it poured down and nodded her understanding. "I read you the first time you walked into the elevator, Biscuit. I'm pretty good in my snap judgments at this point in my life."

Brick shook his head, "You don't know anything about me."

"I know enough," she answered. "You volunteered to help in North Carolina, held your own when I needed you, and you're still here. You're either a good man, or you're a spy. Either way, you wouldn't assault me."

Brick looked at the shower curtain, not sure how to respond to her logic.

"Still here Biscuit?" she called.

"Yes," he said.

"Don't tell anyone you saw me, okay?"

He nodded, then realized she couldn't see him, "Okay."

"Thanks."

He shook his head and collected his things, "No problem."

"You're a peach, I don't care what everyone else says," Gage called as he walked out the door.

Brick slung his backpack over his shoulder as he walked down the hallway and paused when he saw EmEm.

"Is Gage here?" The black man asked, not wasting time on niceties or greetings.

"What's going on between you guys?" Brick changed the subject.

"I don't know what you mean," EmEm looked around, his eyes settling on the women's locker room.

"I mean the dynamic is completely different." Brick responded, "When I started, everyone was thick as thieves, now everyone is avoiding everyone else."

EmEm shrugged, "We go through phases."

Brick shook his head and started walking down the hall again, "Whatever bro."

EmEm went to the locker room, knocked, and opened the door to find an empty room. He turned back and followed Brick, "If you see her, could you call me?"

Brick walked backward so he could look at EmEm, "This isn't my business, I'm not getting in the middle."

EmEm made a face, "Letting me know you've seen her isn't getting in the middle, it's just letting me know you've seen her."

Brick stopped walking, "Okay, I've seen her. She seems fine."

"Where?" EmEm looked around.

"I'm not in the middle," Brick waved his hand dismissively as he walked out of the front door calling over his shoulder, "call me if anyone is bleeding profusely, otherwise, leave me out of it," as the door swung shut behind him.

EmEm looked around again in confusion and went to the computer lab.

Lina looked up when he entered, "Hey EmEm," she smiled brightly, "what are you up to?"

"Looking for our fearless leader," EmEm sighed, "and having no luck."

"Whit is in his office," Lina supplied, "he said he was taking a conference call and didn't want to be disturbed."

"The other fearless leader," EmEm grinned.

"Oh, I haven't seen Gage since she left the club in a huff," Lina looked back down at her computer, "sorry."

EmEm nodded, "This has been the weirdest couple of weeks ever."

"Tell me about it," Lina grumbled.

"What?" EmEm glanced back at her.

"Nothing," Lina smiled brightly, "I'm sure she'll show up to yell at us again soon. Why don't you text Mak? She seemed less pissed at him."

EmEm pulled out his phone, "You're the smartest."

Lina nodded, "I have my moments."

Chapter 45

Mere glanced at her phone when it vibrated. She realized it was a text from Alex and tapped the icon.

Alex: *How are you feeling, Gorgeous?*

She smiled almost involuntarily as she texted out her reply:

Mere: *Much better today. Thx*

Alex: *The waiter was doing something to the drinks. He was trying to steal jewelry or something. I don't know, he was dealt with this morning.*

Mere: *Holy shit, I knew I hadn't had that much to drink.*

Alex: *I'm so sorry, I feel responsible.*

Mere: *No way you could have known.*

Alex: *I'm really glad you left when you did, I wouldn't want to take advantage of you, and I certainly wouldn't want another man to either.*

Mere stared at her phone, not sure how to feel. She was so confused at this point that it was driving her crazy.

Alex: *Are you okay?*

She took a breath.

Mere: *I'm good. Officer Donovan got me home safely. I slept it off.*

Alex: *I'm so glad. I still have your car.*

Alex: *Can I bring it to you?*

Mere chewed her lip.

Mere: *How about you drive it to Craze tonight, I'll meet you there. Maybe I'll even drive you home after.*

Alex: *I can't stop thinking about your lips.*

She smiled.

Mere: *Play your cards right and you might get to taste them again.*

Alex: *Tease.*

Mere: *You love it.*

Alex: *Tonight.*

She let out a little chuckle then headed down into the shop. When she made it to the office, Tessa looked up from Gage's chair.

"Finally, someone actually equipped to do this job," Tessa stood and pointed at a stack of papers on the desk. "I've called and arranged drop off for those people," she pointed to a much smaller stack, "I haven't been able to get through to these customers."

Mere nodded, "Good job, kid. Did you give the drops to Will?"

Tessa nodded, "He's going to need help, there's a lot of them."

"Did he take the tow truck?" Mere asked.

"The flatbed," Tessa nodded, "so he took two cars, he'll be back soon though, he left a while ago."

Mere smiled, "Excellent, good job Tess. You deserve a raise."

Tessa arched an eyebrow.

"Oh, I'm not the boss," Mere shook her head, "I don't control the money."

Tessa laughed, "You're an asshole."

Mere winked, "You know I love you though."

"Uh huh," Tessa turned on her heel, "I'm taking the dogs for a walk." She didn't even finish her statement before Tiny and Killer were sitting at her feet, "Clearly they're starved for affection."

"Well, when your owner's a bitch, it sucks." Mere picked up the small stack of papers and looked through them, "you did good here, kid."

Tessa nodded and headed for the parts closet to get the dogs' leashes.

"Okay, the first two are done," Will came into the shop, "where are my next two?"

Tessa motioned to the office, so Will stepped in as Mere sat down.

"Here's your next two," Mere held up two forms.

Will closed the door behind himself and sat opposite Mere, staring at her expectantly.

"What?" Mere shook the papers at him.

"Tell me about last night Mere," Will responded.

"I went to a party, I danced with a guy, I got a little drunk, so I had Van drive me to his place where I'm pretty sure he put a T-shirt on me so he wouldn't have to stare at my tits." She cocked her head, "Dude has a New York Yankees bedspread. Can you believe that?"

Will looked confused.

"What's got you twisted?" Mere asked.

"You went home with Donovan?"

Mere nodded, "Seemed like a good idea at the time."

"Why wouldn't you just have him bring you home?"

"Because I was drunk, I don't know," Mere shrugged.

"Stop lying to me please," Will said quietly, "I can't take it from both of you. Just tell me the truth."

The quiet pain in his voice gave Mere pause. "I danced with Alex, I'm pretty sure I got roofied and ended up making out with him," she said finally. "Van offered to get me out before I made a bad decision, so I went home with him to avoid you."

Will nodded, "Thank you for your honesty," he stood and took the papers from her.

"That's it?" Mere stood when he turned to leave.

"I just hope you know what you're doing Mere," he said as he moved to the door, "that's all."

"Sorry I worried you, that was a dick move," she looked down.

He nodded again, "Thank you. I shouldn't have waited up. I was just anxious."

She glanced at him with a small smile, "I invited Alex to join us at Craze tonight, you and Lina in?"

Will shrugged, "Maybe this time won't be as stressful, huh?"

"Oh, I invited Gage too," Mere's smile deepened, "I anticipate fireworks."

Will sighed, "Well, I do love explosions," he held up the papers, "be back in a bit."

Chapter 46

That night, Gage was leaning against the wall on the outskirts of the dance floor watching her friends at their usual booth. Will and Lina were cuddled up in the back, laughing at something EmEm just said. Mere was flirting with the bartender to get extra alcohol for the table, and Alex was sitting right beside her at the bar, ordering a drink.

Gage let out a sigh and looked down at her phone to read Mere's texts again:

Mere: *Alex is here with us.*

Mere: *He said he'll leave you alone.*

Mere: *He's into me now. He seems really sweet.*

Mere: *I'm gonna ask him back to the house.*

Mere: *Stop being a dick.*

Mere: *Just come talk to him.*

Her heart was beating in her chest, painfully, with the knowledge that Alex was about to know where she lived. There was nothing she could do about it, without telling her friends about all of her past. She was trying to figure out what to do, and where to go, when she caught sight of Mak out of the corner of her eye.

The Australian was right by the side exit, standing in the shadows with a beer in hand, uncomfortably surveying the crowd. His eyes kept traveling back to her friends, glaring into Alex, before once more sweeping the room. His hair was short on the sides and longer on the top, pushed back off his face.

He was looking rugged and sexy with that haircut complementing the rough five o'clock shadow along his strong jawline. Gage licked her lips and decided it was time to stop fighting her urges for him. It would solve two problems for her tonight. She suddenly knew what to do and where to go. She pushed off the wall and walked through the crush of dancing bodies with a purpose. Most of the dancers moved out of her way, she ignored everyone, even the dancers that bumped her. Her eyes bore into Mak until he looked up and met her gaze.

He watched her walking to him with a mix of confusion and anticipation. It was then that she realized she had on a bubblegum pink chin length wig and her body was covered from head to toe in heavy leather. She unzipped her jacket, revealing her tank top underneath and pulled her wig off, shaking out her dirty blonde hair.

The recognition lit his eyes only a moment before she knocked the beer out of his hand with the wig and jumped into his arms, wrapping her legs around his waist and kissing him hard.

He immediately kissed her back with fervor and his strong arms wrapped around her tightly, exciting her even more.

He pulled back for a second and gasped out breathlessly, "Crikey."

She smiled at him and huskily said, "Take me to your place, now."

He stared into her eyes for a moment as though making sure she wasn't drunk, but he didn't put her down.

She broke eye contact and bit his earlobe, then she whispered breathily, "Please, don't make me wait. I'll let you see the real me."

He cleared his throat but couldn't hide his excitement from her. He put her down, grabbed her hand, and led her out the exit.

~*~*~*~*~

Gage opened her eyes and yawned, she looked around lazily and realized Mak was still sleeping on his stomach with his arm over her midsection. She couldn't help but smile as she carefully wiggled, turning until she was facing him in the small bed. She studied his face silently and scooted close to him, her legs entwined with his.

He let out a contented sigh and pulled her closer with a half-smile, his eyes still closed, "I'm a little surprised you stayed," his voice was gravelly with sleep.

"Really?" She chuckled, "Because you held onto me like a vice all night long."

He opened his eyes and rolled onto his side, "You didn't seem to mind," he responded cheekily, brushing a lock of hair out of her face.

"It's been a while," she acquiesced, "it's nice to be snuggled occasionally."

He grinned, "I'm available any time, sheila."

"My name isn't Shelia" she murmured, pushing him onto his back and cuddling into his side, silently cursing the underwire of her bra as it poked her. Her fingers idly traced crisscrossing scars on his chest.

He ran his fingers through her hair as he held her to him. After a few silent moments, he said quietly, "Well, we both know it isn't Gage either."

She pulled away and sat up, "You're one to talk, Mak," she responded, grabbing her pants and pulling them on.

He sat up too, "I didn't mean to upset you."

"I'm not upset," she responded coolly as she stood up and finished pulling her pants up, zipping and buttoning them. She sat back on the edge of the bed and pulled her boots on, tying them quickly.

"Liar."

She whirled to face him, paused a moment, appreciating his muscular torso, then said, "Stop being all distractingly sexy with your accent and your face." She waved a hand in the direction of his face and stood up, "Thanks for a great time. Now that I'm out of your system, you can move on."

"What the hell are you going on about?" He asked, confused.

"You wanted me, you had me," she responded. "Now, you can let it go. I hoped if I gave you a taste, you would stop acting like you know me."

"I know you used me as an excuse to not go home last night." He stood up from the bed, "I know your mates were drinking with the bloke who strangled you a week ago." She tried to walk out of the room with her shirt in hand, but Mak grabbed her arm gently and pulled her back before she reached the door, "And I know you're scared to be real with me." He backed her up against the wall, "Why is that?"

"I don't know what you're talking about," she responded, surprised that there were tears in her eyes as she looked up into his face angrily. "I don't think I can be more real than I was last night."

He shook his head, "Gage, last night was amazing, don't get me wrong, but you were more real with me outside that stupid club in the rain, than you have been in the three years I've known you."

She was uncomfortably aware of his proximity. She didn't want to admit that her body was reacting to him still. His muscular bare chest was right in her line of vision, even as she carefully tried to keep her eyes elsewhere. She hoped he thought her quick breathing was a symptom of anger, not the heat spreading through her. "I don't know what you mean," she said finally, her voice breathless.

"You know exactly what I mean," he answered, catching her gaze. "You just spent an entire night wrapped up in me, and I don't even know your real name."

She swallowed and fought the urge to kiss him, "I'm not the only one who doesn't tell people their name," she said pointedly.

"Riley Makenzie," he answered matter-of-factly.

When she looked at him in shock, he continued, "Long story, short, my mum loved the name Riley, my dad hated it." Mak swallowed as he pushed on, telling this story for the first time, "Dad reckoned Buck was his son since he's named after him. Which means I'm not his. He found every reason he could to take his anger out on me."

Gage resisted the urge to trace his scars with her fingers again, but her eyes were drawn to the marked flesh.

Mak licked his lips, "'Riley' became a reason. Every time I answered to it, he'd make me bleed. So, I started going by Mak instead. It broke my mum's heart, but my dad liked Mak, it fed his ego, so he lessened up on the ass-kicking. I wasn't allowed to tell my mum what he did, that's why I knew warm compresses work."

She was stunned, unsure how to respond.

"Your turn," he prodded.

"It's about damn time!"

The voice surprised them both, and with Buck in the room, Mak was painfully aware that he was in his boxers and Gage was in leather pants and a bra. Mak turned to face his brother, blocking Gage from Buck's view, "KNOCK!"

Buck grinned broadly and reached over, knocking on the door frame, "You left your door unlocked. You had to know I was going to come in, although I see you were preoccupied when you came home."

With the spell broken, Gage pulled her tank top on and pushed past both men quickly without saying a word, exiting the room, followed by exiting the ground level apartment and heading for the road.

"God-damn-it Buck," Mak growled, trying to find his jeans. When he couldn't find anything fast enough, he simply ran from the apartment.

"I'm so bloody confused!" Buck shouted after his brother as Mak ran out of the apartment and into the street with nothing on but his boxers.

Mak looked both ways, but Gage was gone, "Damn it!" he snapped angrily before turning and walking back into the apartment. He walked up to Buck and punched him in the gut before going back into his room and slamming the door.

Buck doubled over in pain, gasping for breath, he nodded and sputtered, "Yeah, okay, I deserved that one."

Chapter 47

Gage ran until she thought her lungs would burst. She hadn't thought about where to go, she'd just run. Now, she slowed to a walk, trying to catch her breath.

She recognized her garage in the distance and decided she'd go home, even if there was still the danger that Alex might be there. She figured if her friends were there, he wouldn't risk losing his rapport with them by doing something stupid.

"Hello, Bridget."

Alex was behind her.

She didn't turn, she just tried to run again, but then a massive amount of electricity was coursing through her body and everything went dark.

Chapter 48

Whitlock was sitting at the desk in his home office, going through several files. His cellphone lit up, dancing across the desk with an incoming call. He grabbed the phone and stared at it in confusion, the call was from a blocked number. He sent it to voicemail, but it immediately rang again. Then his business cellphone rang at the same time as his hardline.

"What the hell is going on?" He stood up and looked at the multiple security camera views on the monitors mounted to his wall as he answered his cell phone, "Who is this?"

Open the door, mate, we need to talk.

"How the hell did you find my home, Makenzie?" Whit snapped, glaring at the Australian on his monitor. Mak was standing by Whit's front door, staring up at the camera.

You're not the only one with connections. Please open up.

Something in his tone made Whit's stomach twist with an uneasy feeling as he hung up the phone. He hit the button to buzz Mak in, automatically, before he made the conscious decision to do it.

Whitlock sat back at his desk, facing the door, and held his 1911 handgun resting on top of his thigh.

Mak entered the room hastily, his face boarder-line anguished, a backpack gripped in his fist, "Where is she?"

Whitlock remained calm and didn't ask how the Australian knew where in his home to go. He was busy staring at the other man cautiously, "Where is who?"

"You know who!" Mak shouted, throwing his bag into the chair in front of Whitlock's desk, before blowing a breath out as though trying to calm himself. He used both hands to tug anxiously at his hair, "Whitlock, Gage has been on the run from a bloke for several years, yeah?" He didn't wait for Whitlock to respond, noting the obvious recognition in the older man's eyes, "Your team invited him into Gage's home two nights ago."

"What?" Whit put the 1911 on the desk and stood up quickly, "Alejandro Sanchez is in Miami?"

"Has been for some time now. He attacked her a little over a week ago, would have snapped her damn neck if I hadn't intervened." Mak started pacing, "I don't understand why this is news to you, ain't you supposed to be their daddy?"

"Unfortunately, much like a father, my petulant children love to leave me out of the loop," Whitlock responded in agitation, his hand stroked his goatee. He cleared his throat, "Why does this information lead you to me, looking for Gage?"

"She was at my place while your people entertained that bounce," Mak answered. "Sunday morning, she ran out and I haven't been able to find her anywhere." He stopped pacing and stared at Whitlock, his blue eyes scared, "So please tell me you've spoken to her and she's just avoiding me. 'Cause I'm going crazy."

Whit felt the fear radiating from Mak, and it was multiplied tenfold in his own gut, because unlike Mak, Whitlock knew the hell Gage had been put through at Alex's hands.

"Sit down for a minute," Whitlock motioned to the chair in front of Mak, "you're making me fucking nervous." When Mak didn't move to sit, Whit said, "I'll make a call. Please sit down."

Mak sat on the edge of the seat, his leg bouncing anxiously as Whitlock called Mere.

When he hung up the phone, he swallowed as he sat down slowly, "No one at the flat has seen her since Saturday morning."

"So I'm the last to see her," Mak said quietly. He stood up and said, "He's got her. It's the only thing that makes any sense."

"Calm down," Whit held a hand up, "she could just be pissed at everyone and laying low."

"Laying low? Without her friends, dogs, or weapons?" Mak snatched the bag he'd brought from the chair and tossed it on Whitlock's desk; the files the older man had been studying were thrown to the side by the bag's weight. "She left everything at my place." Mak glared at Whitlock, "If you really believe she's laying low, then you don't know her at all."

"I know her a hell of a lot better than you do," Whitlock snapped, leaping to his feet again, "get out of my home."

"No." Mak raised his chin, "You want me to leave? Shoot me. I'm armed, you won't get arrested." The anger left his gaze and his blue eyes pleaded, "Or you can just help me find her."

Whitlock sighed, "I just got this rug. I'm not gonna shoot you." He stared at Mak for a moment before saying, "You're quite taken with her."

Mak stood, chest heaving as he took several deep breaths, he held his hands out as though asking why, "I have no idea what that means, but I'm pretty sure I love her. Have done for some time."

Whitlock smiled slightly, "That's a conversation for another time. For now, let's find our girl." He unzipped the backpack and began pulling items out, he paused when he retrieved an envelope. He looked up at Mak in surprise, "This was with her stuff?"

"In her jacket pocket," Mak responded, "why?"

"No reason," Whitlock stared at the envelope for a moment longer, it was postmarked well over a decade ago.

"Do you know what it is?" Mak asked.

"It's a letter from her father," Whitlock said quietly.

"Her dead father?" Mak clarified.

"Yes, I mailed it for him," Whitlock responded absently, "I knew she hadn't read it, but I thought she'd thrown it away."

"How'd you know she didn't read it?" Mak asked in confusion.

"No reason," Whitlock tucked the letter back into Gage's jacket pocket, "let's look up Alejandro's known associates in the area. That seems like a good place to start."

Chapter 49

Cold water shocked Gage's system again, she woke gasping.

The rope binding her wrists above her head was cutting painfully into her flesh. The addition of most of her body weight being held up only by the rope added to the burn.

She blinked a few times to collect her bearings and stared at the man who had been happily torturing her for what felt like weeks.

"Good morning, Sunshine," he revealed his mouthful of crooked yellow teeth in a grin, that looked more like a snarl, as he tossed the bucket he'd just used to the side.

She stared at him, saying nothing. She'd been trying to wriggle her wrists free every time she was awake, but now she'd lost the feeling in her hands, other than the sharp pain from the rope.

A steady stream of shockingly cold water trickled onto her head and followed her hair down her neck. She was in a constant state of damp shivering.

"Aren't you happy to see me?" Her captor goaded.

"Not sure how you can ask that with a straight face, you pirate mother fucker," her raspy voice made fun of the eye patch covering his left eye. She knew what was coming in response, it was a game they played every time he woke her, but she said it anyway.

His fists met her gut, one after the other, hard enough to force the air from her lungs in a gust. She coughed, barking out, "Avast! Ye scallywag!"

Something hard hit her face, whipping her head to the side, and forcing her whole body to spin in the air, her toes scraping the concrete floor. She tasted blood and waited until her body did a full circle so she could stare at the enraged man in front of her.

"You just don't know when to shut up, do you?" He snapped, a pipe in his hand.

"It's one of my finer traits," she smiled with bloody teeth before spitting in his face. When the pipe swung into her ribs, she felt bones give and cried out involuntarily.

"That's more like it," Eye-Patch sneered, "that's what I like to hear."

She stared at him, trying to catch her breath quietly, wishing her feet weren't anchored to the floor so she could use her legs to break his neck.

"I do believe that Bridget is planning your demise," Alex entered the barren, windowless, room using the only portal to the outside world, a heavy metal door.

Eye-Patch laughed in her face, making her grimace from the smell.

"Of all the torture, I've ever received," she muttered, "THAT was the worst." She coughed and turned her head from the men, "Jesus, man, what did you eat?"

Alex laughed and put a hand on Eye-Patch's shoulder to stop him from hitting her with the pipe again, "Oh Bridget, I really wish you hadn't made all this necessary."

"I know," she stared at him, a mix of rage and fear gurgling in her guts, threatening to spew from her throat. "You wish I would have stayed your good little cautionary tale for all the little girls you kidnapped."

"Kidnapped is pretty harsh," Alex stared at her with the same eyes that she used to find comforting, "I just gave them another option."

"You're right," Gage acquiesced, scraping her bare toes on the ground to try to keep herself from spinning so she could continue to face him. "You just filled their heads with lies and their veins with whatever you were selling at the time until conscious thought didn't need to exist anymore. What better way to keep your customers happy than with powerless girls for them to enjoy?"

"You didn't seem to mind so much when you were one of those girls," his smile was feral, his perfect white teeth almost gleaming, "you always did what you had to for your next bump."

The vomit rose in her throat at the memory of clumsy hands groping at her body, ripping at her clothes. She swallowed and glared right back at him defiantly.

"It's so cute how you think you're so much braver now," Alex said softly, his tone almost apologetic. "I broke you a long time ago baby girl, there is no brave for you."

Gage stared at him, not saying a word, hoping he was wrong.

"Toby, here, has unfinished business with you," Alex motioned to Eye-Patch. "I don't know if you remember, you were pretty fucked up at the time," he reached out to brush a lock of hair from her face but she jerked away from him, "you're the one who took his eye."

She glanced from Alex to Toby in confusion, then realization hit her and she started laughing maniacally.

Toby lunged at her with the pipe in his hand, but Alex grabbed his arm and yanked him back.

"I stabbed you in the eye?" Gage asked breathlessly. "With the knife, he put in my gut," she nodded her head at Alex. "It's your fault," she goaded Toby, "you called him, and he gave me the knife, you dumb-fuck."

Alex held Toby firmly and pushed him toward the door, "Go calm down. We don't want this over too fast."

Toby stumbled toward the door but whirled back to stare at his boss' back, "This is bullshit, you told me I could have her eye! I've waited years for this shit, Alex!"

Alex shook his head with a sigh, staring at Gage, looking her over from head to toe. "Only a man with no imagination would look at this woman, showing us everything she has to offer, soaked to the bone with cold water, completely at our mercy, and only want to take her eye."

Gage swallowed, feeling like cockroaches were running all over her body under his lecherous gaze. She was agonizingly cognizant that she was only wearing her tank top and underwear, everything else had been cut from her body.

Alex pulled his small knife from his pocket and opened it slowly, "Toby, leave me with Bridget now. I'd like some time alone to get reacquainted."

Toby's face was bright red when he slammed out of the door, but Gage didn't see it because she was staring at Alex intently, knowing she couldn't play him like she had Toby.

"I've missed you, baby," he smiled as he brought the knife to her throat and trailed it along her skin to her scarred collarbone, "let's play the games we used to play. You can make it stop if you tell me what I want to know."

"Pink was never your color," Gage said roughly, spitting blood on Alex's pink polo shirt. "You might not want to know that, but you should."

Alex shook his head, "Oh, you're so clever. Your Australian has been filling you with bravado."

"He's been filling me with something considerably bigger than you ever did," she smiled meanly.

His smile disappeared.

"Of course, it's not hard to find bigger than you," she added.

Alex let the blade bite into her skin, watching her blood drip before speaking with a faux calmness as he ignored her words, "A lot of important people seem to think you're involved with a group of misfits who keep showing up on crime scenes across the country. Helping pigs make cases."

"I find that pigs only care about mud and food," Gage responded, swallowing hard when his knife bit into her skin again. "But man, it would be cool to see a pig in court." She laughed hoarsely, "Maybe with a little suit on, its little corkscrew tail would have to be out though."

"I have been informed that you are in charge of PREY," he interrupted her, "as such, you have access to the people who work there." Alex tried to hide his anger, by slowly digging his blade deeper, "It turns out, there's a lot of customers who would love to have that information."

Gage glared at him but kept her mouth shut.

"Especially the leader. What's his name? James Whittier?" Alex carefully sliced a small piece of flesh, making her wince. "There are quite a few people who would pay top dollar for his head. So, you tell me where he is, and I'll stop hurting you."

Gage continued to stare at him, "I definitely don't know a James Whittier," she snapped. "Even if I had that information, which I don't, unfortunately for you, I remember how good you are at keeping your word."

Alex's gaze hardened. "I love it when you play hard to get," he said as he sliced deeper into the muscle of her shoulder. He left his knife embedded as he walked to the metal table, in the center of the small room.

Gage swallowed hard as Alex touched the stick on the table attached to a car battery. "You know," she said with a bloody grin, "I was pleased to see the picana. So often, people watch too many movies and think they can shock you with just a battery." She licked her chapped lips, "It had been a while since I had a good shock session." She gave a rough laugh, "I slept the best I have in years after our talk yesterday."

Alex sighed and brought the torture device to Gage, "Tell me what I want to know, Bridget."

"Okay," she nodded, her eyes wide. "Okay." She swallowed and sighed heavily, as though battling with herself, "He's a LOT bigger th-"

When the electricity jolted through her, she couldn't do anything but scream.

Toby stood outside the door until he heard Gage scream, then he smiled and walked away.

Chapter 50

Buck stood in the shadows, watching the address he'd been given by Whitlock. He was waiting for one of the men, whose pictures he had on his phone, to show their face. He hoped one would show up soon because he'd never seen Mak as obsessed with anything as he was with finding Gage. To be honest, Buck was fond of her, and if she was in trouble, he'd do whatever was necessary to help his brother find her.

A thin man, with hair made stringy by grease and dirt, exited the building into the light, cast by the street lamp, and started to walk down the sidewalk. Buck swiped through the pictures on his phone until it landed on the mug shot of that man, so he started walking.

He texted Mak that he was following one of the marks, then crossed the street to close the space. It wasn't hard to follow the man, he wasn't aware of his surroundings in the least, clearly high on something. It made sense, he was a known associate of Alejandro Sanchez, a known seller of Alex's product.

Buck's phone beeped and he looked down at the response from Mak:

Bastard: *Take him. Bring him to me.*

Buck slid his phone into his pocket and increased his gait, easily catching up to the smaller man.

"G'day mate!" Buck wrapped his left arm around the man's shoulders and pulled him into the uppercut delivered by his right. He caught the man when he crumpled and easily bore his weight, dragging him unceremoniously. When he drew looks from bystanders he smiled winningly, made a drinking motion, and said apologetically, "Two-pot-screamer." He bent down and pulled the man across his shoulders in a fireman's carry so they could disappear into the shadows of the alleyway quicker.

~*~*~*~

"G'day Mr. Watts," Mak was sitting on a table's edge staring at Alex's henchmen when the drug addict opened his eyes.

"What the fuck is this?" Jimmy Watts struggled against the rope that held him to the chair.

"I need you to listen very carefully," Mak responded, his tone even, "I'm in a bit of a hurry and I don't feel like wasting time on you if you don't prove useful."

"Do you know who I work for?" Jimmy shrieked, spittle flying from his lips.

Mak stood from his seat and backhanded Jimmy across the face, "Pull yourself together, I haven't even asked you my question yet."

Jimmy spit blood on the floor and glared up at Mak in silence.

"Good boy," Mak sat back on the edge of the table, "I have only one question for you, if you refuse to answer my question, then I will have one additional question for you."

Jimmy trembled in his seat, his eyes slowly blinking as he stared at Mak intently as though willing himself awake.

"That's it, stay on me, fight the haze," Mak leaned forward, "are you ready for the question?"

Jimmy nodded hurriedly.

"Where is Gage?" Mak asked quietly. When Jimmy looked confused, Mak continued, "Your boss is obsessed with a woman, he snatched her off the street six days ago. He's held her somewhere ever since." Mak stood and began to pace in front of Jimmy, "No body has shown up, so I assume he still has her alive." The Australian stopped pacing and stared at Jimmy, "If she's not alive, things aren't looking so good for you, Mate."

"I didn't have nothing to do with that," Jimmy said hurriedly, "I wasn't even there!"

Mak held up a hand to stop Jimmy from continuing his begging, "You mistake me for a righteous man," he smiled coldly, "I'm a criminal, son. A far more dangerous bloke than your boss. Tell me what I want to know, or I'll ask you my second question."

"Please!" Jimmy whispered desperately, "I can't tell you what I don't know. Mr. Sanchez doesn't tell me nothing! I'm not even gonna be working for him no more, I've been working out a deal with Fernando Cortez."

Mak nodded, "The second question then." He dragged a chair across the floor until the back of the chair touched Jimmy's knees, then he straddled the chair back and stared at Jimmy intently, "Have you ever heard the crunch of a cleanskin's testicles being clamped?"

Jimmy stared at Mak confused.

"I know you're higher than a bloody kite, so I'll elaborate." Mak continued in a conversational tone, "When it comes time to castrate a bull-calf," he reached back to the table and grabbed something metal, "the best way to do it, is to use something called castrating forceps, or an emasculator." He held up the shiny instrument and worked the forceps with his hand as he leaned in, "You use this to clamp down on the flesh just above the testicles. It makes this audible crunching noise." He put his hand on Jimmy's shoulder, "You see, the crunch is how you know you did it right." Jimmy started crying quietly as Mak continued, "Then the testicles die because there's no blood-flow, they fall right off."

"Please," Jimmy whimpered, "I swear, I wasn't there."

Mak smiled, and put the forceps back on the table, "Of course," he nodded, "that's right, you weren't there." He leaned in so close that his warm breath moved Jimmy's hair, "But you bloody well know where he would take her, so answer my question boy, have you ever heard the crunch?"

"No," Jimmy cried softly, tears streaming freely.

"Here's my problem," Mak whispered quietly, still as close to Jimmy as he could be, "I've been castrating bulls with an emasculator since I was six years old. I always wondered how easy a bloke would be." Mak leaned back just enough so he could see Jimmy clearly, "The crunch is the best way to emasculate, it's clean. Momentarily painful, but usually there's no lasting issues." Mak swallowed then continued, "That's too good for the likes of you." He smiled meanly, "Tell me what I want to know, or I will crush your tiny balls in the palm of my hand and rip them from your meager body with a savage twist."

Jimmy's fear radiated from him, and he was distinctly aware that his sweatpants offered no protection, but he decided to try to be brave, "You wouldn't do that. No man would do that." When Mak grabbed him between the legs and squeezed, he shrieked, "OKAY! OKAY!"

Mak let him go and shook his hand beside him, drops of urine hitting the tile floor, "Tell me what I want to know."

"There's a warehouse on the outskirts of town," Jimmy blubbered through his tears, "it has a storm cellar he likes to use for high profile business. She has to be there," Jimmy looked up at Mak, trembling, "it's set up like a goddamn fortress, it only has one way in and out."

Mak stood up, towering over the cowering man, "Address. Now." He leaned in slightly, "You're staying here, if you lie to me, if you falsify anything, I'll come back here, and fulfill my promise to you." He straightened and said, "If you're not lying, I'll be back to talk about your deal with Cortez. That sounds like an interesting prospect."

~*~*~*~*~

"I think I should hire your brother to do all of my interrogations," Whitlock said to Buck as they observed from behind the one-way mirror.

Buck looked disgusted and a bit confused, "You have no idea how good he really is," he responded.

"What do you mean?" Whit glanced over at Buck.

"He's never even seen a bull in real life, we just watch a lot of veterinarian shows on the telly. He wouldn't know how to cut the balls off a bull to save his life." Buck looked at Whit, "Did that little druggie piss on my brother?"

Whitlock stared at Buck while he processed what had been said, then he laughed and looked back into the room where Jimmy was sobbing alone.

"Gear up," Mak entered the room, "we have an address."

"I'm not going anywhere with you until you wash your hands," Buck responded without missing a beat.

Mak grinned and held his hand out to his brother as though wanting to stroke Buck's beard, "What's wrong? You don't like the smell of terror?"

Buck wrinkled his nose, "Wash your hands, I'll get the guns."

Chapter 51

Gage's eyes flickered open of their own volition for the first time since she'd been brought to her own private hell. She was strapped to a table now. Her wrists were still tied tightly with the same rope as before, but now her arms were stretched above her head and anchored somewhere above her on the table. She tried to pull on her restraints, but it was no use, she was stretched so far, she could barely bend her joints. Each foot must have been tied to a leg of the table. Her gut twisted at the thought that her legs were no longer tied together. All the pain she had endured so far had only been physical, she didn't know if she could come back from anything more.

She looked around the room and was struck once more by how barren it was, there was nothing but the table she was on and the hook in the ceiling from which she'd been dangling for most of her time here. She tried to lift her head to look at herself, but she was spread so taunt that she couldn't see much without causing pain in her already tense muscles.

She knew she was covered in cuts of varying depth, courtesy of Alex. She was also aware of the bruises and cracked bones courtesy of Toby, but so far, she didn't think she'd suffered anything fatal as long as she breathed shallowly. She was thankful that the pain distracted her from the tight space, but she wondered when they'd stop toying with her and just end it.

The door opened and Toby walked in with a nasty sneer on his face, "Guess what, Princess?"

She continued staring at him, ignoring the question.

"You don't want to guess at all?" Toby was incredulous, "It's such a great surprise."

She really wanted to stay silent, but couldn't stop herself, "You've finally saved up for a peg leg and you want me to amputate your right leg so you're evensies?"

The anger that bubbled inside of him was visible. It made her sneer meanly.

"That's cute," he spoke with a strained voice after having a clear internal battle with himself, "Alex is gone." He took a step toward her, "So now I get to do whatever I want."

She maintained her angry gaze, trying to keep the terror in her gut from bubbling up.

"He was right about one thing," Toby looked her up and down. "I've been focusing on your eye for so long, I completely forgot about what else I wanted from you back when we were so close."

She gagged visibly but kept her composure otherwise.

Toby walked to the wall behind her head. She couldn't see what he was doing, but she heard a nozzle being turned and heard water rushing seconds before the stream of frigid water struck her body, making her cry out.

"Of course, the movies leave out the real sights and smells of a torture victim," he hosed her down thoroughly, focusing on areas that made her squirm. "If I want to have real, affectionate, fun with you, well, we're going to have to clean you up a bit."

She sputtered and gasped when he brought the hose to her face and let it run, choking her.

"It's so difficult to clean a filthy mouth though," he held the hose directly over her face until the fast stream was practically shooting down her throat. He moved it away when her eyes started to roll.

She coughed and spit the water out, gagging and spewing more from her lungs. It was difficult to breathe because she could only turn her head, all other movement was restricted by the position in which her body was pulled.

"Not so clever now, are you?" Toby growled as he put the hose on her stomach, facing down. She shivered as the water rushed down over her but she didn't say anything because she didn't want to drown on a table in Alex's basement. Toby ran his hand from her thigh to her ankle as he walked to the bottom of the table, by her feet.

"Don't," Gage sputtered, her voice strained.

"What was that?" Toby held one hand up to his ear, the other he rested on Gage's ankle.

"Don't!" She said more forcefully.

Toby laughed, his yellowed teeth making her stomach roil, "Why don't you beg, Princess?"

"Don't do this," she said quietly, "anything but this."

Toby pulled himself up onto the table between Gage's ankles, "I can do whatever the hell I want. And I want to take your eye, while I'm taking YOU." He crawled up the table and brought the hose back to her face. His weight settled heavily on her as he used one hand to hold the hose, practically drowning her, and his other hand tried to rip off her underwear.

Gage tried desperately to move, feeling all of the restraints cutting into her flesh. She couldn't breathe, but a part of her hoped she could just drown and be dead so she wouldn't suffer this injustice. She closed her eyes, tears escaping as she did, and she stopped fighting to breathe. She lay still and let the water fill her. It wasn't the first time she'd felt water fill her lungs. She welcomed the cold spreading through her chest.

He felt her go limp and he threw the hose away, lifting his weight off her slightly. Water dribbled from her mouth, but she didn't gasp for breath as she should have, so he brought the side of his fist down on her chest forcefully. Water spewed from her and she turned her head to the side, coughing viciously as water, blood, and phlegm pooled beside her. Her whole body shuddered with the effort.

Toby settled back on top of her, writhing, "Oh yeah, baby, I love it when you move," he said into her neck with his disgusting breath overtaking her senses.

The sound of gunshots came from somewhere.

They both froze for a moment.

"I'M HERE!" She shrieked as loud as she could, making Toby jerk, "I'M HERE! HELP ME!"

Toby's fist smashed into her face with enough force that she saw stars. The warmth of her blood gushing from her nose stung her frozen cheeks.

When she blinked her eyes to clear her vision all she could see was his knife coming toward her face. She screamed and turned her head away, but felt the blade bite into the flesh above her left eye.

Her whole body was on fire. She strained as hard as she could against her bonds and felt her shoulder dislocate. The pain was excruciating, but it allowed enough space for her to roll her hips slightly, throwing Toby off balance on top of her.

There was too much blood in her vision, she couldn't see anything, but she could feel him regaining his balance. She envisioned the knife coming back for her, but then his weight was gone.

She heard the impossibly loud booms of gunshots in the room, it made her ears ring from the concussions, then there were gentle hands on her.

She let her face be guided by the hands, but she couldn't see anything. Her vision was completely blocked by blood, it was in her mouth and pouring from her nose. She felt like she was choking on it. Her whole body trembled with adrenaline let-down and cold.

"I've got you, Baby," the voice was quiet and Australian.

She laughed roughly, overcome by sheer relief.

She felt him using water to wash her face, clearing her vision. Blinking rapidly, she could finally focus on his face, or at least what she could see of his face. He was wearing a skull facemask over the lower half of his face, but his blue eyes were what drew her sight. They were still clear as the Texas sky, she saw home in his eyes.

"That's it, focus on me, I'm getting you out of here," he said, his eyes angry and emotional. He blinked and reached down to cut her legs free. The relief she felt in her joints, when she could bend her knees again, rushed from her lungs in a sigh.

He moved to cut her hands free but she croaked out, "Leave them, I can't-" she swallowed roughly, "I can't walk."

He nodded and she felt him gently lift her hands from a hook, she cried out when her shoulder moved. She could feel the heat of pure unadulterated wrath radiating from his body as he lifted her to a sitting position and gently put her arms around his neck. She felt his rifle hanging on his back by the sling across his body. The rope binding her wrists helped her hold onto him so he could lift her from the table.

She leaned against him as he stood still, allowing her to get as comfortable as she could in his arms. When she grew still, he picked up his sidearm from the table and emptied his magazine into Toby's already lifeless body.

She couldn't help but smile against Mak's neck, "You finally get to see the real me," she whispered, ignoring the fact that her blood was dripping down his throat, "worth the wait I hope."

She didn't hear his response, she passed out.

Mak put his empty sidearm back in its holster and drew another before walking up the stairs into the controlled chaos in the main warehouse.

"Pop!" Buck alerted Whitlock to Mak's presence with one word.

The look on Whitlock's face when he saw the brutalized woman in Mak's arms made it abundantly clear that she was not just an employee to him.

"Take her," Mak said, "I'll help mop up here."

Whit gently transitioned Gage's tied wrists to his own neck, then carefully took her from the Australian's arms, "Meet me at PREY after."

Mak nodded and transitioned from his handgun to his rifle seamlessly firing one shot through the head of an armed man trying to sneak up on them. "Go. We'll cover yah."

The gunfire that followed reminded Whit of battle overseas, he was fairly certain that the Australians were using far more ammo than they actually needed, but when he looked at Gage's swollen face and blood covered body, he didn't mind one bit.

Chapter 52

"She must be really pissed at us," Mere looked at her phone again for what felt like the millionth time, "she still won't answer."

"Where could she be for a week?" Will asked, clearly worried, "Miami is our home, we have contacts everywhere, how could NO ONE have any idea where she is?"

"To be honest, Gage could be right next to us in a restaurant and we wouldn't know it," EmEm said. "She's a damn chameleon."

"She's never done this before," Tessa was pacing. She'd been pacing for most of the week.

"What about Tiny and Killer?" Mere said, "Even if she'd leave us behind, there's no way she'd leave them."

"She wouldn't leave us," Will snapped, "we're the only family she has."

"Family who invited a murdering, abusive, drug dealer into her home," Lina walked into the flat, her tan face unnaturally pale.

"What?" Will went to her side and grabbed her arm to support her because she looked shaken.

"Alejandro Sanchez, not Alex Santiago," Lina said quietly. "He's one of the predominant drug dealers in America. I found several stories linking him to prostitution of young female runaways, even unsolved murders, and cases of brutal assaults." She swallowed hard, "I think he is who Gage has been running from since we've known her. The timeline adds up," a tear streamed down Lina's cheek. "She would have been fifteen when they met. Alex said they dated for five years then she ran away," Lina's voice cracked, "I'm pretty sure he victimized her for five years and she ran away and had been hiding from him for the six years she's been with PREY."

Realization settled heavily over the group.

"Then we completely disregarded her weird behavior and brought a maniac into her safe haven," Mere said what they were all thinking.

"We suck," Tessa whimpered, tears streaming down her face.

"Well, it seems you're all caught up," Whitlock stepped into the flat using the doorway Lina had just vacated. "Alex is a sadistic piece of filth who has been hunting down the only woman to ever defy him for the last seven years." He glanced at Lina, "She was fourteen when he claimed her. She was running alone for a year before I found her."

All eyes were on their leader, who was uncharacteristically emotional, he was wearing a blood-soaked T-shirt. His hands shook as he held them in front of him, staring at his palms.

"Whit," Tessa's voice broke as she stared at him with terrified blue eyes. She'd never seen him without a collared shirt, there was something unsettling seeing him so disheveled. It was almost more upsetting than the blood.

"She's alive," he responded gruffly, looking up at the group, "why you would trust a stranger over Gage is beyond me." The anger in his tone was palpable, "His goons snatched her outside, here, six days ago. Once he knew where she lived, all he had to do was wait for her to come home," he glared at the table, not making eye contact with anyone. The muscles of his arms and shoulders strained as he made fists, "She wasn't even rescued by her team, by the people she loves like family." When he finally looked up, his eyes were watery and his hands dropped to his sides in defeat, "When she needed us, we let her down," he growled, "so I left her with the people who cared enough to go fight and save her."

The group all stared at him, their faces a mix of anger, sadness, and fear.

"She's-" Mere swallowed hard, "she's okay?"

"What's the damage?" Will asked quietly, his eyes downcast, his voice strained.

"She's taken quite a beating," Whit answered, "she's lost blood, required a lot of stitches, cracked some ribs, and she may lose the sight in her left eye. Only time will tell. She was clearly tortured pretty severely but she's not talking about it."

"Can we see her?" EmEm asked quietly.

"To apologize?" Whitlock snapped, glaring at the younger man. He spoke again before EmEm could respond, "I'm leaving that up to her. I'll pass along the desire." He turned and called out, "We all failed her," as he left.

Brick passed Whitlock and stepped into the flat. He had deep bags under his eyes, blood on his shirt, and an almost annoyed expression which he turned on Mere, "Can you take me to Gage's room?"

"You get to see her?" Tessa squeaked in surprise.

Brick turned his exhausted gaze to the youngest person in the room, "I'm the one who has been trying to treat her, since she's refusing to go to the hospital. So, can someone point me to her damn room so I can get her some clothes and her Tylenol."

Mere stood and headed down the hallway, "She doesn't need something stronger than Tylenol? Whitlock painted a pretty gnarly picture."

"The picture painted is nothing compared to the canvas," Brick grumbled, massaging his left hand with his right, "and trust me, I've tried to get her to take something substantial, she's fighting me over just about everything. She won't even let me give her something for the pain while I'm stitching her up, it's not exactly an ideal situation."

"Sounds about right," Mere opened Gage's door and walked into the room. She picked up a duffle off the floor and started to fill it with some of Gage's personal effects.

"Thanks for this," Brick motioned to the bag, "I wouldn't have known what to grab."

Mere smiled at him sadly, "Sorry we've been such assholes to you, thank you for taking care of her. We won't forget it."

He shrugged, "It's just what I do."

"You didn't have to, we haven't given you a reason to be there for us," she responded as she walked into Gage's bathroom and put some toiletries into the bag.

"I'm on this team whether the team likes it or not," he took the bag from her and slung it over his shoulder, "I figured I might as well show you why I'm useful."

Mere nodded, "Well, like I said, it hasn't gone unnoticed." She rested a hand on his forearm, "Seriously. Thank you."

He smiled tiredly, "Thank me later, I don't even know if I've saved her eye yet."

Mere shook her head, "You didn't harm her, it won't be your fault if you can't fix her. You're one of us now. We're all here for you if you need anything."

"You're all here?" Brick arched an eyebrow.

"I'm here," she said, "if you ever need anything."

"Thanks," he patted her hand and then headed out of the room.

Chapter 53

Gage sat on a bed in her bra and underwear, her chin rested on her knees and she stared into her reflection in the mirrored closet door.

Her left eye was painfully swollen, the stitches itched, she could only see shadowy shapes when she closed her right eye.

A light knock on the door was followed by, "You're going to be okay. You know that right?"

She ignored Mak when he entered the room and continued staring at her injuries. She was healing, she felt stronger every day, but the array of colors and stitches all over her body was distracting.

"Gage?" Mak sat on the bed behind her but didn't touch her. Part of her felt terrible that she flinched when anyone touched her, even him, but she couldn't help it.

She put her feet on the ground and twisted slightly so she could look at him.

"It's been a week," he said gently, "don't you think you've punished them enough?" He put her phone on the bed between them, "They didn't know."

She swallowed and stared at him instead of looking at her phone.

"I got you a present," he pulled a small box from his jacket pocket.

"If that's jewelry, I'll kill you," she said.

He chuckled and shook his head, then looked at her concerned, "Really?"

She smirked and held her hand out. He squinted his eyes at her as though trying to figure her out and placed the box in her palm. Her hand only twitched a little when his brushed it, so he smiled brightly.

"I only ask, because I'm not actually sure if it counts as jewelry or not," he said in a conversational tone.

She made a face at him in confusion before looking down and opening the box. When she realized what was inside, she wasn't sure if she wanted to laugh or cry so she just yelled, "You're such an asshole!"

He laughed when she punched his shoulder as hard as she could, "OW! It's a thoughtful gift!"

She dumped out the box on the bed, at least twenty eye patches all different colors and designs spilled across the bed-spread. She couldn't help but laugh as she looked at each one, they were themed to match all the different wigs he'd seen on her. Her fingers settled on a pirate eyepatch, complete with the skull and crossbones, a tear escaped her right eye and she didn't flinch when he wiped it away gently.

"I didn't mean to upset you," he said softly.

She smiled and glanced at him for a moment before leaning forward and kissing him gently. It was the first time she'd consciously made the decision to touch anyone since she'd woken up at PREY. She sat back after a minute and put on her pirate eyepatch, "Arrrrrr you going to just sit there? Or can you hand me my pants?" she motioned to her clothes folded on the bed behind him.

"I actually like you this way," he said.

She smirked at him, "Sure you do. Who wouldn't? I'm sexy as hell."

Her tone was sarcastic, so he leaned in, gently pulled her face to him, and kissed her deeply. When he pulled back, she was breathless, and he whispered, "You're God damn right you are, don't you forget it." He stood up and poked her nose, winking at her before leaving the room so she could get dressed.

She watched as he left and closed the door before she looked down at her phone to see that she had several dozen missed calls and text messages. She took a deep fortifying breath and stood up to get dressed. "I guess I have a lot of explaining to do."

After she was dressed, she took off her pirate eye patch and put on a somber blue one instead. She picked up her phone and created a group message telling everyone to meet her at the flat.

"Need a ride there?" Buck called through the wall making her smirk.

"No, she doesn't need a ride from you!" Mak yelled back.

Gage laughed out loud when she heard slamming around in the next room. She knew the Australians were wrestling, and that simple everyday action made a weight lift from her chest. She wasn't a broken doll on someone's shelf, she was a friend they could good-naturedly fight over. She pulled her hair back into a ponytail and walked from the room, ready to face her friends and explain everything.

Chapter 54

Gage stood outside her garage, chewing the inside of her lip, and wringing her hands silently, staring at the stairs. She'd passed enough vehicles to know that everyone was already inside.

"You okay?" Mak placed a gentle hand on her lower back, she shivered slightly but was actually thankful for the contact. She looked up at him, nodding, then turned back to the stairs and took a deep breath before starting to climb up them.

When she saw her friends through the glass sliding door, her heart skipped a beat and her foot faltered on the step. Mak's arm went around her quickly and firmly, helping her steady herself. A tear fell down her cheek and her breathing quickened.

"You don't have to go in there," Mak said softly, "but they all love you. You know that. There's nothing you could say to them to change that."

Tiny started barking excitedly and Killer began jumping at the glass, drawing everyone's attention to Gage's panic-stricken face.

"Well, they all love you except Brick," he amended, hoping to make her smile, "but who cares about him anyway?"

She tried to smile, to let him know she was okay, but she was actually panicking. She knew they wanted to rush up to her, but everyone very carefully stayed perfectly still.

Gage took a deep breath and let it out slowly, calming herself. She wiped away her tears and sniffled, raised her chin and walked forward with Mak's arm still around her.

"I'm right here if you need me," he said quietly.

She nodded and smiled up at him momentarily before sliding the door open and stepping inside. Killer jumped into her arms, making her wince due to the impact on her ribs. She kissed him on the head, then let him jump down, before gingerly bending down to stroke Tiny's ears and kiss his snout.

When she straightened, she was painfully aware that all eyes were on her, even though her gaze was on the floor.

Will stood from his chair, closest to her, at the head of the table. He touched her elbow to guide her to the chair but quickly jerked his hand back when she flinched from him.

"Damn it, I'm sorry," she sighed and shook her head. She glanced at his hurt expression and tried to smile reassuringly, but then felt even worse as his eyes quickly adverted from her gaze.

She chewed on her lip again and stared at the floor, her hands started shaking but she felt stuck in time.

"You can sit," Mak said quietly, breaking the painful silence.

Everything immediately burst into action at once.

"I'm so sorry." Will said at the same time EmEm said, "We should have known better."

Tessa jumped up and rushed to get Gage a glass of water, while Mere stood up and grabbed a bottle of Jameson from the bar. Whitlock walked into the sitting area from the kitchen with a tray of glasses and Buck leaned back against the wall smirking at everyone else bumbling around.

Lina was sitting in the corner crying openly, staring at Gage's face.

Brick sat in the back of the room with his arms folded across his chest and a toothpick bouncing on his lip as he chewed it.

Gage slid into the chair Will had vacated and put her hands on the table, palms down. The vicious cuts, burns, and bruises on her wrists from the rope were bright purple and blue against her pale skin. The faint twinges of yellow and green were just beginning to shoot through the bruises, showing the faint signs of healing.

Everyone stopped again and silence filled the room with stifling finality.

Gage blew a breath out and finally looked up, meeting Mere's eyes first she said, "I have a lot to say. I need y'all to let me get it out, or I won't be able to get through it." She looked at each person in turn, "I'm going to start by apologizing."

They all started speaking at once so she slammed her palms down on the table hard enough to make most of the people in the room jump.

"Let me get through it," she said again, enunciating each word carefully as she cradled her sore hands to her stomach. She felt Mak put his hand on her shoulder gently but she stared at the table in front of her, studying the grain intently. She took heart that the touch didn't make her cringe, so she swallowed and continued quietly, "I need to apologize for not explaining myself earlier. I just expected y'all to go about life, like everything was fine, while I was spiraling out, because I was too proud to admit my past." She glanced up at Tessa, "For so long I tried to make up for my short-comings by over-compensating everywhere else," she shrugged and once more her eyes dropped to the table, "it got to be too exhausting, but I didn't take a break or come to y'all like I should have. I just shut down and hid away."

"We should have waited for you, instead of nosing around where we didn't belong," Mere said quietly, staring at the Jameson in her glass. Her pale green eyes lifted and met Gage's gaze, she emphasized, "I should have waited."

Gage nodded her acceptance, then chewed her lip, "I don't know where to start."

"The best place to start, is probably the beginning," Whit said gently, but firmly, as he sat beside Mere at the table and poured himself a glass of whiskey.

Gage sucked in a breath with a slight nod and said quietly, "When I was a kid, like three years old, my mom was murdered in front of me." She let out a breath like the weight of the world had just been lifted. "I don't think I've ever said that out loud before," she laughed nervously.

"Jesus, I knew she died, but I had no idea," Will's face was unreadable.

"My mom somehow knew what was coming." Gage stared into the distance but her eyes weren't focused on anything, "She locked me in a closet, to protect me, but she got shot right outside the door." She continued softly, "I can't remember her much. I remember her hair smelled like lavender and vanilla. My dad used to say I looked just like her, but I don't remember her face. I don't even have a picture of her."

She shuddered, "I remember the gunshot. I remember the thud her body made against the door." She ran her hand across the table, "Her blood came under the door, and I tried to make myself as tiny as I could so it wouldn't touch me." Mak's hand slid off her shoulder, but she still felt his presence, "Because if it didn't touch me, then it couldn't be real." Hot tears streamed down her cheeks. "I spent years after that, not letting anything touch me, so it wasn't real. My dad raised me until he decided to be a hero and go overseas as a contractor. Though being raised by Gabriel Grayson wasn't exactly rainbows and butterflies."

"Did you just say Gabriel Grayson is your father?" Mak asked, looking at Buck with wide eyes.

Gage glanced up at him, "Yes. Why?"

Mak shook his head, "I think I knew him," he mumbled. "No. Can't be the same bloke. Sorry. I won't interrupt again."

Brick had removed the toothpick from his mouth, his blue eyes trained on Gage's face as she answered Mak's question. Listening to her intently with his face carefully blank.

Gage wiped at her face and tried to pick up where she'd left off, "'The world is a dangerous place'," she mocked her father's voice. "Those were his last words to me. He made the world decidedly more dangerous for me since I became an orphan shortly after he left." She sniffed and sucked in a breath, "The only family I had old enough to adopt me was an uncle in New York, but he was busy with his own problem child, he couldn't take me in long-term. So, I bounced from foster home to foster home. Just an angry, violent, whirlwind of teenage hormonal rage," she rubbed her wrist. "I ran away from every home because, of course, I knew better than anyone trying to help me. Then when I was fourteen, Alejandro Sanchez found me." She stood up and started pacing, "He knew just what to say, he knew how to sell me before I even knew I was looking for something to buy."

She glanced at Whitlock, who looked away, "So at fourteen, I tried some painkillers, by fifteen, I was addicted to heroin," she ignored the quiet involuntary noises she heard from some of her friends. "I wanted to be numb," she said louder than she meant to, her voice cracking, "I was so fucking angry all the time." Everything was pouring out of her now, she didn't care what her friends thought, she just needed to finally tell someone everything, "Everyone I loved left me, so I decided to poison myself every day. I didn't give a fuck about myself, why should I? Clearly, I wasn't worth shit." She spoke in a conversational tone, "Alex decided I was going to be his girlfriend. I welcomed it. He gave me free shit sometimes." She gagged slightly, "Other times, he made me work for it."

Her disgust in her own past marred her face worse than the scars or cuts, "I just wanted to stay numb, but after years, it was killing me. I knew I wouldn't last much longer. Not only did Alex beat the shit out of me whenever he felt like it, but I was at his mercy, always." She stopped pacing, "I decided I had to leave, or I was going to die. But Alex had already made up his mind which he wanted," she touched the scar by her belly button through her shirt, "he stabbed me and left me for dead with his second in command to get rid of my body. But he left the knife in my gut." She smiled and acted out her next words, "So I yanked the knife out and stabbed at that asshole blindly." She touched her eye patch, "Apparently, I took his eye, but I didn't wait to find out how I did, I just got the hell out of there."

She took a deep breath, "I convinced my veterinarian foster father to stitch me up, and give me antibiotics, then spent the better part of a year hiding and trying to get clean." She cleared her throat, "Whitlock found me on my twentieth birthday and we started PREY, shortly thereafter. I started collecting friends and projects like it was going out of style, and I decided to lock away my life before PREY." She swallowed, "It just didn't work out like I wanted."

She looked up finally, her gaze falling on Brick, who seemed uncomfortable, "Which is why I don't take pain medication. I'm an addict. I've been clean for a while now, but I can't risk exposure." She looked at Mak, "And I don't show the real me. Because the real me is fucked up, and quite frankly, a disappointment." She looked at Tessa, "But that's why I pretty much adopted you, Tess, because you have the chance to be everything I'm not. You're talented, and amazing, and good."

"You're those things too," Tessa said quietly. "You found me and took me in," she shook her head, "you didn't have to do that. You could have just left me to die, but you didn't."

"I see so much of who I was in you," Gage said quietly, "before I was ruined by the bullshit."

"You're not ruined," Mak interrupted with a gruff voice, "and for what it's worth, I like the real you."

"PREY wouldn't be the success it is, without you," Whitlock pipped up, "as crazy as you are, you make this team work. You created it."

"Thanks, Papa Bear," Gage said quietly. "I guess most of you know exactly why I never wanted any of this to come out." Her eyes slowly rose to meet Mere's gaze, "I know you hate drugs. I know you've seen them ruin lives. I didn't want to disappoint you as much as I was disappointed in myself," she shrugged, "I hated myself enough for all of you."

"No one hates you, Gage," Mere stood from her seat and hugged her friend fiercely, "I'm so proud of you. You fought it. You beat addiction all by yourself. That's amazing, and a true testament to your strength. I'm so sorry that you thought my feelings about drugs could possibly extend to who you are now."

Gage stood awkwardly while Mere hugged her, but her eyes were on the floor.

"You've been there for all of us," Will stated matter-of-factly, "maybe we didn't know about, or expect, this type of past, but you're still our sister."

EmEm nodded, "I wouldn't have you any other way Momma, you're our heart around here."

"It definitely explains some of your quirks," Will added with a smile.

"No enclosed spaces," Tessa stated.

"Window open in the car," Mere added.

"Never look the same twice in a row," Mak piped up.

"Not to mention you're just nuts," Brick said.

Gage actually laughed then, and the tension that had been in the air, lifted. "I'm so sorry guys, I knew I should have told you when Alex first showed back up, but some part of me was terrified that you'd be as disgusted with me as I have been with myself. I didn't want to risk losing you. I couldn't stand it if you hated me."

Will, EmEm, Tessa, Lina, and Mere all hugged with Gage in the middle.

"There's nothing you could do to make us hate you," Tessa said softly, "you're still the same amazing woman we all love."

"You're just a little more colorful than we thought," EmEm added.

"Everything's about color with you," Gage sighed, making everyone laugh.

Chapter 55

Gage walked into her favorite Bistro with oversized sunglasses obscuring half her face. Her hair was a sleek platinum blonde river down her back. She felt overdressed in her jeans and leather jacket, the Florida sun was hot today, but she was self-conscious about her still healing injuries.

She smiled at the hostess, "I'm here for a pickup."

"What's the name?" The young girl asked, looking at her computer.

"Meredith," Gage responded and glanced around the restaurant.

"It will be just a few more minutes," the hostess smiled, "they're finishing your pizza now."

"Okay," Gage nodded and moved to stand just inside the door, where the air conditioner was blowing.

"Hey there, Bridget." The voice was smug and dripping with malice.

Gage stiffened and immediately regretted leaving the flat alone for the first time in over a week.

"I lost a lot of valuable people in that warehouse."

She turned and stared at Alex, who was sitting at a small table inside the door. He'd been blocked from her view by a large planter.

"When I saw Meredith's number come up in the log, I thought I'd wait to see her," Alex smiled charmingly, but to Gage, it was like looking in a shark's mouth.

"You stay away from my friends," Gage said calmly. She was proud that her voice didn't waver at all.

Alex shrugged, "I'm thinking maybe one of them will give me the information I need since you refused to cooperate."

"You stay AWAY from my friends," she growled the words again.

"That Tessa, she's a little old for my usual tastes, but I hear she comes from good drug stock."

He was goading her into action. She knew it. She bristled anyway.

"I heard the Escobars didn't even know Terrence Davenport had another daughter," Alex said conversationally. "Isn't that interesting? That the oldest daughter of such a man is still breathing?"

Gage knew she couldn't give him what he wanted, but it was taking every ounce of willpower to restrain herself. Her muscles were actually aching from the tension.

"You know, I still do dealings with Pedro Escobar," Alex was enjoying this new torture he was inflicting. "Coincidentally, he's one of the ones seeking information about your boss." He settled back against his chair, lazily smiling at his game. "I wonder what he'd give me if I snatched her off the street, pumped her full of heroin, had a couple goes at her and then dumped her in his lap."

Gage was shaking.

"Do you think he'd pay me in cash for the opportunity to skin her alive? Or do you think he'd just give her to his men to rape to death?"

Something inside Gage snapped. All she could hear was the hammering beat of her heart, and all she could see was red as she lunged past the planter and tackled her tormenter out of his chair. He put his arms up feebly to protect himself, but Gage just punched and punched and punched until her shoulder ached. She could hear people screaming and scrambling away.

Alex's goons rushed forward, but by the time they reached her, she was standing over their boss with a Glock pointed at him. They stopped.

Alex moaned on the ground, his face a bloody pulp.

"If y'all would like to live, I suggest you tend to your boss, and let me leave," she stated calmly.

One of the men nodded.

"Good." Gage backed away from the scene until her back hit the counter where her pizza box was sitting. She grabbed the pizza and strode from the building, holstering her weapon and immediately breaking into a run.

Chapter 56

Gage opened the door to the garage, tossed the pizza box onto her workbench, and went directly into the bathroom to wash the blood from her knuckles. She pulled the wig off her head and shrugged out of her leather coat before dropping them into the trashcan to be burned later. She turned the water as hot as it would go and let it run. She took off her sunglasses and threw them into the trash can too, before staring into the mirror, until steam clouded the mirror.

When her vision was blocked, she washed her hands until the pink of her skin was the only discernible color. Once she'd finished with her hands, she washed her face and shook out her temporarily scarlet hair so it fell down her shoulders, then she cleaned the sink with bleach and tied up the trash bag. She settled an eyepatch over her left eye.

She heard the phone ring upstairs and sighed when it was picked up on the first ring. She knew that Tessa would come to yell at her any moment, so instead of worrying about the confrontation, Gage walked across the garage to let Tiny and Killer out to do their business.

She heard the stomping footsteps coming down the stairs and sighed again. She hated always being right.

When Tessa slammed into the garage, her face was almost the color of her hair. The anger rose from her like steam from a hot road in the rain.

Gage turned from the younger woman and busied herself at her workbench fiddling with her tools, reorganizing.

Tessa paced angrily, tugging at her hair as she almost seemed to argue with herself internally before practically shrieking, "Damn it, Gage! How COULD you?!"

Gage winced at the high-pitched noise as she turned to face the girl, "What do you mean how?" She smiled meanly, "I grabbed him by the shirt and punched until my arm got tired," she shrugged, "then I left."

"Are you insane?" Tessa's tone was sincere, "Or just stupid?"

Gage arched her right eyebrow and growled, "Be careful."

"ME!?" Tessa snapped, "You want ME to be careful? You just provoked a first-class criminal into action!"

"I provoked HIM?!" Gage roared, her temper flaring, "Look what he did to me!" Gage snatched the eye-patch off of her face, revealing her left eye which was still swollen shut and a painfully bloody purple color with an angry gash that marred her once smooth face from the top of her eyebrow to her cheekbone. The redhead couldn't help but wince at the sight which had been kept from her since the injury occurred. Gage drew pleasure from Tessa's horrified expression before speaking smoothly as she replaced the eye-patch, "He's lucky I didn't kill him."

Tessa composed herself almost instantly and grabbed Gage's shoulders, shaking the woman. "He's a DRUG DEALER," she snapped, "he won't see this as retribution." When Gage shrugged the girl's hands off and turned her back, Tessa stepped in front of Gage again, "He'll see this as an offensive move." Gage glared at Tessa as the redhead continued, "An offensive move which requires immediate attention."

"So, I'll hit him until he stops," Gage muttered stubbornly.

"Drug dealers DON'T stop," Tessa insisted quietly, "they never stop, are you really so foolish that you don't recognize that?"

Gage glared into innocent blue eyes with her one cold jade one, "I'm not your parents." She made her voice purposely cold, knowing she was hurting the girl, "I didn't steal ice from a Colombian King Pin and try to fucking sell it."

Tessa looked away, her vision blurring with tears, "My father made a stupid decision and my whole family had to pay the price." She forced her gaze back to Gage's face, "For all we know, you've just done the same thing."

"You are a selfish, spoiled brat!" Gage exploded, her voice high-pitched, "I took you in, put you through school, fed you, gave you clothes, all on my own dime. You repay me with all this self-important philosophy crap," she shook her head angrily. "I could have left you to rot where I found you."

Tessa nodded, her eyes fiery, "You COULD have," she agreed, "but you didn't; so now that I tell you what you're doing is dangerous and stupid, I'M spoiled?" She pushed Gage hard, "WAKE UP!"

Gage stumbled back from the girl, startled, and then felt her temper flare even hotter, "I've BEEN awake," she snapped. "I've been living a fucking nightmare for the last four months." Tessa had the decency to look away, which made Gage continue, "You were SO aware of my pain, weren't you, Princess? I was spiraling out of control and all you cared about was going abroad to study, until I was half-blind and carved up like a side of beef." Gage pushed Tessa this time, making the redhead's attention snap back to her, "But now, suddenly, you know better. YOU know what I should do? By all means, enlighten me," she beckoned to the younger woman with her hands, "go on, what is it that I should have done?" She cocked her head slightly, "Should I have let him get away with what they did to me? Should I let him threaten you and Mere?"

"That's not what I mean," Tessa snapped.

"It's exactly what you said," Gage responded, "I should have smiled and thanked him for the stitches, cut flesh and ruined eye."

"Your eye isn't ruined," Tessa started.

"We don't know that," Gage snapped, "I might never see properly again. But that doesn't matter," she said bitterly, "does it?"

"Shut UP!" Tessa yelled.

Gage stood still with her chest heaving with deep breaths as she tried to reign in her temper.

"You should have done the right thing," Tessa continued in a calmer tone, "you should have gone to the police."

"The police can't help me," Gage responded in a strained voice, "the police will charge him. Then I'll be put on the stand and ripped to shreds." Gage held up her hand to stop Tessa from speaking, "I'm an ex-junkie who used to do anything for Heroin. Just because I've changed, doesn't mean anything to them. Even if by some miracle they don't use my past against me, this case will be publicized and I'll never be able to work at PREY again."

Tessa sighed, "You don't know that."

"Yes, I do," Gage retorted, "are you so naïve that you think the world is black and white?" Gage gave a weak smile, "If the world was right, I would probably be in jail."

"Then let's just go!" Tessa said, "Let's just pack up and move somewhere different. We'll change our names and cover our tracks."

Gage shook her head, "I did that before, he'll find me. He always does."

"Then go to the police and see what happens," Tessa insisted, "please, do it for me."

"I just can't."

"Please Gage," Tessa begged, "we have to run or go to the police."

Gage sighed, "He ruined my face. I can't hide, I'll stick out like a sore thumb."

"The police then," Tessa insisted, her blue eyes wide and pleading, "call Van. You know he'll help."

"Van is going to New York," Gage shook her head. "You know there's no one else at the department willing to help us."

"Then let's hide," Tessa circled around in her argument. "Your face isn't that bad. As it heals, it'll get even better."

Gage tucked her chin to her chest and closed her good eye. She stood silently for a moment before muttering. "It's kind of hot in a Mad Max kind of way, right?" She opened her eye and shot a half-smile at Tessa.

Tessa couldn't help the snort of laughter that bubbled suddenly out of her throat, "You really are hopeless."

Gage shrugged, "You know you love me."

Tessa opened her mouth to respond but the rough staccato of automatic gunfire cut off her words.

Gage tackled the younger woman to the ground, shouting, "Down," as she rolled off her friend and covered her head with her arms.

Bullets ripped through the garage without any aim or direction. Oil canisters burst and began spewing their contents. Gasoline rained down everywhere, choking Gage with fumes as heat erupted from somewhere to her left.

The smoke mixed with the fumes, making it impossible for her to see with her one good eye. Her skin felt like it was burning as a mix of hot liquids pooled against her arms on the floor. When the bullets finally stopped, a small explosion rained hot metal down on them.

Gage pushed herself up into a crouched position and tried to feel around for Tessa, "We have to get out of here!" She yelled into the hot haze. She rubbed at her arms to rid them of the shards of metal that were burning her as she searched the haze with her good eye.

It wasn't until she looked down at herself that she realized that her arms were streaked with blood. She looked at her hands and saw that they were dripping. Her heart leaped into her throat as she moved forward on her hands and knees, feeling for her friend, "TESSA! Where are you?"

Panic tightened her chest painfully and the fumes, which were already keeping her breath from her lungs, seemed like a secondary issue.

Her eye caught the sight of a slumped figure and she scrambled to where Tessa was on her side, her red locks across her face.

Gage pulled the younger woman into her lap and let out an inhuman shriek of pain, "Tessa!" ignoring the fact that red hair was matted with blood to Tessa's cheek beside sightless blue eyes, staring into nothing.

"Tess? Tessie? Please Tessie, Please," Gage cried, shaking her friend as the flames grew closer. "Please Tessie, you have to wake up now," she wailed, but Tessa was gone. There was no light left in her usually bright eyes.

The smoke became even thicker so Gage forced herself to gently lay Tessa down. She kissed the girl's forehead and whispered, "I'm so, so sorry," before crawling toward where she could see the smoke pouring into the evening air.

When her hands met the gravel of the parking lot, she forced herself to her feet and stumbled a few feet before dropping hard to her knees and vomiting violently.

She heard running footsteps and felt rough hands grabbing her shoulders, forcing her back to sit on her feet.

"Gage!" Will was shouting over the sound of the roaring fire, but his words didn't seem to break through, "Are you hurt? Are you okay?" She didn't answer, she sat on her feet, staring ahead in shock, even when he slapped her across the face and shouted, "Where's Tessa?"

She felt a hot tear escape her eye and she swallowed before looking at him and choking out, "Dead," in a rough voice.

She stood and walked away from the conflagration which had once been her whole life. The explosions from within the inferno didn't even make her flinch as she climbed into her Torino and the engine roared to life.

Once the shock of that single syllable released his limbs from their paralysis, Will chased after the woman shouting, "Gage! What the hell are you doing?"

Gage revved the engine and the Torino lurched forward, kicking debris into the flames as the garage collapsed in on itself.

Chapter 57

Nothing mattered anymore.

There was no lucid thought in Gage's mind as she drove, covered in innocent blood, to the only place she knew she could find Alex.

She couldn't hide anymore.

She wouldn't run this time.

Consequences didn't matter anymore. There was no right and there was certainly no wrong. Gage was prepared to do whatever was necessary to ensure that no more of her loved ones were hurt or killed because of one man's sick obsession.

Her tires squealed in protest as she slid into the parking lot of Craze, spitting gravel at the line of people waiting to get into the nightclub.

She heard the screams of protest, but she couldn't care anymore, they were just the background noise of a soundtrack in some movie she watched once. She reached across the Torino and opened the glove box before pulling a latch in the corner which opened a different compartment, revealing her two handguns. She pulled them out and climbed out of the car, shoving one into the waistband at the back of her pants, she used that quickly freed hand to put the Torino into neutral and let it roll down the small hill toward the side of the building. She fired one shot through the gas tank and tried not to vomit as the smell of gasoline once more overwhelmed her senses.

She heard people screaming and watched them scatter as she walked toward the front door. She threw her zippo into the line of gas from the car and didn't even wince when it exploded into the side of the building, bricks began to fall and people streamed from the building in terror.

She could see Tim at the front door. He was watching her and ignoring everyone else. She really didn't want to kill him unless she had to; he wasn't such a bad guy, just mixed up with the wrong people.

She saw the personal battle he was dealing with as she approached. Instead of going for the firearm in his shoulder holster, he reached out a hand as though to grab her.

She smirked, grabbed his pinky finger, and twisted it with all the strength in her left hand. She felt it snap and felt him fall off balance with pain; his scream was silent to her ears because as she kicked him out of her way and he fell from the front stoop, she was already continuing on to find Alex.

Inside the nightclub was complete chaos. People were trying to get out, but when they saw her, they turned and ran for the opposite exit. It was only then that she had a conscious thought of how insane she must look, covered in soot and blood.

She surveyed the area and saw three of Alex's goons trying to put out the fire from her Torino. Her gaze was immediately drawn to the middle of the dance floor where the raised section was still partitioned off as though some drunken girl would be trying to go up the stairs to see the owner of the establishment while the club was on fire.

The music was still blaring though the DJ was long gone, and the lights were still flashing with neon, making her stomach drop as she tried to focus on the platform. She was waiting for the familiar face she was searching for to pop into view.

She was the only person on the dance floor; everyone else was frantically trying to push their way into the alley.

"Alex!" She yelled as loud as she could, but her voice cracked and couldn't be heard over the music. She glanced at the DJ platform and fired one shot into the system. It erupted into sparks and a deafening squelch cut through the speakers before going silent.

She glared up at the platform again and waited a moment.

Alex peered down from the railing, his face mish-mashed with bruises and swollen features, "Hey, what's going on babe?"

She swallowed and continued to stare up at him, trying to decide what exactly to do.

"Why'd you shoot my stereo? You know that's expensive equipment, don't you?" His cavalier tone made her insides roil.

She raised her firearm to point right at him.

"What's this?" He laughed, "You really think you can just walk in here, kill me, and walk back out?"

"I don't need to walk out," she rasped, her throat feeling as though it had been charred from the inside.

"I see you got my little present then?" He smiled meanly, "Too bad it missed its mark."

The three men who had been working on the fire dropped what they were doing and ran at her from her right. She drew her secondary weapon and dispatched them without looking away from Alex with her burning glare.

"That was pretty impressive," he stated, "but you could never kill me, Bridget, you know that."

"You missed me," Gage responded, her eye glaring into him with hatred and pain. "You killed Tessa."

That simple statement made Alex's face twist in fear and duck back as a bullet ripped through the air at him. The bullet struck one of his bodyguards in the throat and the large man fell to the ground sputtering and squealing.

She heard Alex shrieking for assistance and heard things being pushed around on the platform. She walked calmly to the circular stairs and began her assent.

She had no doubt that there were armed men above her. Men who would shoot her the second she came into view. It didn't matter. She didn't care anymore. All that mattered was ending this before it killed anyone else who loved her.

She was about to turn the last corner, to walk onto the platform, when an explosion above her knocked her to her knees. She looked around in confusion and saw a man on the stairs behind her, wearing an Americana mask over the lower half of his face and a tactical vest. He winked and shrugged, nodding up the stairs.

She recognized Mak instantly by his swagger and couldn't help but feel glad he was there as she struggled back to her feet before walking onto the platform to see the carnage before her. It appeared that the large man who had been injured by her bullet had crawled, or been rolled, onto the grenade. He wasn't in one piece anymore.

Gage heard Mak's footsteps on the stairs as she surveyed the room, searching for Alex.

She spotted him, hiding behind the couch, at the same moment that she heard and felt the bullet firing from a thug beside him. It hit her in the torso and she stumbled back from the force of it, but she did not fall. She let loose all of the rounds she had left in her firearms into the couch and heard the satisfying sounds of contact before the weapons were both empty. She dropped the useless tools and walked to the couch, ignoring her wound completely. She was running on pure adrenaline and fury. The pain was just a nuisance.

Mak crouched as he entered the room and saw Gage walking to the couch, he saw her two weapons on the floor and picked them up, one by one, and threw them in his bag before moving to support her, should she need the assistance.

She crouched down, disappearing from view and as he rounded the corner, he saw her kneeling beside Alex. The man was sputtering blood; the wound ruining his lung was clearly lethal.

"We have to go," Mak said, "the cops will be here in no time."

"I'm not leaving until he's dead," Gage responded simply. "I want this to be over."

Alex grinned at her with blood stained teeth and then spat at her. His blood didn't reach her however, it just fell back onto his face.

"It is over," Mak said hurriedly as gunfire erupted somewhere in the club, "we have to go."

"You go," she answered quietly, "I'm going to finish this." She drew a knife from her boot and held it up with two hands.

"Are you sure?" Mak asked her, noticing her hesitation.

"He killed Tessa," she stated calmly and plunged the knife into the left of his chest, angled under his sternum, into his heart.

The choking squeal he released when he felt the blade, made vomit rise in her throat but it wouldn't come all the way up. She withdrew the knife and he was still, blood pooling beneath him.

She wiped her blade on Alex's shirt, replaced the knife into her boot, and stood up shakily. Tears streamed from her eyes when she saw Mak, and she really seemed to see him for the first time, despite his mask, "He killed Tessa!" She wailed and moved toward him.

Mak wrapped her in his arms, "I know," he whispered, "but you did good. You did real good, Baby. I've got this handled, but we have to go right now."

She barely heard his words before she collapsed against him. The after-effects of an adrenaline dump, severing the tie of abuse, and her injuries, all combined in the basin of her insomnia and washed away her consciousness.

Mak picked Gage up, carrying her down the stairs and out of the club as the sirens began to wail. "I can see you're going to be a handful," he muttered with a small half smile as he pushed out of the side door and hurried down the alley to Buck's waiting truck.

Chapter 58

It was the smell that brought her back from the abyss in her mind. The smell of her whole life burning, an acrid plume of fumes, which made her stomach roil involuntarily. She opened her eyes and stared at the sky, memorizing the orange glow, so she'd recognize it later when it visited her dreams. She realized she could see fully, her eyepatch was gone and her left eye was no longer straining, that small victory felt like a slap in the face.

"Where's that bloody medic?" His voice vibrated against her back, and she realized she was laying in the grass, against Mak's chest, on the outskirts of her parking lot.

There was some pain from her side, where she felt his hand clutching, but it felt dull. More of an annoyance than true injury. She knew she'd been shot, but the pain in her soul was far more severe. "It's all my fault," she wanted to scream it, but it came out as more of a strangled whispered wail.

Mak readjusted himself so he could see her, now she was laying in his lap. "None of this is your fault," he said forcefully. The tone he used surprised her, so she looked into his eyes as he continued. "You didn't kill Tessa. You sure as hell didn't set your place on fire."

He said it with such conviction that some part of her felt better.

"She just wanted to go to Rome," she said softly, tears streaming down her cheeks.

"I know," he answered gently, cupping her cheek in his big hand, "there's no way to have known this would have happened."

"She saw it coming," Gage answered, staring at the fire, which was barely being contained by the many firefighters on scene.

"No, she didn't," Mak responded gently, "she never knew what hit her. She was gone before she hit the ground."

Gage's face twisted in pain and she let out an animalistic wail that stabbed him in the gut.

Mak wrapped her up in his arms against his chest and rocked her like a frightened child as she cried for what felt like hours.

This was how they were when Mere and Brick arrived, breathing heavy and red-faced.

"Did you run here?" Mak asked.

"There was traffic," Brick responded matter-of-factly as Mere fell to her knees by them.

"She's been shot," Mak nodded with his head to his blood covered hand, "I have no idea where the bloody paramedics are, they were meant to have been here ages ago."

"Probably stuck in the traffic," Brick responded, kneeling beside Mere and motioning Mak's hand away. "It's not so bad," his relief was apparent when he lifted her shirt enough to see the wound. "It looks like a flesh wound," Brick did a quick once over, "she seems in good condition, considering…" he trailed off.

Gage was staring into the flames again, her despair reflected in her eyes as clearly as the flickering lights.

Mere grabbed her best friend's hand tightly.

Gage looked at her hand, then followed the arm to Mere's face. Recognition lit her face and she sat up quickly, "I should have let her study abroad, Mere," she wailed as she threw herself into Mere's arms.

Mere stroked Gage's hair soothingly and made shushing noises, but she was clutching Gage just as fiercely, her green eyes awash with pain.

Finally, two men in paramedic uniforms and a stretcher came running up the alleyway.

"Crikey, it's about damn time," Mak waved at them, "oi, over here."

As they came over, Mak tried to untangle himself slightly, making sure to keep his hand on her wound, but trying to make room beside her.

Gage gripped his forearm tightly when she felt his weight shift, "Don't leave me."

"Never," he answered, "I'm just making space for these blokes."

"What happened?" The younger EMT asked as he assessed her wounds, moving Mak's hand in the process.

Gage gripped Mak tightly as he tried to move again.

"There was a drive-by, which caused this fire," Mak answered. "She was inside and was struck but managed to get out of the fire."

"It helps if she answers the questions," the second EMT stated as he handed gauze to his partner who was tending the wound. "What's your name, Ma'am?"

"They killed Tessa," Gage whimpered, "why would they kill Tessa? She didn't do anything to them."

"Ma'am?"

"She's obviously in shock. Her friends can answer your questions," Brick snapped.

"Look, Buddy, just let us do our jobs," the younger EMT snapped.

Brick stood up, "She just got shot and watched a girl she considered her sister gunned down in front of her. Her home and business are burning to the ground, and you expect her to have any kind of cognizant thought process right now?"

"Just get her vitals," the older EMT said, "you three need to give us some space so we can work."

"Don't leave me," Gage whimpered, "please. Everyone leaves me."

"Right," Mak stared at the older man, "that's your answer then."

The younger EMT looked at his partner, exasperated.

"Okay, but try to stay out of our way," the older man sighed.

"Her name is Bridget Grayson. She goes by Gage. She's twenty-six years old. She's not on any medications or drugs, but she's a recovering addict and claustrophobic." Mere glanced at the man with the computer taking notes, "What else do you need?"

"Does she have insurance?"

Mere nodded, "She does, but I don't know where her card is," she glanced back at the building, "it might be in there."

"That's okay, do you know anyone who would know that info?"

"I'll call our boss once we're done here," Mere stated, gripping Gage's hand as she was transitioned to the stretcher. "I'm sure he'll meet you at the hospital."

"Okay, we're ready to go," the younger EMT looked up, "one of you can ride with us."

"You go," Mere looked at Mak, "we'll meet you there." She looked down at Gage, "We'll meet you at the hospital Mami, Mak is going to ride with you, okay?"

Gage nodded, her green eyes dazed, "Be safe," she said softly.

"We will," Mere smiled reassuringly, "you're going to be okay."

Gage nodded again, clutching Mak's hand as she was lifted and carried to the ambulance.

"Where are the dogs?" Brick asked, "Oh my God, I just realized I didn't see them."

Mere smiled, "They're okay. Will found them running around the fire, trying to get in, he took them back to his place so he could pick up Lina."

Brick nodded, "Good, I don't think she'd survive losing them too."

Mere nodded and pulled out her phone, "Agreed."

Her phone rang once before Whitlock answered, *I'm on my way now, do I need to bring anything other than our insurance information?*

"That's all they asked for," Mere said, "Brick and I will meet you."

Who's with her?

Mere smiled slightly, "Take a guess."

Makenzie is going to be in our lives now.

It was a statement.

Mere nodded, "I hope so."

Chapter 59

When Gage opened her eyes, she didn't recognize the ceiling. She felt a breeze on her face and turned her gaze to an oscillating fan on her bedside table. There was road noise coming from somewhere, but no window she could see. There was a large curtain pulled, blocking where she assumed the door should be.

She glanced to her other side and couldn't help but smile. Mak was asleep in a chair, his head awkwardly thrown back, his mouth slightly open. There was a couch beside his chair; Will, Lina, and EmEm were all sitting on the couch, asleep leaning on each other. Mere was sprawled across their laps. Brick was sitting on the floor against the wall in the corner, using the corner to support his head.

"Are you still feeling alone?" Whitlock's voice came from just past the curtain as he stepped into her view.

Gage looked at him, "Sorry."

"What are you apologizing for?" He sipped from his disposable coffee cup and grimaced, "Other than for making me drink terrible hospital coffee."

She let out a breath that was almost a laugh, "I'm sorry I didn't tell you what was going on. I'm sorry I couldn't save Tessa. I'm sorry for..." She trailed off, tears flooding her eyes. "I'm just really sorry."

"You made your decisions for a reason," Whitlock said softly. "For what it's worth, you don't have to worry about Alex ever again."

"I-" Gage started, but Whitlock held up his hand.

"A woman with bright red hair stole your Gran Torino and did a number on Craze with back up from the Cortez gang. Apparently, they didn't take too kindly to him shooting up your shop on their turf," Whitlock said precisely, making sure each word was carefully enunciated.

Gage looked at her hair, and realized she was blonde again, she looked back to her boss as he continued speaking.

"Alejandro Sanchez was killed in the onslaught," Whitlock said, "along with many of his cohorts. Apparently, there were quite a bit of drugs recovered on the scene by local police." He glanced behind the curtain, "Along with several weapons believed to have been used in the drive by. Isn't that right Officer Donovan?"

Van pulled the curtain back slightly and stepped closer to her bed, "How you doing, Slugger?"

Gage shrugged as she tried to sit up slightly. Her bed started moving into a seated position and she looked at Mak who winked at her as he held the button down on the controller. Once she was seated, she looked back at Van, "I've been better. But I've also been worse."

"Tell me what you can remember," Van said.

"I remember having a fight with Tessa, then I remember gunshots. I tried to get Tessa to the ground, and a fire started. Then I realized Tessa had been sh-" she swallowed hard, "shot." Mak grabbed her hand. She looked at him gratefully, then turned back to Van, "I checked her, but she was gone. Then I crawled out of the fire in time to see my Torino driving off."

"Did you see who was driving your car?"

"Not even a little," she responded truthfully, "it was dark and smoky, plus I was in shock."

"What about you?" Van asked Mak, "Where do you fit in?"

"I've been chasing her skirt for the last few months," Mak nodded at Gage and shrugged, "I pulled up right before the fire trucks arrived. I carried her to the back of her building, away from the fire, and waited with her until the medics arrived."

"Neither one of you have any idea why Sanchez would have ordered your shop shot up?" Van asked.

"I imagine it has something to do with the fact that I left his abusive ass back in Texas," Gage responded, "he never got over it."

"Nothing to do with the body count in Alex's warehouse earlier this month?" Van asked, "Or the fact that he was beaten pretty brutally in a Bistro, not far from your place?"

"No shit?" Gage asked, "What's your city coming to? Rampant with crime. I had no idea."

Van sighed, "So the blood found on the table in the basement of his warehouse didn't belong to you?"

Gage cocked her head, "You mean there's a victim out there you haven't found? That sounds like some awful police work to me."

"What happened to your eye?" Van asked.

"I like to pick fights," Gage stated.

"Someone hit you?"

"Something like that," Gage nodded.

Van rubbed his face with one hand, "Jesus Gage, what happened at the Bistro?"

"I don't know what you're talking about, which Bistro? When?"

"Meredith called in a pizza order, a woman with straight blonde hair arrived for the order, then went berserk and beat Sanchez to a pulp." Van stared at her with tired blue eyes, "Now, who does that sound like?"

Gage shook her head with a shrug of her shoulders, "Maybe she was the victim whose blood you found."

"What's really funny is she took the pizza," Van stated.

Gage laughed, "I guess beating a dude WOULD boost an appetite."

"So, you have no idea what went on at that warehouse, the Bistro, or even at your shop?" Van's tone wasn't hiding his disbelief, "Even though you specifically asked me about this guy before any of this happened." He motioned to the door behind him, "The medical staff informed me that you've taken a pretty substantial beating recently. In fact, there's a story in your skin of prolonged and sustained abuse:

broken bones, interesting scars, some still-healing wounds." Van's jaw was tight as he continued, "Not to mention, the doctors are convinced you have been pretty consistently abused from childhood."

Gage made a face, "Oh yes, let's not mention it." Her body was stiff and she looked away from Van, "I asked you about my abusive ex who'd recently come to town. I was worried he was here for me, but it seems like he was after this other woman."

"You can tell me what happened," Van took a step toward her, "we're friends aren't we?"

Gage nodded and met his gaze, "You're the only cop, not related to me, I've ever trusted, Donovan. If there was something more, I would tell you about it."

"Maybe that woman was outside when the shooting started," Mak suggested, "it's possible she was missed, so she drove off in Gage's car to get her revenge."

"Were the keys in the car?" Van asked.

"Must have been," Gage rubbed her face with her free hand. "I'm usually much better about that, but I've been pretty stressed lately. I have a lot of cars, sometimes one falls through the cracks."

Van nodded, "So your story is you were worried about an ex but kept to yourself. Then he shot up your shop and you just stayed on scene and waited for help?"

"I was shot," Gage stated, "and you always tell me not to take the law into my own hands."

"You picked a hell of a time to listen to me," Van smiled slightly. "Well, a detective will probably be by to collect your statement. But the fact remains we have a useless video of two women who are a similar build, but it's impossible to identify either one. We have some blood left at the warehouse, but nothing to compare it to, and no one coming forward as a victim." Van shrugged, "Every one of the bodies there was a criminal with a mile-long rap sheet. As far as I'm concerned, someone did us a favor." He sniffed, "No one at the Bistro can give an accurate description, and Alex declined our help at the scene, no doubt because he intended to take care of it himself."

"So, you have no idea if he put a hit on my shop, or if I was just caught in the crossfire," Gage pulled her hand from Mak's and cracked her knuckles.

"That's accurate," Van nodded, "we didn't get to speak to him, he was killed shortly after your shop was hit."

Gage nodded, "You have anything from that scene?"

Van arched an eyebrow, "Worried?"

"More curious, I'd like to know who this woman is so I can thank her for her efforts," Gage smiled sweetly. "Though I am quite upset she stole my Torino," she made a face, "is it impounded?"

"The Torino is destroyed, it was used as a distraction," Van continued to watch her face, "she blew it up."

Gage's jaw dropped, "What?!"

Van laughed, "Well, since there were only cameras on the outside of the club, we assume because of the drug activity inside, we saw exactly nothing. Except your car rolling into the building and blowing up."

Gage pouted, "I loved that car. It was beautiful. They made a damn movie about it."

"Our witnesses inside saw a crazy woman with red hair shooting up the place," Van continued, "but none of them saw her face, they were too busy running away." He cracked his neck, "By the time we got there, we arrested a couple of Cortez's thugs, but truthfully, we still have no idea what actually happened. And we have no idea who this mystery woman is."

"That sucks," Gage made an apologetic face, "good thing you're leaving soon, huh? This won't wreck your impeccable conviction rate."

Van laughed, "You're going to be watched closely for a while, the P.D. isn't going to like having nothing. They'll watch to see if you slip up."

"I don't mind audiences," Gage shrugged, "I have nothing to hide from our friends in the police department."

A small smile lingered on Van's lips, "You take care of yourself."

Gage nodded, "Will do."

Van turned to leave just as Mere rolled off her friends' laps and landed with a grunt on the floor.

"God, I was trying to wait for you to leave, but I had to move," the redhead grumbled.

Van shook his head, "I don't suppose you know who picked up your pizza?"

Mere sat up and scratched her head, "I have a standing order every Thursday, if I don't collect it, they give it to the homeless in the area. It's entirely possible one of the people who get it, if I don't, decided to try their luck early." Mere shrugged, "I was on my way to pick it up when I saw the police swarming, so I decided to go somewhere else for lunch."

"Nervous about the police?" Van asked with an arched eyebrow.

Mere laughed, "God, no. I just prefer to stay out of their way while they're conducting their business."

Van nodded, "Yeah, sure. You guys are always in the middle of some trouble, you know that?"

"We're very unlucky," Will chimed in with a voice husky with sleep.

"I don't suppose you saw anything?" Van asked.

Will shook his head, "I heard the gunfire from our apartment," he wrapped his arm around Lina's shoulders. "I was afraid about Gage because I knew she was on edge about Sanchez, so I ran to the garage just in time to see Gage crawl out."

"That must have been very shocking for you to see," Van's tone was unreadable.

"Yes," Will stated, his dark eyes staring into Van's, "I will never forget the feeling of sheer relief. Which was quickly doused by the knowledge that Tessa was gone."

Van lowered his eyes, "I'm very sorry for your loss, she was special."

"Yes, she was," Lina said softly, her red-rimmed eyes making her tired expression even more noticeable.

"I'm sorry to be the one to question you guys so close to this tragedy," Van started.

"Just do your job, Donovan," Whitlock grumbled. "My people are professional. They'll answer your questions."

Van sighed, "I wanted it to be me," he glanced around the room at each of the people inside, "I didn't want you to be questioned by someone who didn't know what kind of loss you've suffered."

"It's appreciated," Gage piped up, "but still unfortunate."

Van nodded, "I get that. I need to know where each of you were when this all went down."

"Well I was inside the garage, then bleeding in the backyard," Gage stated, "I don't remember much other than being an emotional wreck."

"I was on my way to the garage to pick up Gage when I saw the fire," Mak stated. "I got there and told Will to get the dogs, then I carried Gage to the back to get her away from the fire."

"I arrived in time to see Gage crawling out," Will stated, "she told me Tessa was dead and was in a pretty severe shock."

"He slapped me," Gage said, "I remember that part."

"Sorry," Will said sheepishly.

"I needed it," Gage shrugged.

"When Mak got there and he took care of Gage, I collected Tiny and Killer so they didn't go inside the fire." Will swallowed, "They were trying to get inside. I think to save Tessa."

"Thank God they're okay," Gage sighed, "I was worried about them."

"I took them back to our apartment, to get them away from the scene," Will stated.

"I was at our apartment the whole time, waiting for Will to let me know what was needed," Lina said, "we didn't know if it was anything to be worried about." She looked at Gage, "When he brought the dogs home, I tried to calm them, and checked them over for injuries."

"Were they okay?" Gage asked.

"They were frantic but unharmed," Lina said quietly.

"I was asleep at my apartment, completely unaware of anything happening," EmEm said bitterly.

Lina grabbed his hand and squeezed it, "There's no way you could have known."

EmEm shook his head, his dark eyes tearing up, and looked away.

"I was at PREY," Brick stated, "weightlifting." Van made a face at Brick as the younger man spoke, like he was trying to place where he had seen him before.

"I went to PREY to exercise, but got the call from Mak, so Brick and I went to the scene," Mere said from her seat on the floor.

"And I was at my home when I received the call from Will, so I collected the paperwork I thought would be necessary and came to the hospital," Whitlock finished. He looked at Van sternly, "We can all give you written statements to that effect. But at this point, we would like some time to be together."

Van nodded before turning to Brick, "Have we met before? You look extremely familiar to me."

Brick shook his head, "I don't think so."

"Are you sure?" Van squinted at the Corpsman as though trying to read him.

"I've been overseas for most of the last six years," Brick responded, "So unless you're a Marine I patched up, I doubt you've seen me."

Van let out a small sound of disbelief and headed for the door, "Thank you for your cooperation, everyone."

"Hey Van," Gage called after him. When he turned back to her, she smiled, "Good luck in New York, you'll do great. We'll miss you."

Van smiled back at her, "Thanks, I appreciate that."

"Keep us in mind if you ever need help up there," Will added.

"Will do," Van laughed as he left the room.

"So, when can I go home?" Gage asked, looking around the room.

"Well, shit," she sighed, "when can I start looking for a home?"

"I contacted the insurance company," Mere rubbed her face with both hands and climbed to her feet, stretching, "I'm sure that will be a fun conversation, once the adjuster comes out."

"You guys can stay with me for now," EmEm said.

Mere laughed, "I'm not going to live under the same roof as Derek," she shook her head, "no offense."

EmEm shrugged, "That's fair."

"You can stay with me," Brick said, looking at his hands.

When the room was silent, he looked up, "I have a spare bedroom. It's not like I'm asking you to marry me," he added with a scowl.

"That's really sweet of you," Mere smiled, "I appreciate it."

Brick shrugged, "No problem. Might be nice to have company."

Mere grinned, "I snore, just so you know."

Brick smirked, "I sleepwalk, we'll be a fun pair."

Gage sat silently, smiling at her friends as they interacted in front of her like it was her favorite television show.

"You can stay with me," Mak said quietly, standing beside her and stroking her hair back, behind her ear.

Gage looked up at him, "Are you sure you're ready for all this? I'm kind of a mess."

"Never surer of anything in my life," he winked at her.

Warmth spread through her as she hugged his middle tightly, "Thanks, Riley."

Mak looked up startled as everyone stared at him, "What? You had to know I had a first name."

Mere made a surprised face, "Actually we thought you were created, like Whit, and you only had one name."

"Like Beyoncé," EmEm added with a smile.

"You all know my name is James, right?" Whitlock looked around the room.

Everyone put on a shocked face.

"You're all idiots," Whitlock sighed.

"We love you too," Gage laughed as Mere scampered over and hugged Whitlock.

Chapter 60

It had been several days since she'd been released from the hospital. Gage was still trying to finish working through everything that had happened, but it was difficult. She'd spent most of her time at PREY, trying to figure out her next move.

She sat at a computer desk with an envelope laying in between her hands, which were palm down like a naughty school child waiting for a nun's ruler. She chewed her lip, deep in thought, before finally grabbing the letter and tearing it open.

She paused once it was open and lay it back down again. She hadn't expected her heart to start thumping so violently in her chest. She stared at it again, studying every detail of the envelope which she'd carried with her for so long. It was addressed to her, obviously, but the return address and postmark were what always drew her attention.

It was from her father in Afghanistan, dated a week after his death. She knew it was probably his last letter, given to a friend for safekeeping, and mailed to her by unfamiliar hands after the death of her only immediate relative remaining. She'd received the letter when she was thirteen, through her caseworker at the time, who'd apologized for the delay. Apparently, the mail in Foster care worked differently than in the rest of the world, it had been sitting in a box somewhere, waiting for delivery for nearly two years.

She was angry with herself, that she'd never been brave enough to open it, let alone read it. She'd been so angry with her father in those first few years, she didn't care what he had to say in his final moments, because nothing he said would make his abandonment any less painful. She knew all about pride and country and doing what's right, so no pep talk from her dead father was going to improve her attitude.

Then she'd been entangled with Alex, and she knew how disappointed her father would have been in her. That shame had kept her from the last words she'd ever have from him, because it broke her heart to let him down, even just the memory of him filled her with despair. She could see his disappointed brown eyes clearer than anything else in her memories of him. They burned into her soul whenever she thought back to that time in her life.

Even though she'd never opened it, she'd also never thrown it away. She couldn't bear to separate herself from that last piece of him, a piece he'd intended only for her. Destroying it felt like shooting him, as weird as that sounded.

Gage sighed heavily and placed her forehead on the desk, touching the letter, as though trying to guess what was inside.

Now that she'd finally, truly, closed the chapter of Alex in her life, she felt like she could open this letter and know what her dad had to say. She finally felt strong enough to let her father be another chapter closed in her life. Maybe if she could do that, she could actually learn what this 'love' crap was about. Mak seemed interested in teaching her, maybe it was time to be a willing student, instead of a mildly interested tourist.

She sat back in her chair and grabbed the envelope again, yanking the letter from inside. She stared at the folded paper in her hand like it was about to burst into flames, before unfolding it with shaking hands.

The first few paragraphs were what she expected: I love you. I'm proud of you. I'm sorry it had to be this way. All the phrases that made her stomach roil because she'd gone against every single thing he'd taught her for so long.

She dropped the paper after she read the last few sentences.

She snatched the paper back and held it closer, reading the last paragraph over and over until she pretty much had it memorized.

I gave this to the only person I know I can trust. He'll look after you while I'm gone, you can trust him, even though sometimes he's hard to love. I know this will be hard to accept, but Gidget, I'm not dead. I had to go away to create something important. It was too dangerous for me to be with you. I'm so sorry I had to leave, I promise it was necessary, I was needed. After you turn twenty-one you can find me. I'll call the diner, where we went on our dates, every date night after your twenty-first birthday. When you're ready, go there. You'll know the name when you hear it. We have work to do.

She sat in silence, her whole body shaking, as she attempted to process what she'd read.

Finally, she stood up and carried the letter with her down the hall. She walked past Brick and Will in the hallway on her way to Whitlock's office, but she didn't even acknowledge them. If they spoke to her, which she was pretty sure they did, she didn't hear a word.

She opened Whitlock's door without knocking. He was sitting behind his desk, speaking with potential clients.

"What the hell are you-" he trailed off, his anger forgotten at the sight of the distress on her face, "Gage what is it?"

He stood and walked around the desk, hurriedly excusing himself as he ushered her from the room, holding her elbow. He took her into the conference room, where Mak, Buck, and Mere were comparing targets. They all grew quiet when Whit and Gage entered the room.

At this point, Gage had silent tears flowing freely from her eyes, but she was still shaking too hard to use her voice. She pulled her arm from Whitlock's grasp.

Will and Brick entered the room behind them, obviously curious about Gage's state, and Mak moved to comfort her, but Whitlock held up a hand, halting him in his tracks.

"Gage, what is it?" Whitlock asked again, his voice softer than she'd ever heard it.

She turned her face to stare at him, searching him for answers, "Did you know what was in the letter my father sent me?"

Whitlock adverted his gaze, confirming what she already feared.

"You son of a bitch!" She slapped him so hard it made her hand ache.

When he stared at her, his eyes were a wash of remorse, pain, and anger, "You think I liked keeping it from you?"

"I don't care how hard a decision it was for you," she shrieked, "you were like a father to me! How could you keep this from me?"

His voice was gruff when he said, "I had no choice. Gabe made me promise."

"My love, and mental health, isn't as important to you as a promise made to the man who ruined my life," Gage stated it like a fact.

"Sorry to butt in," Mere said slowly, "but what the actual fuck is happening here?"

"My father is alive," Gage responded, still staring at Whitlock, "If I'm not mistaken, Whitlock here was responsible for mailing the letter to me from my supposedly dead father." She held the letter up, "A letter I've been carrying for over a decade because I've been so torn with grief and guilt, that I couldn't bring myself to read it." She handed the letter to Mere, "A letter which tells me, my father CHOSE to leave me, he didn't die." She cocked her head, "A fact which apparently, our fearless leader has been aware of this whole time but neglected to tell me."

Everyone stared at the two of them with wide eyes, afraid to speak.

"Biscuit!" Gage whirled to face the newest member of PREY, "Feel like going on a road trip with me?"

He was momentarily uneasy, staring from Gage to Whitlock to Mak and back again, "Uh, why me?"

"Because I have to go to Texas," she responded, "and what I encounter there will be rather emotional for me. So, I need someone who doesn't give a shit about my feelings to ride shotgun and watch my ass."

He arched an eyebrow and shrugged, "Okay, I'll watch your ass and ignore your feelings, that's easy enough."

"Hey!" Mak yelped but Gage cut him off.

"Good. Pack a bag, we're leaving in the morning." Gage took the letter back from Mere, "I need answers, and my answers should be given on date night. The third Friday of the month."

"That's in four days," Mak said.

"Yes, that's why I have to leave tomorrow morning," she responded before looking back at Brick, "be here and ready at 0600." She left the room leaving everyone in shocked silence.

~*~*~*~

Mak walked into the room he'd been sharing with Gage and sat on the bed in silence. He watched her throw clothes into the duffle bag beside him on the bed.

"I know you don't like this," she said finally, as she moved around the room, "but I need you to trust me."

He shrugged without saying anything.

She stopped moving with a sigh, and stood with her back to him, "You can't come."

He crossed his arms over his chest and leaned back against the wall.

"You care too much about me," she stated.

"You mean I love you," he corrected her, "if you're going to discount me, you could at least use the right term."

She turned to look at him, her jade eyes swimming, "You care too much about my emotional well-being." She insisted, "You'd be more concerned about me, than situational awareness." She shrugged, "I'm sorry, it's just the truth."

He shrugged, "You already made up your mind. I can't change it."

Her eyes were pleading, but for once, he wasn't going to give in, his own frustration was overwhelming. He'd already pulled her from two situations, bleeding and in pain. He worried what might happen to her if he wasn't there.

She closed the door and walked over to him, kneeling on the floor between his legs, she looked up at him, "I wish you could come. You ground me in a way that no one has ever been able to before," she put a hand on his knee, "but you also make me put my guard down. That's never happened to me before." She swallowed when his gaze finally met hers, "You terrify me."

"You kinda like me, huh?" He gave a small smile and her heart lifted.

"Yes," she responded, "I like you a lot. That's a big deal for me."

"That still doesn't explain why you'd rather take Brick with you."

"It's not that I'd rather," she answered, "it's what's the most rational. He doesn't care about me like you do, he won't worry about my emotional health. He'll concentrate on the task at hand," she ran her hand up his thigh, "he won't get distracted," she gave Mak a little half-smile as she leaned into his lap.

"That's not fair," he groaned.

"I don't play fair," she responded, unbuttoning the buttons of his shirt one by one, starting at the bottom.

"Yes, I know," he sighed, "you're too good at being distracting."

"Distract me, instead," she responded, "I don't have to leave for a few hours," she smiled up at him playfully.

He cradled her face in his hands and stared deeply into her eyes, "I love you. If this is your decision, I'll respect it. But I won't like it."

She stared up at him for a moment, searching his face, "Thank you," she said quietly.

"One day, you're going to realize you love me too," he said, "and you're going to say it back to me." His hands moved to under her arms so he could lift her up into his lap, "That will be a hell of a day."

She straddled him and kissed him sweetly before pulling back and whispering, "That WOULD be a hell of a day, Riley."

He grinned at her and rolled her underneath him, "I love the way you say my name," he growled against her lips before kissing her fervently.

Chapter 61

Gage tapped her fingers anxiously on the table, her coke sitting forgotten beside a plate of uneaten eggs.

"You should eat," Brick said between bites, "you're still healing, it's important to stay fueled. Especially since you're barely sleeping."

Gage looked at her plate with disdain before glancing at him, "I'm good. Thanks. It's not my fault you drive like a maniac."

Brick shrugged, "It's actually pretty good food, it could settle your sensitive girlie stomach."

She stared at the melting ice in her coke. The water was pooling around the cup as its condensation created trails of moisture.

"As much fun as this delightful road trip has been," Brick broke into her thoughts, "is it coming to an end anytime soon? I can't wait to drive home with the window open in the Texas humidity."

She shrugged, "Sorry, I like the fresh air, you know that. We're where we're supposed to be. All we can do now is wait." She met his blue eyes, "For all I know, he's died since he wrote the damn letter."

"Well that would be a huge waste of time," Brick sighed.

Gage rolled her eyes, "I'm so sorry my family drama isn't interesting enough for you."

He actually laughed, "Oh it's interesting. Almost as interesting as you choosing me to come with you on this trip. I thought for sure it was your way to get me alone and have your way with me."

She arched an eyebrow at him, "You're not my type."

He smirked at her, "Uncomplicated sex isn't your thing?"

"It used to be," she responded, "I guess maybe I'm growing up," she smirked, "or you just really don't appeal to me."

He shrugged, "I'm an acquired taste, I'll give you that."

The bells on the door chimed, signaling the entrance of a customer. Gage's eyes were instantly drawn to the raven-haired middle-aged woman who entered. She wore jeans and a leather coat even though it was hot outside. She had a tan line where her wedding ring normally sat, and she moved with the grace of a dancer or a fighter.

"What's up?" Brick asked, sensing the change in Gage's demeanor. He tried to look out of his periphery, but the woman was behind him.

"I'm not sure," Gage responded quietly, "something is off."

"Should we go?" Brick asked.

"No, finish your meal," Gage looked back at him with a fake smile plastered on her face as though he'd just said something funny, "let's see where this goes."

The woman sat on a stool at the counter and ordered a black coffee. She put a manila envelope on the counter beside her place setting and pulled her dark hair into a low loose ponytail.

"How's your hand to hand?" Gage asked conversationally.

"It's not bad," he responded, still eating, "I've got my backup piece on my left ankle."

She giggled, as though he'd just said something naughty, "I'm still slowed down from pain right now, I'll favor my right. There's a holstered SIG in the small of my back."

"Got it," he answered, taking a sip of his drink.

The woman glanced their way and met Gage's eyes. Her blue-green eyes widened in surprise and she instantly looked down at her placemat.

"Well that wasn't obvious," Gage grumbled. She was about to stand up and confront the woman when two men entered the diner who were even more out of place. The newcomers stared right at the back of the lone woman and moved to sit near her at the counter, one on either side.

"There's a woman at the counter who clearly recognizes me," Gage said quietly. "Two big ass dudes just entered from the front, it looks like they're here for her, they must be operators of some sort. They're dressed like you were for your interview," she winked at him.

"Another tacti-cool dude entered from the rear," Brick responded, using his fork to move food around on his plate.

Gage sighed, "Don't they know its impolite to enter from the rear without consent?"

Brick choked on his drink and liquid dribbled down his chin as he scrambled for a napkin.

The woman looked at Gage, concern marring her face.

"She's not scared," Gage stated, "she must know how to handle herself okay."

"Or she just doesn't realize they're here for her, because she's here for you and has tunnel vision," he responded, using his napkin to dab at his shirt.

Gage motioned with her head to the exit, and the woman nodded, tucking the envelope into the back of her jeans, under her coat, then zipping the coat shut.

"Rear guard is yours," Gage threw some cash down on the table, "the other two will probably follow us out."

Brick nodded and grabbed her arm as she walked past him, "Try not to kill anyone, we don't know who the good guys are here."

She leaned in as though to kiss him goodbye, "We're the good guys," she whispered, and gave him a peck on the cheek before walking down the aisle and holding the front door open for the strange woman.

Brick picked up Gage's full cup as he stood and chucked it into the rear guard's face as he hurried to rush out of the Diner after his buddies. While he was still shocked, Brick grabbed him by the back of the neck and slammed his face into the metal table with enough force to knock the sense out of him. Then Brick rushed from the Diner after Gage.

When he got outside, the first thing he saw was two men dressed similarly to the man he'd subdued. They were both laying in pools of blood with sightless eyes. Rain was pouring down, washing rivers of blood into puddles at Gage's feet.

"Jesus, Gage, I said don't kill them!" He shouted over the rain, that's when he looked up and saw the gun pointed at him. He put his hands up and glanced at Gage who also had her hands up. The woman from inside had a Glock trained on him, but her eyes were pleading with Gage.

"Please Bridget, I need you to trust me," she said, lowering her weapon slightly "just get in the car."

Gage glared at her, "I don't get in cars with strangers," she said coldly, "you didn't even offer me candy."

Brick moved his hand slightly, testing the level of distraction.

"Don't," the woman snapped, her eyes on him in an instant, with the handgun following, to point at him, "I'm not stupid, do not go for your gun."

Gage side-stepped so that she was standing in front of Brick, "How about you leave my friends out of this," she motioned toward the gun that was now pointing at her chest, "whatever THIS is."

The woman's eyes welled with tears for a moment and her hand shook, "You're so beautiful," she said softly.

Gage arched an eyebrow, "Um, thanks?" She glanced over her shoulder at Brick, then back at the woman, "Now are you going to tell me about my father, or are we just going to wait here for the cops?"

Brick took a step forward slowly, so he was right behind Gage, his hands still up, "I only knocked that dude out inside, he could come to any minute now," he said loud enough for everyone to hear.

The woman cursed and stepped closer to them, "Damn it, Bridget, just get in the car!" She motioned to a blue Corolla parked near them.

When she came close enough, Gage grabbed the Glock, twisted it up and forced it back, making the woman yelp in surprise and pain. When she looked up again, Gage had the Glock pointed at her, and Brick had the handgun from the small of Gage's back also pointed at her.

"I don't get into strangers' cars," Gage said again, calmly.

"I'm not a stranger," the woman cried out, yanking the wig off her head with her uninjured hand, she released a wave of blonde hair, "I'm your mother."

Gage felt dizzy when the smell of her mother's shampoo clouded her senses and she took a step back from the woman, her back hitting Brick's chest.

Brick's free arm wrapped around Gage's middle in case she fainted as he said matter-of-factly, "Well, that's fucked up."

PREY Revelations Preview

Viv, your cover's blown. Get out now! Gabe's voice was strained, he was clearly trying to remain calm for her benefit. Vivian Grayson stood still, her hand resting on her flat stomach as she listened to the phone.

There was shouting in the background, then her husband's voice was back, it was no longer containing the terror. ***Prepare yourself, there's no time to run. I'll be home as soon as I can. They're coming for you. You have maybe five minutes.***

Vivian's heart began to beat rapidly due to his tone. She dropped the phone even though her husband was still calling for her. "BRIDGET where are you baby?" She ran down the hallway to her daughter's room, grabbing her sidearm from a holster hanging on her bedroom's door as she went.

Bridget looked up from her toy cars when her mother entered her room, "Hi Momma," she smiled brightly, her luminous green eyes wide and happy.

"Come to me," Vivian held out her arms until Bridget rushed to her and hugged her tightly, the small girl buried her face in her mother's soft blonde hair, inhaling the scent like she always did.

Vivian squeezed Bridget tightly and carried her quickly down the hall to the master bedroom. "What's wrong, Momma?" Bridget's voice was small and confused.

"You're going to be okay, Baby, I promise. Momma is going to take care of you, okay?" Vivian heard the slamming of a body against the front door.

"Mommy, what's happening?" Bridget whimpered, terrified as the sound got louder.

"Daddy will be home soon, you have to stay here and be as quiet as you can, okay?" Vivian had put Bridget down at the opening to her closet. "Be brave, okay? You have to be my brave girl."

"Okay," Bridget's voice was so small, she didn't think her mother would hear. When she realized that her mother was going to leave her alone, she grabbed Vivian's free hand and tugged it toward the closet, "You hide too, come in here with me."

"I can't, baby," Vivian tucked her gun into the back of her pants and used both hands to touch Bridget's face and hair, she hugged her daughter again, tightly, like she didn't want to ever let her go. Then she forced herself to release and shoved Bridget into the back of the small closet. She slammed the door shut and locked it with a combination lock. She whirled to face her attacker a split second before he brought his gun up.

She rushed at him, knocking his hand away and punching him as hard as she could in the solar plexus. She stepped behind him and kicked him as hard as she could from behind, forcing him against the closet door. Before he could collect his bearing, she fired two shots, one through his heart and one through his skull. He fell to the floor, blocking the door.

She wanted to rush forward and let Bridget know everything was fine, but then she heard more men coming in the house. With one last longing look at the blood-spattered door which housed her only child, she rushed from the room. She made sure one of the men breaking in saw her, then escaped from the house through a window and ran. A small smile twisted her lips when she realized they were all following her. She had to keep them chasing her, so no one would go back and search the house.

~*~*~*~*~

"You're doing great," Brick said calmly as he drove away from the diner, "just keep doing what you're doing. Breathing is good."

Gage was having a panic attack in the passenger seat. Her hands were twisting the seat belt anxiously and her breathing was coming in gasping breaths that couldn't quite fill the lungs in her heaving chest. She was light-headed and trying to force her lungs to work properly, instead of the fleeting bursts of air her anxiety was giving her.

"I'm so sorry, Bridget. I never wanted to leave you, I didn't have a choice," Vivian Grayson was sitting in the back seat. Her hands were zip-tied behind her back and the seatbelt held her back in her seat.

Gage let out a high-pitched noise that was somewhere between a shriek and a wail.

"Maybe you should just shut up," Brick snapped angrily. "You're only here because I didn't feel like explaining to my boss why I let you get arrested."

Vivian had the decency to lower her eyes and fall silent.

"All right," Brick glanced in his rearview mirror, "we're not being followed."

Gage kept clenching and unclenching her fists, staring out her open window, trying to calm herself.

"I've got this, I know what to do," Brick pulled out his phone, scrolling through his contacts he selected the number he wanted and held his phone to his ear.

Is she okay?

Brick let out a strained chuckle, "She's unharmed," he responded to Mak's concern. "Long story, short, she's freaking out. Some crazy shit went down, three dudes attacked us in the diner. She stepped in front of a gun for me, not really sure why. Full disclosure, I had to put my hand in her pants, I'm sorry about that. We're on our way home, but she needs someone to talk to, so here."

Brick heard the yelling as he handed the phone to Gage, but he continued to drive, his eyes forward.

Gage held the phone to her ear but couldn't make her voice work. All she could do was keep trying to slow her breathing.

When Mak heard her, he stopped yelling. In a slow and soothing tone, he began to speak, *Okay Baby, I hear you. She'll be apples, let's focus on breathing. Slow and steady. Deep breaths that fill up your chest. In through your nose and out through your mouth.*

Gage closed her eyes and focused on his soothing voice.

Just listen to my voice. I'll talk a bit, bottler, let me tell you about... he trailed off thinking about a topic. Her breathing started to get rapid again so he spoke again. *Just listen to me, okay. You're going to be fine. You're on your way home. When you rock up, I'm gonna do whatever you need. I can wrap you up and hold you for as long as you want. We'll lock the door, and not let anyone in. Or, if you'd rather, we'll go to the range and you can outshoot me. Or we'll go to the gym and I'll let you beat on me a bit. I'm here for you, I'll do whatever you need.*

Her breathing started to slow as she focused on his voice, she didn't really listen to what he was saying, just the tone in which he said it.

That's it, you're doing bonzer.

She could hear the smile in his voice.

Did I tell you I decided I like your tattoo?

"You hate butterflies," she gasped breathlessly.

That's true, I do. I hate them, but I wanted to tell you that I understand why you chose them to cover your scar. It makes a lot of sense. You used it to cover your past, instead of letting what happened to you define you, you changed it into something different. Something beautiful. Just like a caterpillar becomes a butterfly. That's really amazing when you think about it.

"I was thinking of getting it covered," she said softly, her breathing more normal.

Seriously? You little ripper!

The relief in his voice made her let out a small laugh.

I really do like the symbolism, and the strength you displayed by choosing it.

"You just hate butterflies," she answered with a smile, her eyes still closed, but her breaths were finally getting back to normal.

Better now?

"Much, thank you," Gage rubbed her face with her free hand then stared out the window.

Spiffy. Now can we talk about Brick's hand in your daks?

Gage rolled her eyes, "He only said that to rile you up."

So, he didn't put his hand down your daks?

"Only in the back," Gage responded, "he was getting my gun."

What did he need your gun for?

"To point at my mother," Gage responded quietly, closing her eyes again when her pulse raced momentarily.

Well, that's fucked up.

She nodded, "Yeah. We're on our way back now." She cleared her throat, "All three of us."

You want me to stay on the phone for a bit? I don't have any plans this arvo.

She smiled, "Can you let Whitlock know about Vivian? If it seems like he knew, punch his lights out."

Um, really?

"You don't have to do the punching part, but I'd kind of like it," she responded.

"James doesn't know I'm alive," Vivian said from the back seat.

"Seems you don't have to hit him," Gage said conversationally.

Love you

She took a deep breath and basked in those words before responding, "See you soon." She gave Brick his phone back and stared out the front window, feeling much calmer and more grounded.

"Was that your new man?" Vivian's voice irritated Gage.

A deep raging sadness filled her so she made a dismissive noise in her throat instead of responding.

"Please tell me about your life," Vivian begged, "I've missed so much."

"Whose fault is that?" Gage snapped.

"All mothers who locked their kid in a closet and faked their own death, shut the hell up," Brick's voice was calm but loud. "She just got over the anxiety attack, don't set her off again."

Vivian leaned back in her seat and stared out her window, her blue-green eyes hard, but sad. After a few moments in silence, she said quietly, "You'll understand when you have kids. Raising them is hard when you have a dangerous job."

Gage laughed harshly, "How would you know? You didn't raise me. Do you think telling me that you chose your job over me should make me feel better?"

"My cover was blown," Vivian said, part of her happy that Gage was at least speaking to her, "men came to the house to kill us. I had to lead them away."

"Cool, so you let me be traumatized to protect me," Gage nodded, "I can almost buy that, but you never came back. Dad told me you were dead."

"We agreed that it would be better for me to leave until we could discover the mole who gave up our location," Vivian responded.

"So you never found out, or you just realized it was way more fun to be child-free?" Brick asked good-naturedly.

"Your friend is an asshole," Vivian snapped.

"He's actually not only right to ask, but also more family to me than you are at this point, so how about answering his very interesting question," Gage continued to stare straight ahead, barely containing her anger.

"We still don't know who keeps finding us," Vivian grumbled.

"You're terrible at your job too, huh?" Gage asked.

"What do you mean too? You are amazing at what you do," Vivian sat forward slightly, "I have been so impressed with you, not to mention all you've overcome and all you've accomplished."

"Oh, no," Gage responded. "I'm amazing. I was referring to the fact that you're a terrible mother, and also terrible at your job."

Brick snorted, glancing in the rearview mirror quickly to see Vivian slump in the seat, defeated.

The rest of the trip was uncomfortably quiet and extremely awkward.

About the Author

As a child, I was always drawn to stories with strong characters who wanted to change the world. Every book I read and every movie I watched was immediately transformed in my mind with additional characters and different storylines or plot points. I carried a notebook everywhere I went to jot down experiences, character ideas, or observations.

When I was twenty years old, I was a victim of domestic violence. I still bear the scars, physically and emotionally, from that time in my life. A time when I lost myself and allowed my self-worth to drown in a sea of uncertainty.

At twenty-one, I felt a calling to serve my community, so I became a deputy sheriff on patrol who worked midnights. Over the course of five years, I became a decorated officer who specialized in crisis situations. I learned much about the world, and the people in it, by serving. Unfortunately, I was injured in the line of duty and was forced to medically retire.

Now, with a traumatic brain injury and a Chiari I Malformation, I suffer from debilitating headaches, daily pain, personality changes, and many other symptoms. If not for my family, I would never have found my way back to the words I love. I hope, through my stories and characters, I can help impact one person the way I have been impacted.

Finding my way after losing so much of myself has not been easy. The PREY world has been a project thirteen years in the making. It represents a new path. It is my new beginning. I hope it is as entertaining for you as it has been for me.

I live in Virginia on a small hobby farm with my husband, son, two German Shepherds, chickens, ducks, and rabbits. My husband is a former Marine who currently serves as a deputy sheriff.

Made in the USA
Columbia, SC
20 November 2020